NOT WHAT IT SEEMS

Books by Lisa Jackson

Stand-Alones
SEE HOW SHE DIES
FINAL SCREAM
RUNNING SCARED
WHISPERS
TWICE KISSED
UNSPOKEN
DEEP FREEZE
FATAL BURN
MOST LIKELY TO DIE
WICKED GAME
WICKED LIES
SOMETHING WICKED
WICKED WAYS
WICKED DREAMS
SINISTER
WITHOUT MERCY
YOU DON'T WANT TO KNOW
CLOSE TO HOME
AFTER SHE'S GONE
REVENGE
YOU WILL PAY
OMINOUS
BACKLASH
RUTHLESS
ONE LAST BREATH
LIAR, LIAR
PARANOID
ENVIOUS
LAST GIRL STANDING
DISTRUST
ALL I WANT FROM SANTA
AFRAID
THE GIRL WHO SURVIVED
GETTING EVEN
DON'T BE SCARED
OUR LITTLE SECRET
YOU'LL FIND OUT
IT HAPPENED ON THE LAKE

Cahill Family Novels
IF SHE ONLY KNEW
ALMOST DEAD
YOU BETRAYED ME

Rick Bentz/Reuben Montoya Novels
HOT BLOODED
COLD BLOODED
SHIVER
ABSOLUTE FEAR
LOST SOULS
MALICE
DEVIOUS
NEVER DIE ALONE
THE LAST SINNER

Pierce Reed/Nikki Gillette Novels
THE NIGHT BEFORE
THE MORNING AFTER
TELL ME
THE THIRD GRAVE
NOT WHAT IT SEEMS

Selena Alvarez/Regan Pescoli Novels
LEFT TO DIE
CHOSEN TO DIE
BORN TO DIE
AFRAID TO DIE
READY TO DIE
DESERVES TO DIE
EXPECTING TO DIE
WILLING TO DIE

Published by Kensington Publishing Corp.

NOT WHAT IT SEEMS

LISA JACKSON

KENSINGTON PUBLISHING CORP.
kensingtonbooks.com

KENSINGTON BOOKS are published by

Kensington Publishing Corp.
900 Third Ave.
New York, NY 10022

All Kensington titles, imprints, and distributed lines are available at special quantity discounts for bulk purchases for sales promotion, premiums, fund-raising, educational, or institutional use.

Special book excerpts or customized printings can also be created to fit specific needs. For details, write or phone the office of the Kensington Special Sales Manager: Attn. Special Sales Department. Kensington Publishing Corp, 900 Third Ave., New York, NY 10022. Phone: 1-800-221-2647.

KENSINGTON and the K with book logo Reg. U.S. Pat. & TM. Off.

Library of Congress Card Catalogue Number: 2026935108

ISBN: 978-1-4967-5374-8

First Kensington Hardcover Edition: July 2026

ISBN: 978-1-4967-5376-2 (ebook)

10 9 8 7 6 5 4 3 2 1

Printed in the United States of America

The authorized representative in the EU for product safety and compliance
is eucomply OU, Parnu mnt 139b-14, Apt 123
Tallinn, Berlin 11317, hello@eucompliancepartner.com

NOT WHAT IT SEEMS

Chapter 1

"Gol-dern birds," Billy Huber muttered, balanced on the old extension ladder while stretching to reach the starlings' nest that was clogging the gutter of his barn. With one eye to the storm clouds gathering overhead, he held a trowel in his gloved hand, and he poked at the twigs and grass and bits of paper that the birds had collected, but the nest was a little out of reach.

He leaned a bit farther just as his dog started barking his fool head off. "Not now," he growled, glancing back at his house and noting from this angle that the patches on his roof were about shot. He only hoped they would survive this next storm; then he'd tend to them. And his yard. Geez. From this vantage point, it looked bad. Real bad. Patchy grass, car parts left to rust, the old mower sitting where it died last summer, some rodeo equipment, even carnival paraphernalia. Along with a lot of other things. He'd have to get after the yard, too. Clean it up. He would. When the weather turned.

He sighed. Ever since Linnie had passed, about eight years earlier, he'd let the place go, and in his head, he heard her tsk-tsking. And her voice. Always her voice.

"Bill Huber, what's got into you? Where's your pride?" She would eye the trash in the yard and shake her head, her blond ponytail scraping her shoulders. "I don't know why you collect these things.

Car parts and old washers and whatnot filling the sheds and littering the yard so that the chickens don't know where to feed? Old signs and posters and broken-down furniture you're never gonna fix. And what about them banjos and guitars you ain't never gonna play? And don't get me started on the carnival crap—weird mirrors and the like! What're y'all thinkin'?" Her lips would be pursed, her blue eyes glittering hard as ice. She'd wipe her tiny hands on her apron, then make shooing motions as she ordered, "Now, go on. You fix that fence, and while you're at it, put the mower away. Go on, now, you know you can get a new part for the John Deere down at Wheeler's, so don't you be gittin' lazy on me, y'hear." Then she would nod curtly, turn back to the house and say over her shoulder that she would call him in when the meal was on the table. Just before the old screen door slammed behind her, he'd hear her say, "And don't you dare be late for supper!"

"Yes'm," he said aloud now, as if his dear departed Linnie could still hear him. As if she was still in the kitchen, baking rhubarb pie, or seated in her favorite recliner, mending his clothes or reading from the Good Book. Oh, how she liked to quote the Bible to him. Especially once their daughter had left for college down in Florida and only returned at Christmas and on Linnie's birthday in June.

But that was all over now. Once Linnie passed, Janelle quit visiting, just got to calling him once every week or so—"checking in," she said, but more likely "checking up" on him, for whatever that was worth. Probably just to see if he'd kicked the bucket. It was a shame, really, but he and Janelle had never gotten along. It hadn't helped that she'd married a loud, brash ass of a man old enough to be her damned father. Well, almost.

Rather than dwell on his own mistakes in the fatherhood department, Billy let his gaze wander to the side of the house where the garden had been. Cabbages and string beans, potatoes and squash, musk melons and strawberries, tomatoes and, oh, yes, rhubarb had once thrived in that fenced-in spot. Now it was home to mice and weeds and God knew what else.

She had a way with gardening, his Linnie had. She had a way with a lot of things. He felt that old pang when his thoughts ran to Linda-Sue, gone early. Had to remind himself that what she didn't have a way with was seeing the beauty and value of the items he found at auction or tossed onto the side of the road, or marked "free" and just waiting for him to scoop them up and toss them into the back of his Ford Ranger.

His chest tightened. It was his fault—

The dog barked loudly, interrupted his daydream—or twilight dream, as the afternoon had already bled into evening. "Arlo! Quiet!" Billy yelled from the fifth rung. But the mutt—part Australian shepherd and part who-knew-what—was pacing along the fence line, his hackles up, his eyes focused on the darkening woods surrounding this scrap of land Billy's family had called home for nearly a hundred years.

"You hush!" Billy commanded as the ladder shifted under his weight.

But the dog was nervous, his hackles raised, his growl, when he wasn't barking, low and ominous. Stiff-legged, tail raised, Arlo glared at the shaded woods.

"Darn fool mutt," Billy said under his breath, but he glanced at the copse of hickory and pine that had caught the shepherd's attention. Probably a deer hiding there, or maybe a rabbit or possum. Nothing to get all worked up about.

Nothing out of the ordinary to be seen.

Nothing unusual to be heard.

Nonetheless, Arlo was usually spot-on about danger.

Billy paused from his work, staring at the tree line and listening hard.

Crickets chirped over the hum of mosquitoes and the rustle of dry leaves as the wind picked up. Somewhere near the creek, a bullfrog was croaking. Dusk was leaning into night, the storm on its way.

A shadow moved in the woods.

Billy blinked.

Then saw nothing.

A chill raced up his spine, an icy touch that had nothing to do with the sultry night and a lot to do with his belief that the devil was always watching, always waiting.

Was there someone—be it Satan or someone of flesh and blood—just beyond the cover of pine needles?

No.

He was letting the dog get to him. That was all.

Time to finish up.

The destroying of the darned starlings' nest was his last task of the evening. As soon as it was done, he'd head inside, reheating the remains of last night's supper—Stagg Chili over store-bought biscuits—to be washed down with sweet tea, then topped off with a stiff shot of Jack Daniel's. Maybe two. He just had to get rid of the stupid nest where yet again a determined starling had found a crevice in the gutter.

Ignoring Arlo's sharp warning barks from the other side of the fence near the house, Billy leaned closer to the nest.

If he could just reach a little farther . . .

The tip of the trowel brushed the layer of twigs and grass.

He extended a bit more.

Stretching.

He gave a little poke.

His weight shifted slightly.

Just enough.

The aluminum ladder slid on the uneven ground.

"Shit!"

Billy tried to right it by adjusting his body. Frantically, he grabbed hold of the gutter.

Too late!

The ladder toppled. Falling away.

For a split second, Billy dangled by one arm, the gutter's sharp edge cutting through his glove, finding flesh, then it too gave way, ripping from the building in a horrendous moan of twisting metal.

"Goddamn!" he swore. Hanging in midair, he caught a glimpse of movement out of the corner of his eye again. What the hell?

A wraith, dressed in black, slipped around the corner of the old pump house.

Satan himself, come to claim his own!

With an earsplitting screech, the galvanized steel gave completely away, ripping from the eave.

"Shit!"

He lost his grip, falling fast.

Thud! He hit the ground and heard his ankle snap, the gutter crumpling beside him. An upturned rake impaled his right arm in its jaws. "Yow!" Steel teeth cut through his shirt, slicing into his flesh.

He sucked his breath through his teeth as the pain sizzled through his arm and shoulder. And his ankle. It was broken, sure enough. Throbbing, hot and hard.

He blinked. Staring upward. Hoping he'd imagined the specter.

But in that moment of agony, he locked eyes with Lucifer himself, his dark form looming over him. "Oh, sweet Jesus," he whispered, trying and failing to scoot away.

Beelzebub, the damned Prince of Darkness, had come to claim his soul.

No! He tried to scream as he inched backward over the uneven ground.

No words escaped his dry throat as he saw the weapon—a sharp blade in the wraith's hands.

Oh, sweet Jesus!

Quick as lightning, the demon struck, driving the instrument of death deep into Billy's throat.

As blood gurgled from the wound, the specter grabbed hold of Billy's head, raising it upward just long enough for recognition to dawn in Billy's eyes.

Not the devil, but—

Slam!

The monster thrust Billy's head down and onto the star-shaped blades of a garden tiller left to rust in the rain.

Lights flashed behind Billy's eyes.

Pain exploded in his skull.

Then, thankfully, there was nothing.

Chapter 2

Pierce Reed's cell phone rang through the warm Georgia night. His wife heard it. Even over the buzz of conversation and the music flowing from inside the house, Nikki caught its distinctive tone.

Oh, great.

Here they were, at his best friend's daughter's sweet-sixteen party, dancing on the veranda under twinkling fairy lights strung overhead, and his damned phone had the nerve to ring.

"Don't answer it," she said, as he reached into his jacket.

"Yeah, right." His gaze caught hers, and one corner of his mouth lifted.

He had a point there. As an independent crime reporter, when had she ever ignored a call?

"But—"

He held up a finger to quiet her arguments, then wended through the dancers, away from the crowd and around a corner.

She waited a couple of minutes, but when he didn't return, she cut across the lawn toward the garage side of the house, where Pierce had disappeared. She nearly ran into Naomi, who was walking rapidly toward a kitchen door and away from a tall, lanky man who was just climbing into the crew cab of a large, black Ram truck. His features were illuminated momentarily, dark hair catching in the light, square jaw rock-hard, thin lips set in a grim line. He sent an angry look toward the house, where Naomi was disappearing through a door near the kitchen. Muttering something unintelligible under his breath, he yanked the cab door shut, and he was shrouded in darkness until he turned on the ignition; the big truck's engine roared to life, and the driver's sharp features were visible in the glow from the dash lights.

As Nikki watched, he executed a quick three-point turn, then, with a roar of the big truck's engine, sped down the long drive.

Odd, Nikki thought, just as she caught a glimpse of Pierce rounding a corner.

She took off after him, cutting around a waiter carrying a tray of drinks, following her husband to a brick patio where a waterfall splashed into the large pool and moonlight danced upon the water's smooth surface. Stars glimmered overhead, and the soft hoot of an owl came from the woods surrounding the Kittle estate.

As she reached Pierce, she heard his end of what seemed to be a terse conversation. ". . . Yeah. I'll be there . . ." He checked his watch. "Twenty, maybe thirty minutes."

Nikki's heart sank.

Since the birth of their daughter, Chloe, nearly three years earlier, she and Pierce hadn't enjoyed many nights out alone. Between his job as a homicide detective with the police force and hers as a freelance writer, they were both busy. Lara Kittle's birthday celebration had been the exception.

And yet, she understood.

More than that, she was intrigued, as always, with her husband's work.

As Pierce cut off the call, she asked, "What's that all about?"

"Oh, so suddenly you're interested?" he said, though he wasn't really teasing. His jaw was set.

"Someone was murdered."

"Someone is dead," he corrected.

"But if you're involved," she pointed out.

"There's a possibility of homicide."

"Possibility?"

"Could be an accident."

"Someone from the department called you," she clarified, not about to be put off, "so it's got to be suspicious."

"I don't know yet, but I've got to go."

"I'm coming with you."

"Nikki, please . . ." This was their long, ongoing argument. He wanted to keep his work close to his vest. Police procedure and all that. And she, being naturally curious and a crime writer to boot, was always pushing. He thought she was nosy. She told herself she was just inquisitive. Well, and eager for the next story.

"And how am I supposed to get home?"

"You can get a ride with . . ." His voice trailed off. "I'm sure Jamison has a friend who lives in town and they wouldn't mind dropping you off."

"Forget it." She wasn't about to be pawned off on one of Jamison Kittle's buddies or their stuck-up wives. No way. No how. Though she, herself, was the daughter of a judge—God rest his soul—and her own mother was a known social climber, Nikki had no use for all that nonsense. "I'm coming with you."

"Jesus, Nikki, for just this once—"

"Let's go." She shot him a look, and he clamped his mouth shut rather than continue the argument as they walked through the veranda, where adults were still dancing or sipping drinks, then into the huge recreation room, where most of the teenagers had gathered. Nikki recognized a few, including her niece's horseback-riding instructor, Annabelle Van Camp.

Inside, the music was rap and hip-hop, the kids playing pool or lounging in groups on leather couches and probably drinking on the sly.

A long bar ran down one side of the room, and on the opposite wall was a display of weaponry any mercenary would envy. Jamison Kittle's collection of rifles, bows, swords, and knives ran the gamut from historic, with his great-great-grandfather's shotgun, to state-of-the-art semiautomatic rifles. He boasted all types of weapons, from Revolutionary War muskets to a World War II Luger supposedly taken off a fallen German soldier and a more recent AR-15, all gleaming behind locked glass panels.

A jukebox straight out of the fifties glowed in one corner, and a poker table was off to one side. There were two steps up to the kitchen, where Jamison's wife, Naomi, petite, blond, and in charge, was organizing the servers, making sure the refreshments—sliders and mini pizzas and burgers—were arranged on silver platters.

Through an archway, Nikki spied the dining room, where the table was festooned in pink and silver, a huge cake displayed in the center, while around it were silver platters of cupcakes, confections, and gleaming jars of candy.

At that moment, Lara Kittle swept through the kitchen in a gown of frothy pink. Her hair, piled loosely on her head, was dark, her eyes a deep brown, and her glossy lips were turned down into a pissy frown. "Is this good enough?" she demanded of her mother and poked a finger at her outfit.

Naomi glanced away from a bowl filled with melon balls and eyed her eldest daughter. "It's not how Shirley would have done it, but it's okay, I suppose."

"You suppose?" Lara rolled her large eyes. "Jesu—Geez, Mom, I'm in the damned dress. Isn't that good enough?"

"For the pictures, dear."

"Yeah, yeah, I know." Lara blew out her lips. "Let's get them over with."

"Your sisters aren't ready." Naomi sent a sidelong glance toward Nikki as if to silently convey: *See what you're in for?*

Lara picked up her skirt and, back stiff in indignation, dashed down to the rec room and her friends.

"Where's Jamison?" Pierce asked as Naomi fretted over some prawns displayed on a mound of ice and lemon wedges.

"Who knows?" She stepped away from the counter, where a server was waiting. With a broad sweep of her hand, she indicated that the trays were to her liking and could be whisked away. Yet she was obviously perturbed, her glossy pink lips pinched. She glanced up at Pierce as the waitress scurried off with two trays of appetizers. "He knows we want pictures of all of the girls! Maybe in his office?" With a huff, she said, "That would be just like him! In the middle of Lara's big night, if you can believe it." Then spying a platter of refreshments that didn't meet her standards, she said, "No . . . no, that's not right! Mini pizzas by themselves. Mini burgers on a separate tray! What're y'all thinking?"

Rather than question her further, Pierce peeled off and went through a door to the main hallway, where streamers and fairy lights decorated a wide staircase. Two girls in matching silvery gowns were giggling as they descended, nearly tripping on their skirts. Jamison and Naomi's younger daughters. Shana, the redhead, eleven-ish, was in front, while blond Michelle, the youngest, tumbled after her. Somehow neither tripped as they slid in glittery sandals on the hardwood and rounded the corner, careening into the kitchen.

"Naomi's not going to like that," Pierce said and crossed the foyer to the closed French doors of the den. Through the sheer curtains, Nikki spied Jamison, his chiseled face tense as he talked on the phone. Pierce rapped on the doorframe, and Jamison nodded curtly and motioned for him to enter.

"Got it," he said into the phone. "Be there as soon as I can." He clicked off and grabbed his jacket off the back of his chair. "You heard. About Billy Huber?" he said without preamble.

Pierce was nodding. "Just got the call. On my way there now."

Jamison glanced at Nikki. "And you?"

"I'm tagging along." At the furrowing of Jamison's brow, she held up a hand. "I'll stay in the car."

He didn't seem convinced, and really, it was probably a lie. She couldn't imagine watching from the sidelines.

"She'll wait until we sort out what happened." Pierce was talking to Jamison, and the fact that he wasn't addressing her directly got under Nikki's skin.

"We don't want another incident," Jamison said, and Nikki sucked in a swift breath. Pierce's jaw tightened, and his eyes flashed. They both understood, and a hot surge of guilt swept through Nikki when she thought of Sylvie Morrisette, once Pierce's partner, now deceased. The Texas-tough detective had died while trying to rescue Nikki, who had been investigating a case where she hadn't been wanted, where she shouldn't have been, at least in the minds of the local cops. To this day, many officers in the police department blamed Pierce's pushy wife for the loss of one of their own.

It hadn't been easy for Nikki.

It was much worse for her husband.

"I said, 'I'll wait,'" she clarified, trying and failing to hide her annoyance.

"Good." Jamison turned his attention to Pierce. "I'll be there as soon as I can, but I have to deal with the party. Naomi's insisting on family pictures since the girls are all dressed up." Irritated, he shoved a hand through his hair. "So far, it's been one helluva night."

Pierce agreed. "And it's not over yet."

Jamison gave a curt nod as he headed toward the rec room. "That's the problem, isn't it? Will you contact Augustin?" he asked, referencing Pierce's most recent partner, Sol Augustin. "I think she's out of town."

"Coming back tomorrow morning, but I'll loop her in."

"Good." Jamison seemed satisfied. "Let's roll."

Pierce was already on his way outside, Nikki in lockstep.

"Billy Huber?" Nikki said once they were in the car. She remembered the name from when she'd written about a single-car accident that had taken Linda-Sue Huber's life. Nikki had been a reporter for the *Savannah Sentinel* at the time. "His wife died, what? Six, maybe seven years ago?"

"Around eight, I think." Pierce's headlights cut through the night. "Something like that."

He was wrapped in concentration, and she saw his face in profile, illuminated by the dash lights. In her mind, he was still startlingly handsome. Not a Hollywood he-man, but tall and lanky, with thick dark hair and light brown eyes that could glint gold when he was angry.

Of course, they were often at odds over her career. Though she was now a freelance journalist and author and no longer worked shifts at the newspaper's office, she was always interested in her husband's cases, and that caused friction between them. That said, they never grew tired of each other. Theirs was not one of those steady, by-the-book, everything-on-a-schedule marriages, but it worked. Sometimes their fights were mercurial, but their relationship was never, ever dull. The truth was that Nikki was in love with Pierce now as much as she'd been when she'd first set eyes on him.

Now his eyebrows were drawn together, his jaw set in granite, beard shadow evident. As she studied him, she felt a little thrill. Silly, she supposed, after all these years, but there it was.

As he drove, the illumination from the headlights of approaching cars washing over them, Pierce placed a call to his partner. When Sol Augustin didn't pick up, he left a message and turned deeper into the low country, where traffic thinned and the woods deepened. Pierce was on his phone several times during the drive, each conversation short and clipped, while Nikki continually checked hers, searching for information on William Huber and his deceased wife.

"This must be the place," Pierce said, spying an overgrown lane. Tree branches formed a canopy overhead, weeds and vines created hazards in the ruts of the drive, and through the brush, Nikki saw the pulsating lights of emergency vehicles. They rounded a final corner to a clearing where several police cars were parked. Portable lights illuminated an area littered with debris from last night's storm, the ground already covered by junk of every shape and size. Under the artificial illumination, old washers and refrigerators, tools and equipment, televisions and rusting car parts were visible. Nikki even recognized the front end of an ancient Studebaker, tires included, like the one she remembered her grandfather driving before she'd entered elementary school.

A hoarder's dream.

A fire marshal's nightmare.

"Look at this," she whispered, taking it all in and noticing the fire truck and EMT vehicles idling, drivers at the wheels.

In the middle of it all, surrounded by men and women in uniform, some with flashlights, was the body of a bearded man in jeans and a sweatshirt, lying supine, the back of his head impaled on the blade of a rusted garden tiller. A fallen ladder lay nearby, resting on what appeared to be part of a Whac-A-Mole display.

"Billy Huber?" Nikki asked, focusing on the dead body.

"I assume." Pierce had cut the engine of his Jeep and was opening the driver's side door. He paused, his eyes finding hers. "Stay put."

"I—"

"I mean it, Nikki."

"Don't tell me what to do."

He paused for just a second, his lips tight as conversation and the sound of a barking dog drifted into the car.

"Just don't order me around," she insisted. "Okay? I said I'd wait, and I will."

"Remember. This is police business."

"Got it." From the corner of one eye, Nikki saw the source of the noise, a shaggy shepherd, pacing on the porch and barking like crazy. "Is that dog limping?" she asked, turning to look at the animal, who was separated from the barnyard by a wire fence.

"Don't know." Pierce slammed the car door shut and picked his way around an unruly stack of tires and over the patchy, unmown grass to the area where several officers had collected.

A bit stung by his harsh tone, Nikki eyed the scene through the windshield but couldn't hear the conversation he was having with the other cops. She was trying to tamp down her irritation and keep her emotions under rein. Pierce wasn't being high-handed, she told herself. He was doing his job. But yeah, he could whittle down his authoritative attitude by more than a few notches.

She'd never been one to take orders. He knew that. But he also knew that the last time she'd disobeyed him, the consequences had been traumatic. Deadly. She bit her lip. But the word *disobeyed* stuck in her craw. He was a partner, her husband . . .

And a homicide detective who'd lost his partner.

Because of you, that nasty voice in her head reminded her.

There was a lot of emotional baggage involved in that particular incident. A lot. She counted herself lucky that she was still married.

She absently rubbed her abdomen and watched as the emergency vehicles drove away. No need for the EMTs to stick around, nor the fire department. Billy Huber was obviously dead. And had been for a while, she guessed, noting the dried blood on his body and the tiller's blade.

She scanned the area, turned on the AC, and lowered the passenger door window, letting in a warm breeze that brought with it the scent of pine and earth and something she couldn't quite name.

Death.

That was it.

This whole place appeared as if it were dying.

From the looks of it, Billy Huber had toppled from the ladder, stripping off a gutter that lay near him. And he'd had the bad luck to fall onto the blades. Except that the police were suspicious that a crime had been committed.

She wondered about it, as she stared at the blood crusted in the victim's matted hair. Had someone intentionally knocked Billy off the ladder, then rammed his head into the sharp, spiky disks that reminded her of ninja stars? But who would do this to him? And why? Was it really murder? Or just an awful accident? She squinted at the dead body while vaguely aware of the still-barking dog.

It was hard to see, but it looked as if he'd somehow injured his neck, too. Wasn't that blood at the base of his throat? Some kind of cut?

If only she could get a better view . . .

Over the barking, she heard one burly deputy ask Pierce, "Possibly an accident? You think he fell and hit his head?"

Pierce wasn't convinced. "If so, he was pretty unlucky."

"Was he? If ya ask me, ya fall off a ladder into this mess of a yard, and nine times outta ten yer gonna hit somethin'. Take a look around. Have you ever seen so much shit scattered in a yard? Mother of God, this place is a pigsty. So much goddamned crap. You'd think my ex lived here!"

A woman cop nearby said, "One man's trash is another man's treasure." She was tall and lean, athletic, her brown hair brushing her shoulders, her face pale in the harsh light. Nikki thought she recognized her, had met her at some of the station functions—maybe last year's Christmas party. Her name was Liz something . . . what was it? Martin? No. Maddox. Liz Maddox. Yeah, that was it.

"If you say so." The big man was clearly skeptical.

"I've seen your desk, Swanson," she replied with a huff. "You got no call to judge."

Oh, right, Ron Swanson. He was a deputy, Nikki thought. She'd heard his name before, but had never met him. She made a mental note and wished to high heaven she could hear more. If she could just take a peek around . . .

"Goddamn! Can someone shut that fuckin' mutt up!" It was Swanson again, and he was glaring at the porch, where the dog continued its incessant barking.

She could help with the shepherd. She was good with dogs.

No!

She'd promised Pierce.

She fought a mental battle, but her fingers strayed to the door handle.

She wouldn't be hindering but helping, she reasoned.

"I swear if that damned cur don't stop that infernal racket," Swanson declared, "I'll take care of him myself!"

"I'll call animal control." Maddox was reaching for her cell phone, and Nikki clicked open the Jeep's door to step outside as Pierce, ignoring the bickering and racket, crouched down for a better look at the body.

Nikki slipped outside, closing the Jeep's door softly so that the interior light winked off. "Don't call animal control," she said, loud enough to be heard over the barking and chatter of conversation. "I've got this," and she started for the fenced area around the house. She caught a glimpse of her husband's tightened lips before he gave a quick shake of his head. Ignoring his silent warning, she slipped through the gate just as she heard Swanson say, "Hey! What the fuck is this? Jesus, it's got a number carved into it—Looks like a six or . . . well, maybe a nine, depending on which is end is up."

"It's a rock, Swanson. For Crissakes, look at all this junk," his partner said, waving an arm at the piles of trash only made worse by the broken tree branches littering the area. "One damned rock in acres of this crap, and *that's* what you focus on?"

Nikki shot a look at Swanson, who was holding up a stone in his gloved hand. "It was next to the body. Kinda tucked under it. Maybe dropped out of the guy's pocket. And look at it. Shiny. Probably polished. Like a big agate."

"Okay." Maddox was unmoved.

"But on the other side some kind of mark—I can't figure it out." Swanson was clearly puzzled. "Looks like hieroglyphics of some kind."

"It's a damned rock, Swanson. Do you see what we're dealing with here?"

Nikki strained to hear the rest of the conversation, but she couldn't appear too interested, and she had the dog to deal with.

It watched her as she approached, its black lips pulled back, sharp teeth bared, dark eyes bright from the reflection of the lights. As she approached, it snarled in warning.

"Shhh," she commanded softly, and the beast, a shepherd of some kind, glared. "Quiet." She was calm and steady, moving slowly, but with determination. "It's okay," she said, which, of course, it very much wasn't.

The dog lunged and snapped. Teeth flashing.

"No!" she ordered tautly but didn't back down. She'd been in tighter spots than this. One scared shepherd wasn't going to stop her. She took a step up to the porch, and the dog backed up. "You're okay," she cooed. "Look, if you don't want to end up in the pound, you'd better hush. Got it? You're lucky I'm here."

Another low growl, but finally the dog quieted and slunk away, hiding under a broken chair covered in horseback-riding paraphernalia. Beneath the pile of bridles, helmets, and even a saddle covering the dilapidated rocker, the shepherd's eyes were still fixed on her. But he—or maybe a she—was no longer making a racket. The shepherd was scrawny, its coat matted and dark. And was there blood in its mottled fur? "Oh, let me look at you." But as she neared, the dog snapped before sinking deeper under the rocker. "Okay, okay." Nikki sank down on an ottoman losing its stuffing and spoke in a quiet, soothing tone, all the while straining to hear what was happening on the other side of the wire fence.

She only caught a word or two, phrases, bits of the conversation over the hum of insects and the regular croak of a nearby frog. The cops' conversation was muffled as they tried to piece together what had happened. Flashlights swept over the scene and upward to the roof of the barn, where a piece of gutter was hanging.

Pierce straightened and glanced over his shoulder to the Jeep, then toward the porch, where, in the darkness, she met his gaze. His jaw was tight again, lips flat. Obviously, he was irritated with her, but didn't say anything as she'd managed to stop the barking.

Within minutes, the medical examiner's van arrived, slowing to a stop with a crunch of tires on the sparse gravel. A stern-faced, balding man stepped from behind the wheel, and after a few quick seconds of talking with the officers, he, too, bent down to examine what had once been Billy Huber.

She considered how wise it would be to just walk up to her husband, but before she could make a move, headlights cut through the night, and the crime-scene team arrived.

There was more chatter, more flashlights glowing, instructions issued before Billy Huber's body was zipped into a bag and hauled into the back of the ME's van. The crime-scene team took over the area, taking measurements and digital pictures, combing the area as the deputies backed off, huddling with Pierce, their conversation only a mumble.

Nikki turned her attention back to the space under the rocker, where dark eyes glittered suspiciously. If the dog was bleeding, it wasn't all that much. No blood was dripping onto the floorboards.

It took over an hour before Pierce started back to the Jeep. By this time, the dog had stopped its intermittent growling, but was still regarding Nikki guardedly.

"You coming?" her husband said.

"Yeah, but I want to—"

"We're not taking the dog."

"Of course we are." She straightened off the broken ottoman.

"Nikki, we can't. I mean, how do you think you're going to get him to come with you? And when he does, what about Mikado?" he asked, mentioning their aging husky mix as he opened the driver's side door.

Nikki slipped through the gate and latched it behind her. "But—I think he could be injured."

"Animal control will see to him."

"Animal control. No, Pierce, we need to—"

"We need to let the professionals handle it. First of all, he's not ours. Secondly, who knows if he's had all his shots? And thirdly, we don't need another pet. We've already got a cat and a dog. And if this one's hurt," Pierce added with a hitch of his chin toward the house, "the department will handle it. The answer is no."

He was firm. And, unfortunately, making some sense. Frustrated, Nikki hurried through the mud and grass and around what appeared to be part of an old treadle sewing machine to reach the Jeep. "So he'll see a vet?" she asked, opening the passenger door.

"First animal control, at least to begin with, and then a vet if necessary."

"After that?"

"Then we'll see. After we speak with Billy Huber's daughter. She's the one who called the department to check on her dad. In the meantime, the dog has to be removed from the property so we can investigate the house and yard." He motioned toward the fenced area that included Huber's cottage. "We'll be back in the morning to check out the house."

Nikki said, "Okay, then. I'll come with you."

For once, he didn't argue.

Chapter 3

Sol Augustin stood, barefoot, on the very ground where Billy Huber had lost his life. It was still dark, a few hours before dawn, and she was alone, had ignored his posted warnings and the yellow band of crime-scene tape as she'd parked near the gate and walked to this low-country farm.

The area where he'd lain was clearly marked near the barn, the grass flattened and part of the chalk line still visible.

She wanted to feel his death, to sense what he'd seen, to witness, in her mind's eye, how he'd died. She needed to experience his last moments on earth.

And she didn't want anyone to know that she was here or what she was doing. Especially not anyone from the police department.

No one would understand.

This she knew from past experience.

But she'd covered her tracks and, gratefully, had slipped onto the property unseen. Where she could be one with the dead.

Who was this dead man, and who had killed him so violently?

She took in a deep breath and heard the soft, plaintive hoot of an owl over the creak of an ancient weather vane as it turned in the breeze. She felt the dampness of the earth beneath the soles of her feet and the moisture in the air. Could smell the decay and rust.

There was clutter all around.

Man-made objects that the dead man found dear. She'd caught sight of them in the beam of her flashlight as she'd walked into this barnyard. A rusting, curved arm of a carnival ride—the octopus, she thought. It stretched from one of the sheds to the fence, where rolls of chicken wire and collections of bottles were piled near the toppling frame of a beehive.

Treasures.

Sol slid out of her simple cotton shift, where the white fabric had contrasted with her mocha-colored skin, the coloring she'd inherited from her Haitian mother. Her eyes, too, were large over high cheekbones, but were more green than brown, thanks to her white, missionary father.

It was their combination of genes, island native and deeply supernaturalistic Christian, that had given her the gift that was sometimes a blessing and oftentimes a curse. But it was a gift that she used to her advantage, as she was doing now.

With the dress pooling around her, she closed her eyes.

Whispered a prayer to the gods of the earth and sky, hoping to reach him.

Come to me.

William Jasper Huber, come to me.

She waited and drew in a long breath, smelling the grass and pines. The cool Georgia night surrounded her.

Somewhere, not too far off, a creek babbled.

She felt the flutter of a bat's wings as it darted overhead, chasing insects. She imagined the ruffling of the Spanish moss in the live oaks that rimmed the property, sensed the presence of a rabbit moving through the tall grass . . . but she needed more, and waited for the deceased to bridge the chasm between the living world and the dead.

"Come to me," she called aloud, hoping his spirit would find her, would cross over, and looked into the shadows of the surrounding trees.

She closed her eyes.

There was an occlusion.

Too many voices.

Not only had the police been here clouding the energy, but others, too, had trod upon this very spot. Emotions sizzled through the air. Anger. Curiosity. Fear. Disgust.

Too many voices.

Concentrate, she told herself.

Filter out the noise.

Find him.

She took a deep, calming breath.

Slowed her heart rate.

Her eyelids fluttered, her teeth chattering just a bit.

Then it happened.

The slight tremor in her body.

As if she were experiencing the rising of William Huber's escaping spirit.

Come back.

But Billy's essence didn't stop rising, only paused to look down at the bloody scene and his own broken body.

He wasn't alone. A man bent over him. An angry man who yanked a blade from Billy's bearded neck. Furiously, the man wiped the bloody blade against his thigh before tucking a stone beneath Billy's shell of a body and scuttling away, toward the woods.

Inside, Sol turned to ice, the night curdling cold.

Who is he? Who did this to you?

In her mind's eye, the dead body twisted to stare at her with unblinking eyes.

"Who?" she said aloud.

The dead man's lips didn't move, but she heard his voice, clear as a clarion call: "Who did this to me? The damned spawn of Satan, that's who."

And then he disappeared.

But that wasn't all, she knew.

Billy Huber's wasn't the only death . . . oh, no. She'd caught a glimpse of another soul this night, and she knew, with a blood-chilling certainty, there would be more.

The day hadn't quite dawned when Nikki, unable to stand it a second longer, brought up the investigation. Pierce was just finishing breakfast, while Chloe was propped in her booster chair and giggling as she plucked Cheerios one by one from her plate and dropped them to an eagerly waiting Mikado.

"You're going back to the Huber place?" she asked.

While Pierce had showered, shaved, and dressed in a navy suit, she was still in her PJs and robe, no makeup, her hair caught in a very messy bun, tangled from a bad night's sleep, her thoughts swirling over what had happened to Billy Huber.

"After the office." He no longer seemed angry with her, thank God, but he wasn't chatty either.

"No news?"

"Nikki," he warned.

"Don't say it. Police business. I *know.*"

"Good."

"But as a member of the press," she said, as he finished his coffee and carried his empty cup to the sink, "I could use some information. And you were on the phone last night." She'd tried to overhear the conversation, but the door to his office had remained firmly closed as he'd made and received calls. All of which she surmised were about the homicide of Billy Huber. When she'd asked him about the calls as he'd slipped into bed, he'd tersely explained that Huber's dog had somehow escaped the animal control officer and was nowhere to be found. That was the extent of information he was willing to impart.

But then he'd taken her into his arms and begun kissing her, and for the time being she'd let herself be carried away in a heated, passionate, and emotional wave of lovemaking. Afterward, Pierce had kissed her forehead, rolled over, and begun lightly snoring almost immediately.

Not so for Nikki. She'd tossed and turned all night, wondering what had happened to Billy Huber. Who had killed him and why? That was the crux of the mystery. If, indeed, Billy had been the victim of homicide, which seemed likely because of Pierce's involvement.

Then there was Huber's dog. Why had the animal control officer been so careless? Where was it now? She'd worried about the dog all night, and what little information she'd pried from Pierce this morning hadn't eased her mind or abated her curiosity.

Now Pierce interrupted her thoughts. "The last I heard, you were an independent reporter these days."

"Still a member of the press." She took a sip of her now-tepid coffee, then set the cup down.

"Technically, yes, but you're not on the staff of the *Sentinel.*"

"What's that got to do with anything?" she demanded, then to her daughter, "Chloe, stop that. Mikado doesn't need Cheerios."

"He likes them!" Chloe was delighted by the dog's attention.

"If you want to know more, as a member of the press," Pierce said, "just call the station. Talk to the PIO about the case."

She rolled her eyes as he found his keys on a side table. The new public information officer, Vivian Johnson, was professional and oh-so tight-lipped.

Unfortunately, Pierce was right. From the moment she'd discovered she was pregnant with Chloe, Nikki had given up working at the office, had gone freelance completely, and even stopped writing true-crime books. As she'd suffered a series of miscarriages, she'd been over-the-top in following her doctor's instructions and had decided to turn in her resignation. She'd told herself she needed R and R, though the inactivity about drove her out of her mind. She'd never been one to sit still for long. Athletic and curious to a fault, intrigued by any kind of mystery, she couldn't stand lying at home with her feet up, trying to occupy her mind with watching television, scrolling through the Internet, or reading on a chaise by a pool. She needed action. Excitement. Mental stimulation.

Crossword puzzles, Sudoku, knitting, and the like were all fine and good, but just not enough. Nonetheless, she'd gritted her teeth, forced herself to slow down, and indulged herself in crime dramas streaming on television, listening to true-crime podcasts, and expanding her cooking repertoire, as well as spending more time with her sister Lily and niece Ophelia, "Phee," and yes, even her mother. During the nine months of her pregnancy, Nikki had done everything by the book, and *voilà*, Chloe had been born without any complications. So worth it, but could she do it again? She wasn't sure. Pierce was pressuring her about a sibling for their daughter, but Nikki wasn't convinced they needed to add another baby into the mix. For the moment, she was repeating the mantra "One and done." It sounded good right now, though she wasn't one to say "never."

Now, Pierce bent over the high chair and kissed the top of his daughter's head. Chloe turned her face upward, big eyes bright, apple cheeks creasing as she giggled. "Daddy!"

"That's me." And despite the fact that she had milk smeared all over her face, he picked her up from the chair and hugged her. "Who's my girl?"

Her green eyes twinkled. "Mama your girl."

"That's right, imp, she is, but who's my other girl?"

"Mikado," she said, teasing, showing off her baby teeth, wrinkling her nose in pride at her joke.

Pierce pointed out, "Mikado's a boy."

"Like you!"

"Exactly. And, silly, it's you. *You're* my girl." He gave her a squeeze, and she tossed back her head and laughed gleefully.

"You my boy!" she said.

"You got that right, but right now your boy has to head to the office."

"No, you stay!" she insisted as Nikki drained her cup, then scraped her chair back, arms outstretched for the handoff as Pierce passed his daughter into her arms.

"Gotta work," he explained.

"It's Sunday," Nikki protested, and Pierce arched an eyebrow.

"There's a possible homicide, and when did the weekend ever stop you from working when you were on the trail of a hot story?"

"Fine."

"I'll see both my girls later," he promised. While Chloe squirmed, he pressed a kiss onto Nikki's cheek before striding out the door.

Seconds later, Nikki heard the rumble of the garage door opening and the sound of Pierce's Jeep's engine sparking to life.

Chloe wriggled out of Nikki's arms and toddled to the door to the garage, but was thwarted in her escape as she couldn't yet work the knob.

This was their morning routine, and for the most part, especially on the good days like today, Nikki loved it.

Still, a part of her missed going into the office—well, kind of; she and her editor at the *Savannah Sentinel* had never seen eye to eye, but the kinetic atmosphere in the newspaper office always energized her. Even though actual newspaper sales had tumbled and most of the reporting was done online these days, there was still an electricity to the workplace.

She spent the better part of the next hour getting both herself and Chloe bathed and dressed; then they fed the animals together. As Mikado dived into his bowl and their tabby, Jennings, picked at his food, she thought of Billy Huber's dog, injured and probably scared.

Lily, yawning, appeared downstairs after making her way from the guest bedroom. "There's still coffee, right?" she asked and beelined for the pot, still warming on the coffeemaker's burner. "I don't suppose you've got a ciggie?" she asked hopefully.

"No, and you quit, remember?"

"Ugh. Yes. Bad idea." Nikki's older sister, now an ash blonde, had taken up residence with them. Temporarily supposedly. And part of the deal was that she would give up the long, black cigarettes she loved. Years before, Lily had confided to Nikki that they made her feel "sophisticated" and "continental," though that time was long over.

Lily was, and always had been, impossibly thin, an academic who embraced literature and philosophy and ballet in her younger years and had never had a nine-to-five job. She'd gotten pregnant years before, had the baby, and refused to mention who Ophelia's father was. Maybe she didn't know. It was a secret Lily swore she'd keep to her grave, though Nikki thought that might be impossible these days, once Ophelia turned eighteen and could get her own DNA kit and take a test that would link her to any relatives in the system. So, as much as Lily loved to have an air of mystery about her, that little secret might eventually come to light.

As for her smoking, she'd sworn she'd quit, and to be fair, Nikki had never caught her lighting up. But every once in a while, when her sister returned after being out with friends, Nikki thought she caught a whiff of tobacco smoke wafting in the air, mingling with Lily's perfume.

A thump sounded. Then the sound of running footsteps overhead, on the second floor, signifying that Ophelia had awoken.

Lily said, "I think the dead has risen," as she settled into a chair at the island with her cup. Seconds later, Ophelia, barefoot, her nightgown billowing around her, burst into the room. At eleven, "Phee" was on the gangly side, with light brown hair that was always a mess, freckles bridging her nose, and a wide smile with teeth that were still a little too big for her face. She loved horses and Taylor Swift and was begging to get her ears pierced and her hair highlighted. So far, Lily had resisted.

At the sight of her cousin, Chloe beamed. "Phee-Phee," she said happily and was rewarded by being swung off her feet and twirled into several tight circles. Mikado barked, and Jennings slithered under the couch, while Chloe giggled in ecstasy.

"Where is all this enthusiasm on a school day?" Lily asked, though, in Nikki's estimation, Phee was always cheery and in high gear. As cynical and somewhat world-weary as her mother was, Phee embraced life and was always running at a speed ensured to break the sound barrier.

"Let's go outside," Phee said to Chloe as she set the still-dizzy toddler onto the floor, then shot through the patio door.

"You all right?" Nikki was about to pick up her daughter, but Chloe was already drunkenly toddling out the open door to the patio.

"God, I wish I had Phee's energy," Lily said, eyeing the black coffee in her mug. "But there isn't enough caffeine in the world to pep me up like that." She took a sip. "You know, she reminds me of you when you were a kid." At that thought, Lily pulled a face. "Oh, Lord, I hope she doesn't turn out like you."

"Thanks so much."

"Oh, you know," Lily said with a flip of one hand. "Always getting into trouble, always nosing around, always chasing after nutjobs and criminals and—"

"Oh, whoa, whoa, whoa. That's not *all* I do."

Lily cocked a doubting eyebrow. "Sure. Whatever you say." She buried her nose in her cup and let the subject drop. They talked about the day stretching before them. Lily was going to take the kids to the park and then visit their mother; she hoped to convince Charlene to consider moving to a retirement community, a place where she could be independent until she needed more care. So far, their fierce but frail little mother was balking and had refused. Whenever the subject was brought up, Charlene always smiled sweetly and said, "Oh, bless you, honey. Of course I will. Just as soon as hell freezes over."

"I'll get the girls breakfast," Lily said. "Do we have any Pop-Tarts? Phee is all over them right now. Really into Frosted Strawberry Milkshake or Frosted Hot Fudge Sundae, or something like that, and for God's sake, Nikki, don't give me the evil eye. I *know* it's not the best breakfast in the world, but I'm happy she slows down long enough to get anything into her, and she's getting really picky."

"You were, too," Nikki pointed out. "So is Mom. Still."

"Yeah, yeah. I know."

"Don't worry about Chloe. She already ate. Fruit and cereal."

"Okay." Lily scraped her chair back to rummage in the cupboard and withdraw the box of Pop-Tarts. As she slipped two into the toaster, she asked, "And so what is it you're going to do again?"

"Working on a new book. Might have to go out for some research." Nikki was pointedly vague about her day. The less anyone knew about what she really was planning to do this morning the better. And that included Lily. If Lily needed to reach her, Nikki would have her iPhone with her.

Damn Pierce for being so tight-lipped about the case.

Other than the fact that Huber's dog had escaped, all Nikki had gleaned from him was that a deputy had been sent out to check on Billy on a wellness call after his daughter, Janelle McGowan, had phoned from Jacksonville. Janelle had been concerned, as she hadn't heard from her father in several days after he'd promised to phone, something he did every week. Janelle also had known about the storm that had ripped through the Savannah area, so she'd been concerned enough to phone the authorities.

Bad weather had been the least of Billy Huber's problems, Nikki thought, as she reached into the refrigerator for the remains of Phee's barely eaten hamburger, all that was left from a Happy Meal from a day or two earlier. She rewrapped the burger and dropped it into her tote. Then she gathered her laptop, phone, and notebook, before taking the time to kiss her daughter goodbye, promising to be back by midafternoon.

"Bye-bye," Chloe said, waving from the cradle of Lily's arms. This was their usual morning routine, and so Chloe wasn't distressed. As opposite as Nikki was from her sister, she thanked her lucky stars that she had someone she could trust to care for her daughter while she worked. She gave Phee a quick hug before snagging one of Mikado's extra leashes from a hook in the laundry room and adding it to her oversize bag. As she made her way to the garage, she checked the tote to make certain she had packed a small flashlight, a separate recorder, and a set of lock picks that she hoped Pierce would never find. Tools of her trade.

As she fired up her Subaru, she convinced herself she wasn't really lying when she'd told Lily she was doing research. Not when she had a feeling that Billy Huber's death might be fodder for her next book.

Chapter 4

The drive to the low country and Billy Huber's farm took little more than thirty minutes. The April day was bright, the sun rising and promising heat. She rolled the windows down and felt the wind whip through her hair, then drove past the lane leading to the Huber farm, making certain that no police vehicles—or any other vehicles, for that matter—were on the property.

She couldn't really tell, as the lane curved, but after driving by once, she decided to chance it. Even so, she parked nearly a quarter of a mile down the road, around a corner, on a spur of another drive where the shoulder was wide enough to pull off.

With her bag slung over her shoulder, she jogged back to the lane, which had been overgrown by an untamed hedge of saplings, scrub brush, and berry vines.

The gate was now closed and marked with crime-scene tape that fluttered slightly in the morning breeze. She pushed it open and started along the curving drive to the cluttered, junk-filled yard surrounding the house and outbuildings. Though not as garish as it had appeared the night before, the area was blanketed with all kinds of junk and broken tree limbs.

No dog in sight.

No signs of life.

The air still.

Quiet.

Almost eerily so.

No birds chirping or insects humming.

Oh, get over yourself. It's just a quiet morning.

Nervously, she eyed the woods surrounding the house and barnyard. A forest of hickory, pine, and live oaks separated Huber's scrap of land from the rest of the world. As she studied the woods, her skin prickled. She imagined someone hidden deep in the undergrowth.

Someone watching.

Or maybe the missing dog?

Or maybe nothing—Maybe it was all in her fertile, suspicious mind.

It was a crime scene, the spot where a murder had taken place. Her nerves were just on edge, that was all. Knowing that Pierce would throw a fit if he knew she was here, and that at any minute a police cruiser might roll up the drive and she would have to explain herself, had made her jumpy. That was all.

"Get on with it," she told herself, slipping her phone from her pocket. She started with the matted grass, still stained with blood and the spot where the tiller had been. Quickly, she snapped pictures of the area: the flattened grass and weeds where Huber's body had landed, the torn gutter on the barn, the remaining collection of junk.

Who had wanted him dead?

And why?

Again the question haunted her.

Carefully, she backed up, avoiding the clutter and making a wide circle while taking shots of the barn, sheds, an abandoned chicken coop, a pump house, and a woodpile, where she was certain hornets and squirrels had nested. She clicked off images of the collected rubble, piles of horseshoes, and car parts scattered everywhere.

As she snapped off a series of shots of the cabin itself, she ignored that little tingle of anxiety that crawled up her spine while she called the dog.

Nothing.

No one was here, not even the shepherd.

She was alone.

She was just being a ninny, letting her wild imagination get the better of her, she thought, trying to convince herself as she stumbled over a dirty baby doll that cried out as she stepped on it.

"Dear Lord," she whispered and backed up to the fence surrounding the house. She took a quick picture of the doll, eased through the gate, and made her way along the path to the porch, where last night she'd stayed with the dog.

The canine, of course, wasn't around.

She tried the door.

Unlocked. Probably just like the night before.

So far, so good.

Nerves strung tight, she slipped inside the gloomy interior.

Softly, she called to the dog again, but heard only the steady drip of the kitchen sink. No whine or bark or claws scraping on the floor. The air was unmoving, the scent of old cigarette smoke mingling with a foul odor seeping from the partially opened door of an ancient refrigerator.

A faded floral love seat was pushed against one wall, and a recliner sat in front of an old bubble-screen TV. One corner housed a woodstove, where ash was piled high behind a cracked glass door. And everywhere, on every surface, was clutter. Magazines, books, tools, records, all covered with a thin layer of dust.

She stepped around a stack of old forty-fives and pushed open the door to a bedroom in the same condition as the rest of the house. A double bed with a bare mattress and sleeping bag rested beneath a single window and was surrounded by clothes and more trash. She thought there might be a dresser near the closet, but she couldn't be sure.

A hoarder's delight, she thought, spying the single bathroom that looked as if it barely functioned. Rust and rings on toilet and sink, the floor of the shower stained as well.

She saw nothing that indicated why Billy Huber had been killed.

Who had hated him so much to spark such violence?

She kept snapping pictures as she climbed a rickety, low-ceilinged stairway that wound upward to an attic landing, where one door opened with a shove. Had the police even been inside? It didn't seem so. But they would be. And probably soon. She didn't want to be caught poking around, and she sure as hell didn't want to compromise the investigation. But she couldn't quell her curiosity, and so she carefully squeezed into the dark room, which smelled of mold. When she used the back of her hand to turn on the light, nothing happened, so she swept the beam of her small flashlight over the small space with its sloped, raw-wood ceiling and water stain running down one wall. The single, small window was covered by a black curtain and the ever-present cobwebs.

But unlike the rest of the home, in this room there was no clutter. No bags of clothes or broken furniture or forgotten books. Instead, she found a small table draped in a black cloth and back-dropped by a dusty mirror. Swathed in cobwebs, reflected in the glass were baby items: a rattle, a yellowed onesie, a bit of hair tied with a ribbon, along with a framed picture of a newborn and a hospital souvenir birth certificate with inked footprints.

She sucked in a breath and read: *Caleb Farmer Huber.* The baby's weight, date, and time of birth were listed as well. Her heart twisted, and she swallowed a sudden lump in her throat.

All of the items had been placed around a Bible and a blue ceramic heart.

A small urn.

On an altar.

For an infant.

She forced herself to take a picture, her own ashen reflection caught in the shot. She swallowed hard, feeling the loss of this child, knowing the pain.

Suddenly, Billy Huber's disinterest in life made more sense.

A cool whisper crawled up her spine, the feeling of being watched.

Ridiculous.

She was alone.

No one else nearby.

And yet . . . was that the creak of a floorboard downstairs?

The back of her throat went dry, and she froze, straining hard to listen for any sound.

But the house remained still.

Eerily so.

Enough, she thought, and she hurriedly clicked off a series of pictures of the bare room and the disturbing altar, an area frozen in time.

She paused on the landing, looking over the rail, listening and searching the lower level for any sign that someone was inside.

But there was nothing other than the beating of her own heart.

Maybe she'd been mistaken?

Still on alert, she eased down to the main area and out the door to the porch, where the air was fresh, morning dew still glistening on blades of grass that grew between the scattered car parts and other junk.

She'd spooked herself, that was all. She'd let the dreary house get to her and—

From the corner of her eye, she caught movement, a dark shadow dashing around the corner of the house.

Her heart nearly stopped.

Someone was here?

No. Not someone.

The dog.

No longer barking his fool head off. Now quiet as a church mouse.

Good.

It was one of the reasons she'd come.

She latched the gate before the shepherd could escape and then spoke in soft tones to the cowering animal. It took off, leaping onto the porch to dive under the same rocking chair as it had the night before. As she cautiously approached, it growled, showing teeth, dark eyes focused on her.

"Oh, stop that," she said, deciding that it was more scared than angry.

And, no doubt, hungry.

She reached into her bag, where she found the half-eaten hamburger. "Look what I have for you." Quickly, while the dog continued to stare at her, she unwrapped the remains of the burger, tore off a corner, and tossed it onto the porch.

The shepherd's gaze flicked to the morsel, then to her before he crawled from beneath the chair to snap it up. She noticed the blood on his matted coat and was more determined than ever to get him to a vet.

Before he could retreat, she flicked out another piece.

Again, the hungry dog scarfed it down.

And didn't retreat to its hiding place.

Good.

Carefully, she laid the leash in a circle on the uneven floor boards and placed torn bits of the burger in the circle.

The dog waited.

Nikki didn't move.

After nearly five minutes, hunger overtook fear, and the ratty-looking mutt took the bait, gobbling up each torn bit of hamburger and sticking his nose into the circle of the rope, which, when he stretched his neck far enough, she pulled tight.

Startled, the dog yanked back.

Nikki talked to him in soothing tones, and after immediately surging back against the leash, the dog finally relaxed, all fight gone.

Using the last scraps of the burger, she lured him along the lane and road to her Subaru and the waiting crate inside the cargo space.

Time to see the vet.

Then call her husband.

And face the music.

Chapter 5

"Let me get this straight," Pierce said, his voice tight on the other end of the wireless connection. "You're at the clinic? The veterinary clinic, with Billy Huber's dog?"

"Arlo. That's the dog's name," Nikki said from the privacy of the clinic's parking lot. "At least according to the tag on his collar."

"I told you not to—"

"And he was shot," she said, cutting Pierce off before he went ballistic over the phone.

"Shot?"

"Yeah," she said moving to the shade of a small dogwood tree. "Dr. Vasquez found bird shot in his backside. Right near his tail. Surprisingly, not serious. I told the vet to keep the pellets for the department." He didn't reply and was obviously still trying to rein in his anger, so she barreled on. "They're keeping Arlo here for observation until someone from animal services comes for him, but I was thinking that maybe we could—"

"Stop. Right there. We don't need another dog."

"I know, but Mikado's getting old and—"

"And we have a houseful as it is."

"You're the one who invited Lily and Phee to come live with us," she reminded him.

"I know, but you needed help and . . ." He paused, then added, "Look, I've got another call coming in. It's a 'no' on the dog, and you're not to go back to the Huber place until we're done—no, wait. Don't go there at all. Nikki, seriously, we discussed you staying away from crime scenes."

And they had. But not for a long while. Not since directly after the case of the missing Duval girls had been solved and she'd written the book about it. Now, though . . .

She countered with, "I think we should reopen the discussion."

"Not now," he said, then, "I really have to go."

"Okay. Love you," she said, and she meant it.

He sighed, but added, "Love you, too," then clicked off.

She blew out her breath. She hated these fights, but their marriage was full of the pushes and pulls needed to keep them both aware of each other's needs and wants. Before she went back into the clinic, she called Lily to check on Chloe.

"I'm loading up the car now," Lily told her. "Mom called, and she wants to go to lunch at the country club, if you can believe that."

"You're surprised?"

"No, I guess not. But, God, I hate that place. It's so . . . what's the right word . . . ?"

"Fake? Hypocritical? Pretentious?"

"All of the above."

"It's everything you hate and Mom loves."

"That's it! But if it'll get her to eat, then fine. I'll suffer through the stuffy pseudosophistication and snobby hypocrisy."

Nikki smothered a smile as she stepped onto the sidewalk outside the vet. An older Toyota Camry pulled into the lot and aimed for a handicapped spot. As soon as the car was parked, the driver, a woman with a cloud of white hair, climbed out and retrieved a cat carrier from the back seat.

"Mom just can't get over the fact that she was the wife of a judge," Lily was saying. "Big Ron Gillette. Dad's been gone nearly ten years, and she still wears her rings and the mantle, or more precisely the tiara, of being his missus, if you know what I mean."

"Queen Bee."

"Yeah, that's it. And she called to make sure that I would wear a dress and that the girls would "dress appropriately" as well. No jeans, you know. God, are we stuck in the nineteen-fifties, or what?"

"Maybe the sixties."

Lily asked, "Sure you don't want to join?"

"When you offer it up like that? Hard to resist, but no, I think I'll take a hard pass."

"Fine, but you owe me."

"A dozen times over," Nikki admitted as the woman with the cat entered the vet clinic. "How is Chloe?"

"Bubbly as ever. Babbling about seeing 'Gam-Gam.' But do you think she'll ever say, 'Auntie Lily?' Nope. Not a prayer. She's as stubborn as her mother."

"Well, good luck," Nikki said, still smiling. "I'll catch you this afternoon."

She ended the call, then climbed into the warm interior of her Subaru and drove to the offices of the *Savannah Sentinel*. Even though she was no longer on staff, she had full use of the paper's resources. Tom Fink, who was the editor, allowed her access, though grudgingly, and usually there was a price to pay. He'd never really forgiven her for branching out and writing full-length crime books; she suspected that he harbored more than a little jealousy at her success.

But he hadn't cut her off from access to the paper's computers because he needed her. Nikki's articles were often picked up by national news sources, and it didn't hurt the *Sentinel*'s reputation that she was a crime author of note, her books hitting most of the bestseller lists.

Fink's favorite line was, "You scratch my back, I'll scratch yours." The quid pro quo that always got under her skin because the way he said it almost sounded dirty.

She parked on the street, a block down from the brick warehouse where the *Savannah Sentinel* was now housed. After using a code to gain access to the building, she made her way to the stairs, as the elevators were iffy at best.

On the third floor, she noted that Celeste, the receptionist and Fink's on-again, off-again mistress, wasn't at her desk. Maybe things were off-again.

Nikki slipped past cubicles where a smattering of reporters were at their desks, eyeing monitors, fingers diligently clicking on keyboards. Along one wall dedicated to online content, two employees were seated on stools, checking the news feeds and updating the *Sentinel*'s website and social-media platforms. Conversation hummed over the rumble of the air conditioning and the ever-present sounds of footsteps, keyboard clicks, and ringtones. There was an energy here that, deep down, she missed.

With a glance to the corner, Nikki noted that the door to Fink's glassed-in office was closed, the blinds drawn, a sign he wasn't in.

Good.

She didn't want to deal with him if it could be avoided, as he was always pressuring her for more information than she had. Fink seemed to think that, because she was married to a homicide detective, she had access to privileged information about ongoing cases and therefore should share it with the *Sentinel* and its readership. No matter how many times she'd explained that she wasn't privy to the case files, nor would she share information if she were, Fink never let up.

So she was better off not working here full-time.

"I figured you'd show up," Kendra Phillips said, looking up from the computer screen on her desk. Kendra was relatively new to the paper and a bit of a gossip, friendly enough, but always pumping Nikki for information. Slender and pushing thirty, Kendra wore her brown hair straight, didn't cover her splash of freckles with makeup, and wore a single diamond stud in one nostril. "So, let me guess. You're already on the Huber murder, right?"

"Just doing a little research."

"When Fink's not in. Clever." Kendra sipped from a straw planted deep into the oversize cup she kept filled with Diet Pepsi. "What're you 'researching'?" She didn't use air quotes, but the tone of her voice suggested Nikki was being evasive.

Which she was.

"Just backup information." Nikki kept walking.

"On Billy Huber?" she asked. "You know I heard he killed his wife."

Nikki stopped in her tracks. "Killed her?"

"Walked away from a single-car accident when he was driving. The wife didn't make it. He did."

So it seemed someone else was doing her own research. No surprise there. Kendra was nothing if not ambitious, and with Nikki working freelance, that left only Norm Metzger on the crime beat. And he was half out the door already.

"Ignore her," Roy Lutz whispered as he swept by, papers in his hand. "But be on alert. She's a barracuda, not a guppy."

"If you say so."

"Oh, I do. You know it." Roy's eyebrows raised over the tops of his fashionable glasses. Self-confident and whip-smart, Roy worked on the arts and leisure section of the paper. Everything about him was casual haute couture, from his Dior polo shirts to his Gucci sneakers. "She wants to be you," he confided to Nikki.

"What's he saying?" Kendra wanted to know, but Nikki took Roy's advice and didn't respond, at least for the moment.

Roy said lightly, "Nothing."

Kendra rolled her eyes. "Don't be such a girl!"

"Maybe you should try being one," he said, breezing out the door.

Kendra muttered something under her breath, but picked up her cup and was about to catch up to Nikki when her cell phone rang. Making a frustrated face, Kendra plopped down in her chair and, answering, peered around the edge of her cubicle, her calculating gaze following Nikki as she settled into the desk she shared with several other freelance reporters.

Tuning out the office drama, Nikki logged on and started her search into Billy Huber's life.

The bullet points were quickly organized:

He'd been born fifty years earlier in Chatham County and had lived on the same property for most of his life, aside from a short stint in the army. He'd bought out his mother after his father had died and had been married to Linda-Sue Farmer for nearly a quarter of a century.

As Kendra had alluded, Linda-Sue had died suddenly at the age of forty-seven in a single-car accident. Billy Huber had been at the wheel, and while Linda had been thrown out of the vehicle and was pronounced DOA at the hospital, Billy had survived with minor injuries.

But had he "killed" her? Certainly not intentionally. Still, Nikki made a note to check further.

According to the county records, William and Linda-Sue had two children. The first, Caleb, was born five months after the marriage and died shortly after birth, which explained the sad, nearly forgotten altar in the attic at Huber's house.

His only surviving child was a daughter: Janelle Alice.

She found Janelle's birth certificate and marriage license and current address in Florida, where she resided with her husband; there were no children of record.

But William Jasper Huber had been far from a model citizen. His criminal record included two arrests for driving under the influence, shortly after Caleb's death. There had also been assault charges filed after a bar fight, but those charges had been dropped. Again, within weeks of the baby's death. Then his criminal record had become clean.

However, there were several civil suits filed as well. One was over an altercation with his neighbor during a dispute about the placement of a fence. Huber had ended up paying restitution and promised to move the fence, so the situation had been resolved. In the other, one of his two brothers had sued him for non-payment of a personal loan, a year after the fence incident, around the time of his wife's death. That suit had never gone to court.

Nikki leaned back in her chair and studied the notes she'd taken, including the names and addresses of people she wanted to interview, especially anyone who might harbor a grudge against William Huber. He was no saint, but he wasn't exactly a sinner, either. Most of his transgressions had been after a life-changing experience.

But if, as Kendra had suggested, Linda-Sue's death hadn't been an accident, then all bets were off.

Surely, the police had checked and looked into any life-insurance policies that Billy Huber had held on his wife. She'd double-check as well as talk to the neighbor who'd had the argument about the fence, if he still lived on the abutting property. Then she would check with Billy's daughter and brothers. And with the man who'd accused Billy of assault in the bar fight.

Her cell phone pinged and she saw the text from Lily:

Heading home. I don't know who is more worn out: Mom, Chloe, Phee, or me. Oh, wait. It's me!

Nikki responded with a laughing smiley face emoji and a quick reply:

Thx. I should be home in an hour or so.

To that, Lily texted, with her usual sarcasm:

I won't hold my breath.

The response bugged Nikki more than she wanted to acknowledge, but probably because the remark hit a little close to home. Nikki hated to admit it, but she did tend to lose track of time when she was working, though she didn't feel her daughter was missing out. "Quality over quantity," she said, hoping to believe the old saying, trusting that it wasn't a cop-out.

Fortunately, Kendra wasn't at her desk, and Nikki escaped another conversation.

But as she stepped into the hallway, she spied Fink and Norm Metzger getting off of the elevator.

Great.

She braced herself. Coming face-to-face with Metzger was never pleasant. He was big and a little sloppy, with eyes that could cut right to your soul. He was prone to jeans and baseball caps and never tried to fake friendliness. Unlike Fink. They were like Mutt and Jeff, she thought, outwardly opposites and yet both members of the "Good Ol' Boys Club," despite the women's movement.

Fink was lean, his neatly trimmed hair more salt than pepper these days, and dressed, usually, like today, in a polo shirt and pressed khakis. Metzger might be sloppier, but he was Fink's go-to crime reporter. It didn't seem to matter that long ago Metzger had lost his edge. Though Nikki knew she was a better investigative journalist than the big man, Metzger and his boss went way back.

Golfed together.

Hunted together.

Played poker together.

Well, fine.

Again, she was better off as a freelancer, as she didn't have to deal with office politics. And she felt satisfaction that both men harbored barely concealed envy at her growing independence and success.

She gave a nod to them and hoped to avoid any conversation. But Fink peeled off and caught up with her at the door to the stairs. "Hey, I heard about Billy Huber," he said. At this point, who in Savannah hadn't? The homicide was all over social media.

"You were at his place last night," Fink continued, "at the scene of the crime."

Bad news traveled fast.

"I was."

Fink's brow furrowed. "So he was murdered. That's what the cops think."

"They're investigating."

"Pierce is in charge?"

"I don't know yet."

The elevator dinged, the doors opened, but neither Metzger nor Fink stepped inside. Fink offered what he thought was a winning smile. "Of course you do."

"Look, Tom, you know he won't tell me anything. He never does. In fact, he suggested I talk to the new PIO."

"You want me to hold this?" Metzger called, motioning to the elevator car, where the doors were beginning to shut.

Fink waved him off, his gaze never leaving Nikki's. "We both know there's always pillow talk, right? Bedtime tête-à-têtes." His eyebrows raised suggestively, and she wanted to slug him.

"Inappropriate," she stated flatly. Thank God, she didn't work for him any longer. He was her editor, yes, but her eight-to-five boss? Never again. If she didn't need the contacts the paper provided, she would cut all ties with the *Sentinel* once and for all.

"Oh, come on," he cajoled. "I was just kidding around. You know that. But seriously, you and Pierce, you must talk about—"

"We don't." She yanked open the door to the stairs. "I've got to go." But she paused long enough to add, "You should be a little more careful, Fink. All your 'kidding around' could easily be interpreted as sexual harassment."

"*Mis*interpreted, you mean." His smile faded. "That's the trouble with you, Gillette. The main reason you didn't fit in here. You take everything too seriously."

"And all this time I thought the news was serious business."

"Doesn't mean you can't relax a little, take a joke."

"Right."

She swept into the stairwell and heard footsteps echoing on the floor below. "I'll expect a story on the Huber homicide in the morning. Or maybe tonight," Fink called after her, his voice fading as she hurried down the steps.

She couldn't really argue, much as she'd like to. She used the office and contacts of the newspaper for her articles as well as research for her books.

Quid pro quo.

"My ass," she muttered as she pushed the exterior door open and felt the heat of the afternoon hit her full force. Once in her car, she slipped on her sunglasses and peeled out of the lot, all the while telling herself to cool off. She knew Fink was a jerk, so why did she let him get under her skin? She needed to forget Fink and concentrate on Billy Huber's murder. She had new information, so she should use it.

She drove back to the house with her window rolled down, the wind catching in her hair. No one else was home, so she hurried up the spiral stairs to the attic space under the eaves that she'd converted to her office. Mikado tagged after her. "How would you like to have a brother?" she asked and saw his tail wag slowly. His coat had lost a lot of its shine, and his muzzle had grayed with the years. "Don't worry. You're still the best, my number one dog," she assured him and rubbed the top of his head. "You always will be."

As Mikado curled at her feet, she synced her phone to her laptop, then viewed the pictures of Billy Huber's place, studying the spot where he'd died, near the barn, with the torn, dangling gutter and downed ladder. "Who did this to you?" she said as if the dead man were standing next to her. Slowly, she sifted through the shots, seeing nothing new.

She was about to turn her attention to pictures of his house when it struck her that something was missing.

What was it Swanson had said last night? Something about finding a rock with a number on it? And hieroglyphics? Yet she found no picture of any marked stone. She checked again through over a hundred digital images. No rock. Obviously the police had taken it, so they thought it was something significant.

What? she wondered, absently reaching down to scratch Mikado behind his ears.

Maybe nothing.

And yet, it seemed odd. Out of place. And those little details that didn't fit sometimes were a clue.

Or else she was making a mountain out of a molehill.

It wouldn't be the first time.

And, she thought, probably not the last.

Chapter 6

Reed drove the short distance to the town of Pooler, where he met with Dr. Maren Ito at the state crime lab. She escorted him into the morgue, with its soaring ceilings, bright lights, and high windows, her steps purposeful.

Petite in stature, her black hair pulled severely away from her face in a tight bun, Dr. Ito wore rimless glasses, a pressed white lab coat, and a no-nonsense demeanor as she displayed Billy Huber's lifeless body, which was lying supine on a metal gurney.

"The body's already been scanned," she said, as Reed viewed the corpse.

Tan lines were visible on Huber's arms and neck, his thin torso white, ribs visible, graying hair swirled across his chest. His brown eyes were open, a silver growth of beard covering sunken cheeks and a defined jaw. Along with the wounds from his fall off the ladder, there was the usual Y-shaped incision on his torso and the neat slice across the top of his skull that cleaved his thin, stringy hair.

"I'll work on the preliminary report later today," Ito said. "It'll be a while for the blood work to come back, but here's the rundown: William Huber was dead at least forty-eight hours before his body was discovered. Looks like he fell off the ladder. His internal injuries and broken pelvis, tibia, and ribs are consistent with a fall, as is his brain bleed. Contusions on his upper arm and shoulder."

"He landed on an upturned rake," Reed said. Huber's shoulder and upper arm had been impaled on the curved tines.

She nodded. "His right wrist is broken. But," she added, glancing up at Reed, "here's the interesting thing: It wasn't the fall that killed him. His jugular was sliced by a sharp instrument of some kind." She pointed to the obvious cut to his throat. "A knife possibly, something with a very sharp blade, almost like a scalpel."

"We haven't found a weapon yet. Still searching."

"Look for a long, slim blade, something that would cut clean and deep." She motioned to the back of Billy's head. "And also, see these injuries?"

"Hard to miss."

"They're from where he supposedly fell against the tiller blades, but they're inconsistent with how he would land naturally."

"Meaning?"

"Meaning that I think someone deliberately forced his head onto the blade either very soon after, or right before, his throat was sliced. There are bruises along his jawline where someone held him. Hard enough to break the blood vessels under the skin. Like this." Standing at the head of the table, she placed her gloved hands on either side of the dead man's face and lifted his head from the table. "See?"

"I do."

She was nodding, agreeing with herself, the overhead lights reflecting in her black hair. "This was no accident. Someone was very determined to see Billy Huber dead and viciously so." She set Billy's head down gently, then stripped off her surgical gloves. "I'm no psychiatrist, but I'd be willing to bet that whoever did it was very, very angry."

"You think a crime of passion."

"Just my guess, but either slamming his head against the blade or slicing his throat would have killed him if the fall didn't."

"You're thinking the murderer enjoyed killing him."

"Again my medical degree isn't in psychiatry." She looked up at Reed. "But this"—she gestured to the table—"was literally overkill." She stepped back from the table. "Seen enough?"

More than, he thought, as he left the modern building with its glass walls and manicured grounds. He climbed into his Jeep, where the interior was sticky and hot and a yellow jacket, which had somehow found its way inside, was slamming itself against the windshield in a vain attempt to escape. He lowered the windows and waved at it until it flew away.

Putting on his sunglasses, he called his partner, Sol Augustin. She'd drawn the short straw and been temporarily assigned as Reed's partner.

"Hey," she answered. "You still in Pooler?"

At five-ten and as athletic as she'd been as a basketball player for the Georgia Bulldogs, Sol could be intimidating to some. She was smart and competitive. And had her secrets. A bit of a mystery. She kept things close to the vest, though there were rumors about her, police gossip that suggested she was hard to get along with and sometimes "out there, if ya know what I mean." Reed did. The talk was that she had some kind of ESP, something deep inside that would cause her to be intense one second, then seemingly almost lost when the wave of foresight or whatever it was washed over her.

"On my way back." Reed engaged the Jeep's engine and drove out of the parking lot.

"Find out much?"

"Some." He filled Sol in on what he'd learned about Billy Huber's homicide, how brutal and intentional it had been.

"Slicing his throat wasn't enough."

"Apparently not." Reed slid down the visor as sunlight was bouncing off the road. "Did you visit the crime scene?"

"I did. Early this morning."

"See anything?"

"Just got a feel for the place."

He nodded, though she couldn't see him. He knew Sol liked to visit a crime scene on her own, without any distractions.

She continued, "When I got into the office, I spoke with some of the deputies who interviewed Huber's neighbors and family members. None of the neighbors saw or heard anything out of the ordinary, and they agreed with his brothers that Huber kept to himself. When they dealt with him, it wasn't pleasant. None of them seemed all that broken up that he was dead. The neighbor to the west, just beyond a stretch of woods, Otis Childers, was in a legal battle with

Huber a while back. Lawsuit over a fence, but it was dealt with. Huber moved the fence, and Childers claimed Huber was a—and I quote—'nutjob,' who had come onto his property and stolen some farm equipment. Huber denied it, and when Childers went over in his pickup to confront him, Huber came out with pistol and threatened to kill him." She paused. "That didn't go over so well, but Childers backed off."

"And saw nothing on the night he died."

"Right. The other neighbors were Duke and Frances Wheelan. They, too, claimed Huber wasn't friendly. Apparently, they caught him trying to poach deer and boars off their property, despite warning him to stay away. Wheelan sued him, but the suit went nowhere, as in court Huber insisted Wheelan was the one who had poached on his property. The judge threw the whole thing out. But despite Wheelan putting up NO TRESPASSING signs, Huber kept ignoring them and crossing onto Wheelan's property whenever he pleased."

"So Billy Huber was the neighbor they all loved."

"Yep. The kind you'd want to invite to a party," she answered ironically.

"So what about Huber's family? You said you talked to them?"

"Didn't get much more than I told ya. Again, no one seemed all that grief-stricken about his passing. The daughter, ah . . . Janelle McGowan lives in Florida now, Jacksonville. She reluctantly agreed to come and ID the body, but she wasn't keen on it. Didn't say much, but I got the feeling she'd rather spit on his grave than leave any roses on it. No love lost there. And she's his only kid. He had a son who died right after birth, and his wife has been dead for around eight years."

"Siblings? Parents?"

"Parents are both dead. Natural causes. First the father, then the mother a few years later. He's got a couple of brothers, one older, one younger. I talked to them on the phone. Neither unhappy or surprised that he died or that someone killed him, which was odd. The older brother, Terence—he lives in Plano, Texas, by the way—he didn't say much. Quiet, I guess. But not shocked that someone killed his brother. His comment was, 'So Billy finally pissed the wrong guy off, eh?'"

"What about the other brother?"

"A couple of years younger. Billy was the middle child. So, uh—Robert, he goes by Bobby—he really went off when I brought Billy up. Didn't seem bothered at all that his brother was dead or had been killed for that matter. From what I got out of it, Bobby loaned Billy ten thousand dollars about the time Billy's wife, Linda-Sue, died, around eight years ago. Bobby had to take money out of his retirement account, pay taxes on it, and he swears he's never seen a dime back. Resents it. There's bad blood there, let me tell you. Bobby claims he's gonna sue the estate if Billy didn't, in his words, 'Have the decency to leave him the value of the loan with interest.'"

"Did Billy have a will?"

"We're still lookin'."

"What about life insurance?"

"Unknown," Augustin said. "But, again, we're looking into it."

"Good. We need to know who profits from Billy Huber's death."

"On it," Augustin assured him.

They talked a bit more, and by the time they broke the connection, Reed was within the Savannah city limits and driving past Forsyth Park, busy now with people jogging or walking. Women were pushing strollers, and young couples walked hand in hand as they strolled on sun-dappled sidewalks beneath live oaks draped with Spanish moss. He glanced at the majestic fountain, newly restored, its spray glinting in the sunlight.

At the station, he parked in the lot, his thoughts still filled with the homicide. Who held such a deep-seated grudge against Billy Huber that they wanted his death to be brutal? Everyone who knew Billy seemed to have a reason to dislike him. But had someone's hatred been so deep that it would propel him to murder and to kill with such savagery?

Nikki's stomach rumbled. She glanced at her watch and saw that it was already after two. She was about to call her sister and check in on Chloe when she received another text from Lily:

The girls wanted to go to Leopold's. I thought, "Why not?" After lunch with Mom, we all need to pamper ourselves. Since a spa treatment and double margarita weren't possible, ice cream and some time in the park was the next best thing. Be home in an hour or so.

Lily added an emoji of a face rolling its eyes.

Nikki sent a text back, before heading downstairs and making herself a tuna sandwich with pickles. She ate quickly, popped the top of a can of Dr Pepper, then nearly sprinted up the spiral stairs to her office, where she scooted out her desk chair and speed-dialed her contact in the police department, a friend from high school.

Even though Nikki was still considered by some at the station to be persona non grata, there were a few deputies in the department who remained friendly and would, with prodding, give her guarded information. The rest of the force would probably never forgive her, would forever blame her for Sylvie Morrisette's death.

Understandable.

Didn't she blame herself?

She just refused to dwell on the guilt that could have consumed her. It's not what Morrisette would have wanted, and it was definitely not what she wanted for herself.

Still, in the middle of some sleepless nights, there it lay. Waiting. Reminding her that, because of her reckless actions, a woman had died.

A mother.

It was in those restless evenings that Nikki would creep into the nursery and watch Chloe sleeping.

The accident that had taken Morrisette's life had also resulted in Nikki miscarrying yet another baby, which had torn a hole in her heart, a hole she'd tried desperately to conceal from the world, and from her husband. She'd been far more careful during her subsequent pregnancy, and even so, it had been touch and go for a while, but eventually, Chloe Victoria Reed had arrived, red-faced and screaming, into the world. Chloe's birth had been a jubilant event, but each time Nikki remembered the miscarriages, a lump would fill her throat, and a bit of sadness would steal through her heart.

"Nikki Gillette. I figured you'd call," an annoyed female voice answered. Jill, Nikki's longtime schoolmate, was very protective of the department.

"I was just looking for information on the Huber homicide."

She scoffed. "You know I can't tell you anything more than you could get from Viv. Remember her? She's the PIO. Better yet, talk to your damned husband."

"All I need to know is if Billy Huber's next of kin have been notified."

"Shit," Jill said under her breath, then, "Yes. This morning."

"Thanks."

"Next time, call the PIO. Make it official. You hear me, Nikki? I'm serious. Just because we were in Brownies together, and and we took martial arts together in grade school, and you were my rock when Kurt Hendricks dumped me for Sara Tillis right before senior prom, or, or . . . that you put in a good word for me with your husband when I needed a job here at the department after Seth walked out on me and the kids . . ." She stopped for a second, as if counting up the favors and realizing Nikki had always had her back. "Well . . . well . . . Oh, it doesn't matter! I know you've been a good friend. But that doesn't give you the right to call me and try to weasel information from me."

"You're right. I do hear you."

"Oh, sure," Jill said, not bothering to hide her sarcasm.

"Thanks again," Nikki said, but the line had already been disconnected.

No surprise there.

Since she'd already gotten Janelle McGowan's phone number, she punched it into her cell. Five rings later, she heard a rough female voice answer. "Hello?"

She quickly introduced herself, saying she was a reporter with the *Savannah Sentinel*, which wasn't a lie but definitely was a bit of a stretch, and offered her condolences about Janelle losing her father.

"Oh, God, a reporter. Already?" was the response. Nikki heard what sounded like the rush of wind and music, as if Janelle were driving. "I just heard from the cops a couple of hours ago. Y'all don't waste much time, now, do ya?"

"I'm looking into your father's death."

She snorted. "Well, according to the cops that showed up on my door, he was murdered." She said it matter-of-factly, without the grief, anger, or concern Nikki had expected. "'A probable victim of homicide,' that's what they said. So somebody offed him. To tell you the truth, it doesn't surprise me. Billy was weird as weird can be."

"In what way?"

"*Every* way. After Mom died, he just lost it. I mean, really lost it. He always was a hoarder, and if you ever saw his place, you'd know what I'm talking about. But once Mom passed, it just got worse and worse. He should have gotten help, but that wasn't Billy's way—hey, Al, could you turn down the radio, for God's sake? Can't you see I'm on the phone here? I don't need to be competing with Brad Paisley while I'm tryin' to talk to this reporter here. . . . Excuse me," she said more loudly, and a male voice responded something unintelligible, then, "Listen, Ms. . . . what did you say your name was again?"

"Nikki Gillette."

"Gillette?" she repeated, and Nikki wondered if Janelle had seen her name on a book and recognized it, could even be a fan. "Like the razor blades?"

So much for her fame. "Yes. Could I ask you a few questions?"

"Not now. I'm not gettin' great reception. We're on the road. Coming to Savannah to tie up the loose ends and all. The police said they'd be done searching Billy's place today, if you can believe that. Dear Lord, if you ask me, it would take years to search that place proper, but what do I know? They also want me to ID his body. I guess I can do that. Not lookin' forward to it, I can tell you that much." She sounded resigned and irritated that her life in Florida had been interrupted, even though her father had just died and been the victim of a vicious homicide. She sighed and turned away from the phone and said, "Light me up one, will ya, hon?" A moment, then she was back again. "Looks like I've got a shitload of junk and a damned dog to deal with. God knows if he still has goats or whatever up there. Hell, what a mess. Look, if you want to talk to me, maybe meet me there—at his farm—in the morning?"

Again, Nikki heard a male voice say something to Janelle. "Yeah, I said, I know," she responded, then into the phone once more, "We'll be there by ten."

"About the dog—" Nikki started, but Janelle had already cut the connection.

"You find anything of interest at the Huber place?" Jamison Kittle asked as he slipped into Reed's office and pulled the door shut behind him, effectively cutting off the sounds of voices, ringing phones, footsteps, and the general din from the hallway.

"We found lots of stuff," Reed said. "All of it junk. You've been out there?"

Reed had been at his desk for a couple of hours after returning from Pooler. He'd grabbed a quick lunch, a basket of fried chicken and biscuits from a vendor on the street, when he got back to the city, and had had enough time to catch up with his partner and read through the statements from people the police had interviewed, all of which had confirmed what Augustin had told him over the phone.

"Yeah, finally made it out to Huber's farm last night. I guess I just missed you." Jamison leaned against the doorframe. "Naomi was pissed that I left the house. Even a murder wasn't a good enough excuse to leave Lara's sweet-sixteen party."

"You only turn sixteen once."

"And you only get murdered once," Jamison shot back, with a smile. "And as for the teen years? The teen years. We're all lucky to have survived." He nodded at Reed, who nodded back in complete understanding. They'd known each other since college, long before Jamison had served in the army, moved back to the area, and swept Naomi off her feet, causing her to break her engagement to a local guy and marry Jamison Kittle instead.

Reed smiled at the memory. He'd been best man at Jamison's wedding, usurping the role usually assigned to a brother. Jamison had four younger brothers whom he'd named as groomsmen. Rather than choose one of his siblings, he'd opted instead for his best friend.

Now he said, "So bring me up to speed. You're convinced we're dealing with a homicide?"

"Don't you think so?"

"You're the investigator. I'm just the ADA."

"Just," Reed said with a small laugh. Jamison had moved up the ranks quickly. With DA Katherine Okano permanently retiring after being on the job twice, there had been opportunities available in the district attorney's office, and Jamison had taken advantage of them. It didn't hurt that his father, Harrison Kittle, had paved the way. Harrison senior had once worked in the very office Jamison now occupied and, after being elected DA, had eventually become a federal judge.

Jamison seemed to be on the fast track, following in his father's footsteps.

"So how about we get a cup of coffee, or sweet tea, or whatever, and you fill me in?" Jamison suggested. "I've been cooped up all day. Missed lunch."

Reed grabbed his jacket before following Jamison outside and across the street to a local coffee shop, where Jamison ordered a sweet tea and a shrimp po'boy with a side of fried green tomatoes and Reed settled for a regular coffee.

"As I said, I missed lunch," Jamison explained as they sat at a shaded table in the back of the bistro. Birds hopped from the branches of the trees overhead or picked at crumbs that had fallen to the brick patio. A small waterfall gurgled in one corner, and potted plants were strategically placed to give the illusion of privacy, though the area was nearly deserted. As soft jazz played from hidden speakers, a woman in her twenties sat in the corner, earbuds visible in her ears, her concentration on her open laptop as she sipped coffee. Another couple was picking at pastries while paying attention to no one but each other.

A waitress brought their order, and Jamison tucked his tie into his shirt before digging in. As he ate, Reed brought him up to speed on the investigation, including what they'd discovered at the scene, their focus on Billy Huber's ever-growing list of enemies, and the circumstances of how he'd died. "I'll be getting a preliminary autopsy report today, possibly tomorrow morning, but Ito was convinced someone killed Billy Huber, probably someone with a serious grudge. As it turns out, we could have more suspects than usual. Estranged family members, neighbors who didn't get along, acquaintances who didn't like him." Reed sipped from his cup and watched as the woman in the corner closed her laptop and tucked it into a case. "You know, a lot of times we hear what a nice guy the murder victim was, how they didn't have an enemy in the world. This time, it's just the opposite. Billy Huber didn't seem to get along with anyone."

"That right?"

"So far, no one has a kind word to say about the guy."

"Anyone at the top of the list?"

"Not yet." He shook his head and leaned back in his chair. "We're trying to weed out anyone who could possibly have been in the area.

But the time of death is uncertain, his body having started to decompose and with the storm and all. The lab is still working on it, testing the condition of his stomach contents and his eyes. It'll take a while for the blood work."

Jamison finished his sandwich, wadding the checkered paper and tossing it into the trash. "Anything else interesting?"

"Nothing certain, but there is one thing that bothers me."

"Only one?" Jamison asked, smiling.

"There is an oddity."

"What kind of oddity?"

"Probably nothing, but there was a stone that seemed to be wedged under the body. One of the deputies noticed it."

"A rock?"

"Take a look." Reed pulled out his phone and sorted through several pictures he'd taken at the scene. When he found the shots of the rock, he handed the phone to Jamison. "The stone is clean. Polished. The weather has been bad, lots of rain and wind, debris everywhere. And there were no insects or larvae or eggs under it. Nothing but bent grass. It might have come from Billy's pocket . . . but . . ." Reed thought hard, watching a white cat slink behind a potted palm. "Like I said, probably nothing."

"You think it was placed under the body by the killer?"

"I wouldn't go that far yet, but it seemed out of place, even with all the clutter in the barnyard." Reed watched the cat hop nimbly onto a table and then the top of the fence. "Huber was an odd duck, no doubt about it. A hoarder. Junk everywhere, except for paths and walkways and a small clearing where the body was found."

Jamison narrowed his eyes as he studied the picture of the rock. "What's the significance of the number? Nine, right?"

"Or six. Impossible to tell."

"A rock with a number scratched into it . . . hmm."

"Not scratched. Etched. Probably with some kind of specialized tool," Reed added. He'd learned that much from the lab where it was being tested. "We're trying to make sense of it." He pointed to his phone. "Take a look at the next shot of the other side of the rock."

Jamison swiped the screen and squinted at the image. "Writing of some kind."

"Looks like."

"A message?" Jamison frowned as he handed the phone back to Reed. "That someone, presumably the killer, placed under Huber's body?"

"Maybe it's just another piece of his junk collection."

"Or a talisman?"

"A talisman?" Reed shook his head at the thought of the stone being a good luck charm. "If it was, it was a piss-poor one. The only luck Billy Huber had was bad."

Chapter 7

"Oh, look at you, Chocolate Face," Nikki said, taking Chloe from her sister's arms. Nikki had heard the car approach and hurried down the stairs and out the front door just as Lily released Chloe from her car seat.

"We ran out of wipes," Lily explained, squinting against the lowering sun. "I thought I had an extra pack in my bag, but as it turned out, no."

"No worries, I'll clean her up."

"Ice cream," Chloe said, a grin splitting her messy face.

Nikki nuzzled her little cheek. "I can see."

At that moment, Phee climbed out of the car. Wearing earbuds and clutching her iPhone, she bopped her head to music only she could hear as she walked into the house.

"Taylor Swift," Lily explained, as they headed into the house. "I swear she knows the lyrics to every song."

"Like you did. Only it was Michael Jackson or Justin Timberlake."

"J.T.," Lily said, remembering. "Okay, fine." Lily agreed, walking inside, where the air conditioning was rumbling. She dropped her bag onto the floor in the hallway next to the console table and warned, "I'm not cooking. I know it's my night, but I figure I did my duty with Mom."

"How is she?"

"Irascible. Picky. Snobby. Basically the same. And that country club . . ." Lily gave a fake shudder. "The worst. Shoot me if I ever start turning into her."

"No chance of that."

"I don't know. Remember Janey Cartwright? She was in Andrew's class, I think." Lily paused and whispered, "God rest his soul." Their older brother had been gone for years, but his early death still brought with it a low-level pain and grief from which their family had never quite recovered.

"Janey Cartwright? Not ringing any bells," Nikki said.

"In high school, she smoked and drank and was always high. God knows what drugs she was on, and she dressed—well, she kind of had this whole Madonna Goth vibe going on. Fingerless gloves, skirts over jeans, thick eyeliner, and dark eye shadow, like that."

"Okay."

"Janey embraced it," Lily said. "Big-time. And she was always in trouble with the police and suspended from school. I was surprised she even graduated. But I think she was a lot smarter than she acted."

Nikki was at the kitchen sink, trying to wipe the smudges from Chloe's face with a damp paper towel. Chloe was having none of it and wriggled in Nikki's arms, turning her face this way and that, trying to avoid the dreaded towel. "No, Mommy. No!"

"Yes," Nikki insisted firmly.

"Anyway, I saw Janey today," Lily went on as she reached into the cupboard for a wineglass. "At the country club. Good Lord, I barely recognized her. She's turned into this . . . this country club Stepford wife. A younger clone of Mavis Greenlee." Lily eyed her sister. "Don't tell me you don't remember Mavis."

"I know Mavis." Mavis was a country-club mainstay, a pseudo friend of their mother's who was also active in their church.

"No!" Chloe insisted.

"Fine." Nikki tossed the wet towel on the counter and set Chloe onto the floor. The minute her feet touched down, Chloe scrambled off toward the stairs, probably in search of Phee. Mikado, who had been lying in his bed near the fireplace, struggled to his feet and took off after her, his toenails clicking on the hardwood.

"Hey," Pierce said and kissed Nikki on the cheek. "This looks so . . . uptown."

"Looks can be deceiving." She nodded to the empty box on the counter. "Don't expect too much. Embellished, but pre-packaged."

"Smells wonderful." He wrapped his arms around her waist and whispered against the back of her neck, "And so do you."

"Take it upstairs!" Lily called from the dining area.

"What's this all about?" Nikki asked as he released her.

"I thought maybe I was too hard on you earlier," he admitted and picked up a slice of apple.

"Those are for your daughter."

"She won't mind."

Nikki nodded just as a rush of tiny footsteps on the stairs heralded Chloe's arrival. "Daddy!" she screamed, her lips, a vibrant red color, split into a wide, delighted smile. Iridescent green eye-shadow covered her eyelids, and black mascara was thick over her usually pale lashes.

Pierce scooped her off her feet and, as he had done earlier in the day, twirled her in the kitchen, while Mikado padded over for some attention. "What happened to you?" he asked his daughter, and she giggled.

"Phee made me pretty!"

"You're always pretty," he told her as he placed her on her feet. "You don't really need any makeup." He gave Mikado a few pats on the head, and the dog's tail wagged slowly.

"Why don't you let Phee know that dinner's ready," Nikki suggested to her daughter. "Wash your hands."

Pierce added, "And maybe your face," but Nikki shook her head. "Let it be."

"She looks like she's auditioning for *Ru Paul's Drag Race*."

"At two?"

Lily chimed in, "Almost three, and you know they start early these days."

Nikki found the nearly empty bottle of wine and held it up in offering, but Pierce shook his head and opted for a beer.

"I'll finish it." Lily swept the bottle from Nikki's hand just as she heard the pounding of little footsteps, the girls returning, with Chloe leading the way.

Lily was opening the refrigerator door. “Janey’s blond now. Pla inum.” She retrieved a bottle of blush-colored wine. “And her make up is less David Bowie and more Doris Day, if you know what mean.” She poured herself a glass and held up the bottle. “Want a splash?”

“Sure.” She found a stemmed glass and waited as Lily filled it “Ooh. That’s enough. Too much.” She took a sip as Lily shoved the cork back into the bottle. “Doris Day?”

“The whole sheer makeup, fresh-faced thing . . . definitely not the Janey I remember. Anyway, cheers,” Lily said, clicking the rim of her glass to Nikki’s.

“Cheers.”

“How’s the work going? Figured out who killed that man, whatever his name is?”

“Billy Huber. Not yet, but working on it.”

“And how does Pierce feel about it?”

“What do you think?” Nikki kicked out a barstool and sat at the counter.

She made a face.

“That’s about right, I think.”

She nodded. “Remember, I’m ceding my chef rights to you tonight. Now, if you’ll excuse me, I’m going to have some much-needed me time.”

With that, Lily swept outside and around the corner, where, Nikki guessed, she might be sneaking a cigarette. An afternoon with Mom at the country club while trying to engage Phee and corral Chloe could turn almost anyone into making questionable choices. A smoke was the least she probably needed.

By the time that Pierce walked through the door, Nikki had managed to doctor up a box of Helper with sausage—forget the hamburger the package suggested—and tomato paste and some fresh herbs from Lily’s herb garden on the back deck. The salad was sparse, but it did the job as far as greens were concerned, and she found a loaf of bread that she warmed in the oven. She even cut up slices of apples and bananas for Chloe.

It wasn’t exactly an epicurean delight, but it sufficed.

Lily had relented and set dinnerware on the table, then added a vase of cut flowers she’d snipped from the garden.

"I see you've been practicing your art," Lily said to her daughter as Phee scraped back her chair and Nikki placed Chloe in her booster chair.

When Phee didn't respond, Lily touched her daughter on the arm, then motioned to her ears. "Not at the table."

Reluctantly, the girl took out her AirPods.

"Not at table!" Chloe repeated, shaking her head. "No, no, no!"

"She's such a little 'ruleser,'" Phee said, sending Chloe a just-stop-it glare.

"And after you put all that effort into making her look special," Lily chided.

Pierce settled into his chair and said, "I hate to ask what a ruleser is."

Nikki warned, "Don't."

Too late.

Phee, still sending Chloe dark looks, explained. "It's a little twit who loves to tell someone else what the rules are!"

"Okay, okay." Lily waved her wineglass.

"Let's eat," Pierce said, deliberately changing the subject. He passed the casserole to his niece and said to Nikki, "This looks great."

"Restaurant quality." Lily smiled before burying her nose in her glass.

Nikki ignored her sister, her mind moving past the meal to hover on questions about Billy Huber's murder. What had the police discovered? Were there any serious suspects? Who would gain from Billy's death? What about witnesses? With an effort, she took the first bite.

Restaurant quality?

Hardly.

Epicurean?

Not a chance.

But it was nice that Pierce could enjoy her efforts.

With the dog under the table and Jennings atop the back of the sofa so that he could watch them, Nikki made sure Chloe managed to eat rather than just play with her food. She tried to bring up Billy Huber, but Pierce deftly changed the subject every time she mentioned his name. She had to let it drop.

For now.

After the table was cleared, the dishwasher loaded, Chloe was bathed and wrestled into pajamas, was read two bedtime stories, and finally fell asleep on her back, her little lips moving slightly, reddish curls splayed around her head. Nikki kissed her clean little forehead and whispered, "Sweet dreams," as she tiptoed out of the room. The house wasn't completely quiet, as Lily and Phee were watching television in their room and Pierce was in his den on the phone, but the day was winding down.

Nikki climbed the stairs to her office, where she went through her notes and, for what seemed the dozenth time, perused the pictures she'd taken of the Huber place, with its mountains of junk.

Had Billy Huber had any girlfriends? she wondered. Maybe one with a jealous husband? Or was there someone who held a serious grudge against him? A friend? More likely, an enemy? Maybe someone who would gain by his death? Who had motive and opportunity?

She heard Pierce on the stairs and Mikado's paws scraping the floor as the dog followed him. "Thought I'd find you up here," he said as he entered her study.

She rotated her desk chair and watched as he settled himself into the window seat that overlooked the backyard. He held her gaze. "Let me guess. You're working on the Huber case."

She laughed. "Ah, gee, you must be an ace detective or something."

"Or you might be pretty transparent."

"That, too," she admitted, as Mikado found his bed near her desk. "You got anything for me?" she asked. "Fink is all over me for a story."

"And he thinks you can get information from me."

She lifted her brows. "Can I?"

He shook his head. "Nothing to tell."

"Oh, come on. Really?"

"Really." He held up his hands, palms out, as if in surrender, as he stood again. "Look, when I can tell you something, I will. You know that. Now, though, I'm heading to bed."

"Want company?" she asked.

A smile inched across his chin, and she noticed the beard shadow covering his jaw and the twinkle in his eyes. "Always."

She clicked off her computer, took hold of his hand, and tugged, pulling him to the stairs.

* * *

"And whatever you do, do it heartily, as to the Lord and not to men, because . . . no, as to the Lord and not to men, that's it"—he murmured under his breath, remembering the verses he'd learned as a child—"not to men knowing that from the Lord you will . . . you will receive the reward of the inheritance. Because you serve only the Lord Christ."

Not exactly word for word of the New King James Version of Colossians 3:23–24, but it would suffice. He loved to whisper Scripture as he worked, here in his basement, a private space, *his* space, carved beneath one of his sheds.

His tools surrounded him, all hanging on the stone walls, or arranged perfectly on the table next to his pistol and his open Bible. Chisels, hammers, and mallets. He felt a warm pleasure and a glow of anticipation as he fondled the stone, smooth now that the edges had been honed and polished in his tumblers.

And there was the antique bookcase with glass doors, behind which he kept his Bibles.

Yes, all was in perfect order.

He smiled, satisfied that he'd recovered his stolen property. Over the noise of the tumblers, humming and turning the stones, music was audible via the old stereo he'd refurbished, playing his father's cherished vinyl records. Chamber music filled the small space.

Mozart.

For a second, he closed his eyes, listening to the woodwinds and piano.

His music collection was eclectic, what he played depending upon his mood. Everything from country to rock, jazz to blues, heavy metal to folk, hip-hop to ska. Whatever his mood dictated.

Tonight, he needed Mozart's melodic strains.

He hummed along as he picked up his etching tool and began to engrave, only to freeze as he heard his dogs.

Barking madly.

Growling.

Sounding angry.

A warning.

Apprehension crawled up his spine on spidery legs.

Had he been found out?

But how? He'd been so careful . . .

For a second, his throat went dry, and everything—the rumble of the tumbler, the music—was drowned out by the sound of the dogs and his accelerated heartbeat.

But it couldn't be.

He waited.

His anxiety mounted, his fingers still grasping his etching tool in a death grip.

And then it was quiet.

The hounds had given up their baying.

Maybe it was nothing. Some creature had gotten over the fence and prowled too close to the kennels.

That was all.

And yet . . .

He couldn't be too cautious.

Not now.

Not when his sacred work had just begun.

He slid the Glock from its holster lying on the table and carefully, quietly mounted the ladder-like stairs; waiting near the top rung before sliding open the trapdoor, hoisting himself into the shop, then moving swiftly and silently across the old hickory floorboards to the window. Through a slit in the blinds, he studied the gravel yard between the kennels and the stable.

The horses were restless.

Shuffling in their stalls.

But the dogs . . . quiet now.

Good.

Beneath the warm glow of the security lamps, he saw nothing more than a bat swooping from the surrounding pines, and . . . wait! What was that? A shadow darting past the old pump house. A man? Crouching low?

No—two small men.

Crouching low.

His fingers tightened over the gun's grip.

How . . .

Sudden movement.

His heart clenched for a second.

Before realizing he was wrong.

As he focused on the movement, he recognized a lone coyote throwing its shadow against the aging boards of the kennel.

Yes, that was it.

Now, the beast was apparently downwind and out of sight of the kennels.

He aimed the Glock at the narrow nose and glowing eyes.

Bit his lip.

But he didn't pull the trigger. Couldn't risk the blast.

Tense, pistol in hand, he kept his gun aimed as the scrawny coyote trotted past the kennels.

Again the damned dogs sent up their warning howls! Baying loud enough to wake the damned dead.

Good-for-nothings.

Not even hunting.

But she liked them. So . . . fine.

Miserable curs.

Once the coyote disappeared, the hounds settled down again. As did his racing, reactive heart.

He lifted the trapdoor again and made his way down the stairs, checking his watch. He had little time. Would have to work faster.

He'd almost shot the marauding coyote, which would have risked everything. He couldn't afford to be reckless. Not now.

He told himself he was just nervous.

Anxious.

Juiced by anticipation.

Back in the basement, he slid the pistol into its holster and glanced at the stones—shining and ready, sorted neatly by the open Bible. Repeating his favorite verse, he changed the music on the old stereo's turntable.

Led Zeppelin.

"Stairway to Heaven."

As Robert Plant wailed and the music filled the room, he slipped onto his stool, picked up a small chisel, and went back to work, carefully etching the number into the stone's gleaming surface.

And then?

He glanced over to the vials propped in their rack. All neatly labeled. All with purpose. All shimmering dark red in the light.

Perfect.

But he needed to pick up his pace, he thought, as the song faded and he eyed the glossy photo he'd tacked to the bulletin board.

A headshot.

Of a woman.

Who didn't know what was in store for her. Didn't realize that she would soon meet her maker.

Judgment Day was coming for her.

And coming fast.

Chapter 8

"You can have the dog," Janelle McGowan told Nikki as they stood at the edge of the fence surrounding Billy Huber's house and yard. It was afternoon and hot, mosquitos and flies buzzing over early-blooming weeds and wildflowers. Nearby, on the sparse gravel lane, a huge RV was idling.

"You're serious?"

"Yeah. Just pay the damned vet bill." Janelle, a large woman in a tank top and shorts, surveyed the property, staring out at the piles of junk. "Either you take him or I put him in a shelter or whatever. I said as much to the vet—Dr. Whatever."

"Vasquez."

"Sounds right." Frowning, sweat running down her temples, Janelle added, "And that goes for anything else you want." She gestured to the yard. "Dear Lord Jesus, how am I supposed to get rid of all the junk so I can sell the place?"

It was a rhetorical question, Nikki knew, and one for which she had no answer.

"I suppose I could light a match to the house and call it good. Maybe the old coot had fire insurance on the place."

The old coot being Billy Huber.

Janelle shook her head, sunlight catching in the strands of blond visible in her short, brown hair. "Just kidding, but, holy shit, what a mess." Turning toward the idling motor home, she yelled, "Al!"

When there was no response, she muttered something under her breath, then shouted more loudly. "Al!" A beat, then, "Albert, come out here!" She stomped her sandaled foot in frustration and kicked up a puff of dust.

A big man came lumbering down the two steps of the motor home. "Hold your horses," he drawled as he crammed a Stetson onto his balding head. A plaid, western-cut shirt was stretched over his belly, pearly snaps barely holding the fabric together. "What's the matter?"

"I'll tell you what's the matter! Do you see this?" She swept a meaty arm expansively to indicate all of the Huber property. "Do you? It's a mess, that's what it is! And now I've got to do something about it? Oh, good Lord! By the way, this is—Mickey Gillette. She's with the press."

"Nikki. Nicole," Nikki corrected as the big man tipped his hat.

"Okay. *Nikki*. But, Al, what the hell am I gonna do with all this junk?"

"You don't gotta do anything, not today," he said and slung a long arm around her shoulders.

"Except talk to the cops. Goddamn, if someone else hadn't done it, I swear, I woulda killed Billy myself, if I'd seen how bad this all was."

Not exactly the grieving daughter.

As if she had read Nikki's mind, Janelle clarified, "Look, Billy . . . he wasn't my dad, okay? I mean he was. Biologically. But—" She made a face. "Between you and me, he wasn't much of a father. Ever. I don't think Mom ever really loved him. I should've done a DNA test to find out if there was any blood connection because I sure didn't have anything in common with him, but, hey, it's too late now, and I get to go down to the morgue and ID his body, make it official, you know. As if I didn't have anything better to do."

"Do you know anyone who would want to see your father dead?"

Janelle looked at her as if she were an idiot. "Didn't you hear a word I said? He was a loser. A snake in the grass—knee high in this case," she said as she gazed at the weed-choked pasture. "He was someone who would steal from a blind guy. So, yeah, I think anyone he met might want to kill him."

"Anyone in particular?"

She dismissed that with a wave of her hand. "He didn't get along with people in general. Not his family. Not his bosses, when he had them, not his neighbors, not anyone."

"What about friends?"

"Did he have any?" Her face was blank. "None that I know of." She glanced at her watch. "Look, I've got to get on the road. As I said, I've got a dead body to identify, and then there's a lawyer in Savannah and . . ." Her shoulders slumped, and she sighed loudly. "I don't need this."

"We'll get through it," Al said, and again squeezed her shoulders. "One day at a time, and well, you got the property."

Janelle looked over her father's place again. "It's worth something, I guess," she said dubiously. "Fine, fine. Let's get on with it. And you"—she added, shrugging off his comforting arm and pointing at Nikki—"deal with the damned dog."

"I will," Nikki promised and wished she'd learned more than the obvious facts that Janelle Huber McGowan hated her father and seemed to be mad at the world.

Like the man who'd sired her.

Maybe the apple doesn't fall so far from the tree after all.

"So here's what we know about that rock from the William Huber crime scene," Clint Darden, one of the lab techs, said, his deep voice clear through the phone connection at the station. Reed had been about to leave the office when he'd gotten the call and now was seated at his desk again, pen in hand.

From his chair, he kicked the door to his office closed, blocking out the sounds of the department, the incessant ringing of phones and chunk of the fax machine over the buzz of conversations.

Darden continued, "The mark on the back of the polished stone is the number nine. In Hebrew. When you hold the stone upright to read that number, then rotate it side to side, it reveals the number nine in Arabic, or the numbers we use today."

"If we assume that the numbers are the same."

"Yes."

"And we don't flip the stone end over end?" Reed said, thinking aloud.

"Again, yes," Darden agreed, and Reed considered it, wasn't going to rule out that the Arabic side wasn't a six. Yet.

"But that's not the most interesting thing about the rock," Darden told him.

"What is?"

"We can tell that it's been tumbled or polished, smoothed and made to shine, and the numbers were etched into it deep enough to be visible. But—here's the interesting part—that visibility was enhanced by blood. Stained, I guess you'd say."

"By blood," Reed repeated, feeling his pulse tick a little faster as he leaned closer to the desk phone. "Intentionally?"

"Looks like it. Because the blood is only in the crevices that are etched into the rock, almost as if it was painted into the etchings."

"Why?" Reed asked, even though he knew there was no definitive answer yet.

"Possibly to make the numbers more distinct, so that they appear more clearly in the stone?"

So as not to go unnoticed. The killer, or whoever laid the rock beneath Huber's body, wanted someone to find it with its hidden message. Or so it seemed. "Ink or paint or any other dark liquid could have stained the rock."

"Probably."

Reed tossed the idea of the blood over in his mind. If the killer left the stone purposefully, which seemed all the more likely, he was intent on making his message known. "What kind of blood?" he asked, wondering if somehow Billy Huber's blood had been smeared onto the rock's slick surface.

"Still working on it."

"Let me know the minute you get anything on it—kind, type, DNA, whatever."

"You got it."

He hung up and tossed the information over in his mind. The number nine. In Hebrew and Arabic. On a polished stone. Left under Billy Huber's body. He didn't like it. Yeah, it was a mystery that intrigued him, but if the killer had left his mark and was intentionally trying to convey some kind of cryptic message, then there was more to Billy Huber's death than simple murder.

He almost laughed at himself as he reached for his suit jacket. Was murder ever uncomplicated? The death of one human being by another. Even those killings that were acts of passion weren't simple.

Patting his pants pockets to make certain he had his wallet and keys, he slid on his jacket.

Outside, the day was starting to cool. A spring breeze ruffled his hair as he unlocked the car remotely and then spied his wife standing next to her Outback. She was holding Chloe, who lit up when she saw her father. "Daddy! Daddy!" she called.

Picking up his pace, he noticed that the lift gate to the Subaru's cargo area was open. Inside, lying on a dog bed in Mikado's kennel, was Billy Huber's dog.

"Oh, no," he said, shaking his head as the shepherd, chin on his paws, looked up at him with forlorn eyes. "We're not taking this dog home."

"Daddy!" Chloe stretched her chubby arms in his direction.

"Nicole," he said, eyes trained on his wife as she transferred their child to him and the little girl giggled as he broke eye contact and swung his daughter around. "Hey, there, princess," he whispered against her neck, and she laughed, her curly hair bouncing, her eyes bright as she wrinkled her nose.

"Arlo!" Chloe proclaimed, pointing at the cage in the back of Nikki's car. "Mikado's friend."

"Arlo," he repeated, arching an eyebrow at his wife, who in turn stubbornly lifted her chin.

"Uh-huh!" Chloe nodded sagely as he stopped the twirling.

"Well, Mommy and Daddy need to talk about this."

Nikki nodded. "We do. At home."

"Fair enough," he said, deciding to argue later. They did not need another dog. But he bit his tongue for the time being as he loaded Chloe into her car seat.

After he'd buckled in his daughter securely, he straightened and found Nikki standing beside him. She handed him a plastic bag with what looked like a dozen or so silver pellets.

"Bird shot," she explained. "Taken from the dog."

He slid a glance at the animal. Vicious and snarling last night. Demure and quiet now. Possibly still sedated?

"Dr. Vasquez had actually neutered him a couple of years ago.

Also, I met with Huber's daughter, Janelle, who, by the way, told me to keep him. She has no use for him and had planned to give him to a rescue."

"Which wouldn't be that bad of an idea."

She ignored him. "Will the pellets help in the investigation?" she asked.

"Don't know," he admitted, "but they won't hurt."

"Do you think the killer shot the dog?"

Pierce lifted a shoulder.

"Mommy!" Chloe said through the open door of Nikki's Outback.

Nikki nodded. "Coming." To Pierce, she said, "We can talk about this at home." She slammed the hatch to the cargo compartment closed, while Pierce said to his daughter, "See you at home," before closing the open door.

Nikki paused to look over the roof of her car. "Arlo is really a sweet dog, and he's going to be a great pet, once he trusts us."

"And he's still under the effects of anesthesia?" Pierce asked, peering at the shepherd and noticing that the dog's back and hips had been shaved to expose the stitched wounds where the bird shot had been removed. The dog eyed him, and he said, "Looks like you've got a new home," as Nikki slammed the cargo door shut.

Nikki smiled up at him from behind the wheel.

Resigned to another pet to add to their ever-growing menagerie, Reed stepped back onto the curb and watched his wife wheel out of the lot.

Pick your battles, he reminded himself, as he climbed into his Jeep and started the engine in order to roll down the windows and turn on the AC. He figured this particular fight was lost before it even got started. Did he really care about another animal joining the family? Not really. As long as the dog—Arlo, he reminded himself—was healthy and not dangerous.

But as he rammed the gearshift into drive, he remembered the snarling beast of the night before with his suspicious eyes and flashing teeth. That wouldn't do. Nor would the fact that Nikki was always challenging him, sometimes to the point of going behind his back.

Chapter 9

". . . I'm just saying that it's time," Ina insisted on the other end of the wireless connection. As Nikki's literary agent, Ina was always pushing Nikki to write another book. "Surely, you have some ideas, probably lots of them!"

Phone to her ear, Nikki eyed the books she'd written, the spines visible on the bookshelf in her office. They were all true crime, all about cases in which she'd been personally involved.

"*The Third Grave* came out last summer," Ina prodded, and Nikki pictured the fiftyish woman with jet-black hair, dark eyes, and a throaty, cigarette-raspy voice. "I thought you might have a new project."

"Maybe, but I'm not sure," she admitted, thinking there might be an interesting angle to Billy Huber's murder. "A case is developing, but it's still in the beginning stages."

"And an investigation can take years. I watch *Dateline*. You need to strike while the iron's hot, or at least still warm. I'm sure you can come up with something."

Maybe. Maybe not. "I'll work on it," Nikki promised before ending the conversation. But, she had to admit, Ina was right: Who knew how long it would take before Billy Huber's killer would be brought to justice? Possibly never. And it might not be "juicy—a big story," as

Ina had always described her books. Sighing, she eyed the open newspaper on her desk and saw her byline under the article about Huber's homicide. It had been short and to the point, no more information in the article than what she'd gotten from Viv, the public information officer.

Dry and simple.

For once, Norm Metzger hadn't complained about Nikki taking over his territory or, as he so sweetly remarked, pissing in his pot. The truth was that Metzger, always on the lazy side, was eyeing retirement.

And the story had gotten old.

It had been over a week since Huber's body had been found, and in that time, his daughter had identified his remains and returned to Florida. The police had contacted all of Billy's known acquaintances, and though Pierce had admitted there were a plethora of suspects, progress was still slow.

Fink wanted something new on the murder.

So far, there wasn't anything.

Ina thirsted for a new story.

Again, Nikki was drawing blanks.

She stood and stretched, hearing her back pop and seeing Arlo scramble to his feet. After their argument, Pierce had relented; she could keep the dog after she'd vowed not to ever take in any strays again, not without first consulting with him. That was fair, she decided, and if the situation ever arose again, she'd deal with it then. No need to borrow trouble.

The other caveat Pierce had insisted on was that Arlo needed to be a docile, non-aggressive family dog, one that would obey simple commands and never attack anyone.

On the issue of the dog's temperament, she and her husband were in complete agreement.

For once.

"Come on," she said to Arlo now, but the dog was already shooting past her and down the stairs.

He'd come a long way in a week.

From the snarling, matted mess she'd found at Huber's house, to a shy, but seemingly loyal dog to Nikki and Chloe. Fortunately, the bird shot hadn't affected his gait, had only been superficial, and already his coat was beginning to grow back a little.

Mikado had been a little standoffish at first, but had begun to accept the new member of the family. Jennings wasn't as keen on Arlo, his little pink nose definitely out of joint. If the dog got too near, the tabby had taken to hissing and arching his back, then slinking into the shadows to curl up with Phee and ignore Nikki completely. As if she were a traitor.

Now, on the first floor, Arlo beelined for the back porch, and Nikki let him outside, where he romped onto the grass and rolled in the blades, grunting in pleasure as the day bled into dusk. Mikado wandered outside, and Chloe, in footed pajamas, squealed in delight and sped past Nikki to join the dogs.

Pierce was right on his daughter's heels. "It's bedtime soon, right after dinner," he said, but Chloe, giggling, flung herself down on the grass. "So much for the bath."

Nikki couldn't help but smile at her daughter's joy and her husband's good-natured frustration. Pierce managed to corral their daughter and hauled her inside just as Lily and Phee returned from Phee's horseback-riding lessons. While Phee took off her helmet and kicked off her riding boots, Lily placed two pizza cartons on the kitchen island.

She stated, "This counts as my turn making dinner. And we're using paper plates. I know it's not ecologically sound, but there's no way I'm doing dishes." She located napkins and plates from the cabinet next to the table. "Oh, here we go—all we have is Fourth of July and Christmas . . . oh, and one Halloween. What do you say?" she asked Chloe, once Nikki had settled her into her booster chair and snapped a bib over her already grass-stained PJs. "Black cats?" Lily held out two plates, an orange one decorated with black cats and witches' hats, and a second with an image of a deer with a red nose and matching scarf. "Or Rudolph?"

"Cat!" Chloe declared.

"There ya go." Lily set the paper plate on the table in front of Chloe as Nikki cut up one piece of the Hawaiian pizza with its paper-thin slices of ham and chunks of pineapple, then dropped the bite-size bits onto the plate.

Phee washed the grime of the horse stables from her face and hands before sitting at the table, where the adults had divvied slices of Hawaiian and vegetarian pizzas.

"Anything new on the case?" Lily asked as she picked at a slightly charred artichoke leaf.

"Huber homicide?" Pierce shook his head.

Nikki pointed her pizza slice at her husband. "He wouldn't tell us if there was."

But maybe there just wasn't anything to discuss. Nikki had been going over her notes and making calls, but all she'd come up with were dead ends. She'd talked to everyone she could think of, and her only new angle was about Huber's wife Linda-Sue's death. In the single-car accident, Billy had swerved to avoid a deer that had darted into the road, but the doe had been hit and killed, the truck skidding into a telephone pole, and Linda-Sue had been pronounced DOA at the hospital. Not exactly the purposeful tragedy Janelle had hinted at and blamed Billy for.

Was there more to the story?

So, far, Nikki didn't think so.

But she would keep digging.

Chapter 10

Seated on her tufted vanity stool, Mavis Greenlee frowned at her foot, specifically her right foot and the polished nail of her big toe. It was painted a shimmering shade of coral, the precise color of her lipstick, and, of course, her fingertips.

But there was a flaw in the polish, a tiny chip, just noticeable enough that she couldn't possibly wear open-toed shoes to the Honeywells' patio party. If she couldn't wear her gold sandals, then her entire ensemble would have to be rethought. The peach-colored, frothy blouse and beige skirt and jacket needed the glitter and dash of *je ne sais quoi* that the sandals and her coral-tinged toes provided.

"Damn it all to hell," she muttered, as Princess, her cat, wandered into the bathroom and hopped lithely onto the vanity. Absently, Mavis stroked the Persian with the beautiful lilac points on her long, creamy fur. A lovely creature who usually distracted Mavis from her problems.

But not today.

Not with this horrendous toe, for God's sake!

It was the fault of the girl who had applied the color. The girl at the salon. The one who could barely speak English. The girl whom Mavis had deigned to let apply the polish because Marta, that little sneak, hadn't been in this afternoon. Even though Mavis had a standing appointment with her.

Marta was good with toes and gave the most delicious calf massages.

Marta understood exactly what Mavis wanted.

Marta would never have let Mavis leave the shop unless the polish was set and hard.

But then Marta hadn't been in the salon this afternoon, and the watery excuse that she'd felt ill didn't sit well with Mavis. Not at all.

Well, nothing did.

Because not a thing, not one blessed thing, was going right!

Just take the other day, about a week or so ago. It had been a nightmare. First thing in the morning, the blender had died, so no perfectly balanced smoothie.

To make matters worse, her Mercedes coupe had decided to die, right there in the garage, making her late and forcing her to drive Arch's pickup, as he, of course, was already driving his Aston Martin.

Unbelievable!

Then there had been the horror of the lunch at the country club. Not only had the kitchen run out of shrimp bisque, but also that revolting Charlene Gillette had shown up with her artsy-fartsy daughter and granddaughters, only one of whom was legitimate, mind you. The little one, with the curly reddish hair and big eyes. She at least had a known father. But she was a brat if there ever was one. Just like that mother of hers. Nicole. The reporter. Mavis couldn't help but sneer when she thought of "Nikki." A pushy little tart, that one.

But it was Charlene's older daughter who had shown up at the club with her kid. A "tween" or whatever you called them these days. The rail-thin granddaughter seemed churlish and uncouth, just like her mother, Lily—that head-in-the-clouds heathen who had dared have a child out of wedlock and raise her as a single mother.

As if she had that right!

Faux avant-garde, that was who Lily Gillette was. A horrid piece of work, just like her mother, Mrs. Hoity-Toity, the widow Gillette, still mourning for "The Judge," as she'd referred to Big Ron. Mavis scoffed. Ronald Gillette was a womanizer if there ever was one.

Mavis should know.

And she did.

Oh, she surely did.

Her lips curved a bit at the memory of slyly sneaking away with Ron at one particular Christmas party, right under Charlene's perfect little, surgically sculpted nose. Mavis and Big Ron had nuzzled behind the oversize fir tree with its sparkling lights and glittering garlands. If she tried, Mavis could still smell the scents of evergreen boughs and juniper berries and feel the heat of Big Ron's lips upon her décolletage. She'd wondered then, as she did now, if the "Big" in his name referred to something other than his stature. She smiled because she knew it was true.That night, right before the dinner bell had been rung, she'd let him hold her close. His moustache had tickled her skin, and she'd grown warm deep inside . . .

Dear God!

She snapped back to the present.

Dismayed, she caught her image in the vanity mirror. In the glow of the Hollywood lights surrounding the reflective glass, she noticed her face had flushed at the memory and she was breathing a little too hard. With a cotton pad, she dabbed at the little beads of sweat that had sprouted on her forehead, then, slowly, let out her breath. "Give me strength," she said in a whispered prayer and touched the necklace with its tiny cross that she always wore around her neck and, she knew, close to her heart.

She felt an immediate sense of calm. That's better, she thought, admiring her reflection.

As Princess leaped onto the floor to disappear into the bedroom, Mavis tucked an errant curl away from her face and back into the chignon at her nape. Her thoughts roved to what had been a miserable week. Her schedule had changed at the whim of everyone else. The mahjong game had been canceled on Tuesday because Florence's flighty daughter had decided to breeze into town unannounced. Then the wine tour had been rescheduled due to some plumbing problem at one of the vineyards. On Sunday, she'd been assigned to find drivers to deliver meals to the housebound members of the church. She intended to talk to Reverend Stark about that! And now . . . now her damned toenail!

She should go back to the salon.

Demand a refund or a touch-up from that smarmy little girl who hadn't let the polish set properly. She had been too hurried, too rushed, handling Marta's clients as well as her own.

And, damn it, she had left the wretch a hefty tip.

Mavis stood, intent on marching back to the salon when her grandmother's voice wafted through her mind.

"Say a prayer, Mavis dear, talk to the Lord. Learn patience. It's just a little flaw. All God's children have flaws. No one will notice."

"Of course they will!" she said aloud, as if her dearly departed grandmother from Appalachia could hear her. Grammy never had to deal with Savannah society! Ora-Jean would never have understood how important it was that she look perfect.

If not for herself, then for her friends.

And if not for her friends, then for Archer.

At the thought of her third, philandering husband, Mavis felt her teeth clench nearly as tightly as her fists. That son of a bitch. She should have known. Once a cheater, always a cheater. Right? But, still, just because he and Mavis had gotten together when they were both still married, that didn't give him the right to play around on her! Who did he think he was, flaunting *that woman* around his club?

And she'd heard they'd gone horseback riding.

Really?

Horseback riding!

Archer hated horses. And riding. And anything outdoorsy aside from hunting, and that was when he was younger. But what could he do if not indulge that little slut? A woman who was only nineteen! A scheming little bitch who was barely more than a girl. Over forty years his junior, for God's sake! Younger than his damned daughter, and, oh, God, almost as young as his granddaughter. What kind of a monster did that?

It was . . . disgusting. And maddening. And so, so humiliating! She slipped back onto the tufted stool and felt like . . . what? Crying? Weeping like a spoiled child? Well . . . yes. But she wouldn't.

But now, *now*, her goddamned nail was chipped!

Holy Mother of God, it was amazing she hadn't ended up in a mental institution with what she had to put up with.

But it was too late to go back to the salon, as it was now closed.

Angrily, Mavis scooted back the small stool, caught a glimpse of herself in the mirror, and quickly, forcefully, changed her expression. The scowl produced lines around her lips and between her eyebrows, and that would never do. She wasn't due for another Botox treatment for two more weeks . . . and oh, those dark circles.

No, no, no! Would nothing ever go right?

Well, surely not today.

"Take a deep breath, dear."

"Oh, shut up!" She hated hearing Grammy's voice these days.

"And pray." Well, she'd done that. She was a God-loving Christian, for goodness' sake. Just ask Reverend Stark. How many times had she chaired the Birds of Paradise, which was the ladies' aid society for the church? She'd tried to change the name but had been steadfastly voted down by those old bitches—biddies who'd been around since the seventies when girls were called "chicks" or "birds" in England—and Paradise was in reference to heaven, of course.

Duh!

Maybe it had been cute years ago, but now it was just a stupid, silly name. Despite all the good the society did.

Disgusted all over again, she strode out of the master bath she'd so meticulously designed and rushed down the curved staircase to the living area, where the drinks cart was waiting. With trembling hands, she poured herself a stiff shot and took a long, satisfying swallow. Then another, polishing off the vodka in her glass before taking the time to fill her short glass with ice cubes from the kitchen refrigerator. Then she poured herself another—just a quick one to steady her nerves—as her cell phone rang, the sound coming from a distance.

What the hell now?

She scrambled to find the damned thing—where had she left it? Oh, hell, it was upstairs? Cautiously, so as not to spill her drink, she mounted the inlaid steps bathed with elegant light from the crystal chandelier suspended high above the staircase.

In her bedroom, she was relieved to find her cell where she'd left it, flung onto the bed in her hurry as she got dressed. Right next to Princess, who stared at her with wide, blue eyes. Mavis scooped up the phone, recognized the number on the screen, and sighed heavily.

Her mother.

Just what she needed.

Blanche was in a private home, where Mavis paid the women who watched after her a small fortune. Yet still her mother called. Maybe with the help of one of the aides. Maybe by herself. Having just celebrated her eighty-fifth birthday, Blanche still had the wherewithal to hit the speed-dial number for her daughter. And only to complain.

"Fabulous," Mavis muttered sarcastically.

She thought about answering, then decided against it. She wasn't in the mood to deal with Blanche's resentful comments about her care.

Not today.

She had her own problems.

Mavis would call back later.

Tonight—no, tomorrow.

She let the phone ring and sipped her drink as the call went to voice mail.

"She's your mother. My daughter." Grammy's reproachful voice was haunting her still.

Well, too damned bad.

Tomorrow morning was soon enough to listen to Blanche's litany of complaints about the food, the caregiver, the house, her aches and pains . . . "Ugh," Mavis whispered just as she heard a noise.

From downstairs?

But she was alone.

Except for Princess, who was still on the bed.

And it was the maid's day off.

She cocked her head toward the open door of her bedroom and the landing beyond, but the house was still. And getting dark. Shadows of the late afternoon crawling across the floor.

Could Archer have come home?

At the thought, her skin crawled. He was an appalling man who had let himself go to seed. While Mavis toned herself with a personal trainer and worked out with hand weights, took a Pilates class, and even spent an hour a week doing tai chi, Archer satisfied himself with rounds of golf.

Still, though she found him reprehensible in so many ways, that didn't mean she would let some little whore come sneaking into his bed as well as his heart and, most likely, his wallet. And, to be honest, he'd been starting to trim down a bit, probably because of that *girl*! And, of course, the horseback riding! Honest to God!

"Hello?" she called down the stairs, still straining to listen.

Nothing.

She ignored the uptick in her pulse.

Was that a soft footfall on the first floor?

"Archer?" she yelled a bit louder, the fading light from the skylight high overhead offering little illumination.

It was times like these when she wished they still had the dog. A Labrador retriever like the one Archer took hunting when they were first married, but Buddy was long gone, and Mavis had refused to have another dog in the house. She didn't need the dirt tracking in, and then there were the fleas and ticks . . . no, thank you. Princess was enough of a pet. But now, feeling edgy, she would have liked the dog with his sharp nose and ears.

"Honey—are you home?" she said, forcing the endearment out.

The house remained still as a tomb.

And yet she sensed someone or something in this sprawling manor. She and Archer were long past playing cute little tricks on each other—like surprising each other. That playfulness had only lasted a few months into the marriage.

So . . . ?

Best not to take any chances. These days, you couldn't be too careful. Just last week a local man had been murdered. At least, that's what Mavis had read. In two separate articles in the paper, written by Charlene Gillette's snippy little reporter of a daughter. Even though she didn't know the man who had been killed; he lived outside the city. Still within several miles. Close enough to be worrisome.

One had to be aware. And cautious. And armed. She walked to her bedside stand and opened the drawer. There, nestled on its matching pillow was her pink pocket pistol. Cute. Compact. But deadly.

And loaded.

Always.

She swept it up and clicked off the safety, then moved stealthily from the bedroom to the wide landing at the top of the staircase.

She squinted down the curved steps.

Nothing moved.

But did she feel a draft?

Had a window or a door been left open?

Every muscle in her body tensed. Every nerve ending came alive.

She glanced across the landing to the opposite wing of the house. Archer's domain. But the double doors to his suite were closed tight.

And then something clattered to the marble floor below.

She didn't hesitate, but started down the stairs.

The marble was imported. From a quarry in Italy. Rare. Gorgeous. Beyond expensive. If anyone was marring it, they would pay for it, and—

Wait!

Was that a shadow on the landing just above her?

But how—?

She spun quickly, pistol raised, and saw him.

A looming figure.

She gasped!

No!

He lunged.

Pushed her, big hands on her shoulders.

Her feet went out from under her.

She fired.

Just as the gun flew from her hand.

The shot went wild.

Tumbling backward, she saw the chandelier, with its dimmed lights, swirling above her, then she hit the stairs. Hard. Something cracked. She mewed in pain as she tried to catch herself, but momentum kept her rolling, over and over. Slamming into each step.

Her shoulder.

Her pelvis.

Her head.

Bam!

Bam!

Bam!

With each hit, a new pain erupted to scream up her body.

Her chignon unraveled.

The vaulted ceiling whirled overhead.

Crack!

She landed hard, the side of her face slamming against the glorious marble, a horrible crunch assuring her that her cheekbone had shattered, momentum throwing her onto her back.

Agony rippled across her face, pain searing through her body. Her legs were tangled on the stairs.

Could she move? Not yet. And her phone . . . oh, God where was her phone?

She heard him.

Felt the vibrations of his footsteps as he slowly descended.

She had to get away. To escape!

Lying on her back, her skirt bunched at her waist, her legs untangled of their own accord. Now her feet pointed to the landing above. She needed to turn over, to crawl away, but couldn't make herself move.

Come on, come on, come on!

She willed her legs to shift, even just an inch. To push herself backward, away from his slow but determined advancement.

Nothing.

Oh. Dear. God.

Her mouth turned to dust, and her eyes widened in dread. She tried to scream but was unable. All she could do was to turn one blurry eye up at this monster who had invaded her home. She blinked. Tried to focus. But only saw the image of a man in black and something in his hand. It glinted in the fading illumination from the chandelier, and her heart stuttered.

A knife?

He had a knife?

Or . . .

He raised the glittering weapon as he approached.

Mother of God—No!

She let out a weak croaking sound just as he reached her.

"Meet your maker," he whispered, before . . . before . . . spouting some kind of Bible verse, or was it a song? Her brain was too dazed to think clearly. But she knew she was about to die, about to feel the puncture of that wicked blade into her eye or nose or throat or wherever he chose to thrust it.

"No, please—" she forced out in a gurgle of salty blood, but was saved from the pain as she blessedly lost consciousness.

Chapter 11

"Is this how you found her?" Reed asked as he stared down at the broken body of Mavis Greenlee.

Her husband, Archer, stood near the open front door of their mansion. In a polo shirt and pressed khakis, the tall man was huddled against the sidelight of the massive double doors. Archer could do nothing more than nod, his gaze glued to the crumpled mass that had been his wife.

Blood had pooled on the marble floor beneath Mavis's blond head, a wide puncture wound at her neck, legs splayed upward on the stairs, one of her arms at an impossible angle, no doubt broken. Probably in several places. On the fifth step, a small pink pistol rested, and there appeared to be a bullet hole in the ceiling, right next to a massive chandelier.

The foyer itself was crawling with EMTs and police, the walls reflecting the blue and red flashes from the police vehicles parked in the wide, circular drive outside.

"You didn't move her?" Reed asked.

"No, no, should I have?" Archer's big eyes rounded, and he was sweating, drops glistening through his thin comb-over. "I thought you were never supposed to . . . I mean, I saw her, called to her, but I knew she was dead. I, um, I did go near and check for a pulse. I told that to the 911 operator, but there was nothing." Now he was shaking his head more violently, his voice rising, "And she wasn't breathing. I put a finger under her nose. I checked for a pulse. I did. I checked. But I knew. Oh, God, how did this happen?" He seemed genuinely distressed.

"Okay." Reed crouched low, staring at the once-beautiful woman. He knew her, had seen her at several charity functions over the years. Mavis Greenlee was synonymous with Savannah society.

"Can I . . . Can I go now?" Archer was inching toward the open door and the circular drive, beyond where the first responders had gathered near the fire trucks and emergency vehicles.

"Go where?"

"We have another house," Archer said quickly, fidgeting with his keys. "Out on Tybee Island. Until . . . well, until you're finished here and . . . and she's gone." He swallowed hard and waved a hand at his dead wife. "I just can't stay here. It's too . . . well, you know."

Reed did know.

He'd seen it all before.

Those left behind not wanting to stay in the home where a murder had taken place.

From somewhere above came a loud, pitiful cry.

"What—?"

"Princess," Archer said, glancing up at the closed double doors at the top of the stairs. "My wife's cat. Oh, God, what am I going to do with her?"

At that moment, Sol Augustin returned to the foyer. She'd ridden with Reed to the Greenlee mansion but, after a quick view of the crime scene, had stepped outside to take a call.

She was just disconnecting and stuffing her cell into the pocket of her slacks. "What do you mean?" Sol asked, her gaze shifting from Archer to the dead woman.

"Not her. Not Mavis," Archer said, realizing what Sol was probably thinking. "The cat. What the hell am I going to do with that damned thing?"

As if she'd heard, Princess gave up another long, pitiful wail.

"You're worried about your cat?" Sol said slowly.

"I just don't need another damned thing . . . I mean I . . . I have to get out of here."

"He's leaving?" she asked, turning her attention to Reed.

Reed explained. "They've got a place out on Tybee."

"Do you? Well, that works out, now, doesn't it?" she said, turning her gaze on Archer. "And no room for a cat out there?"

"I can't—I just can't! Oh, God. It—she—hates me. Spits and hisses and runs away. She's Mavis's damned Persian and I . . . no, no I can't have that . . . that thing with me. No."

To Reed, Augustin said, "Just got off the phone with the ME's office. They're on their way."

"And Forensics?"

"Should be here any minute." Sol then turned her attention to Archer Greenlee. "Where were you again?" she asked, studying the nervous man. "Earlier tonight."

"I told you. Or—I mean, I told the cop—a deputy, I think. I can't remember his name. Big guy. Black. He was here when I first got here."

"Deputy Freeman?" Reed asked. "Marlin Freeman?"

"Yeah, yeah. That sounds right. I, uh, I think so." Archer said, blinking rapidly and wiping a hand over his forehead.

"You have cameras here? A security system."

"Yes, but the original cameras are old, and the newer ones were too good, picked up everything that went on. A rabbit, a bird, whatever, so . . ."

"They're not functioning, is that what you're saying?" Augustin asked.

"Yeah. This is a safe community." Archer was nodding, but did manage to look sheepish. "I mean it was."

"What about your neighbors?" Reed asked.

"I—I don't know." Archer shrugged. "I, um, I suppose they do. At least some of them."

"Already got deputies checking," Augustin said, "and interviewing the neighboring places, and the stores and street cameras." To Archer, she asked, "Where were you tonight?"

"Me?" At first, he seemed offended, and then he cleared his throat. "I—I was downtown at the Stag and Boar, had a few beers with some friends. Knox and Otis and Stoney and a couple of others will tell you I was there." His Adam's apple worked wildly. "You can call any of them. They'll vouch for me and tell you I was there. Or talk to the bartender, Max . . . no, Mac. Yeah, call down there, talk to Mac. He knows I was there." Archer's frantic gaze moved from Sol to Reed. "We meet down there once a month or so, sometimes after the rifle club. You know, just target shooting." He was visibly sweating. "You can call any of them. They'll vouch for me. You believe me, don't you? You don't . . . I mean you can't possibly think I had anything to do with this." His skin was white and stretched over his features, his eyes wide.

Reed said, "We'll need a formal statement down at the station."

"Do I need a lawyer?" he demanded, stricken. "Oh. Christ. You all, you all think I'm behind this? Holy shit! I knew it. I just knew it! The husband is always the primary suspect."

To her credit, Sol didn't roll her eyes. "If you think you need an attorney, then by all means, call one."

"I don't . . . I mean, I didn't do this . . . I wouldn't . . . never . . . but . . ." He looked panicked and pulled at the collar of his shirt.

Reed stepped in. "Go down to the station, make a statement, and then you can go to the house on the island."

"Okay. Okay. I will." Archer was nodding frantically. "I will. And . . . what about the house?" His gaze darted throughout the interior, to the living area off the foyer, and across the hall to a large den filled with books and a wide mahogany desk situated in front of a marble fireplace. The entire house, Reed guessed, was filled with what Archer considered valuable items.

"We won't be finished here for a while."

Again there was a plaintive meow.

"And the cat? Can someone . . . ?"

"We'll handle it," Augustin said.

"Good. Good. So. Um. Can I get my things? From my suite upstairs?" Archer waved a hand toward the top of the stairs and the landing where a huge portrait was visible, a slimmer, younger Archer with a full head of brown hair. In a suit and tie, he stood slightly to one side of his wife. One of his hands rested on her shoulder as Mavis, dressed in a shimmering silver gown, her chin lifted, sat in a high-backed chair, a dog, a golden Labrador retriever, resting at her feet. Archer said, "I can use the back staircase if you want . . . so as not to disturb . . ." His voice fell away as he glanced down at Mavis again, then looked quickly away.

"Do you have enough personal items at Tybee?" Reed asked. "We'll need to go over the entire house."

"Oh." Archer was backing toward the door. "Okay. Yeah, yeah, I guess I can make do with what I've got on the island."

"Good. Do that. 'Make do,'" Augustin said coolly. "And while you're at it, make certain we can get in touch with you."

"I—I gave you my cell number. I have it on me." He patted a pants pocket, making sure the phone was where it was supposed to be, then, as if he expected Reed to change his mind, Archer scooted out of the door, and within seconds, the sound of a sports car's engine roared to life.

"Must be nice," Augustin said as she scanned the wide entry hall with its soaring ceiling, curved staircase, shiny floor, and, of course, dead body. She picked up a vase on a side table and then, as if she realized she wasn't wearing gloves, quickly replaced it. "About the cat?"

Reed watched as she quickly put on a pair of thin disposable gloves. "Call someone from animal control, and maybe they can get in touch with a shelter." He hated to think what would happen if Nikki found out about another abandoned pet. Though his wife hadn't shown up at the crime scene yet, it was only a matter of time until she found out that Mavis Greenlee had been murdered. Then she would no doubt discover that Mavis had left behind a cat that her husband didn't want and that Nikki would move heaven and earth to adopt.

"Okay," Sol was saying, making a note about the animal before crouching down and studying the victim with a critical eye. "What's that?" she asked.

"What?"

"Under her skirt. There." She pointed to the hem of Mavis's skirt, which had ridden up to her waist in her fall, and there was an unlikely bulge in the tight, tummy-shaping panties.

"I don't know," he admitted.

Augustin leaned forward and, with gloved fingers, carefully pulled down the waistband low enough to show the edge of a polished stone, gleaming under the light from the chandelier suspended above.

Reed's gut tightened as she took a quick picture of the item in place; he nodded to Augustin and watched as she extracted the rock. A number was clearly visible.

"Five?" she murmured. "Or . . . or possibly an S." Turning the stone over, she straightened, then held the rock out for Reed's inspection. "Marked on the other side."

"Just like the other one found at Billy Huber's," he thought aloud. "So it's probably a number, not a letter. A five in Hebrew and the other side a five in Arabic."

Her eyes slitted as she studied the stone. "It looks like we've got ourselves a serial killer. Right here in genteel Savannah."

Reed didn't like the thought, but he didn't disagree.

She replaced the stone and stood. "Random victims?"

"Unlikely."

Reed looked around the opulent house, with its neatly arranged furniture, polished antiques, and gleaming surfaces. Nothing out of place.

Except for a dead woman.

"What the hell do Billy Huber and Mavis Greenlee have in common?" he muttered.

"A killer," she said, following his gaze and most likely his thoughts. "But who?"

"That's what we have to figure out."

Her eyes scanned the rest of the foyer, her gaze running up the carpeted stairs to the landing. Had it not been for the grizzly gash in Mavis's neck and the gun on the stairs, one might have assumed she'd tripped near the top step and tumbled head over heels to her resting spot at the base of the stairs. But her slashed throat and the polished stone told another story.

His phone buzzed, and he expected the caller to be Nikki. Instead, he saw Jamison Kittle's number on the screen. Reed stepped onto the porch to take the call and felt the cool of the night against his skin. "I take it you heard," he said as he answered.

"Yeah. But I can't believe it. Another one?" Jamison sounded gobsmacked. "Are you kidding me?"

"Not kidding."

There was a pause before Kittle said, "I know Mavis Greenlee. I play golf with her husband. And Naomi—she'll be devastated. She knew Mavis from the country club and church. God, I think the Greenlees were supposed to be at the Honeywells' party tonight. We were there, and Naomi mentioned it was odd that Mavis and Archer didn't show, then she said something about them having some marital problems, but I didn't think much about it. I mean, who doesn't? Then I got the call, and I phoned you to confirm. I don't want my wife to hear it on the news. She'll . . . God knows what she'll do."

"I can confirm. It's Mavis Greenlee."

"Damn," Kittle muttered, barely loud enough for Reed to hear over the conversation going on between two firefighters and a deputy standing near the collection of vehicles in the drive. "Same killer?" Kittle asked.

"Looks like. It won't be confirmed for a while, but yeah, I'm guessing."

"Keep me posted," Jamison said. Then he added, "Better yet, I'll be there."

"We've got it handled."

"I know. But as I said, this is personal."

The forensic team arrived and ushered everyone out of the house and into the night. Augustin joined Reed at the top of the circular drive, and when one of the team came out with the cat in a carrier, Augustin said, "I'll handle this" and caught up with the deputy.

Reed watched as she took the carrier and hauled it down the drive and past the open gate to her truck, which was parked across the street, its front grill just visible past one of the gateposts.

As she was returning, the van from the coroner's office arrived and was waved through the gates so that it could be parked close to the house. A few curious neighbors tried to follow, but deputies kept them at bay on the other side of the barrier cordoning off the Greenlee house.

Within minutes, Jamison Kittle showed up, leaving his car outside the police barricade and walking up to the house. For once, he wasn't dressed in a suit and tie, but showed up in slacks and a long-sleeved, black T-shirt, his hair slicked back and still damp as if he'd just stepped out of the shower.

On the steps of the house, he greeted Reed, who asked, "You tell Naomi?"

"Yeah. Before she heard it on the news." Kittle rubbed the back of his neck. "She was beside herself. Wanted to come here with me, but I talked her out of it, and she finally agreed. Someone had to stay with the girls." His gaze searched the exterior of the home, past the azaleas and dogwoods and planters overflowing with phlox and petunias to the brick wall enclosing the estate. "How the hell does this happen?"

"We're trying to figure that out."

Kittle peered through the open door and eyed the foyer of the house, where Mavis's corpse was being placed inside a body bag. He shook his head. "Unbelievable," he said under his breath. "MO the same as the Huber homicide?"

"Yeah. But Mavis had a gun."

"Did she?" He didn't seem surprised as the bag was zipped and loaded onto a stretcher. "And it didn't help?"

"No." Reed sketched out what they knew, and together they watched as Mavis Greenlee's body was hauled out of the house, whisked into a van, and driven away.

"We need to find this guy," Jamison said as his phone buzzed and he checked the screen. "It's Naomi." He let out a breath. "I'd better go. Keep me informed," he said again, then held up a hand to say goodbye as he started jogging back to his car, answering the call on his way.

As Kittle passed through the gates, Reed saw the first camera crew from a local television station arrive.

He wasn't in the mood to deal with reporters. Not yet. Not until he had answers. Until then, he didn't want to try to deflect or dodge their questions. He'd have to deal with enough of that at home.

Time to call it a night. He caught up with Augustin, who told him she wanted to check Archer Greenlee's official statement at the station and then double-check his alibi. "I can handle it. I'll report what I find out in the morning."

He didn't argue. It had been a long day, and he could do some follow-up from home. And there was Nikki. With her ear to the ground, she probably already had heard about the new homicide and would demand answers. It was better that he deal with her at home rather than have her show up here at the scene.

He wouldn't put it past her.

She'd done it before. His jaw flexed as he remembered the last time, at the Beaumont estate and how Sylvie Morrisette had paid the ultimate price for his wife's dangerous, uncompromising need to investigate.

God, he missed Morrisette, he thought, as he climbed into his Cherokee and drove away from the flashing lights and unanswered questions at the Greenlee estate.

Morrisette, like Nikki, had been a rule breaker. Or at least someone who would bend the law to the breaking point. For all the right reasons. Morrisette had been as tough as old leather, unconventional to a flaw, and determined to, as she so eloquently put it, "Lock those fuckers behind bars, no matter what it takes."

He'd had a few partners since, none of whom he'd really connected with. Not like Morrisette.

Maybe Sol Augustin would change all that.

Augustin was good. Insightful. Didn't miss much.

But there was something about her that bothered him, something he couldn't quite name. On paper, she was a stellar police officer. She'd landed a four-year scholarship to college and had been consistently on the dean's list. The same held true when she'd sailed through the police academy, and in the five years since graduating from the academy, she had proved herself.

Her work with the department had been exemplary. She was smart but quiet, hardworking, and private. Her thought pattern didn't quite follow his, so she observed things he missed. She came at every case from a different angle. She wasn't pushy, but held her own. She managed to always keep her temper in check and never, so far, had flown off the handle. Her emotions were always under control.

Unlike Morrisette, who had always gone off half-cocked.

In many ways, Augustin was a far better cop. More methodical. More controlled. Whereas Morrisette ran on emotion, Augustin ran on . . . what? He didn't know. It seemed as if she was calm, calculating, and competent, that she relied on common sense and strategy and good old logic.

And yet . . .

He sensed there was something more. Something hidden. Something secret.

Don't we all have our secrets?

Of course.

But some were more dangerous than others.

He rolled down the window as he drove through the city streets, the rush of cool Georgia air invading his Jeep, the misty glow of streetlamps lighting his way. He caught a glimpse of the moon as he passed the park, then, just a quarter of a mile before he reached his house, he pulled to the curb. As traffic eased by, he let his vehicle idle for a few minutes, retrieving his cell phone from his pocket to punch in a quick text:

Hey. Just checking in.

How're things?

How about we meet this weekend?

It sounded lame. Even to him. But he hit send and hoped for a response from Toby Yelkis, Sylvie Morrisette's seventeen-year-old son. The kid had struggled in school, even before his mother had died, but since then, things had gotten worse. If it hadn't been for Pierce stepping in, the angry teenager would've ended up in juvenile detention—and, possibly, still could. While Toby's sister, Priscilla, was now studying at SCAD, the Savannah School of Art and Design, and shared her own apartment with roommates, Toby was still slogging his way through high school.

Toby still lived with his deadbeat dad, Bart, Sylvie's much maligned loser of an ex. But Pierce had to tread carefully, as Bart Yelkis didn't like anyone getting too close to his kids. Oh, he'd take the tuition money that Nikki had put aside for their education, but he made sure it was known that he didn't want or need Pierce's "interference" in his children's lives. Though Priscilla was making her own way, blossoming despite losing her mother, the same wasn't true of her younger brother.

Pierce stared at the screen, hoping to see bubbles appear, indicating that Toby was responding. No such luck. The screen remained unchanged. "Great," Pierce muttered under his breath, and he put the Jeep into gear before driving the few remaining blocks home. As the wide garage door clunked downward behind him, he heard a cacophony of barking. Both dogs. Once he stepped inside the house, they greeted him in tandem. Mikado, head down, tail sweeping side to side, and Arlo, eager and wriggling; despite Pierce's reservations, the new dog was fast burrowing into his heart. "Yeah, yeah, I missed you both," he lied, as he hadn't thought of the dogs all day.

His wife?

Yes.

His daughter?

Of course. But the dogs? Not so much.

Now as he peeled off his jacket and dropped his keys onto the small table near the back door, he took the time to scratch each one behind the ears and nearly tripped on Jennings, who had scuttled into the hallway.

The tabby. Right. And now there was another feline who was soon to be an orphan. Mounting the stairs to Chloe's bedroom, he hoped beyond hope that Nikki didn't get wind of Mavis Greenlee's Persian. The last thing they needed in their menagerie of a home was another abandoned animal.

He saw flickering gray light seeping from beneath the door to Lily and Ophelia's room and the low rumble of the television's audio. Another bit of illumination slipped down the spiral stairs from Nikki's study, but before he climbed up, he wanted to check on Chloe. The door to her bedroom was slightly ajar, and he pushed it open far enough to ease through. In the glow of the night-light, he made out her shape in the crib, saw her tiny lips move and a bit of moonlight catch in her tangled curls. His heart filled.

"Hey," Nikki's voice was soft, but he visibly jumped as he hadn't heard her pad into the room. She joined him at Chloe's bedside and linked her fingers through his. "You okay?"

"I am now," he said.

She tugged on his hand, and together they walked along the short hallway to their room. Once there, she closed the door behind her. "I heard about Mavis Greenlee," she said, big eyes searching his.

He wasn't surprised.

"What happened?"

"Still working on it." He took off his jacket and tossed it onto the side chair near the window.

"Pierce?"

"Looks like a homicide."

She nodded. This wasn't news. As ever, she was not far behind the police when it came to local violent crime.

"The husband?"

Shaking his head, he said, "We don't know. But, no, I don't think so. He was pretty shaken up."

She was leaning against the closed door. "Any chance that her murder is connected to Billy Huber's?"

"Why would you think that?" Did she already know about the wound in each victim's neck? About the engraved stone found near the bodies?

"Timing."

He wouldn't lie. Nor would he compromise the investigation. "Unknown," he evaded, loosening his tie.

"But maybe?"

"We'll see."

But, because of the engraved stone, he knew there was a connection, that the killer was one and the same.

"You think they're connected," she said, reading him. "Because of something . . . on-site?"

"Stop," he told her.

"Ohh . . ." He watched her put two and two together and was annoyed yet proud of his irrepressible wife.

"Don't say it," he warned.

"Another rock . . . maybe?"

"If you start spouting your theories, everyone in the department will think I'm talking to you."

"You'll just have to convince them otherwise."

"I'm not saying you're right, but there are parts of the investigation we want to keep under wraps. You understand?"

"I won't compromise you. I promise."

But she couldn't help the grin that spread across her face. When he tried to argue some more, she put a finger to his lips and, with her free hand, grabbed hold of his tie, leading him on quiet tiptoes to the bed.

"Nikki . . ."

"Shhh." She then pushed him playfully onto the mattress.

Well, okay. They could argue more later.

Then his cell phone pinged, announcing that a message had come in. He yanked the phone from his pocket, intending to check the message later, but as he set it on the nightstand he read the message glowing brightly on the screen. Two words. From Toby Yelkis.

Fuck off.

Chapter 12

The dogs were restless. Pacing in their kennels. Occasionally whining.

With a harsh command, he shushed them, then slipped past the cages to the door secreted in the floor of what had once been a granary, when his grandfather had owned this land, long before the barn had been converted to the kennels where his hounds now paced.

Satisfied the dogs had settled, he quietly unlocked the trapdoor and slipped down the stairs. He was still excited, his blood pumping, exhilaration in his nerves and muscles. He tried to quiet his accelerated heartbeat, but the electricity sizzling through his body made calming himself impossible. He still could see the look of surprise and horror on that supercilious woman as he'd plunged his knife into her neck. And to think she had actually tried to wound—no, kill—him with that ridiculous little pocket pistol.

Pink, no less.

The gun was a vanity object, like her false eyelashes, bleached hair, and ridiculous, expensive feline—all trappings of the life she led. The fake life she paraded to the world. Holier-than-thou and a sinner of outrageous proportions.

It had been oh so satisfying to watch her realize that she was dying, that she would leave this earthly world and have to face her own personal judgment day as she met her maker.

All her sins would be revealed.

Locked in his private space, he reminded himself not to fall into Mavis Greenlee's trap, that he shouldn't revel in his own accomplishments, not even if he was doing God's bidding. There was no time for personal glorification.

He lowered himself onto a coarse straw pillow on the floor, bowed his head, and closed his eyes, reminding himself that he was but a vessel of the Lord, that he should not and would not allow his ego to overshadow his mission.

"I am your servant. All that I do is for you," he whispered over and over as his mantra, until the adrenalin rush in his veins had evaporated and he was breathing evenly again, his composure intact, his mission clear.

His was not a blood lust.

His was a calling, and he had to remember that.

But just in case he got ahead of himself, he leaned backward and opened the cabinet where his weapons were stored.

He eyed them all.

The mace.

The whip.

A coil of barbed wire.

The branding iron.

The cat-o'-nine-tails.

Ah, that last one would do. He could use it and hide the welts.

He retrieved the weapon with its nine leather braids and hard knots. He thought of the braids as snakes and imagined them on pagan Medusa's head as he felt the smooth wood handle. Removing his clothes, he decided that twenty lashes would suffice.

Then his mother's voice echoed through his brain: "Really? Twenty? Do you think that's enough for all the sin in you?"

He felt a quivering in his soul whenever he remembered her standing above him, looking down, the cross at her neck winking in the sunlight streaming through the windows as she stood, holding a butcher knife in one hand and tapping it sideways against the palm of her other. Silently threatening. Causing a chill to run through his guts.

"I don't think so."

"Shut up."

He closed his eyes, pushed her disapproving words out of his mind, refused to remember the downturn of her pale lips, the disappointment in her wide, gray eyes.

He wouldn't think of her. Or of what she did.

He would deal with the here and now and cleanse the world. One sinning mortal at a time.

But first . . .

He raised the gleaming whip overhead, paused a second to contemplate his own sins, then cracked his wrist. "One."

Snap!

Nine little bites on his back muscles. He flinched, grimacing, his body jumping with the first blow. Good. Of course, he couldn't get as much power into the strokes inflicting the wounds himself, but it would do.

Again.

"Two."

He struck. Hard as he could.

Felt the sharp pain. Sucked in his breath.

Again.

"Three." He felt the first hot bloom of blood. The stinging cuts.

Again.

"Four." His jaw tightened as the pain sharpened. Increased.

But he did not, would not stop.

He bit his lip to keep from crying out, then stopped before he drew blood and hence the possibility of attention. No. He would suffer in silence and control himself.

Again.

"Five."

He kept at it.

Again!

Again!

Again!

With each stinging, successive blow, his knees became weaker, his resolve began to dilute, and he cried out.

At nineteen, he stumbled. Nearly passed out. Braced himself.

Again!

The cat-o'-nine-tails whirled above him and then flayed his bleeding flesh. "Twenty," he croaked, the pain radiating. Still, he forced an agonized grin. He'd met his goal, but he wouldn't gloat, wouldn't revel in it; otherwise, he would have to mete out more punishment. He let his faltering smile of triumph fade, and he dropped to his knees to pray again.

His back was on fire.

Yet still he prayed.

Only when he was completely humble once more did he rise and step under the cold shower to rinse away the blood and sin. Afterward, he awkwardly applied some salve to his shoulders and back as best he could, then dressed again.

"Not good enough," his mother's voice mocked.

But he ignored her, set his jaw, and resumed his work.

He felt sufficiently obedient and humbled once more. Able to concentrate.

He rifled through his carefully catalogued vinyl records. Now that his rebellious, prideful fire had been smothered, he flipped past the heavy metal albums of the seventies and eighties. No Black Sabbath or Megadeth—they wouldn't do. Not tonight. Nor would Metallica.

He kept searching until he found a choral arrangement of folk songs. Not his usual cup of tea, but appropriate for his mood.

With gentle fingers, he lowered the LP onto the turntable of the old Pioneer and switched it on.

A few scratches sounded as the record spun, and then the blended voices and intricate harmonies filled the room. For a second, he pretended to be leading the ensemble, his imaginary baton sweeping in rhythm, his head moving as the music swelled. Once the music filled him, he sat at the stool near his workbench and reached into his pocket for the small vial of blood he'd prepared earlier. Painstakingly, he applied the blood to the smooth stone with a thin brush, meticulously tracing the number 1.

The music stopped, and he was forced to get up and flip the record over before the calming harmonies filled the space again.

Patiently, he waited for the blood to soak into the etching, then, satisfied, even a little proud, despite pride being a sin, he repeated the process, so he had two similar, if not identical stones. Satisfied, his back still burning, he left one of the finished stones on his workbench, then, with the other in his hand, walked to the closet with the secret back panel. His fingers found the niche in the wall to slide the panel aside. Beyond, there was just enough space for a small stool and a corner curio cabinet. Once settled onto the stool, he placed the newly finished stone next to the first two already gleaming in the cabinet under a strand of battery-powered lights.

Now there were three.

Though, of course, he was jumping the gun just a bit as the third sinner had yet to meet her maker.

But he planned to remedy that soon.

Very soon.

And these three polished rocks were just the beginning.

When his work was finished, there would be a collection of ten perfect tiny headstones. All inscribed. A perfect set.

"The only perfection is God," his mother reminded him unkindly before he picked up the knife again. "To think otherwise is a sin."

At four in the morning, the house was quiet, though the high-ceilinged foyer still blazed with lights from that oversize monstrosity of a chandelier. But all the techs were long gone, and the husband was on Tybee Island. Sol knew. She'd checked.

Now, with the deep blue of night still clinging to the town, she slipped through the wide front door, locked it behind her, and clicked off the lights. The foyer instantly darkened; there was only a minimal glow from the kitchen, where the oven's clock gave off a weak blue illumination. She was lucky the house was down a long, twisting drive bordered by thick trees and shrubbery; no one should notice the house had suddenly gone dark.

Pulling a towel from her backpack, she quickly shed her clothes. Who knew how much time she had? Patrols had increased in the area, and she'd timed her visit carefully. Still, she didn't want to be interrupted.

Or found out.

She eyed the bloodstain, still visible in the near darkness: an inky splotch coloring the thick carpet runner on the stairs and down to the marble floor. Stepping forward, she let her bare feet sink into the still damp, sticky pool where Mavis Greenlee's head had landed. She felt the residual blood darken her soles.

Closing her eyes, she took a long breath, concentrated on evening her breathing, clearing her mind, slowing her heartbeat.

Quiet.

So quiet.

And then . . . she felt a twitch in her cheek. A quivering of her eyelids.

A shudder sizzled through her, crawling up her spine.

In an instant, she felt Mavis Greenlee's presence, the bit of soul still lingering, as the woman's final moments rippled through her.

Panic!

Fear!

Pain!

Her knees buckled and she was on the floor, her knees slamming into the coagulated blood.

Who did this to you? Sol silently asked, wincing.

Who is he?

Why did he leave his calling card in the form of a smooth, marked stone?

In her mind, she heard the blast of a gun, felt the world reel, the renewed, sharp agony of Mavis's head cracking against the floor. Somewhere, a cat was crying, and the assailant flew down the stairs, his face in shadow, the blade in his hand glinting under the incandescence of the chandelier.

A scream erupted.

He struck.

Hard.

Fast.

The knife flashed.

Hatred.

Anger.

The blade dripping in blood.

Trembling, Sol tried to hold on to her own presence as she reached across the void attempting to connect, but Mavis's soul was rising, that scrap of her that remained, leaving.

No!

Not yet!

Who is he?

Who did this to you?

But that final bit of Mavis twirled ever skyward.

"Who?" Sol yelled, slamming her fist onto the bloody floor.

And then she heard it.

"Lucifer." The name of the devil whispered through the cavernous foyer, but in her mind's eye, in her vision of Mavis dying, Sol realized the dead woman's lips never moved.

She began to shiver.

Was suddenly cold to the bone.

She blinked.

Caught her breath.

She would learn nothing more. Unsteadily, she rose and, once the vision had passed completely, cleaned her feet and knees as best as she could, then dressed and swiped the towel across the bloody marble. She wasn't worried about fingerprints. She'd left some earlier in the day. She might have to come up with some explanation about the disturbed bloodstain, but she didn't think so. The police were done with the scene, and she doubted Archer Greenlee would notice or care. She tucked the stained towel into her backpack and turned on the foyer lights again, then hurried outside to the spot where she'd hidden the bicycle she'd ridden through the town. She hadn't risked driving her own vehicle, didn't want anyone or any street or neighbor's camera to have caught it as she'd driven by or parked at the Greenlee estate. She was dressed in black, wearing a mask, hiding her own identity, just as the killer might have.

She was only three blocks down the street when she looked over her shoulder at the sound of a car engine. A police cruiser had turned onto the street behind her and was slowing near the entrance to the Greenlee home.

Quickly, she cut down an alley so as not to be seen. She had every right to be at the crime scene as an investigating officer, but she didn't want to lie nor have to come up with any kind of excuse.

Not yet.

She'd save that for later if anyone noticed the disturbance in the blood within the house.

She avoided what little traffic there was, but noticed, as she reached her apartment house, that the city was coming to life. The early-morning risers had turned on lights and were probably already making coffee. She noticed a couple jogging a few blocks ahead, their reflective shoes and wristbands glowing in the dark. From several streets over, she heard the rumble of garbage trucks starting their rounds. A delivery van rolled down the street in front of the building, and the old guy who lived in a condo across the street was walking his ancient Labrador retriever as he did every morning before dawn.

Sol rode in a wide circle to avoid the parking lot's camera, then slipped into the back of her ground-floor unit unnoticed. After parking her bike in the hallway and locking the sliding door behind her, she took the bloody towel from her backpack and shoved it to the bottom of her under-the-sink trash can. She made her way to the bathroom, stripped, lathered her entire body, then stood under a steaming, hot spray until the blood on her feet and knees had completely washed away and the cold she'd felt in her soul had finally dissipated.

With water streaming down her body, she leaned her head against the wet tiles of the small shower stall, whispered a prayer, and was finally able to center herself again. Twisting off the taps, she took her towel from its hook and dried off before wrapping her wet hair in a turban and donning her white sack dress.

In her bedroom, she lit a candle, drinking in the cleansing smells of cedar and lavender before sitting cross-legged on her bedroom floor and again praying. This time not to the Christian God but to any spirit who would listen. "Help me," she murmured. "Help me find this madman before he strikes again." She breathed deeply, hoping her prayers had been heard and would soon be answered, but inside her soul, she feared that the gods were quietly reminding her of the lessons she'd learned in her youth: "Find strength in yourself, Sol. We are here only to guide you."

"Then, please do it. Guide me."

She heard no answer, but knew in her heart the horrible truth: The murders had just begun.

This killer was far from finished.

Chapter 13

"You're kidding!" Lily said the next morning as she was filling the coffeemaker with water. Her hair, piled on her head, was a mess, and she was still in a robe and slippers, while Nikki, carrying Chloe, was dressed for the day. "Mavis Greenlee is dead? Someone killed her?"

"It's all over the news. Pierce took off over an hour ago."

"Really?" Lily said around a yawn. "Didn't hear him leave. Guess I was dead to the world."

"He couldn't sleep. Too wound up over the case."

Nikki and Pierce had turned on the television in their room when the first newscasts were being aired before dawn this morning, and sure enough, the murder of Mavis Greenlee, one of Savannah's socialites, had been on every local station.

They'd discussed the homicide before falling asleep. Though Pierce hadn't come right out and said so, she was almost certain that the killer had left his calling card at the scene, an etched rock. So, the two murders were related. And it was shocking, stunning, really, that someone in her mother's social circle was one of the victims, killed by the same person who had attacked and murdered Billy Huber, a man who was far removed from the Greenlees in about every way possible.

"What's the connection?" she'd asked her husband, but he'd simply shaken his head. She took that to mean the police hadn't figured it out yet . . . although Pierce was also growing a little tired of her questions by that point.

But they had a serial killer.

In Savannah.

"Wow, I missed it all." Lily was shaking her head as she measured ground coffee into the basket of the brewer. "Hard to believe that awful woman is gone, that someone killed her, though, Lord knows, she made more than her share of enemies." When she caught Nikki's surprised expression, Lily pulled a face. "Come on, you know what she was like." As she pressed a button on the coffeemaker, she added, "I'm not one of those people who creates saints out of sinners just because they're dead."

"I guess not."

"Making them martyrs just because they're dead is pure crap." Lily opened a cupboard, found her favorite mug, and, realizing Nikki hadn't agreed with her, said, "What?"

"I don't know," Nikki replied. "I guess I'm just surprised at your attitude." She set a wriggling Chloe onto the floor, and the girl dashed to her aunt.

"You're a Mavis Greenlee fan?"

"No, but—"

"Oh, come on, Nikki. You know what I mean. It's a shame Mavis is dead, and it's really, really awful that someone killed her, but again . . . truth. Okay? Mavis Greenlee was pretty dreadful."

Nikki couldn't deny it. Although Mavis had been involved in all kinds of charitable events within the city, she had a reputation of being self-involved and cold, even with her own family.

"Up!" Chloe demanded, tugging on her aunt's robe, raising her chubby little arms.

"Just a sec, sweetie." Lily found the creamer and sugar and set it next to the cups as the coffeemaker gurgled to life, coffee drizzling into the glass carafe. "Okay, come on, you." She picked up her niece and burrowed her nose in Chloe's soft cheek.

Chloe giggled. "Stop!"

Lily grinned at her. "So, how're you this morning, Little Miss Sunshine?" she asked, giving her cheek another buzz.

Laughing, Chloe ordered, "Dance!"

"You got it. Hey, Alexa, play some . . . dance music from . . . uh . . ." She looked at Nikki for help. ". . . oh, I know. Alexa, play Beyoncé!"

"Shuffling songs by Beyonce," the virtual assistant announced, as the coffeemaker hissed, filling the air with the scent of warm java. Soon the distinctive beat and intro to "Single Ladies (Put a Ring on It)" filled the room. "Ooh, I love this song," Lily said, swinging Chloe around as the little girl squealed in delight.

"You're dating yourself," Nikki observed.

"You like it, too."

"So you're dating us both." Nikki spied the dogs on the patio and walked to the French doors. "Come on in, guys." Arlo sped inside with Mikado, tail slowly wagging, following at a more leisurely pace.

As the song ended, Lily, breathing hard, set Chloe onto the floor. "Go wake up Phee," she suggested, "And when you get back, we'll make pancakes."

"Mickeys?" Chloe said.

"Sure. Mouse pancakes." Lily was already reaching for the filled coffeepot as Chloe, bare feet flying, sprinted toward the stairs.

"Phee's not gonna want to get up," Nikki predicted.

"I know, but tough. She has to get up for school. I mean, we'll probably be late as it is." As she heard Chloe clambering up the steps, then the rapid footsteps streaking down the hallway overhead, Lily lowered her voice and said, "So what happened? To Mavis, I mean. Like how and where?"

Nikki filled her in on what few details she had gleaned from Pierce and the early news reporting, leaving out her own deductions. At least this time someone else had broken the story. It bothered her that she hadn't been the first on the scene, so to speak, but at least it put off her eventual head-butting with her husband over her reporting.

"Is this killing related to the other one, with Billy What's-His-Name?"

Nikki shrugged. She wasn't going to go there with Lily.

She found a travel mug and poured coffee into it just as her phone buzzed. Pulling it from her pocket, she saw that the caller was Fink and didn't answer. Again. He'd called once already. She'd sent that call to voice mail and ignored the three subsequent texts—all about the Greenlee homicide. As she capped her cup, she said to Lily, "Look, I've got to run . . . You've got everything, right? With the girls, I mean."

"Yeah, yeah." Lily, leaning against the island, sipped from her cup and nodded as she eyed the clock. "No doubt about it, we're gonna be late." She walked to the bottom of the stairs. "Ophelia?" She waited a beat. "Come on! Get up. Now! Hurry up! Rise and shine like you've never shined before."

"That should do it," Nikki drawled.

"It better."

Chloe was taking the steps deliberately, one at a time, as she descended. "She told me to 'Go way,'" she complained, pouting as Nikki reached the staircase.

"Did she, now?" Lily said. "I guess it's time for Drill Sergeant Mom to take over. You can come with me, Private Chloe."

"Wait a sec." Nikki picked up her daughter and kissed her curls. "Look, honey, Mommy's got to go to work. I'll see you later."

"You're with me," Lily said, taking the girl from Nikki. "Let's go slay the dragon."

"What dragon?" Chloe asked.

"Phee."

"I heard that," Ophelia yelled from their shared bedroom.

"Ah," Lily said, "Sleeping Beauty awakens."

"You're mixing up your fairy tales," Nikki pointed out.

"Am I? Does it matter?" Lily said, then to Chloe: "It's really late. Let's forget pancakes, okay? Mickeys maybe tomorrow. Today we're gonna make waffles."

When Chloe squirmed and seemed about to protest, Lily added, "I'll let you press the button on the toaster." And as she carried her niece back to the kitchen, where she retrieved a box of frozen waffles from the freezer, she threw over her shoulder to Nikki, "Looks like another Eggo morning. Now, you, go."

"Okay. Later." Nikki scooped up her oversize bag and laptop from the table, then heard Lily say, "Oh, wait a sec. Who's going to tell Mom about Mavis?"

Nikki had her hand on the door handle. "I was hoping that you—?"

"Nuh-uh-uh. Not me. I already did my duty this week. And she's probably heard the news already, but someone's going to have to deal with the fallout, and it ain't gonna be me."

"I have to—" Nikki started to argue, but saw Lily's warning look. "Okay. Fine."

"Good. Now, go!" Lily insisted. "I've got this." She headed for the base of the stairs again. "Phee!!! I'm not kidding! Get up. Now!"

Nikki's phone buzzed, and Arlo, speeding in from the family room, caught up with her. "Not now," she told the dog, watching his head droop a bit. "Later."

In her car, she eyed the screen, hoping the caller was Pierce with more news, but it was just Tom Fink again. She let the call go to voice mail, then listened to the message. He was just asking for more information, so she figured she'd call him later.

Maybe.

"Let Metzger fill you in," she said to the empty car. "He's your damned crime reporter." She had a lot to do today, interviews to conduct.

But first she had to visit her mother.

"Brace yourself," she warned, because dealing with Charlene Gillette was never easy.

"Aside from the numbers, the stones are nearly identical," Sol said over the noise from the outer hallway, where the buzz of conversation, punctuated with laughter, drifted in over the click of computer keys. "But they're being tested in the lab, along with the blood coloring them. They're also matching the shell casing retrieved off the stairs to the bullet found in the ceiling, checking Mavis Greenlee's DNA, along with all the rest."

Reed leaned back in his desk chair. He'd figured as much, and he was still trying to find some connection between Billy Huber and Mavis Greenlee. The homicides were linked by the etched rocks, but that was all he had so far. The two victims were as socially distant as they were geographically, and on first glance, they'd never met nor had any mutual acquaintances; nor, for that matter, had they known each other even existed.

But they had both been murdered by the same killer.

Why?

Reed drummed his fingers on his desk as he glanced again at the data on Mavis's background, all visible on his computer. She'd been born Mavis Crawford, had attended private schools, married right out of college, was divorced twelve years later, then married again within the year. That union had crumbled after seven years. And then there was her latest husband, Archer.

"Have you checked with the Tybee Island police?" he asked.

"Oh, yeah," Sol said from her desk. "I spoke to Officer Montero, who checked with the patrol. From the looks of it, someone is there. More lights on than usual, though the garage doors were shut, so if Archer's car was there, it wasn't seen."

She was looking at her computer screen and sipping some kind of tea. "What've you come up with?"

"So far, no connection to Huber. Still hunting for a will, but most likely everything is held jointly with her husband."

"She's from money, so he would inherit," she surmised aloud.

"Presumably. Unless she made some special arrangements. Like a trust or whatever."

"But no kids?"

"None of her own. Stepkids, of course. Archer has a daughter, and Mavis has one brother who lives out of state, and her mother is still alive."

"Ooh. That's a hard one. Outliving your kids," Sol said.

"Yeah." Reed thought of his own little girl and couldn't imagine losing her. He wasn't all that great at reaching over an emotional chasm as proven by the text he'd received from Toby Yelkis just last night: **Fuck off.**

Not likely.

But he'd give Sylvie's kid some space.

For now.

"I can run down the exes," Sol offered, finishing her tea and crumpling the paper cup.

"You got names? Addresses and numbers?"

"Yep. They're both still in Savannah. Radley Bowers, her first husband, is the golf pro at the country club where Mavis was a member. He's the senior pro, probably close to retiring. There's a younger guy who gives most of the lessons, especially for the kids. Junior instructions and the like. But Bowers still gives a few to the older guys, the senior members, I guess. And he works in the pro shop." She checked her notes. "Bowers has a family. Grown daughters who've moved away—one in Augusta, the other in Myrtle Beach, and his second wife, Kelsey. As for Mavis's husband number two? Leonard Armstrong. He's still single. Never remarried. He works down at the First Coastal Bank and Trust, handles high-end accounts. From what it looks like, Mavis was still married to him when she hooked up with Archer Greenlee, another wealthy client of the bank's investment department."

"She always had money, and Billy Huber barely had a pot to piss in," Reed muttered.

"I checked his finances. He didn't just owe that brother, Robert. He'd taken out a loan on his property."

"Don't suppose it was with First Coastal?" Reed said, hoping for some kind of thread connecting the victims, no matter how fragile.

"A bank wouldn't touch that mess of a place. Private lender: Horace Denton Investments. Super-high interest rate. Personal loan. The deed to the property was put up as collateral."

"Let me guess," Reed said. "Billy was behind in his payments."

Sol nodded. "I talked to Gina Mercado, the receptionist, who told me that Horace Denton was 'unavailable' and that he would call me back. So far, he hasn't." Her lips twisted downward. "I have this sneaking suspicion he won't pick up the phone, so I'll pay him a personal visit." Her cell rang, and she snagged it from the desk, looked at the screen, and said, "Gotta take this. It's the bartender from the Stag and Boar, the one who was on duty last night when Archer Greenlee claimed he was there. I went by the place last night, and he'd gone home." She answered, and Reed turned back to his computer, where a picture of the two stones was now visible.

Therein lay the connection. Somehow those rocks, with their cryptic messages etched in blood, were the answer.

"Mavis Crawford was two-faced," Charlene admitted with a scowl. She was sitting on a tufted chair near the French doors of her apartment while sipping tea from her favorite Hermès teacup. She cradled the cup, decorated with fanciful horses and a shiny gold interior, as if it were precious. But then Charlene always had a tender affection for some of her most prized possessions.

Nikki didn't argue with her mother as she sat on a barstool at the peninsula separating the kitchen from the living area. No reason to try to sugarcoat the truth, she thought, as she forced a smile at the woman who had raised her. Frail and thin, Charlene was still concerned about her appearance. Her snowy hair was neatly wound in a French braid, her slacks pressed to a knife's edge, her creamy sweater without a snag, a pearl necklace lying gracefully around her throat.

The same attention to detail went into her living space. Her apartment was spacious and airy, with a bank of wide windows facing the garden. Blooming azaleas looked as if they were on fire, and beyond her private patio, a manicured lawn rolled down to a lake, where a pair of swans swam lazily past scattered lily pads. Charlene watched them glide through the water. "Beautiful, aren't they?"

"The swans? Yes," Nikki agreed. "But, Mom, Mavis's name was Greenlee." She checked her watch. It was after eleven, as she'd spent some time at the newspaper office before deciding to visit her mother. "Mavis was married to Archer Greenlee."

Charlene snorted. "She traded husbands like baseball cards."

"Mom!"

"Well, it's true. Just ask your brother. He knew her, you know. Did all her yard work."

"Kyle?" Nikki was surprised. Her brother was a loner, and though he lived in the same town, she rarely saw him. He barely even showed up for Christmas gatherings. In fact, she wasn't certain he'd ever met Chloe.

"Of course Kyle." Charlene seemed perturbed, her thin eyebrows colliding. "He held a very low opinion of Mavis."

Nikki felt the unlikely need to defend the woman she'd barely known. "Being married three times isn't that big of a deal these days, and certainly not a sin."

"Not a faithful bone in that woman's body."

"Aren't you the one who always said you shouldn't speak ill of the dead?" Nikki asked. She'd given her mother the news about Mavis, and Charlene hadn't seemed surprised. And now this disparagement.

"I always told you to tell the truth," Charlene countered, "and

Mavis was nothing but a headache for her mother. Oh, Blanche would never admit it, but that's the way it was."

So much for needing to console Charlene. "If you say so." Nikki's gaze moved to the swans; one had peeled away from its mate and was chasing after an intruding mallard. The swan's neck was extended, his wings stretching wide, as he gave off a hissing growl. The duck quickly took flight.

"Tundra swans," Charlene said. "Very territorial and, like Mavis Crawford, beautiful but hostile." She sipped from her cup. "Unlike her, though, tundras mate for life." And then setting her cup on a small, glass-topped table, she added, "You probably don't need to know this. Few people do. But Mavis and your father"—her fingers fluttered a little—"they . . . they were involved a long time ago."

Nikki gave her mother a long stare. "What?"

"I don't mean to shock you, but it's the truth."

"But—"

"It was a long time ago," Charlene cut her off. "Water under the bridge, you know."

"I . . . didn't know," Nikki admitted, a bit stunned. In a town the size of Savannah, with Ronald Gillette having been active in local politics, there had been bits and pieces of rumors surrounding him all of Nikki's life. But she'd never heard Mavis Greenlee's name attached to him.

"Oh, neither of them thought I knew about their little affair, but I did." She pinned a cold smile on her lips. "So, no, I'm not overly grieving about her, though it is sad for Blanche. It's never easy to bury a child. I know about that." Sorrow stole over her features as it always did when something said or done touched on her remembrance of Nikki's brother, Andrew, gone so many years. His death had been a tragedy, a combination of cocaine, booze, and a faulty deck from which he'd tumbled to his death years before. "Nonetheless," Charlene continued, "I call them as I see them, and Mavis was not a kind soul, no matter how many charity events she put on through the church. She may have fooled Reverend Stark and all of the rest of the women's aid society, but she didn't fool me."

With that, she picked up her delicate cup again and took a sip. "Not once."

Chapter 14

Her mother's bitter attitude about Mavis Greenlee, following as it did Lily's sharp assessment of the woman's character, dogged Nikki as she drove through the city, where graceful live oaks offered shade and trolleys filled with tourists slowed traffic.

For years, Nikki had suspected that her father hadn't been faithful; she remembered women who had been impressed with his wealth, or his bearing, or the fact that he'd been a successful lawyer turned judge. But she hadn't known how much truth there was to the rumors or if they'd been all just idle gossip. As a journalist doing research on old cases, she'd come across her father's name often in the archives, and the Gillettes had graced the society pages more than a few times, but she'd never given in to the urge to dig deeper into her father's life or her parents' marriage. She'd known that there was strife, and that there were times when he hadn't come home when expected. And that, when he did finally return, it was always with a quick excuse and a kiss for his wife, a blasé act like nothing was wrong, despite Charlene's icy demeanor, which often lasted for days.

She slowed for a stoplight and watched as a young mother pushing a stroller, a second child in tow, crossed the street, then eased onto the gas again once the light had changed.

She hadn't realized her mother had known of his affairs and even been able to name at least one of his lovers. It had been many years ago, but obviously Charlene Gillette wasn't one to forgive and forget; her ability to hold on to a grudge was legendary. There was no water running under the bridge as far as Charlene was concerned. No, sir. The dark river of her grievances ran too deep and was far too wide to span.

Nikki took her foot off the gas as she drove past the turn into Huber's farm, noticing a torn strip of yellow crime-scene tape fastened to the old gate now flapping in the breeze. She didn't need to visit the Huber's acres again, but had decided to interview some of the neighbors, especially the ones she knew had not gotten along with Billy Huber. She'd made phone calls, but they'd been ignored, and besides, she wanted to talk to the people who had lived next to the dead man and look them in their eyes. There was so much more you could gain from a face-to-face interview, where emotions were less likely to be successfully masked.

She started with Duke Wheelan, the neighbor who had been in a property dispute about Huber's poaching on his land.

As she pulled into a short drive flanked by crepe myrtle, she saw a tall man repairing a chain-link fence with some kind of stretching tool. The fence separated a yard where chickens chortled and scratched on the dry earth, a henhouse visible, while other outbuildings were scattered around a large, gravel parking area. One large live oak offered a bit of shade near the house, its thick branches stretching over the wide porch.

At the sound of her Subaru's approach, the man glanced over his shoulder, abandoning his task to watch her park near what appeared to be a garage.

He shaded his eyes as she climbed out of the Outback and approached him. "Mr. Wheelan? Duke?" she asked.

"Yeah."

"Nikki Gillette." She stretched out her hand. "I'm a reporter. Freelance, but I write for the *Sentinel*."

"That so?" he asked, as he removed a leather glove. He clasped her palm in strong fingers and met her gaze with his own steely stare.

She guessed him to be somewhere around fifty, flecks of gray in his thinning brown hair, his face weathered from years of working in the sun.

"I'd like to ask you some questions about your neighbor, Billy Huber."

He closed his eyes for a second and gave a little shake of his head. "Look, Ms. . . . Gillette, was it?"

"Yes."

"I told the police everything I know, which isn't much. I didn't hear anything or see anything." He motioned to the farmhouse, where a slim woman with a single, long blond braid and wire-rimmed glasses had walked onto the covered porch. She held the screen door open, allowing a tired-looking hound to hobble through. "Frannie," he called, "would you come on over here for a minute?"

With a perturbed expression, she took off the apron she'd been wearing and tossed it over the rail of the porch, then walked resolutely along a stone path, the old dog following slowly.

"This is Nikki Gillette, she's a—"

"I know who she is," Frannie snapped.

Once more, Nikki stretched out her hand, but Frannie, her face set and hard, ignored it.

Huh.

Wheelan went on, "She wants to know if we saw or heard anything on the night Billy Huber died."

"Of course she does. She's just like the rest of them. They've all been callin' and harassin' us. How in the world would we know what happened? His farm, if that's what you could call it, is on the other side of the woods." She shot her hand outward, motioning to the thick wall of trees in the distance. "And no, I didn't see or hear anything out of the ordinary. We already said as much to the police. Didn't you tell her?" she charged Wheelan.

Nikki interjected, "I'm not with the police."

"I heard that. It's not the point," Frannie said. "Get your information from them! I don't have time for this. I've got dinner on the stove." She skewered Wheelan with her stare. "It's after noontime. Goin' on one."

Wheelan explained, "We've always had dinner midday, and Frannie's on a schedule."

Frannie's eyes flamed. "If you expect me to cook for you, then—"

"I know. It's all right." Wheelan patted the air as if to placate her.

With a huff, Frannie turned, whistled to the old dog, and started for the house.

"Did you know Mavis Greenlee?" Nikki called after her.

Frannie hesitated. Then turned around again. "Only through the church. Reverend Stark introduced us once at the Christmas pageant, a couple of years ago, but, that's all. A shame about her. A real shame."

Nikki asked Wheelan, "What about you?"

"I was at the same pageant. She thanked me for helping rebuild the life-size crèche that is always on display during the Christmas season. Part of the stable and two of the wise men had been destroyed."

"Vandals!" Frannie said indignantly. "Defacing the nativity scene like that? Who would do that? I don't know what gets into some people!" And, with that, she turned back to the house.

And, Nikki noted, Frannie seemed far more incensed at the vandalism than at the murders of her neighbor and church acquaintance.

"There's really not much more to tell you," Wheelan said, his gaze following Frannie's backside as she marched onto the porch, where she scooped up her discarded apron and swept through the screen door, the old hound skittering through just before it banged shut.

"You were in a dispute with Billy Huber," she said to Wheelan.

"Who wasn't? He didn't get along with anyone, including his family."

"He trespassed?" she persisted.

"Yes. Hunted, well, actually poached off my property." He pointed to the forest at the edge of a field where sheep and goats were grazing, the same stretch of woods that Frannie had indicated earlier. "Huber's acres run through that stand of trees over there, and he couldn't seem to stay on his side of the fence, no matter how many times I posted signs against trespassing and told him face-to-face to stay off my property." Scowling slightly, Wheelan added, "He was the kind of man who just wouldn't listen."

The screen door opened again, and Frannie yelled, "Duke! Dinner's on!"

"Coming!" he shouted back, waving at her as she reentered the house. He said to Nikki, "Look, I've got to go, and that's really all I can tell you."

And with that, he left her and headed inside. The short interview was over.

As she drove away, Nikki couldn't help feeling as if she were leaving with more questions than answers. She decided to check with the neighbor to the south, Otis Childers. It might be his dinnertime as well, but she didn't care. Like Wheelan, Childers had never returned any of her calls. And like Wheelan, Childers had had a bone to pick with his neighbor.

It took less than five minutes to pass Huber's property and roll into the Childers' place, where all of the outbuildings were painted white to match a low-slung ranch house with a wraparound porch. As she climbed out of the car, she heard a cacophony of dogs barking, three rushing to the chain link fence that separated them from the parking area.

"Hey! Hey!" A man bustled out of a freestanding shed and shouted toward the kennels. "Hush! Robey! Sam! Hush, I said. And you, too, Elvira!" He was large and heavy-framed, his face florid. Strands of brown hair escaped from under a faded Georgia Bulldogs baseball cap, and the sleeves of his work shirt were pushed up, revealing tanned, meaty forearms.

The dogs did quiet, only one giving up a rebellious whine before they all waited, ears pricked near the gates of their cages. "Darn fool mutts," he muttered, scowling at the dogs. "Go on in!" He snapped his fingers and pointed at the kennels, where all the dogs—German shepherds, or mixes thereof—immediately turned and entered their individual doghouses. "That's better," he said. "Now I can hear myself think." He yanked a rag from the back pocket of his jeans and wiped off the dirt and oil that had collected on his fingers. "How can I help you?"

Nikki introduced herself and explained why she was there, and he acknowledged that he was, indeed, Otis Childers. "Well, you're not the first reporter to come out here, and I s'pose you won't be the last."

"You were involved in a lawsuit with Billy Huber?"

"You got that right. Look, I hate to speak ill of the dead," he began, but something in his eyes gave away his true feelings, and he let loose, "but Billy—he was no good. I mean it. Big-time trouble. A real pain in the backside. And I'm not the only one who got into legal trouble with him. Billy, he wasn't right. Nope, not right at all."

"What do you mean, 'not right.'"

"Didn't seem to have any decency. Didn't know the difference between right and wrong, if you ask me." Scowling, he glanced up at the sky to squint at the early-afternoon sun, as if gauging how many hours of daylight remained. "I wish Daria was here. She'd tell you. The way she found him ogling her. Indecent, that's what it was." Childers rubbed the stubble on his jaw, and his eyes narrowed. "Oh. Wait. Here she is now. She can tell you herself." Gravel crunched behind them, and Nikki turned to see a big, black SUV pull up to a space in front of the garage. The dogs streamed out of their houses to start their racket again.

Another word from Childers and they stopped, but stared expectantly at the slim, tanned brunette who stepped from behind the wheel. Wearing tight jeans, a plaid shirt, and sunglasses, she opened the lift gate of the Suburban, which was piled high with grocery sacks and bags of dog food. She walked up to them, and Nikki noticed her necklace and the small gold cross that dangled from a matching gold chain. "What's going on?" she asked.

Childers made quick introductions and added, ". . . she's here about Billy Huber."

"That old lech." Daria Childers gave an involuntary shudder. "He was always prowlin' around, lookin', ya know. And things around here went missing."

Nikki questioned, "You think he stole them?"

"Wouldn't put it past him," Daria said.

"Did you ever catch him?"

"Heck, no," Childers said. "He was too slippery for that. And it was before we had a security system set up. I mean I've lived here all my life and never needed one. But after Daria caught him watching her, we changed all that."

Nikki registered the camera mounted high over the kennels.

"He was a pervert," Daria said. "A real weirdo."

"How so?" Nikki asked.

"One time I was out working in the garden, over there, just this side of the orchard." Daria pointed to a tilled area on the far side of the house, where a neat row of shoots was just appearing. "It was hotter'n than all get-out that afternoon, and I was just in my bra and shorts. I looked up from hoeing and caught him standing on *our* side of the fence, watching me. He had a rake in his hands like maybe he was gonna try and get some peaches off our tree—steal them, y'know—but then I caught his eye, and he just smiled that weird smile of his, and he ran his hands up and down the handle of the rake, real slow, then rimmed his tongue around his lips. Ugh." She held Nikki's gaze. "If you ask me, he was a psycho."

"What did you do?"

"Told him to get off our property or I'd call the sheriff."

"Did he leave?"

"No. He just laughed at me and kept running his damned fingers up and down the shaft of the rake. I got the meaning, all right."

Otis nodded, his eyes narrowing, added, "I came home from work about then for dinner, saw what was going on, and told him to get off our land and keep his eyes to himself and his dick in his pants and not to come back."

"Did he leave then?"

"Oh, yeah, he took off then. Probably because I was carrying my granddad's double-barrel Winchester with me. He couldn't get away fast enough. Scrambled over the fence and never came back that I know of." Otis rubbed the back of his neck. "I mean, nothin' I can prove, but like I said, we did put up a couple of cameras, but we found them disabled not long after."

"You didn't fix them?"

"Nah." Otis shook his head. "By that time, things had cooled off with Huber, and between the dogs and the cameras being mounted and visible, I figured that would keep people away. We got into a lawsuit over the fence line when Huber built one on my property, but the court forced him to move it, and from that time on, we didn't have much to do with each other."

Nikki asked, "And neither of you heard or saw anything the night he died?"

"I was out of town," Daria said. "I work for a lumber company, and that week we had a corporate retreat in Atlanta."

"And you?" she asked Otis.

"I was here, but as I told the cops, I didn't hear or see nothin' out of the ordinary. I wish I could tell you more, but I can't, and I know it's not the Christian thing to say, but I'm glad Huber's gone," Otis said. He added, "Whoever took him out did the world a favor."

If Nikki expected Daria to take the edge off her husband's words, she was disabused of that idea because Otis Childers's wife seemed to be in complete agreement.

"He was a real freak," she said, "that's all I know."

"Did either of you know Mavis Greenlee?"

"Oh, yes!" Daria brightened for a second, then sighed as if suddenly remembering what had happened to Mavis. "A shame about her. She was a good woman. Very involved with the church."

"You're a member?"

"All my life." She glanced at her husband, then nudged him with her elbow. "But Otis here, he doesn't attend."

"Daria," he warned, "you know I'm a believer." His voice was stern, and he explained to Nikki, "Not that it's any of your business, but God and I, we have our own private arrangement."

"That's so arrogant." Little lines formed around the corners of Daria's mouth, and Nikki guessed this wasn't the first time she and her husband had been involved in this argument. "And arrogance is a sin. Proverbs 16:19 says—"

"Don't you go quoting Scripture and verse to me, woman," he muttered, his voice low, almost a growl.

But Daria didn't back down. She didn't quote from the passage again, but she lowered her sunglasses and arched one eyebrow as if to remind her husband that he was going too far. "I think we're done here," she said shoving her shades back onto the bridge of her straight nose. "I'm very upset about Mavis, and I'm over all this talk about that miserable piece of . . . that horrid man. As I said, he was a real whack job. Dangerous." Motioning to the SUV with its lift gate gaping open, she added, "Otis, you can unload the car." To Nikki she added, through tight lips, "Have a blessed day," before turning on her heel and, with her back ramrod stiff, stalking quickly past the dozing cat and into the house.

"Daria's right," Otis said, though he still seemed to be seething. At his wife? Or Nikki? She wasn't sure. He cast a furious look at the house, scowled, then turned his gaze back to Nikki. "We are done here."

Chapter 15

For the next five days, Nikki was stymied. All of her investigating hadn't turned up much. Though she and Pierce had agreed to share information—she promising not to print anything without the department's approval, he saying he'd give her an "exclusive" first interview once the cases were solved—she was stuck in the house. Chloe had come down with a cold. Both Lily and Phee were battling runny noses and wet-sounding coughs. Her only break had been when Phee had been well enough to go to her riding lesson and Nikki had taken her to the stables to spend the next two hours watching Phee learn from the older girls. Her favorite instructor was Annabelle Van Camp, a friendly girl with rosy cheeks and an athlete's body. Annabelle could ride a horse as if she'd been born to do it, seemingly at one with the animal as it sailed over fences or streams.

Phee had been exhilarated to have gone riding, but probably she shouldn't have gone and relapsed slightly the next day.

As difficult as it was, Nikki worked from home, alternately making soup, taking Chloe's temperature and reading to her, and doing what research she could via the Internet. She brought her laptop downstairs so that she could manage the household and set up a work space at the dining room table while Chloe was wrapped in blankets on the couch, Lily was curled in a nearby chair with the TV on low, and Phee was cloistered in the bedroom she shared with her mother. The dogs took up spots by the fire, while rain peppered the windows and Jennings found a spot on the chair next to hers, his long tail twitching slightly as he slept.

By the sixth morning, Nikki was about to go out of her mind, as Pierce had admitted that the investigation into Mavis's death was hitting roadblocks. The same was true with Billy Huber. "All the alibis have checked out," he'd told her just this morning as he'd stood in front of the bathroom mirror while adjusting his tie.

"You mean her husband's?" Nikki had asked.

"Times three. Not only was Archer where he claimed to be, but Radley Bowers was—"

"Her first husband?"

"Yes, he was with his wife. And as for number two, Leonard Armstrong? He was in Atlanta at a Braves game with clients."

"And none of them had a connection to Billy Huber?"

"Not that we've located."

"What about the alibis of everyone else who held a grudge against Billy Huber?" she asked, meeting his gaze in the mirror.

"Still double-checking. It seems he pissed off about everyone he met."

She grunted an assent. "Including his daughter."

"Right. So, we'll see." He eyed his reflection. Satisfied with the knot, he brushed a kiss against her forehead. "I'll see you later, Nurse Nikki."

"Very funny," she said, hearing him laugh as he headed downstairs.

But later in the morning, after she'd seen a twinkle in her daughter's eye when Chloe had asked for hot chocolate with marshmallows for breakfast, Nikki checked the little girl's symptoms. Thankfully, she was no longer running a fever, and her little nose had stopped dripping, and yes, Nikki had allowed the cup of cocoa.

Even Lily, who stumbled downstairs later than usual, admitted that she was feeling better. "Thank God. For the first time in, like, forever, I actually got a good night's sleep," she admitted, making a beeline for the coffeemaker, where half a pot of coffee was steaming. She poured herself a cup and added a shot of cream. As Chloe was still picking melting marshmallows out of her mug, Lily clicked the rim of her cup to her niece's.

"Cheers!" Chloe said brightly.

"Back at you." Lily rumpled Chloe's curls, and the little girl giggled.

"No!" she objected, tossing her head out of the way, but still grinning widely.

Lily said, "I guess we can call off the quarantine," before pouring more cream into her cup and adding a teaspoon of sugar. She tasted her brew again and sighed contentedly. "That's better. Why don't you get out of here?" she suggested to Nikki. "I know you're going batsh . . . er, crazy cooped up here when you could be out, poking around and getting into trouble."

"You make my job sound so glamorous. You sure?"

"Yeah. I'm keeping Phee home one more day, just to play it safe, but she's feeling better, too, and caught up on her homework. Isn't the Internet wonderful?"

"A lifesaver," Nikki said and didn't argue any longer as she was pulling at the bit to get out of the house. While packing her tote, she said, "The dogs and cat have been fed. Don't believe them if they tell you differently. They lie."

"I've heard that about dogs," Lily said, "but cats?"

"Slyer. Much more duplicitous."

"There you go with your big words again." She saw Nikki hesitate at the back door. "So go, already. We're good here. If there's an emergency, I'll call you. Promise."

"Okay. Oh, wait! Did you know that Kyle has emerged?" She realized that between all the sniffles and coughs and cleaning up, she hadn't given Lily the news about their brother.

"What?"

"Yeah. I forgot to mention. I'll fill you in later, but suffice it to say that he seems to have decided to join the living, or maybe the family, or maybe just connect with Mom, but he's communicating with her."

Lily's lips twisted. "Will wonders never cease?"

"I know. Gotta run."

And, with that, Nikki was out the door. Nearly a week cooped up in the house with two unsolved murders to dig into had totally frustrated her. She'd submitted a couple of stories to the paper, all Pierce-approved, and spent hours on her computer or the phone. She had called everyone on her list, people associated with either Mavis Greenlee or Billy Huber. She seemed to be failing to connect with any of them. They'd either been away from their phones, not answering, or in some way or another unavailable. Worse, Fink was demanding a more "in depth" story about the crimes, and then there was Ina, who had gotten wind of the two murders and the possibility of a new book in the works. "This would be perfect," she'd enthused the day before in a Zoom call. "Two murders within days of each other in Savannah . . . such a beautiful, historic city and . . . well, if the crimes are connected, you know, by a serial killer, so much the better. You could expose the dark underbelly of the city." Lighting a cigarette, she'd added, "And by the way, serial killers are hot."

"Yeah, right," Nikki said now as she drove through the glistening streets. It had rained during the night, but the morning sun was finally daring to peek through thin clouds overhead to reflect on the pavement. As for Ina's suggestion, it was ridiculous. Nikki was a long way from writing a book about the recent murders. First, the homicides needed to be solved, then positively linked; then the killer had to be revealed, arrested, and convicted. It could take years, and that was *if* the crimes were solved.

That thought had occurred to Ina as well. "So, you keep notes on those, but in the meantime, we need something fresh, something you can deliver in the next six months."

Impossible! Nikki had actually laughed. "Let me call all my serial-killer friends. I'm sure they'll sit down and fill me in."

"Make fun all you like," Ina had replied, "but I'm serious. Your editor and your fans are eager for another book. You should be flattered."

"I am," Nikki agreed, "but everyone will just have to wait a little longer." Or a lot longer, if her new book was to be about whomever was behind the Billy Huber and Mavis Greenlee murders.

To that end, she was about to interview Mavis's mother, Blanche Crawford, and hopefully get a little insight into the dead woman's life. She figured Blanche's perspective could add a human element to her story and maybe give Nikki some insight into Mavis's character, and why anyone would want her dead.

As for Billy Huber, she'd learned his relatives had little social-media presence and few friends. While spending most of the week at home, she'd left messages for his brothers, Robert and Terence. Then there was Calvin Smith, aka Smitty, the man with whom Billy had been in a bar fight years before, after the death of his son. She'd found out that Calvin had been in and out of jail, an angry man who had lived in the area years before but now was in the wind. She made a mental note to find him, and surely Pierce could help with that. She had left a message for Smith's parole officer, but again was waiting for a call back.

She was starting to get irritated.

Didn't anyone use a cell as an actual telephone these days?

Now, as she drove down the shaded street to Blanche Crawford's home, her thoughts returned to Mavis Greenlee, and Nikki wondered about the dead woman's finances. Who inherited? Most likely her husband, who was currently holed up on Tybee Island. Were there any life-insurance policies? If so, who were the beneficiaries?

Follow the money was the axiom, but that was only if financial gain was the ultimate goal of the killer. That seemed unlikely, considering the fact that she believed, as the police did, that the murderer of Mavis and Billy was one and the same. If monetary reward was the objective, then Billy Huber was a poor choice of a victim.

What was the link?

She slid her Subaru into an open spot on the street in front of a single-level ranch-style home straight out of the fifties. A silver Lexus was parked in the drive, nose to bumper behind an older, dented Honda minivan, white but dirty, with *Wash Me* written into the grime by an unsteady finger.

Getting out of the car, Nikki noticed that the curtains were drawn around the large bay window of the house, but the front door was wide open, and a heavy-set man in khakis and a polo shirt was pushing a frail-appearing woman in a wheelchair. With some trouble, he was attempting to circumvent a crack on the cement ramp that had been built near the three stairs leading to a leaf-strewn porch, but the wheels of the chair kept catching in the uneven surface, wet leaves collecting in the spokes.

The man, sunlight glinting off his bald head, caught a glimpse of her walking toward him, and a perturbed expression crossed his fleshy features. "Can I help you?" he asked, continuing to maneuver the wheelchair to the bottom of the ramp, where a brick path wound toward the drive. The walkway was covered in leaves and twigs, and once more, he had trouble pushing the chair.

"I'm looking for Blanche Crawford."

"You found her," the woman said with a wry, thin-lipped smile. Her papery skin stretched tightly over sharp cheekbones and a pointed chin. She appeared to be in her eighties, her fingers clutched tightly around a small, well-worn Bible. An apricot-colored pantsuit hung loosely over her thin body, and a lap blanket covered her legs. Her puff of white hair was tamed by tortoiseshell barrettes, while rimless glasses covered sharp blue eyes that narrowed as she assessed Nikki. "You're Charlene Gillette's daughter," she guessed and pointed a gnarled finger in Nikki's direction. "The younger one. A reporter."

"That's right. I'm—"

"Nikki Gillette," the man cut in with an audible sigh. "Why am I not surprised you're here? This is about Mavis, isn't it? Well, we have nothing to say. Nothing." He was blustering, obviously irritated, his dimpled chin extended defiantly. He sent Nikki a scathing glance and said, "Come on, Mother."

"Maybe your mom can speak for herself," Nikki suggested a bit coolly.

Blanche chuckled. "You always did have spunk! Drove your mother crazy and got you into quite a bit of trouble." She swiped at a strand of hair that had crossed her cheek, her hand trembling slightly. "Now, stop, Oliver, I might want to talk to her. This," she motioned upward to the man, "as you may have guessed, is my son." With a glance up at him, she added, "She's helped solve a lot of crimes in this city, you know. She might actually be able to aid us in finding out what happened to your sister." Then a pause, and her gray eyebrows pinched, confusion evident on her features. "Where is Mavis?"

"Mother," he said, with exaggerated patience. "She's gone. Remember? We talked about this. Three times now. And I don't think Ms. Gillette can help. It's a police matter." His shoulders sagged a bit at the confused look in Blanche's eyes. He turned to Nikki. "Look, this is a hard time for us. I just realized what was going on here." He ran a hand through the few wispy hairs covering his head.

"Mavis was supposed to be taking care of Mom. She was the appointed guardian, but . . ."

He flopped an arm toward the house. "I live in LA, and I just hadn't gotten back here since she moved Mom and sold the family home. But . . . I mean, I believed her when she said Mom needed help, and I just let her handle it." A look of consternation mingled with regret caused wrinkles to appear over his eyebrows. He glanced back at the house. "I can't believe she had Mom living here with such limited care." Then he seemed to give himself a quick mental shake. "Well, it's water under the bridge now. And I'm fixing things. Come on, Mom, let's go." He started pushing the chair again, and Nikki noticed movement by the open front door.

A skinny, thirtysomething woman, with stringy red hair and tattoos running up her arms, appeared. She was lugging an overflowing laundry basket and deftly edged her way around the wheelchair to the dirty minivan, where she loaded the basket, shoving it inside.

"We need to get going," Oliver said. "If you want to speak to Mom, try later this week. She'll be at the Riverview Towers. Room four twenty-seven."

"You're moving?" Nikki asked Blanche.

She blinked, squinting a little as she angled her head up toward her son. "Am I?"

"Yes, Mom. We talked about this."

The redhead slammed the door of the minivan and got behind the wheel.

Oliver said, "We really have to go." Jaw set, he rolled his mother over the bumpy bricks to the passenger side of the Lexus, and as he did, Nikki walked up the steps to the open door. Peering inside, she noticed that the old carpet was stained and the brick fireplace darkened by smoke. Several pieces of sagging furniture were scattered around the living room, and boxes were piled near the doorway. The acrid scents of cooking grease, wood smoke, and urine hung in the air.

This was where Blanche Crawford had been living.

She started to step inside, but Oliver yelled, "Don't!" He'd already strapped his mother into the passenger seat of his sedan and had dumped the wheelchair into the car's trunk. He slammed the lid and walked briskly up the brick walkway again. "Please," he said, breathing hard. "Don't go inside."

Before Nikki could step over the threshold, he hurried up the steps with more agility than she could have imagined, then pulled the door shut. "I—I don't know what to say. Mavis moved my—our—mother last year, and I . . . I hate to admit it, but I had no idea what kind of squalor . . . well, it's over now." He withdrew a set of keys from his pants pocket and locked the door, double-checking the handle to make certain the lock was engaged. "As I said, I was remote, and Mom's care fell on my sister. But . . ." He scowled at the front door, where there were scratch marks from some long-ago pet. "I shouldn't have trusted her. A similar situation happened after my dad had his first stroke. I shouldn't have abdicated."

"You feel you abdicated?"

"I have a life in LA, okay? A busy life. I'm the office manager for a construction company. Big one. Lots of jobs going at the same time. And the truth of the matter is that my wife and my mother have never gotten along, so . . ." He shrugged as he shoved the keys into his pocket again. "Mavis told me Mom had dementia, that she needed round-the-clock care and it was expensive, but she was handling it. With money from Dad's estate." He studied the rundown house again. "But if this is where Mom was living . . ." His voice trailed off, and he shook his head. "Mom isn't that bad. Yeah, she sometimes isn't as sharp as other times, and she can't walk on her own, but . . . well, she'll do fine at Riverview. There's a nurse on duty twenty-four seven and staff to look after her and good, nutritious meals and other people. There are classes—art, exercise, that sort of thing. And activities. Field trips. Some of her friends live there, so it'll work out." He sounded as if he were trying to convince himself.

"I really would like to talk to her."

"We've got to get going. You saw how she goes in and out, right? As I was putting her in the car, she told me that Mavis would be mad at me. Really angry. For moving her." He rattled the keys nervously in his pocket. "Okay . . . fine. I'll meet you at Riverview. She'll be fine there," he said, as if still trying to convince himself. "There are people at the Towers. So, yeah." He pocketed the keys and hurried down the path to the car again, where his mother was waiting. Meanwhile, the woman in the minivan had rolled down the window and was vaping, blowing thick clouds of vapor into the spring air.

Oliver started the Lexus, hit the gas, and backed onto the street. As soon as he was off, the minivan started backing up as well.

"Wait!" Nikki said through the open window and the redheaded driver hit the brakes. "You took care of Mrs. Crawford?"

"Who wants to know?"

Nikki introduced herself. No sign of recognition showed in the woman's disinterested brown eyes, so maybe that was a plus. "I'm Sherry," she said. "And yeah, I was hired, just this last week, a temp fill-in, but now it looks like I'm out of a job. Again." She took another puff from her e-cig. "Story of my life."

"Who hired you?"

"Mrs. Greenlee," she responded. "I heard she's dead. Somebody offed her."

"That's right."

"Huh." Another drag. "She was a real bitch. Ignored her mom and left her here. Lots of time all alone. With the TV and a remote and a microwave dinner." Then, as if hearing herself, Sherry changed her tune a bit. "I mean, I didn't really know her. Forget I said that. She gave me a job and all, and now that guy—" She hitched a thumb toward the empty driveway where Oliver's car had been parked. "He's payin' me to clean this dump up. So I guess I shouldn't complain. And at least now someone will look in on Mrs. Crawford." She snorted in disgust. "Her livin' here alone. It's criminal. That's what I think."

"So no one was here with her?"

"Not all the time." Sherry lifted a shoulder and tucked her e-cigarette into an open bag beside her. "Look, I gotta get goin'. I'm haulin' some of Mrs. Crawford's things to her new place." Without waiting for a response, she shoved the van into reverse and hit the gas, screeching onto the street before throwing the vehicle into drive and heading off, leaving a disappearing trail of black exhaust.

Rather than leave herself, Nikki walked around the small house with its overgrown vegetation and broken side gate. The backyard was patchy, a cracked birdbath situated on a covered patio in serious need of power washing. She peered through the slider door, got a glimpse of the kitchen, and saw that the counters were covered with boxes and the sink was filled with dirty dishes. The dingy carpet showed tracks from the wheels of Mavis's wheelchair, and a neglected vacuum cleaner rested near the open door of the near-empty pantry.

She tried the slider, but it was locked. As she walked back to her car, she spied a raccoon scurrying through the brush and rustling the leaves of the overgrown shrubbery. She wondered about the sad state of Blanche Crawford's home and was about to get inside her car when a white pickup pulled into the drive, parking where the van had just been. The driver's door opened, and Nikki froze as she recognized her brother, slightly over six feet and showing signs of silver in his hair. "Kyle."

He paused, hesitated a second too long, then said, "Hey, Nikki."

"What're you doing here?" Her brother was the last person she'd expected to run into.

"Maybe I should ask you the same question." His smile was a little crooked, and it brought back memories of growing up with him, of his exuberance, of his enthusiasm, of his sense of adventure. With bright red hair and a cute, gap-toothed smile, Kyle Gillette hadn't ever met a dare he wouldn't take. He'd jump from a bridge that towered over the river. Climb the highest tree. Sneak booze from their parents' cabinet. Ride the neighbor's wild bull. Whatever.

Until they'd lost Andrew.

Then the no-challenge-too-big fire that had burned within Kyle had been extinguished. It was as if when Andrew died, so had part of him. The laughing, gleefully devious boy was suddenly gone, replaced by a recluse.

"Oh, wait, I get it. You're looking into Mavis Greenlee's death. That's why you're here."

"And you?"

"Hired by Oliver Crawford to clean up the yard," he said. "You know, repair the sprinkler system, or replace it. Check for other damage."

"You know him?"

"Oliver? Nah. But he got my name from Archer, I guess."

"He left about half an hour ago. But you know Archer Greenlee?"

"I take care of his yards. The one here in town and then out on Tybee." At the mention of the island, he suddenly clammed up. Like he'd said something he shouldn't have.

"Mom says you've been by."

"Yeah." He was nodding as he pulled a baseball cap from his back pocket and squared it on his head.

"Why now?" she asked, unable to stop the question that was uppermost in her mind.

"Figured it was time."

"Because . . ."

His cell phone buzzed, and he glanced at the screen. "Gotta take this and get that estimate going." As he put the phone to his ear, he started eyeing the house, ignoring Nikki completely. She had a million questions to ask him, but she had her own job to do. "Later," she called over her shoulder; then, once in her car, she muttered, "Weird." *Why now* was just the start. She wanted to ask him about his life. Was he involved with anyone? Was he working with someone or on his own? How had he connected with Mom again? Was he still in the apartment near the river? Would he like to meet Chloe? What, what, what was going on in his life?

"Stop it," she said aloud, as she slowed for a stop sign near the Cathedral Basilica of St. John and stared up at the twin spires knifing into the blue spring sky. She reminded herself that Kyle was a grown man and had the right to his privacy. If he'd decided it was time to reconnect with the family, she should curb her curiosity and, yes, even her suspicions, and welcome him with open arms. Unfortunately, that wasn't exactly her nature, and as she watched tourists climb onto a trolley, she couldn't help wondering about her brother. "Get over it," she advised herself, but she doubted that she really could.

Chapter 16

Nikki drove the few blocks to Riverview Towers, a five-story building a block from the Savannah River. It was more modern than some of its counterparts, and the upper stories did have a view of the water.

She parked in an adjacent lot, made her way inside, and was stymied by a wide reception desk and the stark, smartly dressed woman behind it. With a bouffant of gray hair, narrow eyeglasses connected by a gold chain that draped around her neck, and a steely smile that showed off slightly overlapping front teeth, she asked, "May I help you?" But when Nikki explained that she wanted to speak with Blanche Crawford, the gates went up. "She's just moving in today, as you probably know, and until we can get an updated approved list of her visitors, you'll have to wait until I can speak with her. So, it might be better if you would come back at another time that's convenient for you both."

Nikki tried to put up an argument but access to "the *private* towers" was denied. She clearly needed to see Blanche before Oliver had time to change his mind about allowing her near his mother.

"You understand, I'm sure, that for privacy and security, we have to be very careful," she was told. Behind her slim lenses, the receptionist's flinty eyes brooked no argument. "We keep lists of people allowed to visit," she pointed out and checked a computer screen, before scanning notes spread on her desk. Spying a form, she ran her finger down the page and even upside down, Nikki read Blanche Crawford's name on the heading. She followed the polished fingernail that paused over several names, again upside down. The list included Oliver Crawford, Wilda Gains, Sherry Engles, and Reverend Westin Stark.

The lobby elevator chimed, the doors opened, and Oliver appeared, his phone in his hand, his attention on the slim screen.

Nikki flagged him down. "Hi!" she said, and he looked up, his eyebrows knitting. Afraid she was about to be turned down in front of the receptionist, she said hurriedly, "You told me to come here."

"I . . . did . . ." He seemed about to argue, but then shook his head. "Okay, fine. Sherry's putting her bedroom together now so Mom can rest after lunch. He glanced toward the steely receptionist, then back to Nikki. "I'll take you up there." Pocketing his phone, he filled out a quick form at the desk, then escorted Nikki to the elevators. As they rode up to the fourth floor, Oliver said, "I just can't believe Mavis left Mom in that rental house. I just thought she was in a private home with round-the-clock nursing care. I expected it to be . . . well, not like that."

It was clear he was looking to excuse himself, so Nikki said, "This place seems very nice."

"Yeah. Yeah, it is."

Once the elevator doors opened, he guided Nikki around a corner and knocked softly on a half-opened door before stepping inside a large, overheated apartment with floor-to-ceiling windows and a broad view of the river and Hutchinson Island.

"Isn't it lovely?" Blanche Crawford asked as she rolled out of the bedroom in her wheelchair and came to a stop near an oversize recliner piled high with boxes and bags. "You're . . . ?" she asked, then a look of consternation crossed her thin features. "I know, I know, don't tell me. Oh, oh, I know. Charlene's daughter?" She seemed to have forgotten they'd met less than an hour before.

"Yes. Nikki."

"Not the artist . . ."

"I'm a reporter."

"Ah," Blanche said, as if she understood, but the clarity Nikki had witnessed on the walkway at the other home had faded.

"I wanted to talk to you about Mavis."

"She's not here now . . . oh, goodness. I think . . ." She looked suddenly confused, clutching for her son's hand. "Norton, I think something's happened to her."

"Hey, Mom. I'm Oliver. Remember?" her son corrected her. "Dad's gone. He has been for a while now."

"Oh." She blinked, focusing hard, her hand falling back to her lap to grip the Bible with its worn leather cover again. "That's right." Her smile, once strong, trembled on her lips.

"And Mavis . . ." Oliver placed a steadying hand on his mother's shoulder. "She's gone, too. Remember, I told you."

"Oh . . . yes. Someone killed her?" She was uncertain. "And where am I?"

"This is your new home. Sherry's making your bed up now and putting your things away. You remember her, don't you? And Wilda will be back next week. She'll be staying with you during the day."

"Wilda?" Blanche looked from one end of the room to the other. "Where is she?"

"Home resting. She had a little surgery, remember? Nothing serious, just a mole removed, but she took the week off. She'll be here tomorrow."

"No!" Blanche shook her head violently.

Oliver said, "But she takes care of you."

"She does not! She's cheap and lazy," Blanche declared.

"Mavis chose her."

Blanche glared up from her wheelchair. "No Wilda! I tried to tell Mavis, but she didn't believe me. Because she wouldn't pay for decent help. Even though she saw how that lazy woman didn't bother keeping the place up! Wouldn't wash a dish. Wouldn't dust a table. Wouldn't mop a floor. Just sat on the patio with her phone, playing games and texting and whatever it is they do now. Sat there and chain-smoked. Didn't care a lick about the house nor the filth. Just look at it!"

"Look at what, Mom?" Oliver asked, bewildered.

"The house!"

"We're in your new apartment now. Remember?"

Blanche turned her head from side to side.

"You've moved now. So Wilda will come here and—"

"No, no, no!" Blanche actually moved her foot from the pedal it had been resting on and stomped on the carpet. "No Wilda. You tell Mavis, I will not have her," Blanche insisted stubbornly, rubbing the frayed edges of her small Bible in agitation.

"Mom." Oliver was obviously trying to hang on to his patience. "Mavis is gone. I told you."

"Well, where the hell is she?"

"I told you. She passed." When Blanche's upturned face registered no emotion, he added, "She passed away."

"Passed away?"

"We discussed this earlier."

"But."

"Knock-knock," a voice called from the open door, and Nikki looked over her shoulder to see Westin Stark, dressed all in black, a clerical collar around his neck. It seemed as ill-fitting as a dog harness on a fish, but she kept her thoughts to herself. He was tall and fit, his still-blond hair neatly combed, his smile gentle, but, she felt, practiced.

"Oh!" Blanche was suddenly beaming and turning her chair to meet him.

"I heard you moved," he said. Then, his eyes meeting Nikki's, he said, "Nicole."

"Hi, Westin."

"It's been a while."

Not long enough, Nikki thought, even as she tried to banish her bad attitude about the man. They had a long history, none of it pleasant. He was a minister now, a man of the cloth, a person who had vowed to give his life to God.

Maybe.

If he remembered how he'd traumatized her in elementary school, he didn't show it. In fact, he'd never acknowledged all the pain he'd caused as a belligerent and violent youth.

"Come in, come in," Blanche said, waving him from the hallway into her unit. "Don't mind the mess. That Wilda, I tell you, she won't lift a finger."

"Mother," Oliver said in a gentle, but warning tone.

"I just came to pay my respects," Westin explained. "And to offer some support."

"Support?" Blanche asked. "Do I need support?"

"He's talking about Mavis, Mom."

"But she's not here."

"I know, and I'm so sorry," Westin said, kneeling next to Blanche's chair and taking her hand. "My condolences to you and all of your family. I thought maybe we could pray together and read a few healing passages." He lifted his Bible.

"Mavis should be here," Blanche said a bit petulantly, hugging her own Bible close. "It might help her. She could use some Bible-studying."

Westin's smile didn't waver. "I see." He cast a knowing glance up at Oliver. "Let's pray, shall we?"

"A little prayer would be nice," Blanche agreed, but Nikki wasn't sure the older woman understood, as she seemed to be falling in and out of reality. Sometimes Blanche seemed sharp as a tack; at other times, she seemed completely at sea.

But based on the attitude of the receptionist/sergeant at arms manning the desk downstairs, it was likely this would be Nikki's only chance to get information. So she stayed, bowing her head as well and listening as they read several Bible verses before Westin said a prayer, then made his excuses to leave. With a pat on Blanche's shoulder and a smile that was meant to be beatific but merely looked condescending, he said, "Good to see you again, Nicole. Perhaps we'll see you on Sunday."

Not on your life.

"Probably not," she said and held his gaze until Oliver showed him the door.

Once the pastor was gone, Nikki motioned Oliver to one side and asked in a low voice, "Do you know if your sister knew a man named Billy Huber?"

"Who?" Blanche called sharply. She'd been staring out the window at the watercraft on the river, but now she eyed Nikki suspiciously. "Billy who?" When Nikki repeated the name, Blanche frowned, struggling. "Never heard of him."

"Mom, it was on the news. He was—"

"I said I don't know him," Blanche cut in. "And Mavis? You'll have to ask her. Barely see her, you know. She doesn't come and visit. And neither do you." She pointed a gnarled finger at her son and let out a snort.

Nikki turned to Oliver. "Do you know anyone who would want to harm Mavis? Did she have any enemies?"

"Her husband!" Blanche said clearly and whipped her wheelchair around to face Nikki. "He's having an affair."

"Mom! You don't know," Oliver snapped, holding up his hands, as if to fend off an attack.

"It's true!" Blanche seemed certain, her eyes clear again. "I've seen him at the club, ogling the girls. The young ones!"

"Mom, you're talking about Radley, and that was years ago."

"Snake in the grass," she growled. "Never did like him. Never trusted him."

"Mavis is—was married to Archer. Remember? Archer Greenlee? You went to their wedding."

Blanche's brows slammed together as she thought. "Archer. The sawmill man?

"That's right, he did own a mill before he retired," Oliver agreed.

"Not the golfer?"

"No."

"Or, um, the . . . oh dear Lord. The banker fellow."

"No. That was Leonard. Leonard Armstrong. They divorced. Then she married Archer Greenlee."

"The sawmill man," Blanch repeated.

"Yes, that's the one." He glanced at Nikki. "Archer inherited a couple of sawmills and a rock quarry, but he sold them a couple of years ago. Retired."

"Mavis never did have any taste when it came to men." With a flip of her hand, Blanche said, "She was boy crazy as a teenager, and I don't think it ever stopped."

Nikki hoped to keep them both engaged as she tried to turn the conversation back to Mavis's first husband. "So Radley and Mavis didn't get along?"

"Fought like cats and dogs," Blanche insisted, but behind his mother's back Oliver was shaking his bald head as he held Nikki's gaze. And he was sweating, beads drizzling down his cheeks. Was it from a case of nerves or because the heat in the apartment was cranked up?

"What about her second husband?"

"Len?" Oliver answered quickly. "Oh, he was a good guy. Adored Mavis."

"Low-life banker!" Blanche cut in. "Norton—that's my husband—they're friends. But I never trusted that man. Smarmy lowlife, if you ask me. Always had an eye on the family money."

Oliver looked weary. "No, Mom, he just did some investments for us, that was his job."

"That's what he wanted you to think."

"He loved Mavis," Oliver argued.

"Nearly twice her age. Robbed the damned cradle, if you ask me."

Oliver pointed out, "Mavis was the one who filed for divorce." To Nikki, he said, "This just doesn't seem right, talking about my sister's life when she can't defend herself. I think it's time for you to leave."

Nikki put in, "The police will want to know."

He found a box of tissues on a side table, took one, and swiped his forehead. "They've called and asked to speak to Mom already. I said they should wait until we moved over here, but I think they're coming this afternoon. I only hope that she's . . . well, you know."

Blanche whipped her chair around, nearly running over the toe of Oliver's leather shoes. "I heard that!" She aimed an accusing finger up at her son, then, with a crisp nod, said to Nikki, "I'm fine."

"Sure, Mom, sure. Of course you are." Oliver threw his arms up before walking to one of the wingback chairs near a faux fireplace and plopping himself down.

Triumphantly, Blanche turned to Nikki. "You asked about Mavis having any enemies?" she said, arching her eyebrows over her glasses.

"Yes. That's right."

"Maybe you should talk to that Charlene Gillette," she said coyly.

"What?" asked Nikki. What did her mother have to do with anything?

"Mom, don't," Oliver warned, suddenly on his feet again.

But Blanche ignored him. "She's a cat, that one. And she never quit blaming Mavis for her affair with Big Ron when it was Ron who seduced her." She clucked her tongue and shook her head, cotton candy hair coming out of its clips. "He's a major player, that one."

"Mom!" Oliver was horrified. "Don't listen to her!"

"Well, it's true. Trust me. Ronald Gillette never let a pretty one pass. They did more than catch his eye, let me tell you."

Oliver made a strangled, frustrated sound. "Mom, please, you know that he was a judge and—"

"Doesn't matter!" she snapped.

"—and this is . . . this is his daughter," he explained, having paled slightly.

"Is she?" Blanche eyed Nikki speculatively. "Then she should know just what kind of a womanizer her father is!"

"Was, Mom. Ronald Gillette died a while ago."

"Serves him right!" With that, she wheeled herself back to the bedroom and began barking orders at Sherry, who was still dutifully hanging clothes in the closet.

"I'm sorry," Oliver apologized and looked like he wanted to disappear.

"Don't worry about it."

"I just . . . I just don't know what I'm going to do," Oliver said, following Nikki's gaze in the direction his mother had gone. "She's always been difficult, but now, she goes from being sweet and pleasant and knowing what's going on to . . . to being either out of it or angry." He swallowed hard. "I can't leave LA, and she refuses to even consider moving. So, for now, this is the best solution. Mavis never told me. She said she was handling everything and Mom was fine, but Mom is definitely not fine, and the fact is that she was living in near squalor without much supervision."

"Why was that?"

"Money," he said, without hesitation. "This place will cost a small fortune, but Mom has the funds, and the money is hers. Mavis didn't necessarily have that viewpoint."

"Do you know anyone who would want to harm your sister? Or kill her?"

"Besides me?" he asked sarcastically. Then, "No. Well, I don't think so. A lot of people didn't like my sister, but did anyone hate her enough to kill her?" He shrugged. "I don't know. I mean, it happened, right?"

And so the answer was yes. Someone did hate Mavis Greenlee enough to end her life. The same with Billy Huber.

But who?

And why?

And how on God's green earth were they connected?

Chapter 17

". . . all I can say is that he was a loser, okay?" Robert Huber's voice was raspy over the wireless connection. Seated in her Subaru and sipping from a to-go cup of sweet tea, Nikki had pulled onto a side street a few blocks from the river. With the sunroof open, she felt the heat of the day seep into the car. She'd put in several calls to people who knew Billy Huber, and finally his brother in Atlanta had returned the call.

Robert continued. "I would never have loaned him a dime, but he was my brother, and hell, I liked his wife. I felt sorry for him about their kid dying and then the accident with Linda-Sue, but it was a mistake. Terry told me not to do it, but I guess I'm a soft touch, and Billy promised me that when the life insurance on Linda-Sue came in, he'd pay me back. Like that ever happened." Robert Huber's voice was raspy over the wireless connection. "And now he's dead, and I'm out ten K. Not counting interest. Unless I can get it back from his estate, but I've seen his place. It's gonna cost more to clean it up than it's worth, if you ask me."

Nikki didn't argue.

"When is the last time you saw your brother?" she asked.

"I can tell you to the day. Christmas Eve eight years ago. That was when the first payment was due. I went to that hellhole he called home, and he wasn't there. I waited. He came back near midnight drunk as a skunk. We got into it, and he promised he'd get me the money the next week. Of course, that was the end of it. I mean, what can you expect from such a lowlife? Merry Christmas and screw you, that's all, excuse my French."

"And after that you never came back?" Nikki asked, staring out the window and watching a bicyclist weave in and out of traffic.

"Nope. I was afraid of what might happen. Billy had a temper, fought with just about everybody he knew aside from Linda-Sue, and I'm not proud to say that I've got one, too. So I thought it was best to let sleeping dogs lie, though I was about to take him to court, even go on one of those TV judge shows if I had to. Well, that won't work now, will it? Guess I waited too long. Seems like Billy pissed off someone who took it a step too far."

"You have any idea who that might be?" The biker turned a far corner as shadows stretched across the street.

A bitter laugh erupted. "Anyone who came across him. Just go through his phone contacts, and go down the list. I'll bet the son of a bitch is someone he knew."

She asked a few more questions, got no more information, and ended the conversation with Robert Huber promising to call her if he thought of anything else that might help.

As for his suggestion about checking Huber's contacts, she was certain the police had that covered. The same went for Mavis Greenlee. A shame the two victims didn't run in the same circles. It would have made her job, and Pierce's, a lot easier.

She drove to the newspaper office and grabbed an open desk, where she called Billy Huber's daughter, but Janelle McGowan was just as unpleasant as she had been when Nikki had met her at her father's place.

"I don't see why I would bother with a funeral," Janelle told her. "Who would come? It's not like Billy had any friends."

"I just thought people might want to pay their respects to your father," Nikki said as she'd hope to attend and see exactly who would show up.

Janelle barked out a laugh. "Who would that be? Huh? Tell me who respected Billy Huber? Not even his own damned brothers. In fact, I heard Uncle Bob once call him a jerk-off on steroids. How's that for some kind of epitaph? Maybe I should put that on a tombstone."

Nikki tried another tack. "It seems to me your dad was religious. He had a lot of Bibles."

"Oh. Well. I'll bet you dollars to donuts he got them on some kind of super sale somewhere or found them in a donation bin. Or even stole them from the local church's aid society, the one my mom belonged to. What was it? Birds for Christ or something? But, come on, religious? My old man? Not much. Mom—yeah, she was a true believer, even after my brother died, maybe even more so, I don't know. I wasn't there. But, Billy? No way. Whatever deal he had with God was . . . let's just say 'unique.' Okay? Oh, I know he claimed to believe the whole Christian thing, you know. Jesus being the son of God and all that, but he sure didn't live his life in Christ's footsteps, if you know what I mean."

Nikki did. The one thing that Billy Huber seemed to have in common with Mavis Greenlee was living a pretty non-Christian life and yet displaying the trappings of faith.

"Just ask Reverend Stark how many times he saw Billy in church," Janelle went on. "I bet it wouldn't be more than a three-fingered lumberjack could count on one hand." She laughed at her own joke. "So, no funeral. Instead, I'm having the old son of a bitch cremated, and I'll probably spread his ashes over all the crap he collected, just before I sell it or have it hauled off to the junkyard. And don't try to sell me on an obituary for your damned paper. Okay? Not interested." With that, she ended the connection, but it wasn't a total loss, as Nikki was left with one new piece of information. Not only were Mavis Greenlee and Billy Huber mutually despised by just about everyone, but they both were connected to the All Christian Church, where Reverend Westin Stark was the pastor and where her own mother attended services.

"Good to see you again, Nicole," she murmured, sarcastically repeating the pastor's quiet rebuke earlier, as she searched the Internet and newspaper archives for more information on the pastor. She quickly learned he'd gotten into trouble in high school, serious trouble that had landed him in juvenile detention. It was no surprise that his elementary school bullying and harassment had continued; the court records had been sealed, but she knew enough about his misdeeds to read between the lines. And, while serving his sentence, lo and behold, Westin Stark had found God, which led to his current career.

Once he was a free man and an adult, apparently he'd discovered preaching and that he was not only good at it, but there was money to be made and social status to be gained. The newly reformed sinner had gone on to school and joined the clergy, and now not only had he returned to Savannah and accumulated an adoring flock, he'd also begun his own podcast, which provided counseling, prayer, and religious guidance to thousands of people all over the country.

"Impressive," she said under her breath as she tried to equate the preacher with the kid who had pushed her into the boys' restroom in elementary school and forced her head into the grossest toilet she'd ever seen.

He'd paid for that particular sin by being expelled. Rumors were that he'd gone on to stealing cars and breaking into houses.

All before finding Jesus. Hallelujah and praise the Lord! Nikki thought unkindly, as that particular childhood trauma could hardly be forgotten or forgiven.

"No luck?" Roy asked, breaking her out of her nightmarish reverie as he breezed past her desk. Seeing her expression, he backpedaled to pause and drape an arm over the panel separating her cubicle from the next. His striped shirt was pressed, white collar starched, and he was wearing horn-rimmed glasses for a very studious and put-together look.

"Luck?" She shook her head. "Not today."

"Any day?" he teased.

She smiled. "It's not that bad. Some days are better than others."

He leaned down and whispered, "Be careful. Fink is in a really bad mood."

"When is he not?"

Roy's voice lowered even more. "Someone messed with his baby."

"What?" she whispered, heart clutching. Tom had three kids, a daughter who was around Nikki's age from his first marriage and two other children now in junior high. "Oh, God."

"Oh, no," Roy was quick to interject when he saw her reaction. "His kids are fine, far as I know." He lowered his voice even more. "It's worse than that."

"What could be—"

"Someone keyed his car."

"The Corvette?" she whispered and saw Roy trying to smother a smile.

"Yep." He nodded and managed to mold his lips into a frown. "It's sad."

"You know who did it," she accused.

Roy held up both hands, palms out. "I do not. But"—giving a shrug—"I can't help appreciating the sentiment."

"Someone left a message?"

He leaned closer. "Yes." His eyes glinted with a deliciously evil light. "They wrote: *Man-whore*. Along the driver's side. Scratched all the way through the paint."

"Oh, dear God." Fink loved his car. Drove it around town with the top down in all weather.

"If you ask me, it's his wife. You know they're split, right? D-I-V-O-R-C-E. Gasp!" he said theatrically.

She had heard.

"Or maybe it was Celeste. She's been waiting for years, and he's just strung her along. So maybe she's had it," Roy mused. "Who would blame her, and even if he is getting a divorce, she might have decided enough is enough."

"And vandalized his car."

"You know what they say about hell's fury and a woman scorned. So . . . just a reminder: Fink's on the war path."

"Not PC," she said, as Roy straightened.

"I know. I'm not. Gotta run. Forewarned is forearmed. Right? But just be careful. Who knows what Fink will do."

"What's that supposed to mean?"

"Oh, Nikki, you know he's had it in for you for years."

"You think he would fire me? He can't. I'm freelance."

"I know. He's just really ticked off." He smothered a smile. "Which I happen to love. Later!" With a wave, he was off, wending through the cubicles and out the front door. Nikki glanced over at Fink's glassed-in office where, through the half-opened blinds, he was fuming at his desk. As if he felt her gaze on him, he glanced away from one of his computer monitors and caught her eye. And then he kicked back his chair and was through the door, marching toward her desk. Was Roy right? Would Fink send her packing? She felt herself bristle. *Let's just see.*

"You have a new article?" he asked. "Something on the serial-killer cases?"

He knew she didn't. She'd called him from the road before landing here and had explained that she was "working on" a story. That wasn't really a lie. Not really. "I don't think the Huber and Greenlee cases have been labeled as serial killer."

"Oh, come on. They're too damned similar not to be linked. Don't the police have some connection between the victims? Haven't they come up with a profile on the psycho who committed the crimes? Isn't there some piece of evidence that was at both crime scenes or a calling card or something?"

She furrowed her brow and spoke the half lie convincingly, she hoped. "Not that I know of."

"Yeah, right," he spat, disbelieving. Then his eyes narrowed. "You know, Gillette, you used to be a good reporter."

"Used to . . ."

"Right. You'd do anything for a story. But you've gotten soft. I can see it. You're not the all-balls-out reporter you used to be. Ever since you had that kid, you haven't had the same dedication, that edge that made you stand out."

"Gee, I didn't think you noticed." She was holding on to her temper with an effort.

"Well, it's gone now. And before you argue with me, remember my back is up against the wall, just trying to keep this paper going. I don't need excuses. I don't need platitudes, and I certainly don't need fluff pieces. What I need from you is the same hard-edged reporting that you did when you made a name for yourself. You know what I'm talking about, so come up with something good. No. Strike that. Come up with something deep, perceptive, and honed to a razor's edge. Something great, in fact. You covered some of the most bloody and bizarre homicides in this part of Georgia. And now? Another one is dropped at your feet, and you're married to the lead investigator, and so far you haven't come up with jack shit!

"And if I don't come up with something you think is 'deep, perceptive, and honed to a razor's edge'?"

"Then I guess we'll be calling you a has-been."

"Wow."

"Exactly." With his jaw rock-hard and his lips thin as that razor he'd been talking about, he stalked back to his office.

She should quit completely. Tell Fink to take a hike or worse. She was seething, but she tamped down her fury. For now she needed to . . . let it go. There was something to be said for revenge being served up cold . . . well, if she could, she'd ram an iceberg of rage right down his throat. But . . . but . . .

But better to write the best damn story she could come up with and offer it to a rival paper. Maybe one in Atlanta. Or Charlotte, or *anywhere*!

She had some ideas, but they hadn't gelled, and she didn't have enough information to create the piece she was planning. Yet. And she couldn't go behind Pierce's back. Nor could she give up on a story. She thought of the rocks that had been left at the scene, polished stones with numbers inscribed on them, but she'd only learned of the first one because she'd been at Billy Huber's place when they'd discovered the stone under his body. From Pierce, she'd heard about the second one, found on Mavis Greenlee, but she'd been sworn to secrecy until such time as Pierce told her she could write about it. For now, the police were keeping that piece of evidence hidden from the public, something only they and the killer knew about, to weed out the people who called in and claimed to be the perpetrator.

She really, really wanted to tell Fink to shove it, to take his bad mood and get out of her face, but she held her tongue and gathered her things. She'd spent two hours going through old newspaper stories, learning about Mavis Greenlee, who had cultivated her public persona to reflect a Savannah socialite with Christian values who dedicated her life to helping others, while neglecting her own mother and making enemies. But unlike Billy Huber, Mavis Greenlee had no criminal record, nor any civil lawsuits leveled against her.

What was most disturbing was what she'd found out about her own father and how her family was linked to Mavis.

Big Ron was long dead, the affair decades past, and her mother was capable of a lot of things, but . . . what? Hiring a psycho to murder an old rival? And what about Billy Huber? Why kill him? To throw off the police?

In that vein, her thoughts turned to Kyle, her ghost of a brother, who had suddenly reappeared in their mother's life and who'd admitted to working for Mavis's husband. What was that all about? she wondered. Gathering her things from the desk and seeing Fink, now wearing his driving cap as he stormed out of the office, she nearly running into Roy on the way out.

"What did I tell you?" Roy asked as he reached Nikki's desk, then glanced over his shoulder to the far door swinging closed behind Tom Fink. "Guess he's not getting any."

"What?"

"Well, Celeste dumped him, just last week."

"Again?"

"Um-hm. And I heard that his wife had finally had enough. Kicked him out."

"And possibly scratched his car?"

Roy gave an exaggerated shrug. "Who knows?"

"Oh, God, you didn't do it, did you?" She was already starting for the exit.

"*Moi?*" he said, motioning to his chest in mock horror. "You know me better than that. I would *never* mar anything vintage. Not even a muscle car." He gave a little shake of his head. "Not my style."

"If you say so," she called over her shoulder, but she wondered what actually lay beneath Roy's overtly perfect facade.

"Oh, for the love of God," she muttered, angry with herself as she took the stairs to the first floor and walked into the afternoon sunlight. Now she was second-guessing Roy. And her brother Kyle. And just about anyone else she came into contact with. Running in circles on this damned case was getting to her, that was it. And then she saw Tom Fink's Corvette as he wheeled out of the lot, the ugly message *Man-whore* scratched into the otherwise pristine paint.

Chapter 18

"You're not my father, so just back the fuck off!" Toby said, irritated that Reed had found him loitering on the steps of the red-brick apartment building where his sister was living. Dusk was approaching, the streetlights were beginning to wink on, and the courtyard where Reed had caught up to the boy was empty.

And Reed wasn't in the mood to be berated.

Not by the kid.

Not by anybody.

After a long day of chasing down leads, sorting through anonymous tips that had come through the department, and dealing with the brass who wanted answers about the two homicides and wanted them now, he didn't have time for any bullshit from anyone.

He probably shouldn't have tracked the kid down.

But he felt obligated, especially after the call from Sylvie's sister, Claire, who lived in Texas but was concerned about her nephew. "I just want to talk to you," he said calmly.

"I got nothin' to say to you!" Toby looked him up and down, glowering at him.

"Don't you?"

"No!" Gone was the Mohawk of a few years back, replaced by long hair curling around his ears and a scraggly, wannabe beard. Nearly eighteen, he was dressed in a wrinkled T-shirt and baggy shorts. He was still lean, but filling out a bit in the shoulders and now was almost six feet tall. He would have towered over his petite, hard-edged mother had she still been alive and was a few inches taller than his sparkplug of an old man, Sylvie Morrisette's ex, Bart Yelkis.

"I heard you moved out."

"From who? Oh, don't tell me," Toby sneered. "Someone over at child services."

"Your aunt. She says you've been couch surfing. Crashing with friends. Skipping school."

Toby's eyes narrowed. "It's none of her business. Or yours."

"Where're you planning to live?"

Toby shrugged, his gaze moving to a squirrel that dashed across the flagstones to scramble up the massive trunk of a live oak. "What's it to you?"

"Wanna know if I can help."

Toby made a disgusted sound as he brought his attention back to Reed. Obviously, he wasn't getting along with his dad, but if he had any bruises, they weren't visible, and the kid wouldn't let him know if his piece-of-crap father had used him as a punching bag. Reed had never seen evidence of it, but Sylvie had been protective of her children, insinuating that Bart was at least emotionally abusive. That was bad enough.

Without proof, Reed couldn't do anything "We've got an apartment over our garage," he offered, though he'd never brought it up before. Then again, Toby hadn't been almost eighteen before. And Nikki probably wouldn't care. Hell, didn't she have a habit of taking in strays? Sure, they were usually in the form of dogs or cats, but she never really consulted Reed about the adoption, just hauled them home. "You could stay there. Long as you want."

"Oh sure. Like that's gonna happen." Before Reed could say anything else, Toby added, "Isn't your wife the reason my mom is dead?"

That cut deep. Because there was more than a little truth in it. "Your mother died in the line of duty."

"Yeah, because your stupid-ass wife was where she wasn't supposed to be and my mom saved her so she didn't drown! That's why my mom . . . Shit." His eyes glistened a little, and he scrabbled in his pockets for cigarettes and a lighter as, high overhead, the squirrel began to scold.

Reed's jaw was so tight it ached, but he held it together as the teen lit up and took a deep drag, while cars passed, the beams from headlights flashing through the open front gate. "So where are you living?"

"My business."

"You're not eighteen."

"Big deal. A few months." More petulant smoking. More cars going by, headlights flashing through the courtyard's open gate.

Two girls pushed through the doors of the apartment building, and Toby looked up, expectantly, but they passed by, both engrossed in their phones, not even glancing his way.

Reed said, "You haven't been in school."

"For fuck's sake, how do you know that?" He answered his own question. "Oh, right, you're a cop! You can do anything."

"Your aunt's worried," Reed said, irritated by the attitude. He knew the boy was hurting, but Reed wasn't setting himself up to be a whipping boy. "Your aunt Claire said you could live with her."

"Well, she can just forget it! I'm not moving to goddamned Plano, okay?" Toby nearly shouted, his eyes flashing. "Why don't you just fuck off and leave me the hell alone?"

"I promised your mom—"

"She's dead! Right? We just went over this! I don't want you in my life, and I don't care about whatever guilt or responsibility or whatever the hell it is you're carrying around with you. That's on you!" He jabbed at Reed with his cigarette, then thought better of it and backed up a step. "Back off, man, just . . . back the hell off." His voice cracked a little as he tossed his cigarette onto the sidewalk, crushed it out with the heel of an army boot. "Leave me alone!"

"You know, this attitude isn't getting you anywhere."

The boy's fist bunched, and Reed saw his eyes spark. Electricity sizzled through the air and, with it, way too much testosterone. Toby, coiled tight as a pit viper, was itching for a fight, ready to strike. "I told you to 'fuck off.' Are you deaf or just dumb?"

Every muscle in Reed's body tensed. If the kid wanted to fight, Reed could give him one. A good one. As the squirrel continued to scold and traffic rolled by, Reed felt his jaw tighten, and he held the boy's gaze, saying without words, *Go for it, you little prick. Take me on.*

For a split second, Reed thought Toby would attack. He knew the boy wanted, maybe needed, to use Reed as a punching bag, to wail on him, fists flying, letting loose all the pent-up frustration burning through him.

So be it.

Reed was ready.

He understood.

Hadn't he once been a rebellious, mad-at-the-world teenager himself? Hadn't he wanted to beat the living tar out of anyone who tried to tell him what to do? Hadn't he been fired up by alcohol and machismo and self-righteousness?

"Do it," Reed warned, egging the angry-at-the-world teen on, his lips barely moving, his eyes focused hard on Morrisette's boy. "See what happens."

Toby's fists clenched again. He began circling Reed, searching for a soft spot, ready to throw the first punch. "You'd like that, wouldn't you? Then you'd have an excuse to arrest me."

"Try me," Reed said, keeping the kid in his sights. "Let's see what you've got."

The door to the apartment building burst open, and three girls, silhouetted by the lights in the building's lobby, stepped onto the sidewalk.

Toby caught sight of his sister. He froze for a second, still sizing Reed up. Then, suddenly, he lowered his arms. "Hey!" he called to the group.

Priscilla, in the middle of the group, saw him, said something to her friends and approached. Like her mother, she was petite and compact, and her hair had once been as blond as Sylvie's. Now, though, she sported an uneven haircut—shaved on one side of her head, and on the other, chin-length strands tinged green. A nose ring glinted in one nostril, and she was sporting what appeared to be a new, vine-like tattoo running up her forearm. "What're you doing here?" she asked her brother as she spied Reed, her eyebrows knitting slightly. "What's going on?"

Reed managed a faint smile. "Toby here was about to show me some of his cage-fighting skills."

"What? No! Tobes . . . Oh, wait. I get it. You're kidding, right?" She laughed a little, unsure, because she, of all people, knew how volatile her brother could be.

"Right," Reed said and caught Toby's eye, daring him to argue. Reed had always gotten along with Priscilla.

"He wanted to fight me," Toby announced and jutted out his chin.

One of Priscilla's neatly plucked brows raised. "Probably not a good idea, Tobes," she admonished. "What—what are you doing here?" she asked again, then when Toby didn't immediately answer, she put two and two together. "You got into a fight with Dad, again, didn't you? And he kicked you out. Damn it, Tobes, I told you to just put up with it a little longer. You graduate in June. That's only a few months . . . oh, shit, you didn't get kicked out of school, too, did you?" She rolled her eyes and shook her head, her lips flattening and reminding Reed of his ex-partner. "God, why can't you just roll with it for a few more weeks?"

"You don't understand."

"Oh, yeah, I do!" She looked over her shoulder to her two friends, who were watching the display. "Go on," she called to them. "I'll catch up."

One of the friends took in the scene. "You sure?"

"Yeah, go. Go!" Then as the two left, she turned back to her brother. "You fought with Dad again. Admit it," she demanded as the squirrel, tired of chattering, climbed higher in the tree.

"Nah. I was just in town."

"And you brought along Mom's partner?" she said in disbelief, underlining her words as she motioned toward Reed.

"He just showed up!" Toby said, then snarled, "Probably following me."

Reed said, "Your aunt called. Toby's been missing some school."

"You got no right to butt in!" Toby shot back. "And don't give me some bullshit about you caring or whatever. He only checks on us cuz he feels guilty!"

"It's not guilt. It's a promise I made to your mom."

"Like paying for my schooling?" Priscilla asked. "I checked."

The conversation wasn't going the way Reed had hoped. "That's different."

"How?" Priscilla wanted to know.

It was complicated. Most of the funding for her kids' college came from Sylvie's death benefit; she'd set it up that way. The rest was paid by Nikki. Because she felt responsible. So, yeah, that wasn't too far away from guilt. He said, "I always told your mom I'd look after you two." He moved a finger between the siblings. "She asked, and I agreed, and I told her I'd make sure you got to go to whatever university or trade school or whatever you wanted after high school."

"What if I don't want to go to college?" Toby threw out.

Reed said, "Why don't we wait and see after you graduate?"

"So that's why you're following me. Cuz you think you're my counselor or something!"

"I don't think that's it," his sister said.

"Hey!" The two girls Priscilla had been with had returned. "Are we going to Drake's or what?" the taller of the two asked, while the shorter, heavyset redhead kept her eyes on her phone while her fingers moved quickly over the screen.

"Yep." Priscilla nodded. "Toby?"

Her brother gave a furtive glance at Reed. "Just wondered if I could crash here tonight."

"At my apartment? Sure, but why . . . ?" she started to ask, and then her gaze moved back to Reed as well. "Doesn't matter. Yeah. For sure. We're going over to a friend's place now. You can come, I guess."

The kid seemed to want to decline, but with one last glance at Reed, said, "Yeah, sure," and as Priscilla waved at Reed, Toby, head down, hands deep in the pockets of his oversize shorts, stalked off.

As Reed walked the block to his Jeep, he chastised himself for almost letting the kid goad him into a physical confrontation.

He'd have to do better next time.

Because whether Toby liked it or not, Reed wasn't giving up.

"So Archer Greenlee left the group early," Nikki clarified, driving through town and talking on the Bluetooth connection in her Subaru. For most of the day, she'd been interviewing people who had known either Billy Huber or Mavis Greenlee, and she felt like a dog chasing its own tail. Getting nowhere and fast.

But maybe things would change now that she had Mac, the part-time bartender at the Stag and Boar, on the line and he was telling her that Archer Greenlee's alibi wasn't as rock-solid as she'd thought.

"He was here at the bar that night, like he said. With his usual group."

She remembered that Archer had claimed to be at the Stag and Boar with some friends, including Otis Childers, as well as a couple of others, Knox Quinlan and Stoney Tripp, whom she had yet to interview.

"But he left early. I remember because he bragged about winning some kind of shooting contest with them the last time they'd been out to the rifle range, and the guys at the table complained that he should be paying for their drinks," Mac said. "And anyway, it wasn't like him to leave early when he had bragging rights."

"And he left about what time?"

"Geez, I don't know. I'd been on my shift for a couple of hours, so maybe seven? The guys usually hang out till ten at the earliest, sometimes midnight. I remember once they were even still here at closing."

Mac didn't have much more to offer, but it was enough to convince Nikki to turn around and find out for herself. She wanted to see Archer's expression when she asked about it. Worry was more likely camouflaged on a phone conversation than it was in a face-to-face conversation. Nervous tics, beads of sweat, fidgety hands, and eye shifting couldn't be so easily hidden,

At the next corner, she pulled into the parking lot of a mom-and-pop grocery, where two crows were fighting over a bit of garbage and one of the checkers, apparently on break, was leaning against the building and scrolling through her phone. Disgruntled, the crows cawed loudly and flapped out of the way, while the checker didn't bother looking up.

Nikki barreled out of the other entrance to the lot, nearly cutting off an older Impala inching down the street, then turning onto Victory Drive, which was part of Highway 80, leading to the island.

Finally, with finding this chink in Archer's alibi, she was getting somewhere.

At the city limits, she called her sister through the Subaru's Bluetooth connection. When Lily answered, Nikki explained that she had one more stop and then she'd be home.

"Sounds good."

Nikki squinted against oncoming headlights and asked, "So everything's okay?"

"Right as rain, whatever the hell that means," Lily said, using one of their mother's favorite phrases. "Phee's doing homework, and Chloe has already had a bath and is in pajamas. We're good."

"I should be home in an hour, maybe an hour and a half. It all depends. If I'm any later, I'll text or phone."

"Okay."

"And I don't know about Pierce."

"He called. On his way home. But don't worry about anything. We're good here. Phee cooked tonight. Boxed mac and cheese. Better than instant ramen, which was her first choice. I told her 'no way.' She can make that for herself and her roommate when she's in college."

Nikki laughed as she clicked off. She thought about calling her husband and at least letting him know where she was going, but decided against it. The less Pierce knew about her research, the better. And so far, the day had proved uneventful.

Earlier, she'd driven to the country club where Radley Bowers was the golf pro and where her own family had been members for generations. The grounds were manicured, lush azaleas in full bloom in shades of pink, purple, and orange. The fairways stretched away from a rambling, stone clubhouse flanked by blossoming magnolia trees.

She'd pocketed her keys and strode across the parking area to the pro shop and walked in as two women in skorts, sweaters, and visors were walking out. Radley was inside, arranging putters by size on a display rack.

He turned to face her when the door shut behind her. A broad smile was plastered across a narrow, tanned face, but before she could utter one word about Mavis, the welcoming grin faded as he recognized her. "Oh, Jesus," he whispered under his breath, and the clubs he'd been arranging fell and scattered around his feet like the thin plastic sticks from a game of Pixy Pick-up Stix. "Nikki Gillette!" A tall, fit man in a yellow Izod shirt and knee-length shorts, he crossed his arms over his chest. "Don't tell me, you're here because of Mavis." To Nikki's surprise, he kicked one of the putters, and it went sailing into a display of jackets, only to tumble to the plaid-carpeted floor. "I knew it. I just knew it!"

"I just want—"

"To ask me a few questions. I know." Radley snagged the thin club he'd booted and tossed it onto the pile. "Just so you know, that woman was the bane of my existence. You hear me, the goddamned bane." He pushed the putters with one foot into a more orderly stack, but didn't bother trying to arrange them. "But other than seeing her here at the club on occasion, I had nothing to do with her."

At that point, Nikki realized she hadn't even asked him a question. Just the mere sight of her—knowing she was a reporter—had set him off.

"God, I thought I was done with her." He ran stiff fingers through his hair, still thick and sandy-colored, his palm white against a darkly tanned wrist, evidence of hours playing golf in the sun. "If you'll leave me alone, I'll tell you what I told the police, okay? Mavis and I were married right out of college, then, about eight years later, we weren't. That was decades ago. She was out of my life. End of story."

He didn't display any modicum of grief for his dead ex-wife. "Why did you divorce?"

"A lot of reasons. Irreconcilable differences."

"That's pretty broad."

"Ancient history, Nikki." She waited, and his face hardened. He finally spit out, "I can tell you got ideas. Go ahead. What're you thinking?"

"I think she had an affair."

He snorted and shook his head. "One? That's rich." He snorted. "Look, I don't want to speak ill of the dead, okay?" He bent down and started sorting the clubs again as if the interview was over. "Yes, she cheated."

"With my father."

He froze for a second, then stood, still holding a child-sized putter. "Yeah." Nodding, he nervously tapped the club onto the floor. "That was the straw that broke the camel's back. I found out and filed for divorce the next day. To her credit, she didn't fight me."

Nikki got right to the point. "And you were home, with your wife, on the night that Mavis was killed?"

His gaze held hers. "That's right. I'd had a meeting at the church after work. Then I came home; we had a quiet dinner, later than usual, I think, and watched TV. There was a game on and then some reruns of *Seinfeld*, I think. Or *Modern Family*. I can't remember, we rotate the old stuff we like, but I do recall that Kelsey was more than a little miffed. The Honeywells were having some sort of patio party, and we weren't invited. Kind of ticked her off. But—that's beside the point." His eyes narrowed. "Anyway, if you're asking me if I killed my ex-wife, the answer is '*no*!'" He tossed the child's putter back onto the unsightly pile. "Divorcing Mavis was the second best thing I ever did. The first was marrying Kelsey. Now, if that's all, I'm working here."

"What church?" she asked.

"What do you mean?"

"You said you were at a meeting at the church."

"Yeah. The All Christian, off of Oglethorpe."

"Where Westin Stark is the pastor?" Nikki asked, thinking the minister's name kept haunting the edges of her investigation.

"Yes. Reverend Stark."

"He was there?" she prodded.

"At least for part of the time. Why? What's this got to do with Mavis?"

"The reverend didn't stay for the entire meeting?"

"Had to leave a little early," Radley said. "That matter?"

She ignored the question. "Can you verify who was at the church meeting?"

"Four of the elders. Knox Quinlan and Otis Childers, Norm Metzger and me. And, of course, Reverend Stark."

"Norm Metzger is an elder?" Nikki couldn't believe the miserable grump of a man she had worked with for years was an elder in any church, Christian or otherwise. For all the years she'd worked with him, she'd never heard him mention any kind of faith.

"That's right. Now I need to get back to work." He started to turn away.

"Did you know Billy Huber?"

"Uh . . . The guy who was killed a week or so ago? I read about it. Your story. But no. Never heard of him until I saw it in the paper and later on the news," he said, then, "Why? Are the murders connected?"

"That's what I'm trying to figure out," she said as the phone to the pro shop rang.

Radley looked in its direction. "I gotta get to work."

Nikki nodded. She'd gotten what she'd come for, even if it did appear to be a big, fat nothing. As she exited the shop, she heard the phone keep ringing and looked over her shoulder to see Radley on his cell, the incoming call and the pile of strewn putters ignored. As she climbed into the warm interior of her Subaru, she couldn't help but wonder if after dismissing Nikki, Radley had put a call into his wife, just to secure his alibi.

She'd started the engine, seeing a gray-haired man park his golf cart near the glass door and head into the pro shop. Through the window, she saw Radley hold up a hand in greeting, quickly ending his call, never bothering to answer the pro shop's phone.

Not exactly taking care of business.

"One more stop," she told herself, pushing thoughts of that earlier meeting aside as she drove across the Bull River Bridge to Tybee Island. She caught a glimpse of the lighthouse, with its beacon, as she rounded the north end, winding through streets until she found the oceanfront Greenlee property.

The sprawling house was painted a fanciful aqua, trimmed in white and rising three full stories, the lowest of which, at sea level, was a triple garage, its doors firmly closed. Tall palms flanked the house and were illuminated by garden lanterns, light washing upward to the shifting fronds high overhead. No car was parked in the driveway, and only a faint, wispy light glowed from windows whose shades were drawn.

She climbed up the wide staircase to the main level with a wraparound porch and rang the bell near the double doors. Though she heard the chimes ringing inside, no footsteps followed. Undeterred, she knocked firmly on the wide front door, but wasn't surprised that, again, no one answered.

So where was Archer?

Had he left town, after telling the police that he would be out here? As far as she knew, he hadn't returned to the house in Savannah and he was retired, but he could be anywhere, having dinner with friends or by himself, or out of town, or anywhere.

She may have just missed him.

She began walking along the wide porch, her footsteps resounding on the planks. She stopped at each window, trying to peer in, but wasn't able to see past the shades.

It was a little eerie walking around in the dark, with only some of the landscape lights illuminating the night. She heard the dull roar of the ocean beyond the chirp of crickets and hum of mosquitoes, but no sounds of life came from within the house. Since the porch seemed to encircle it, she kept moving and told herself she wasn't really trespassing. She'd knocked, after all.

As she reached the back of the house, where a wide staircase led down to a large swimming pool, shimmering in the moonlight, she felt more than a little nervous and told herself she was being silly.

But the thought of two murders having been committed in the area did tend to put her on edge. The pool at the base of the stairs was dark, but a nearby hot tub glowed a shimmering aquamarine, and farther to the east, beyond a band of white sand, the inky Atlantic was ever-moving.

Usually, the scent of the sea and the restless waves rolling to shore calmed her.

But not tonight.

With one last glance at the house, she made her way down the back stairs to the pool and walked along its rim to the hot tub. A couple of towels hung from hooks mounted on the trellis surrounding an exterior shower, and a pair of glittery flip-flops poked out from beneath a chaise with striped pillows. A bottle of wine and two stemmed glasses had been left on a nearby table. One of the stemmed glasses had a smudge of lipstick on its brim.

A woman?

But not Mavis, Nikki surmised, as there was no dust on the glasses, whereas the tabletop was covered with a thick, filmy layer.

She felt the hairs on the back of her neck raise slightly and felt as if unseen eyes might be watching her.

Was there a disturbance in the air?

Was that new noise the swoosh of a sliding door opening? Quickly, she studied the house again.

Nothing.

Was there another light on? Dim, like a night-light?

Her pulse ticked up, but she ignored it. Told herself she was imagining things. Still, she was on edge.

She picked up the wine bottle.

Empty.

Had Archer been entertaining? Some unknown woman. Who—?

This time she definitely heard a noise, like the soft pad of a footstep.

Nikki froze.

She'd been certain she was alone.

But—

More footsteps.

Nikki spun.

Raised the bottle.

And found herself staring at a slim, athletic woman in a short robe and sandals. Her face was in shadow, but she saw that her dark hair shined as if wet.

In her clasped hands was a large pistol.

Aimed straight at Nikki.

Chapter 19

"Who are you?" the woman demanded, her voice loud but trembling slightly, her two-handed grip on the pistol less than steady. "And what the fu—What're you doing in my backyard?"

"Your backyard?" Nikki repeated, her eyes trained on the gun, every muscle in her body tense.

"Yeah. You're—you're, like, trespassing!"

But she didn't sound convincing, her voice high-pitched to the point of squeaking. Just how old was she?

"I thought this was Archer Greenlee's house."

"It is."

"And you are?"

"I asked you first," the woman said childishly, and Nikki knew then she was even younger than Nikki had guessed.

Archer had a daughter, she knew that much, but Caroline Greenlee was in her thirties, and this woman—this *girl* wasn't far past her teens, if that. With a sinking heart, Nikki had the feeling that she knew her.

"I'm Nikki Gillette, and I'm looking for Archer Greenlee. I'm—"

"Oh! Oh, my God! You're Ophelia's aunt? You're that reporter!" The gun lowered as the girl stepped closer, her face suddenly illuminated by the glow from the hot tub. "And you wrote those books about murders around Savannah! I know. I read the last one about those three girls who went missing!"

"Yes, that's right." Oh, Lord. Nikki did know her. She was sure of it. But why couldn't she place her? And how was the gun-toting woman-girl connected to Phee?

"It was really, fu—I mean really, really creepy," she said enthusiastically. "I read all kinds of books like yours, and I'm a major fan of Ann Rule. And, oh, Erik Larson. And even though most of his books are fiction, I *adore* Stephen King! I mean talk about creepy. Like, to the max! They scare the living shi—daylights out of me!" She was smiling broadly by this time, babbling wildly, and though her features were still shadowed, Nikki was starting to place her. "I watch *Dateline* and *Forty-Eight Hours* and all that true-crime stuff, too. I know it's kind of weird. None of my friends are into it, but I can't help myself. I love scary stuff! You know, they say truth is stranger than fiction, and I believe it. I really do!"

"Right." It was rare that Nikki met a fan, even though she lived in the city where the crimes took place. And it was stranger still that it was while she was investigating a crime.

"Could I—could I get your autograph? Like on one of your books? I mean, I asked Ophelia for a signed copy of one, but I guess she never asked you. Or maybe you don't do that?"

Again Ophelia's name. And this is what they were discussing? Nikki's books? After the girl had threatened to blow her away?

And then as the girl tilted her head, her profile catching in the shifting light from the hot tub, her long, black braid reflecting the watery illumination, Nikki finally put a name to the face. "You're Annabelle." Ophelia's riding instructor. And a girl Nikki had seen fleetingly at Lara Kittle's sweet-sixteen party a few weeks earlier. On the night Billy Huber was murdered.

"Yes! Annabelle Van Camp. But mostly I go by Annie. I'm a couple of years older, but, yeah, Lara and I took group riding lessons together back in grade school, like a long time before I became an instructor. Lara and some of the others dropped out, but I just adore horses, I *love* working with them, so I kept at it. Now I get paid to do what I love! It's so cool! Kinda like you must love what you do, right?"

"Right," Nikki said, noting the girl's enthusiasm and the disturbing fact that she was still holding the pistol, though now she was gesturing with her hands. The gun was no longer leveled at Nikki, but Annabelle still held one finger on the trigger. And she was so excited, who knew if she might accidently fire it. "So, Annie, why don't you put that gun down and we can talk?"

"Oh! God! Yeah!" As if she hadn't realized she was still holding the heavy pistol, Annabelle quickly set it on the table, knocking over one of the wineglasses as she did. "I don't even really know how to use it. Really. I've never shot a thing in my life. I mean I'm a vegan. I don't eat animals. Not even fish! Ugh! Like nev-ver! And I certainly don't shoot them!" She righted the glass again. "Anyway, Archer, he thinks I—we—need a gun. For protection. He's been super freaked out ever since someone, you know, killed his wife."

Nikki finally set the wine bottle next to the pistol and asked, "Where is Archer?"

"Oh. He just went out to get some takeout. There's this *incredible* sushi place here, and they have, like, the most *incredible* avocado rolls and vegan California rolls. To die for."

"So he'll be back."

"Yeah. Any time now. In fact, I thought you were him. I was in the shower and thought I saw someone out of the window. Then I realized it wasn't him, so I grabbed the gun and came out."

"You should be careful about that. Pointing a gun at people, you know."

"But you were out here prowling around."

"You could wait for the police," Nikki suggested, though she cringed inside at the thought of someone from the department coming by and Pierce finding out that she'd been here. Worse yet, she might be arrested and he'd find out that way. Maybe it was better to change the subject, find out what she could, hopefully talk to Archer and leave. "You said you live here?" Nikki clarified. "You called this place your house."

"Uh-huh."

"With Archer?" Just to be sure.

"We've been kinda seeing each other," she admitted with a little shrug. "And before you get all he's-old-enough-to-be-your-father on me, I already know that." She folded her arms under her breasts a little defensively. "I've already heard that enough," she said under her breath.

"So people know about the two of you?" How long had this been going on?"

"I guess. Maybe some people Archer knows." Another shrug and Nikki felt the wind pick up. The stars overhead were beginning to be shielded by gauzy clouds. "And my parents. My dad is pretty butt-hurt about it, and Mom, geez, she's *always* pointing out that Archie is older than Daddy, but"—she sighed wistfully and looked past the pool to the beach and inky ocean beyond—"we love each other."

"You do?" Nikki said and withheld judgment. Annabelle was more likely to give her information if Nikki went along with the girl's perspective, even though she couldn't imagine this young, vibrant woman with Mavis Greenlee's widower. "So, how long have you two been seeing each other?"

"Three months!" Annabelle announced proudly. "We've been together three months and eleven days . . . well, not really together-together, you know, because he was married and all."

So she did understand.

"Hey, wanna go for dip in the tub?" Annabelle asked, as if the conversation had grown a little too uncomfortable. She padded quickly over to the hot tub, where she pressed a button for the jets and the water started bubbling and swirling, frothy waves appearing on the surface. "It's *so* cool at night. We come out here all the time. Archie and I love it."

Nikki eyed the wine bottle and glasses, evidence of a private party, and one of the participants was underage. "I'll pass."

Annabelle was already stepping into the tub. "You can borrow one of my suits or, you know, we can skinny-dip." To prove it, she dropped her robe, displaying a young, supple body with smooth muscles, taut skin, and full breasts between which a small cross nestled. It hung from a tiny gold chain, catching in the light from the pool and glittering against her tanned skin as she settled into the water. "Oooh, I'd better warn you, it's pretty hot in here. Yikes!" She sucked in her breath.

"I can see that." Steam was rising from the water's shimmering surface.

"But, seriously, it's *incredible*. I love to come out here after a long day of riding or working at the horse barns and just soak, you know."

Surreal, Nikki thought. But she stepped closer to the tub so she could continue the conversation over the noise of the Jacuzzi's motor and the churning water from the jets. Balancing on the tub's rim, where the scent of chlorine wafted from the water, she asked, "How did you and Archer get together?"

"It was fate!" Annabelle vowed, twirling in the water. "I swear! He, um, dropped his granddaughter off for riding lessons when school started last September, and we just like started talking, you know, about the girl and her riding skills and what horse would be best for her, stuff like that." She floated to the middle of the tub, her braid snaking out behind her. "We really didn't hook up until after Christmas. Because, you know"—she wrinkled her nose and wobbled her head from side to side like a silly little girl caught in a naughty act—"he was married and all."

"That was a problem?" Nikki asked, though, of course, she knew the answer.

"Yeah. Kinda. For me, but not for him. But he was really unhappy, so they were divorcing."

"Ah."

"And it just happened. We fell in love." She chased around some of the bubbles and tried to capture them." It doesn't matter how old you are," she went on. "Love isn't like that." Submerging her chin, she blew some of the frothy bubbles out of the way just as, over the rumble of the Jacuzzi's jets, Nikki caught the sound of a car's engine. A quick wash of illumination splashed across the front of the house and down the side yard. A car turned into the drive.

Annabelle noticed it, too. As the car's engine was cut, she cried, "He's back!" She jumped up and down a little in the tub. Like the kid she was. "Oooh, I'd better not let him catch me like this." She pulled a worried face, then grinned a little wickedly. "Archie doesn't like it when I'm naked around other people. Especially other men. He gets jealous."

"Okay." Sometimes the best plan was to just let the person talk.

She started to step out of the hot tub, when a male voice cut through the night. "Annie?"

"Oops, busted!" Annabelle said under her breath the second Archer Greenlee rounded the corner of the house. He was carrying a white sack in one hand and pocketing his keys with the other. He stopped dead in his tracks at the edge of the deck when his gaze landed on Nikki. "What the hell?"

Annabelle scrambled for her cover-up.

Nikki was already walking up the path and stretched out her hand as she introduced herself. "I'm Nikki Gillette. With the *Sentinel*."

Archer took one look at her, then swept his gaze to the hot tub, where Annabelle was cinching up her short robe. "Oh God," he whispered and, ignoring her, zeroed in on the girl. "You've been talking to her?" he accused. "Didn't I tell you not to . . . oh, dear Jesus." His gaze had landed on the table to take in the pistol, wineglasses, and empty bottle.

"She writes those crime books I like!" Annabelle explained. "And she's one of my student's aunt."

"She's a reporter!" he strangled out, dropping the white bag onto the ground. "I told you not to talk to anyone."

"You said the police," Annabelle argued, a bit petulantly.

"She's married to the detective in charge of . . ."

Nikki waited as his voice faded.

Archer cleared his throat. "Ms. Gillette's husband is a homicide detective, and she," he went on, pointing a condemning finger at Nikki, "is here to try to create some kind of story where there is none."

"But we've got nothing to hide," Annabelle said, walking up and snaking her still-wet arms around his waist.

As if she'd burned him, he pushed away from her embrace, taking a step backward. "Don't," he warned. "And you," he added, squaring off with Nikki. "I have nothing to say to you."

"You left the card game early," she pushed, sensing this might be her only chance to interview him. "I checked with the bartender at the Stag and Boar."

"Wait a minute." Annabelle appeared bewildered as she bent down to pick up the sack that Archer had dropped. "What's she saying?"

"I'm talking about the night Mavis was killed," Nikki explained and positioned herself between the man and the table where the gun lay. Just in case anyone got trigger-happy with her line of questioning. "Archer wasn't where he said he was."

Annabelle's pretty face clouded. "You lied, Archie?"

"I didn't lie," he snapped. "I was trying to protect you." Sighing, he raised his eyes to the cloudy heavens, as if for searching for divine intervention.

"I don't need protection." Her fingers curled over the edge of the sack, which was now turning brown, something inside leaking.

"Yes, yes, you do. *We* do. Or we did. Dear God. Don't you get it?" he snapped, dropping onto a chaise near the bubbling tub. Distraught, he held his head in both hands. "I just wanted to keep Annabelle out of this," he explained.

Nikki said carefully, "I don't see how that's possible."

Then, as if silently conceding defeat, he sighed and glanced up at her. "Look. Annabelle and I are involved. We have been for a little while."

"She told me."

"Not involved," Annabelle corrected, slamming the sack down again. "In *love*."

"And I was trying to be discreet, to save Mavis some embarrassment."

And save your own ass, Nikki thought, but held her tongue.

He went on, "As you've probably figured out, I was with Annabelle that night, before I went back to the house to pick up a few things and attend that stupid thing Mavis wanted to go to, a barbecue or some kind of party at the Honeywells. I'd gone to my usual card game, swung by here, and then, went home and found . . ." He closed his eyes and swallowed hard. "I found Mavis." His voice had lowered to a whisper, and even in the dark night, it was obvious that he paled at the memory. "I panicked for a second or two before I made the call to 911 and . . . and waited for the cops to arrive. I was hoping that this"—he motioned to the space between himself and Annabelle—"wouldn't be found out."

"Is that why you tried to get me to move back home?" Annabelle demanded, as if she suddenly understood the implications of their affair and Mavis's homicide.

"Temporarily," he said.

Her eyes narrowed suspiciously for the first time. "Are you *ashamed* of me? Or, or, of us?"

"Of course not!" He jumped to his feet, hands outstretched. "Annie, honey, you know how I feel."

"Do I?" Crossing her arms under her breasts, pushing them upward so that her cleavage with the little cross was in full display, she pouted at him.

In frustration, Archer plowed the fingers of both hands through his hair. "I'm done talking," he said to Nikki. "I didn't kill my wife. I . . . I was hoping to divorce her, yes, but I never . . . I never would have done anything to hurt her." He sighed into the night. "I didn't want Annie to be dragged into this mess. I was just protecting her."

Beside him, Annie seemed to thaw a little, her smile faltering as she stared up at him adoringly.

Her hero.

Tarnished and rusty as he was.

"Did Mavis know?"

"Yes. Yes, she knew."

Nikki couldn't discern if he was telling the truth about that or not.

"That is all you need to know," Archer said with finality as he looped an arm around Annie's shoulders and she nestled closer to him. "I didn't kill Mavis. I know it looks bad, but that's the truth." His arm tightened around Annie, and his backbone stiffened. "Why don't you do us all a favor, Ms. Gillette, and find Mavis's real killer instead of bothering us?"

"I have a few more questions," Nikki said.

"And I've got no more answers. Nor does Annabelle, so please leave, right now. Otherwise, I'm going to call the cops."

She thought about calling his bluff, but couldn't really, as he'd already called hers.

Neither one of them wanted the police to show up.

Also, she knew, Archer Greenlee had told her all he was going to.

And she thought he was mostly telling the truth.

No matter how in love he was with Annabelle, whether it was the real thing or just a post-midlife fantasy, he hadn't pushed his wife down the stairs, cut her throat, and placed a stone on her body. She couldn't see Archer Greenlee filled with the anger and fury the killer had exuded.

She was mentally scratching Archer Greenlee from her list.

But if he wasn't the killer, who was?

Chapter 20

Two victims. From two different worlds.

In her office, the lamps lit, night closing in beyond the windows, Nikki thought about Mavis Greenlee, an icon of Savannah society, childless, rich, and outwardly living the perfect life. A woman who'd once had an affair with Nikki's own father, which, of course, did bother her, though it had been decades before and Big Ron was long dead. A woman who was divorced twice and whose third marriage was on the rocks.

She leaned back in her desk chair and wiggled the pen in her fingers, clicking it on and off as she thought about Billy Huber. Unlike Mavis, he'd wed just once, was a father, and a collector of all oddities, a hoarder, who made no bones about getting along with anyone and was in debt up to his eyeballs and beyond.

The only thing they had in common was that no one liked them. Not their families, not their neighbors, and not their so-called friends.

As far as Nikki could see, the only person who had crossed both their paths was Westin Stark, the preacher at All Christian. But while Mavis Greenlee was very much a part of the church community, Billy Huber hadn't set foot through the wide double doors leading to the vestibule since he buried his wife. At least as far as Nikki knew from her conversations with other parishioners and Westin Stark himself.

The reverend.

The reformed sinner.

The born-again Christian.

A man with a mean streak that ran deep.

She chewed on her lip and tossed her pen onto the desk.

Reverend Stark wasn't the connection.

He was just the only person who seemed to know both victims, and he was a person Nikki still didn't like. "Get over yourself," she said aloud, and Arlo, ever-vigilant, was on his feet in an instant. While his fur was starting to grow in near his tail, he still looked a little rag-tag. But she loved him.

The shepherd had taken to her since she'd brought him home to become a part of the family. Mikado had accepted the newcomer after a few days, and now they spent their days together. Phee, who loved all things animal and was currently praying nightly for a horse, had fallen in love with Arlo, and Chloe had been delighted with another pet. Even Pierce had grudgingly admitted that he "kind of" liked the dog. The only real holdout was Jennings, who avoided Arlo as if he were a demon sent straight from hell. Only when the dog was occupied elsewhere would the tabby deign to sit on Nikki's lap and not treat her as if she were a traitor. "You'll get used to him," Nikki had assured him just three days earlier, but when Arlo had bounded into the room, Jennings had hissed and scrambled away, clawing so desperately that he'd scratched Nikki through her shorts.

Jennings might never truly accept him.

So be it.

Getting nowhere on the case, she decided to call it a night, heading down the spiral stairs to the second floor, where she checked on Chloe, who was sleeping soundly in the glow of an angel night-light. How could this little girl have changed her life so deeply? Nikki had lived over thirty years without her, and now, at the thought of ever losing her . . . well, she just wouldn't even consider it. Heart full, she bent down and kissed Chloe's soft cheek and watched in wonder as the little girl's lips moved a bit. "Sweet dreams," she whispered, nearly tripping over Mikado on her way out, as he was curled up near the crib.

In the hallway, she noticed flickering light beneath Lily's door.

Nikki rapped softly, opening the door and sticking her head into the room. Her sister was propped up in her bed, her floral duvet tucked around her as she read from a paperback. The corner TV was tuned to some DIY home repair show, the volume muted while Phee was fast asleep in a twin bed positioned beneath the window.

"Hey," Nikki said softly, and Lily looked up and motioned her inside.

"Just wanted to say good night and let you know I'll be out tomorrow evening again."

"So you have a hot date, or else you're doing some investigating."

"It's the hot date; don't tell my husband," Nikki joked, then thought of Archer Greenlee and his affair, and, of course, Mavis's long-ago involvement with their father. She pushed that particular thought from her mind. "Can you watch Chloe?"

"No problem." Lily dog-eared the page, then set her book aside. From the looks of the cover, it was another romantasy novel, Lily's new favorite genre, which blended romance with fantasy. "I've got errands in the morning, and I'll take Chloe, then after her nap, I'll pick up Phee from school," Lily agreed. "Maybe you can run them to horseback lessons to give me a break. I'm in serious need of a mani-pedi." She showed off her unpolished fingernails. "See? And then you can do dinner."

"It's a deal," Nikki agreed, as she sat on a corner of the bed. Chloe loved going to the stables, though she had more interest in the ponies and llamas and goats than in watching her cousin learn how to ride. But now, because of Annabelle Van Camp's intimacy with Archer Greenlee and her willingness to talk, Nikki had a renewed interest in Westside Riding Stables. Though she'd crossed Archer off the suspect list, he still knew Mavis, supposedly better than anyone, and as Tom Fink was always suggesting, a lot could be learned from "pillow talk." Maybe Archer had said something to Annabelle, though that was unlikely. "We'll finalize plans in the morning." She picked up the book. "This any good?"

"Well, it's not a Nikki Gillette crime story, but yeah, it's great." Lily grinned. "Especially if you like mean fairies and war and take-no-prisoners heroines. And let's not forget the heroes to die for."

"If you say so."

"Like I said, not like yours."

"Don't remind me about my next book. Ina's all over me about it." She tossed Lily's novel back onto the bed.

"Something about making hay while the sun shines?"

"Actually, she brought up the age-old 'striking while the iron is hot' cliché."

"I like that better," Lily said, tapping the cover of her novel. "Something they literally do in this one."

"Perfect."

"And it was also a euphemism for . . . you know." Lily wiggled her eyebrows suggestively.

"Yeah, I do know, and now I'll never forget it. Speaking of which, did you know Dad had an affair with Mavis Greenlee?"

Lily rolled her eyes. "Doesn't surprise me. Who didn't he have one with? Who told you? Mom?"

"Yeah. And she's not forgiven either one of them."

"That's Mom. Never lets go of a grudge. What's the old saying? That a grudge only hurts the one who's holding it or something? No, wait, I think it was Carrie Fisher who said something about resentment being like drinking poison and hoping the other person would die?"

"Sounds about right." But she thought about the saying and applied it to Mavis Greenlee and Billy Huber. Who would have a grudge deep enough to kill them and then stage the scene? It hadn't been good enough to take their lives. Whoever was behind their murders held a deep-seated anger and was making a point. She just had to figure out what that point was, and then she could connect the killings and hopefully unmask the sicko behind them.

She climbed to her feet and glanced to the bed, where Phee, hair wild on her pillow, was sleeping. With one arm flung over the edge of the bed, her iPad discarded on the carpet, and her covers bunched around her waist, she sighed and rolled over.

"They're so innocent and angelic when they sleep."

"I know. Looks can be deceiving, can't they?" Lily said with a chuckle, as Nikki whispered, "Good night," and headed to her own bedroom, where Arlo was waiting, lying on his dog bed. He lifted his head, his gaze following her as she changed into pajamas, then walked into the bathroom, where she piled her hair onto her head and washed her face.

He thumped his tail when she returned and, for once, obeyed when she pointed to him and whispered, "Stay." Somewhere along the line, someone, maybe even Billy Huber, had taught the dog some commands. She hurried downstairs and found Pierce in the den, shoulders hunched as he stared at his computer screen.

"Hey, Detective," she whispered into his ear. "Maybe it's time to call it a night?"

"Just a few minutes." He was tense. She saw it in the muscles at the back of his neck, the taut way his shirt stretched over his shoulders. The case and the lack of progress was getting to him.

To both of them.

She'd been hearing from Fink that she needed to come up with an in-depth story on the cases, as the *Sentinel* was keeping the story alive. It had been several weeks since Billy Huber's body had been found, over two for Mavis Greenlee's murder.

"All work and no play . . . ," she said, leaning over his back and wrapping her arms around his neck.

"You should talk."

"I know, but come on up to bed." Her head was next to his, and she brushed a kiss over his ear.

"You've got twenty minutes to cut that out," he said, and she laughed, but her gaze had traveled to the computer screen, where he was reading an e-mail.

"What's that?"

"Private police business."

"About—?"

"Nikki," he warned.

"We have a deal."

He sighed. "It's nothing really. I'm waiting for a report about the stones we found at the scene, and it hasn't come through yet."

"What kind of report?"

He clicked off the screen and turned around so that he was facing her. "Let it go. The report's been hung up due to some technical problem in the lab and the fact that the main lab assistant is down with the flu. Information we should have had weeks ago."

"You're dodging."

He pressed a finger tip to her nose. "And you're pushing. If something big happens, I'll let you know."

"Will you?"

"As long as you stick to our agreement," he said, and then, before she could argue, he twisted and pulled her onto his chair.

"Oh!"

"You were teasing me," he accused as he positioned her so that she was straddling him.

"A little."

"A lot."

Then he kissed her. Long. Hard.

His tongue probing.

She melted inside. Warm and wanting.

And beneath her, she felt Pierce's arousal. "For once, you're right," he said. "We do need to play. Come on!" Still holding her tight, her legs wrapped around him, he stood and carried her to the stairs.

"Don't," she warned. "Pierce, you'll trip."

"Worth the risk."

"I don't think so."

"Come on, Nikki, where's your sense of adventure?"

More easily than she could have imagined, he mounted the stairs, while she clung to him, burying her head in the curve of his neck. They reached the second floor, and he swept her into the bedroom, somehow managing to kick the door closed with a soft thud.

Arlo whined on the other side, but Nikki barely noticed as she and Pierce tumbled onto the bed together.

For the moment, she forgot the rest of the world.

Long after the day shift had gone home and the night shift had settled into its more quiet routine, Sol walked out of the station, the two stones in her pockets feeling heavy as gold bricks, but no one stopped her as she made her way to her rattletrap of a pickup. The Ford was nearly twenty years old and needed new struts, but for now, it would have to do.

It had served her well for fifteen years; she figured it had another five in it. Or maybe more. If she made all the repairs it needed.

One of the reasons she liked the old F-150 was because it was innocuous. It fit into the landscape. No one thought twice about a dented and dusty older-model truck in or out of town. And it looked like it belonged in the woods.

She rolled down the windows and thought about the case. Make that cases. Obviously, Billy Huber's homicide was tied to Mavis Greenlee's, and so far, the only serious connection the department had found was odd: the polished stones left on or near the bodies. The killer's calling card, one he wanted the police to discover, one that meant something special to him, if not to the victims.

Ever since most of her colleagues had gone home to their families, Sol had stayed at the station, drinking coffee, cherry cola, and Red Bull, using the caffeine to fire her blood. She had a long night ahead of her, and she'd need to stay awake as she read through every report, affidavit, and statement on the two homicide cases for the second and sometimes third time, looking for something, *anything* that would spark a new avenue in the investigation. She was through with the done-by-the-book investigating. At least for tonight.

As she drove, the city disappeared behind her into the low country, where wax myrtle and loblolly pines created a blind and she knew of a seldom-used road, one where she would have privacy. She found the turnoff, stopped to open the rotting wooden gate, and drove through.

The lane was little more than ruts, with potholes and tall grass that scraped the undercarriage, but her headlights cut through the darkness as the truck bounced along what had once been a long drive to a sawmill. She heard the whistle of spring peepers and the chirp of crickets, barely audible over the sound of the Ford's engine.

Sol drove for nearly half a mile to a clearing on the soggy banks of an old sawmill pond, the main building near it now in ruin, a skeleton of what had been as large as a barn. No longer was there a roof on the building, and the waterwheel beside it creaked slightly as she stopped the truck and cut the engine. Through the windshield, she noticed clouds moving, partially obstructing the crescent moon and stars.

She snagged her oversize bag from the worn bench seat next to her and stepped outside and into the thick night, where the crickets' music crescendoed and the frogs gave full-throated accompaniment. She felt at one with the earth here.

Using the flashlight on her phone, she followed an overgrown path leading away from the dilapidated structure, through a copse of trees to a ring-shaped, open area. In the middle of the clearing, someone had created a fire pit, the ring of jagged stones now blackened by the soot of previous fires, the logs within the pit charred. She reached into her bag, brought out dry kindling and a week-old newspaper, which she crumpled, then placed in the pit; then she turned the partially burned logs over to expose the dryer underside. With a shot of lighter fluid from the can in her bag and the flick of her lighter, she started the fire. Rocking back on her heels, she watched as the newspaper, with Nikki Gillette's story on Billy Huber front and center, her byline visible, curled and burned. Then the kindling caught, eager flames crackling hungrily skyward.

Satisfied, Sol wasted no time. She removed her clothes and kicked off her boots. With the damp ground pressed against her soles and the grass and soil squishing between her toes, she removed the polished stones from the pockets of her jacket, the stones she'd "borrowed" from the lab. Now, she held each in a hand.

Sol stared into the fire, sensing the energy in the stones, and whispered, "Come to me," adding her voice to the frog and cricket symphony. "Come to me."

A breeze blew across her face, and the leaves in the nearby trees rustled. She smelled the scent of longleaf pine and saw the gossamer Spanish moss hanging from the live oaks dance, pale and ghostly.

Slowly, she closed her eyes, her concentration on the weights in her palms, her fingers clutching each stone gently at first and then more tightly, her caress turning into a death grip. She felt the sharp indentations of the etchings pressing into her flesh, and as she did, she heard the pitiful bleat of a goat and the pained moan of a cow. And then another, more distinct sound, a human cry. A hiss of sorts. Like the swift intake of breath when one is surprised or feels sharp, unexpected pain.

Her own blood seemed to congeal in her veins, her own nerves twitching.

"Who are you?" she murmured quietly, trying to slow her own heartbeat, hoping to hear the sounds of the night, to sense the aura of the stones. "Who did this?"

A sizzle crawled up her spine, like the wispy touch of a butterfly's wings quickly skittering over her bare back, from the curve of her buttocks to the nape of her neck.

Slowly, she brought her hands together, clasping her fingers around the two stones, hoping to meld the tortured spirits she felt trapped inside. "Tell me," she intoned. "Tell me who did this to you?"

The breeze picked up. Stronger now.

The frogs lost their voice.

Even the crickets grew eerily silent.

Sol felt a cold needle of fear in her heart.

The rocks grew hot in her hands.

A tremor ripped through her body.

"Who?" she repeated as her skin prickled.

And then he came.

The figure of a man—dark and looming. His face was blurred as if he were masked, his voice muffled.

But she understood the meaning.

It whispered through her brain like a serpent's hiss:

"The consequence of sin is death."

And then a cold wind blew through her soul, and she cried out.

The wraith had disappeared and yet . . . she felt his breath, and by instinct, as if pulled by a spiritual magnet, she turned to face west. Deeper into the woods. Toward the swampland.

Somewhere in the darkness, she sensed evil lurking.

She stared into the night. "I see you," she said, but spied no eyes catching in the moonlight, heard no breathing.

And yet . . .

He was moving.

Quietly.

On measured footsteps.

The scent of blood in his nostrils.

On the hunt.

Chapter 21

Murmuring incantations, Jeanne LaRoux lit the candles on the altar, watching the charred wicks tremble with light, tiny flames casting shifting illumination on the grayed walls of the hut she'd constructed by hand half a century earlier. The boards were rotting here, so near the swamp, but this was still her sanctuary, where she connected with the spirits.

Whether they were good or evil.

One by one, the candles began to glow.

For power.

For wisdom.

For cunning.

There were dozens of them, all flickering quietly, tapers and pillars and votives stacked upon the altar where the bleached bones of sacred animals appeared to stare at her from dark, knowing spaces where once there had been eyes.

She loved them all.

Remembered them as living creatures.

Revered them in death.

A red-shouldered hawk with its wicked beak and wide, filigreed wings.

A snake, its flexible skeleton coiled.

An alligator's skull, missing a few crooked teeth.

And on the highest level, centered over the crossbeam, was the deer skull. A white-tailed buck, his antlers stretching wide over the altar below.

Jeanne LaRoux had known these creatures in life.

Felt their blood, slick on her fingers.

Tasted their flesh.

And now, honored them in death.

Once all of the candles were lit, she touched the tip of her match to the tinder in the age-old fire pit with its blackened ring of stone, a place she had come for peace and to pray for most of her seventy-odd years. This little hut was her sanctuary, her private place where only a few were allowed in, only those tortured souls who needed her guidance.

Around the perimeter of her shrine of glass jars and crystals she had gathered during her lifetime, the shifting flames made her humble little hut pulse with luminescence as she lit the incense:

Eucalyptus for clarity.

Dragon's blood and patchouli for inner spirituality.

Cinnamon for strength.

Closing her eyes, she sensed the planet ever-turning on its axis, felt a connection to the very earth.

And a disturbance.

Something moving.

Something duplicitous.

And evil.

A shudder ran through her soul. Her gaze shifted to the highest point of the altar. There, surrounded by flickering votive candles, was a framed picture of the Sacred Heart of Jesus. The picture was a gift from her mother, the Christian depiction of the Son of God with his visible flaming heart.

Jeanne, like her mother before her, believed in Christ.

Was she pagan?

Yes?

Heathen?

No.

Her skin tingled, and she knew the time had come. It was urgent that she bridge the great chasm between this world and that of the spirits. She watched smoke from her fire rise past the crossbeam to the hole in the roof, where she caught a fleeting glimpse of the dark night: clouds had gathered, a storm brewing, the spirits restless.

Softly, she whispered. "*Venez à moi*." Come to me.

She glanced to the open doorway where creatures beyond these rotting walls lived. Often, she'd caught the reflection of eyes always watching her—nocturnal creatures who inhabited the undergrowth, rabbits and opossums, otters and raccoons.

But there were also predators and spirits hidden in the darkness. Sometimes, the twin eyes of a bobcat or a coyote caught in the light before the beast scampered away. More often, an alligator's reptilian orbs reflected as it scuttled to the waiting swamp only feet from this small shack.

But none frightened Jeanne LaRoux, not like the malevolence that would soon arrive.

Slowly, she lowered herself on a pillow and sat cross-legged, took a calming breath. Steadying herself.

She closed her eyes, listening past the sounds of the lowland, the frogs croaking, the gentle lap of water nearby, and a soft breeze wafting through the cypress, all punctuated by the hoot of an owl, low and steady.

And more.

Quiet footsteps over the now-accelerated beating of her heart.

Le démon.

Approaching swiftly.

His evil presence moving as stealthily as a water moccasin through water.

"*Donnez moi de la force*," she whispered, praying for strength.

Beneath the worn cushion lay a weapon. A sharp little machete she had never before used. One she had hoped she would never need.

Her falchion.

Shorter than most, hand-carved by her great-grandfather, the curved, deadly blade of her unique machete would serve its purpose.

She heard the slightest scrape of leather upon the uneven boards that provided a walkway over the soggy ground.

Somehow *he* had discovered it. *L'être maléfique.* The evil being.

The air in the hut shifted.

Candles flickered.

And evil, like a black wraith, seeped through the open knotholes and spaces between the boards of her sanctuary.

He was here.

Calming her heartbeat, she slowly reached below the pillow, withdrew her weapon, and pushed herself upright. Though in her seventies, she was, and had always been, athletic.

"*Quitte cet endroit, diable!*" she hissed, before he stepped foot inside, "*et je pourrais te laisser vivre*."

Machete in hand, she eyed the doorway. Did he understand that she called him the devil? That if he left now, she would let him live?

Did it matter?

If he didn't know the translation, he surely understood her meaning.

For a heartbeat, everything quieted.

The frogs quit croaking.

The owl no longer hooted.

Bat wings stilled.

She gripped her weapon.

She would cleave him in half should he—

The demon himself flew into the room.

Dressed in black, his face in darkness, his eyes glittering, he growled, "Die, Sorceress."

She swung.

Hard.

The devil in black danced away.

She attacked again.

He twirled back to the other side of the fire, where his face was illuminated in gold, the flames reflecting in his eyes. She knew this monster. Dear Jesus.

He leapt over the flames.

She raised her weapon. Sliced downward. Felt her blade find its mark, only to glance away.

With an unworldly growl, he grabbed her wrist. Holding it in steely fingers. Bending her hand backward.

Pain screamed up her arm, the pressure pure agony.

She heard the snap of ligaments and then the brittle pop of her bones breaking as she dropped the falchion.

It clattered against the floor as she screamed.

"*Allez en enfer*!" she commanded, damning him to hell as she was forced to her knees.

"You go first!"

With his free hand, he picked up her largest amethyst crystal, the one with several polished points, the blessed rock she used for clarity.

For protection.

Its lavender facets sparkled.

She sent up a prayer.

Too late.

With bared teeth and evil gleaming in his eyes, he raised the sacred stone over his black-cloaked head.

"Die, heathen," he spat, his arm slicing through the air.

She cringed. Turned her head away.

Thud!

The amethyst smashed into the back of her skull.

Pain exploded behind her eyes.

Sheer agony ripped down her spine.

He let go of her wrist, and she fell.

"Now we'll see who goes to hell," he said, though his words were a blur, pain throbbing through her brain. She felt the warmth of her blood flowing and matting in her hair.

Suffering, she found her pride. She twisted her neck. Saw his image turn red as blood streamed over her eye. Still, she hurled her last words, damning him. "*Je maudis ton âme à tous les niveaux de l'enfer, pour que tu sois damné à jamais.*" Then, fighting the black veil of unconsciousness, just so that he understood, she spewed a curse in English. "I condemn your soul to burn in all the fires of hell forever!"

She thought she saw him flinch, just before she caught a glimpse of the knife he withdrew from a pocket. Its blade gleamed as if it were the soul of Satan.

With his lips pulled back in a rictus smile, he inched closer. The point of his knife pricked at her skin.

Thankfully, the gods were kind.

As blood began to flow from her throat, a curtain fell over her eyes.

Chapter 22

He was agitated.

And wounded.

That psycho-pagan bitch had cut him with her ridiculous weapon!

But then, he'd been foolish.

Prideful.

Again.

He slipped down the stairs and tried to find solace in his private workplace, his sanctuary, but the cut on his arm burned, and there were other problems as well. Not just the authorities; he could handle them and make them chase their own tails. But the reporter. That was another matter. She had no rules to follow. No laws that couldn't be broken. No code of ethics.

In the dimly lit room, he dumped out his bag, the glorious, shining stones catching in the weak light. These rocks should have delighted him with their sharp points, flat planes, and sparkling facets, but not tonight. Because of the pain, he couldn't truly appreciate them.

Later he would study their unique and dazzling features.

Now he ignored them and searched through his medicine cabinet, which he kept cool, as it was the spot where he held all the vials of blood, along with salve and bandages, old-fashioned iodine, and a few other herbs and medicinals. He'd collected them for years, and they'd come in handy.

He slipped off his shirt and examined the cut.

Not so bad, he decided. Nothing that a little antiseptic, salve, and a hidden bandage wouldn't solve. The flesh was cut, yes, blood coagulated over his wrist, but the wound was shallow, and when he flexed his hand and moved his fingers, everything worked perfectly. The pain was but a sting. The deeper wound was to his pride. He hadn't anticipated the old witch would be so spry, so deft, so agile.

He'd have to be more careful.

More humble.

And, he reminded himself, he would have to change his schedule. He had plans for those he would send to their maker, a time line that he hated to alter. But adjustments had to be made.

He tended to his wound, sucking in his breath at the sting of the iodine, as he carefully applied it. Next the salve, and then the small bandage that would be easily hidden beneath his clothing.

Tonight, there would be no music.

Tonight, he would bow down to necessity and polish a new stone. One he'd planned for much later in his agenda. He'd etch it with precision, let the blood of those who had been sacrificed stain it, and then he would put his new plan into action.

He sent up a prayer, placed several stones in the rock tumbler he'd retrieved from that thief Billy Huber, and waited, listening to the hum of the machine and the clatter of the rocks.

Despite the noise, the sound of his mother's voice came to him, just as it always did. "Have you atoned, son?" she asked. He ignored her.

But she persisted. "I know you're doing the Lord's work," she wheedled, "but taking a life is a sin."

He knew that. They'd been over this before.

"The first commandment," she said. "Oh, no, I'm wrong. It's the sixth, is it not?"

"It's not a sin if it's ordained by God," he said to the empty room and would not allow her perception of right and wrong to influence him. He *knew* that God had asked him for these sacrifices. The word had come to him as he'd asked for guidance. God had spoken to him. Over and over.

"And was it not a sin when you first took a life?" She was taunting him.

Once more.

And forever.

He'd thought that, once she was dead, he would never hear her voice again. That had been vanity. Her demise had only intensified her voice, causing it to be everywhere. While she was alive, he'd been able to escape her, but now there was nowhere he could be rid of her. She was with him always.

"Your cross to bear, my boy."

"Stop!" he screeched. "Just stop!"

He scraped back his stool and crossed to the stereo, switched it on. Nerves jangled, feeling as if he might jump out of his skin, he rifled through the records, his father's treasures, until he found an LP he thought could drown out her voice. With trembling fingers, he set the record onto the turntable and . . . dropped the needle. *Scrriitttch!* The needle skidded noisily across the vinyl, and it was all he could do not to scream. He couldn't ruin this, one of his father's prized albums from the early seventies.

Sending up a quick, quiet prayer, he tried again and closed his mind to his mother's taunts.

"Haste makes waste, boy. Can't you see? You're not good enough. You will never be good enough. Nothing you can do will ever be good enough."

Biting down on his lip, he carefully set the needle onto the spinning record once more and cranked up the volume. This time, over the continuous click of the tumbling rocks, the thunderous beat of Led Zeppelin's "Immigrant Song" echoed through his sanctuary. Seconds later, Robert Plant's howling scream shook the rafters and burned through his brain.

To no avail.

His mother's cigarette-rasp of a laugh was louder than it all.

"You'll never drown me out. No matter what you do, son, I'll be with you until your dying day."

Chapter 23

"It spit at me!" Chloe cried, dismayed. Nikki was holding her daughter, letting Chloe's feet balance on a fence rail so that they could observe some of the other animals at the stables where Phee took riding lessons. One male llama had obviously taken offense, laid his ears back, and hurled a wad of spit in Chloe's direction. "Icky!" Chloe proclaimed, about to burst into tears.

"You're okay." Nikki smothered a laugh as she swiped the bits of detritus that had landed on her daughter's shirt.

"Am not okay!" To her mother's horror, Chloe spat back at the animal, but by this time the llama had lost interest and was wandering toward a small herd of alpacas nearer the barn.

"Hey, no, honey," Nikki said. "We don't spit."

"The llama did." Chloe crossed her pudgy arms over her chest and glared at the offending beast, who had long forgotten her.

"I know. He was mad or scared or something." Nikki plucked her daughter from the railing. "Come on, let's watch the rest of Phee's ride."

"I hate him."

"We don't hate," Nikki corrected. She set her daughter onto the gravel path. "Let's go."

"I hate him," Chloe repeated indignantly. "He's not nice."

"Okay. You hate him. Now, come on."

Chloe threw one last angry glance through the rails at the offending llama, then followed Nikki into the covered arena, where the smells of horses—oil, leather, dung, and urine—mingled with the dust that was forever kicked up as the riders guided their mounts through obstacles and over jumps. The ceiling rose over twenty feet or more, thick crossbeams supporting fluorescent lights, while open-air windows allowed breezes to flow through the expansive space.

The arena was attached to the stables, separated by a short flight of stairs leading to an office and reception area with windows that overlooked the entire complex.

"There she is," Nikki said, once they were on the bleachers that lined one side of the building. She held her daughter so the girl could see over the barrier between the riding and viewing areas and Chloe could get a better view. Nikki pointed to the middle of the arena, where Phee, tucked low in the saddle, guided a sleek bay gelding over a jump.

"Ooh!" Chloe said.

"Isn't she doing great?" Nikki asked, but her attention was drawn to the instructor in riding top, breeches, boots. A small glittering cross was at her neck, a long, dark braid down the middle of her back. Annabelle Van Camp. On the sidelines, encouraging Phee, urging her on and praising her as she trotted, then cantered, the bay around the vast oval.

Just as Nikki had hoped.

Just as she'd planned when she'd offered to pick her niece up earlier in the day. "I'm taking Chloe to the park this afternoon anyway, so I may as well just grab Phee on the way home," she'd told Lily, who was grateful for one less errand.

"No argument from me," Lily had said.

Now, as Phee's lesson was finished, Annabelle approached horse and rider, then patted the bay's shoulder as Phee dismounted. "Great job," she told the girl.

"Thanks!" Phee, a little breathless, was all smiles.

Quickly, Nikki carried Chloe down from the viewing area, but at the sight of her approach, Annabelle visibly stiffened. "Looks like you had an audience," she said to Phee.

"Hi, Aunt Nikki!" Phee, her cheeks rosy, her eyes bright, waved to

Nikki and Chloe before taking off her riding helmet. "I'll be a few minutes."

Nikki knew the drill from her own days of learning to ride. After the lesson the rider was expected to take care of the horse, cooling him down and removing the tack, and seeing that he was comfortable. All part of the lesson.

"We'll wait," she said, as Phee was already leading the gelding through the long, wide hallway to the stables, the horse's hooves echoing as he followed. Chloe spied a speckled pygmy goat in an enclosure next to the main, barnlike doors and was distracted while Annabelle started for the half flight of stairs to the office.

Nikki flagged her down. "Hey," she called out, "I'd like to talk to you."

"I don't think so." Pausing, she lowered her voice and cast her gaze around to be certain she wasn't overheard, her single braid flipping over her shoulder, a horsefly buzzing around her head. "Archie said not to talk to you. Or . . . or to anyone."

"You didn't confirm that you were his alibi."

"I don't know what you're talking about." She tossed her head. The horsefly flew off, and Annabelle's snake-like braid settled back into place, down the middle of her back.

"On the night Mavis was killed."

"He already told you. We were together."

"Except for the time when he went to his house. To get some things, I think he said."

"But he didn't do anything! He just found her there. Look, I've got to go. I have another lesson in, like, ten minutes."

"And he never mentioned anyone who would want to do her harm?" Nikki asked, one eye on her daughter, who was pushing loose straw through the wire fencing to the goat.

"No," she asserted, more than a little defensively. "But no one liked her. Not even her own family."

"And not Archer?"

"What're you suggesting? Oh, crap! He didn't do it!" She rolled her expressive eyes. "God, haven't you been listening?"

"Did he ever mention Billy Huber?"

"Who?" she asked, seeming bewildered for a second. "Oh. That guy who got killed out on his farm? No. He told you that."

Another instructor was leading a tall, dappled gelding with a girl of about ten or eleven balanced in the saddle. Red hair poked from beneath her helmet, and as she passed, Nikki thought she recognized her. A classmate of Ophelia's possibly?

"Look, I really have to go," Annabelle said, as the big horse and rider passed. She took a couple of steps toward the door to the office. "Archie said to tell you to leave me alone or we'll . . . we'll call an attorney!" She gave a quick, sharp nod. Gone was the effusive, talkative girl in the hot tub. Now the friendly "I-mostly-go-by Annie" had been replaced by scared Annabelle.

Archer had obviously laid down the law.

"Just leave me . . . leave *us* alone!" She turned quickly and dashed up the five steps to the office, her boot heels ringing, a bell over the door tinkling as she dashed inside and yanked the door shut behind her.

Through the large viewing windows, Nikki could see her talking excitedly with a severe, fiftyish woman whose keen eyes looked over half glasses. Her hair was the color of steel and pulled back into a tight, small knot at the base of her skull, and her colorless lips were drawn into a hard, disapproving line. Nikki guessed she was a manager or supervisor or possibly the owner of the riding academy, and right now, she was staring straight at Nikki, her expression nothing less than hostile.

Great.

If it hadn't been before, her impromptu interview with Annabelle was definitely over. Too bad. Though Nikki had been more than happy to spend the afternoon with Chloe and take Ophelia to her riding lesson after school, she'd had an ulterior motive, planning to "bump into" Annabelle and press her about Archer's alibi on the night of Mavis's murder. She hoped to glean more information because so far she'd only come up with dead ends, which, she had to admit, probably included all of Mavis's exes as well as Archer.

Not really surprising, she thought, picking Chloe up again and walking out of the building toward the parking area where she'd left her Subaru.

But she was quickly running out of leads.

As were the police, as far as she knew.

Pierce had been working late, pressured by the powers-that-be in the department to locate the killer. Nothing seemed to be working for him as well. What she'd learned from the little conversation they shared was that no link could be found between the victims. No alibis had cracked, except for Archer Greenlee's, as he'd been protecting Annabelle. Also, there was some kind of glitch getting information from the lab about the blood on the stones left at the homicide scenes. So far, there had been nothing suspicious caught on CCTV footage, nor on any of the neighborhood cameras that, unfortunately, didn't include the Greenlees' secluded estate.

It was almost as if the killer was a phantom.

Which, despite the tales of haunted houses, ghost stories, and voodoo lore woven into Savannah's history, Nikki didn't buy. She didn't believe any of it for a second. She was, and always had been, a realist.

The killer existed.

He would be found.

Nikki just had to figure it all out.

Someway.

Somehow.

"By hook or by crook," she said under her breath as she reached her SUV. Her daughter, riding on her hip, looked at her quizzically.

"What?" Chloe asked.

"Nothing. It's silly," Nikki replied, but she wasn't really paying attention to the question as she spied a small woman just getting out of a large black pickup parked at the end of the lot. Her blond hair caught the rays of a dying afternoon sun as she made her way to a white Mercedes convertible.

Naomi Kittle.

Jamison's wife.

And the black truck was the same Ram crew cab that Nikki had spied on the night of Lara Kittle's sweet-sixteen party when she'd been searching for Pierce.

Then she realized the redheaded girl on the large dappled horse was Naomi's middle daughter. Shana. A classmate of Phee's. That's why Naomi was here. To drop off her kid. But she wasn't waiting for the lesson to end. As the truck took off, Naomi climbed behind the wheel of her white Mercedes and, within seconds, was following the pickup down the magnolia-lined lane that connected the stables with the main road.

"Odd," she said aloud, but this time Chloe didn't comment. She was looking at the field where the alpacas collected near a pine tree and the lone llama, her recent nemesis, stood a few paces off, his head raised, ears pricked forward, silently staring at the two vehicles disappearing around a corner.

Nikki thought about going after the two vehicles, strapping Chloe quickly into her car seat, ordering Phee into the car and hitting the gas, but her niece was nowhere in sight, and the truck and white car were already turning onto the main road. Both in the same direction.

By the time Ophelia did appear, lugging her bag of gear, both vehicles had long disappeared. Too late to follow. However, Nikki couldn't resist a stab at it. Maybe they'd pulled off a mile or two down the road.

After tossing Phee's riding gear into the back of the Subaru and ensuring that her niece was buckled in, Nikki drove down the lane a little faster than usual and turned onto the road in the opposite direction from the city. West. Into the sun.

"Where're we going?" Phee asked.

"Just a little side trip." Nikki adjusted the car's driver's side visor.

"Why?"

"For fun," she lied, then changed the subject. "So tell me, how was your lesson?"

"Good. You saw," Phee answered with more than a little pride in her voice. "I got Reggie to jump. First time . . . I mean for me. Reggie does it a lot with the more advanced riders."

"Right. Great job." Nikki glanced in the rearview to catch a glimpse of her niece, who was already taking her phone from her bag.

"I saw one of the Kittle girls, I think it was Shana, riding a big dappled horse and just going for her lesson."

"Oh, that was Fred."

"Fred?" Nikki repeated, still thinking of the man in the truck.

"Yeah, we call him Freddie. Beginners ride him."

Oh. Of course. The horse.

"So you know Shana, right?"

"What?" Phee glanced up from whatever was fascinating her on the cell. "Oh, yeah. Sure."

"She's in your class at school?"

"Uh-huh." Phee was nodding, but still studying the screen. "She started riding lessons later than I did, so she's in another riding group. The beginners."

"And her mother drops her off?" Nikki asked, one eye on the road, the other on Phee's reflection.

Phee lifted a shoulder. "I guess. Yeah, I think so."

"I saw Naomi there, but she left. Looks like she met a man in a big pickup. A black one."

"Maybe. I dunno." Phee was scrolling through her phone. "Yeah. I think."

"Has it been here before?"

"Uh, I don't . . ." Her eyebrows knitted as she thought. "I think so, but . . . maybe."

"Do you know who he is?"

"What?" She shook her head. "No. Shana and I don't really hang out. We know each other, but we're not really friends."

"Not friends?" Nikki asked, as she drove around several corners and past two forks in the road. No hint of either vehicle. Even though she'd known the chances were slim that she would discover them, she'd held out more than a little hope. "Thought you might be. Horse riders and all."

"No . . . I dunno. She's . . . I don't know." She met Nikki's gaze in the rearview. "Does it matter?"

"No. Of course not." Nikki let the subject drop and gave up the chase. No sense going any farther. She realized they weren't far from the Kittles' house, where only a few weeks earlier she and Pierce had been at Lara's sweet-sixteen party, on the day Billy Huber's body had been found. She drove past the long driveway to the home, but decided against it. What would she say? She had no excuse, and she had both girls in the car with her.

Another time, she told herself, turning at the end of the Kittles' lane.

The large house wasn't visible from the road; it was set back nearly a quarter of a mile, with thickets of pine and oak keeping the property of over fifteen hundred acres private. According to Pierce, Jamison's tract was only part of the original parcel owned by the Kittle family for generations. Pierce had mentioned that Harrison Kittle,

Jamison's father, had split the acreage between his five sons. Though Jamison had ended up with the house and the lion's share of land, the estate had to have been immense.

"Can we get ice cream?" Phee asked from the back seat, breaking into Nikki's thoughts. "I'm starving."

"Sure. As long as you don't tell your Mom and eat whatever we're having for dinner."

"Okay." Phee agreed quickly.

Nikki reminded herself that whatever Naomi was doing with the mystery man in the black truck was her own business. The guy could be her brother, or someone who worked for Jamison, or a friend of his. It probably wasn't a big deal.

Still, her curiosity was on high alert. She only knew the Kittles through Pierce, as he and Jamison went way back. From their freshman year in college, she thought, as she drove through low-lying farmland back to the city and parked just off of Reynolds Square. She then walked to Leopold's Ice Cream and stood in line with locals and tourists, all eager to try the unique and ever-delicious flavors.

Once inside, Phee ordered a cone of Chocolate Chewies and Cream, and Chloe chose her usual scoop of plain old chocolate. Even Nikki couldn't resist and opted for a Caffè Leopold, which was a shot of espresso over an ice cream scoop, in this case, Savannah Socialite, which was a blend of chocolates with pecans and bourbon-infused caramel. Not only was it divine, but it also reminded her of Mavis Greenlee, who had indeed been a Savannah socialite.

And was now dead.

The victim of a vicious homicide.

No. Make that the second victim.

Billy Huber was the first.

She only hoped that there were no more.

Chapter 24

"This is nuts!" Chalice Brown told herself as she steered her sister's older Chevrolet down the ruts of this narrow lane through the swampland. The Impala jolted and rocked over the sparse gravel and potholes, then shimmied over an exposed root. Worse yet, vines and limbs scraped the exterior, and the headlights caught in the eyes of a raccoon before it lumbered out of the way. Why had she listened to her sister, Dorothea? When had Dotty shown even the semblance of sanity?

And yet she'd been desperate, and here, far from her home in Detroit and while visiting Dotty, she'd caved on her sister's harebrained scheme, taking over her appointment with some kook who claimed to predict the future out here in the middle of no-damned-where.

Oh, sure.

And there in the car's headlights was the wooden gate with the no trespassing sign. Just as Dotty had told her. She parked and wished she'd worn boots, as the ground was soggy here, and it would only get worse, as the fortune-teller or seer or high priestess or whatever she was only did her readings in the middle of the effing swamp.

Why oh why had she listened to Dotty?

Well, the answer was simple, really. She *had* to know. Had to! Her life depended on it. At thirty-eight, she wasn't getting any younger, and she wanted marriage and a child. Hopefully before she crossed the Rubicon of Four-O, and time was getting short. But how had she let Dotty talk her into this fiasco? And at dusk? Wasn't that the time when all those nasty nocturnal creatures like bats and possums and, God forbid, snakes came out?

"Stupid, stupid, stupid," Chalice chastised herself as she felt in the pockets of her jacket for her phone, while trudging along an overgrown path. The flashlight app would come in handy as it got darker. And it would, she knew, feeling a little cold inside.

"This is a goddamned fool's mission," she said aloud as she swept her gaze from side to side. There were alligators in this part of the South and all kinds of snakes, like rattlers and cottonmouths and corals and, oh, good Lord, she didn't know what else. But nothing good, she knew that much.

Just keep moving.

She walked through the thickets of cypress and pine, tupelo trees and thorny blackberries, and tried not to notice the Spanish moss that floated, ghostlike, from the huge branches of the live oaks surrounding a small clearing.

She wouldn't let her imagination get the better of her, she told herself, as she noticed the cottage, if that's what you'd call it, and several smaller buildings surrounding the open area. All of the structures were dark, no light showing in any of the windows. A rocker moved on the porch of the cottage, pushed by the wind that stole through the surrounding trees and caused the hairs on the back of Chalice's neck to lift.

Just get on with this. Meet the fortune-teller, have her read your palm or look into a crystal ball or whatever, and get the hell out. You've come this far; no backing out now.

With more than a little trepidation, Chalice walked up to the door of the cottage and knocked sharply.

No answer.

"Hello?" she called, the sound of her own voice raising goose pimples on her skin.

She heard a few cackles and peeps from a small chicken coop, then answering low snorts and grunts near a long, low building that, she guessed, housed pigs.

Awesome.

Just freaking awesome.

A deserted pig and chicken farm in the near dark.

What the hell was she doing here?

She was about to turn around when she saw the faintest of lights past the shimmer of a waterline, and with the setting sun as a guide, she followed a well-worn path that led to the swamp's edge.

Ancient-looking boards formed a rickety bridge that spanned the brackish water to a small island of sorts, where a hut had been constructed. She heard the swoop of bats and told herself to keep calm as she stepped onto the bridge.

Don't go there. This is too weird.

So what if Jaiden never proposes?

Do you think talking to some witchy woman in the middle of the Georgia swamp is gonna change anything?

"No," she said aloud, but continued to move forward. She hadn't come all this way for nothing. She'd better just keep going. Finish what she started.

The old boards creaked under her weight, reminding her, like almost everything did, that she should lose twenty pounds—well, maybe thirty—but it wasn't happening tonight as the last, dying rays of sunlight pierced the branches of the thick cypress and tupelo trees growing right out of the water.

She heard a splash and nearly jumped out of her skin, only to realize it was a fish that had risen to the surface, trying to feed on the myriad of insects that were flying and buzzing around her.

If Dotty hadn't paid for her visit in advance, Chalice would never have come.

"You'll love it," Dotty had insisted. "I'm not kidding you. And you'll love Madam Jeanne. She's fantastic."

"Madam," Chalice had repeated. "Like the madam of a whorehouse?"

Dotty had laughed, throwing back her head. "Nothing quite so salacious."

"Just weird as shit." At that point, Chalice had taken a long puff off her e-cigarette and ignored her sister's wrinkling of her nose.

"I'm telling you, she's the real deal. Predicted I was gonna have a baby girl before I even knew I was pregnant with Marie! And then there was the time I won the lottery—remember that thousand-dollar scratch-off ticket? Well, Madam Jeanne had told me not three weeks before that I was gonna have some good luck! And that I was coming into some money, and oh, right before Mama died, you know? Maybe like a week or two before, Madam Jeanne said she sensed a dark cloud coming my way."

Chalice hadn't bought it. "How can you, a woman of faith, a Christian, believe all that nonsense, Dorothea?" she'd asked using Dotty's given name to add weight to the conversation.

"Because I think Madam Jeanne is touched by the hand of God," Dotty had answered sincerely. "There are all kinds of things we can't explain on this earth, Chalice, but we all know they're God's doing. He knows all."

Chalice had let out a huge cloud of vapor, and for once Dotty hadn't waved the mist away. "Is she God-fearing? Madam Jeanne, I mean."

"I don't know what she is, or what she calls herself."

"A witch maybe?"

Dotty had shrugged. "She, like you and me, is one of God's creations."

And so here Chalice was, in the middle of the damned swamp and feeling as if she were playing the fool in one of Dotty's ridiculous one-act plays, just as she had all through grade and high school. Which was just plain crazy. You'd think that at thirty-eight she might have wised up, but oh-the-fuck-no.

As she edged closer, she eyed the hut, if that's what you'd call it. Maybe a shack? Or a shanty? Whatever kind of handmade hovel it was, it was decrepit, the boards loose and gray, knotholes and gaps in the plank walls showing. In Chalice's opinion, the hut seemed to be close to rotting completely away, soon to be swallowed by this ever-darkening swamp.

Not one light showed . . . no wait, there was a weak orange glow that she noticed through the holes in the siding, but rather than urge her on, the eerie light gave her pause and made her insides congeal a bit. All the while, a damned voice in her head whispered that she was walking into danger.

Maybe she should just bail. Backtrack. Drive Dorothea's old Impala back to her, hand back the money Dotty had paid, and admit that she couldn't go through with it. Her older sister would mock her, but she was used to that.

But, damn it, Chalice *did* want some insight into the future. To find some validation that the six years she'd spent with Jaiden were worthwhile, that they weren't a lost cause.

"Hello?" she called out, her voice seeming to crawl over the water. "Anybody home?"

Of course not. This is not *someone's home.*

At least she hoped not. This place was too small. Too unlivable.

"Hello? Mrs. . . . er, Madam Jeanne?" Why did she feel so foolish calling out the name? No one was around. No one could hear her. And maybe that was the problem.

This whole setup was weird, and her nerves were on edge, tightening with every step she took. She wasn't easily frightened, but dusk in the swamp? Anyone would think twice. "I'm Chalice," she said more loudly and cleared her throat. "My sister, Dotty . . . she made an appointment."

The door to the place was just a dark space, like the opening to a tepee, the sides of the doorway slanted, and Chalice would have to bend to walk in. "Hello?" she said again and heard the tremor in her own voice. She smelled wood ash and cinnamon and eucalyptus.

She took out her phone. Turned on the flashlight app and stepped inside. "Anyone here?" She swept the phone's faint beam through the small space, where an altar was covered in candles that had burned down to nothing but pools of congealed wax. There were crystals everywhere reflecting the flashlight's beam, and in the center of the room a round fire pit, where a few glowing coals peeked from beneath charred logs. And over some of the rocks, a pool of dark red.

Drip.

Drip.

Drip.

Blood?

Oh. God.

A beam overhead creaked.

Chalice's heart stilled.

"What the—?"

Fear shafting through her, she shined her flashlight up to the rafters, past the macabre skeletons and skulls of dead beasts to the roofline and the crossbeam high above.

Hanging from the timber was a body.

A woman.

Her head was at an odd angle, her eyes bulging, blood staining her long dress.

No!

Chalice screamed.

Panic shrieking through her body, she dropped her phone.

Then she was running, her feet pounding over the makeshift bridge, her heart pumping wildly. She clambered over the bridge, the image of the dead woman chasing her.

"Oh, God, oh, God, oh . . ." Gasping, she sped across the clearing to the path. Breathing hard, she scrambled over brambles and vines, tripping once, then again before she got to the old Chevy. What the hell? What the . . . She threw herself inside the car, switched on the engine, and rammed the gearshift into reverse. Feeling as if Lucifer himself was chasing her, she pressed on the accelerator, the tires spinning, as she looked over her shoulder and expected some ghoul or axe murderer to leap out at her at any second.

Go. Go. Go!

What if someone was in the back seat?

She hadn't checked.

Or the trunk?

She'd left the keys in the ignition. Anyone could have gotten in and—

"Oh, please Jesus, if you're listening, help me," she prayed aloud.

Pushing on the accelerator, she kept reversing, swerving, driving like a bat out of hell down the long driveway, looking over her shoulder, the car bouncing and shuddering in the rutted lane. Branches scraped the doors and windows, tires hit rocks and potholes. She didn't let up, just backed through the gate, not slowing down as she reached the road. There she jammed the gear into drive and hit the gas to fly down the highway, the engine rumbling, tires humming.

That woman!

That dead woman!

That effing dead woman!

Hanging like that, neck crooked, eyes bulging, blood draining from a hole in her neck!

Spooked out of her mind, Chalice took a corner too fast, and the car skidded into the oncoming lane, where a pickup, heading in the opposite direction, nearly collided with her. She cranked the Impala back into her lane as the driver of the truck laid on the horn and flipped her off.

She barely noticed, just kept driving.

Faster!

Faster!

For what seemed like miles.

"Help me, Lord Jesus," she whispered, just as she spied a gas station at the next corner. With an eye on the rearview mirror, as if she expected to see the monster who had hung that poor woman like an animal carcass in a slaughterhouse, she hit the brakes and squealed to a stop under the fuel-island canopy, slamming the car into park. Without cutting the engine, she raced, stumbling into the mini-mart, where a pimple-faced kid in a uniform stared, gape-mouthed, at her.

"Call the police," she ordered, breathless and panting, feeling as if she were jumping out of her own skin. "Call them." When the kid didn't move, she pounded the counter, making a jar of pickles jump, "Right now! Call them! 911."

"But—"

"I said call them!" The kid, pale and staring at her as if she was out of her mind, backed up.

"Do it!" Chalice was frantic. "I just saw a dead woman! Hanging from a damned beam, in a hut out there in the swamp!" She gestured wildly to the tall windows that faced the gas pumps that were illuminated by the fluorescent lights and where Dotty's scratched Impala idled. She advanced on the kid and grabbed his shirt, bunching it in her fist. A plastic tag with the name Gary was pinned to his shirt. "Listen, Gary, if you don't call the goddamned police, I will." She dropped her death grip on his uniform, then spying the phone on the counter, snapped the receiver up.

The kid, terrified, backed up farther, probably to hit a security button or a camera or maybe to grab a pistol from under the cigarette counter. She didn't care. With shaking fingers, she punched out the number. "Don't even think about grabbing some kind of gun and shooting me," she said, and the kid froze, eyes wide beneath a fringe of dark hair. Chalice pointed to the vials of e-liquid near him with her free hand and motioned frantically at the vape juice. "And, and give me two of those—the caramel-vanilla ones."

"Wha—what size?"

"I don't care! Any size! Do it!" Chalice ordered.

The kid jumped as the 911 operator answered, and Chalice sank to her knees.

Thank the ever-lovin' Lord!

Chapter 25

"Looks like another one," Sol said, stating the obvious as she and Reed stared up at the corpse hanging from a crossbeam in this shack filled with all kinds of weird, religious artifacts, a mixture of Christian and pagan. Though they had not verified the cause of death, the hole in the dead woman's neck appeared consistent with the murders of Billy Huber and Mavis Greenlee. "I bet if we search hard enough, we'll find another stone with a number scratched into it."

"Lots of stones here," Reed said, eying what appeared to be an altar for the occult or some kind of fortune-telling or witchcraft, with all of the dead animal skulls, candles, and altar positioned around a fire pit.

"Crystals," Sol corrected, looking more closely at the stones reflecting the harsh light from the high-intensity lamps, "and some are missing. Or something is. Look on the top shelf. And then on other parts of the altar." Sure enough, there were spaces in the organized clutter, places where dust had been disturbed, evidence that things had once been positioned on the boards, outlines of other artifacts.

"And the woman who reported this?"

"In a car at the side of the road and completely undone."

"Don't blame her."

"Oh, here we go." Sol motioned to the digital photographer and the videographer. "Get shots of this." She pointed to the victim's hand, the fingers clutching a polished stone. "What'd'ya bet this is our killer's calling card?"

"In her hand?"

"Maybe he broke her fingers or waited for rigor to start to set in so that it would remain where he wanted it?" Her jaw tightened. "He's one sick son of a bitch."

Digital pictures were snapped, a video recorded the entire crime scene, the tech crew going over every inch of the space.

Once the body was taken down and examined by the assistant ME, Reed bent over the remains of the dead woman. With gloved hands, he carefully dislodged the polished stone, so like the others found at similar scenes.

"The number one," he said, studying the stone, carved on either side.

"But she wasn't the first."

He turned the stone over in his hand. "No, but let's hope she's the last."

Sol sent him a disbelieving glance. "Unlikely. Unless we find the killer before he strikes again."

"There could be more that we haven't found yet." He didn't like the thought of that, but it was possible that the killer had been at his work much longer, that other bodies had yet to be discovered. "Let's go talk to the person who found her. What do we know about her?"

"Other than she's scared out of her mind?" Sol bent over to leave the hut, and they started single file down the old boards that spanned this part of the swamp, heading toward a cluster of small buildings that, according to the county records, belonged to Jeanne LaRoux, seventy-two and, now, deceased. Sol had already checked with the DMV database, which noted the address of this parcel of land and offered a picture of the owner, which, of course, helped identify the body. "Jeanne was married to Albert LaRoux, but he's been dead a long while. They had one son, Granger, who is a charter fisherman and lives out toward Tybee."

"The victim? Was she ever in any trouble?"

"With the law? No. Once she was pulled over for plates being out of date." The property had been cordoned off, the buildings checked and secured. Whoever had killed Jeanne LaRoux was long gone and, if Sol was right, had taken items from the hut.

But this wasn't a robbery.

This was another homicide by the same murderer.

Using flashlights, they walked along the dark lane to the county road, where half a dozen police cars and emergency vehicles were parked. One deputy was posted at the gate, another in a car with the woman who had reported the crime, a person identified as Chalice Brown, who lived in Detroit and was visiting her sister in Savannah. Chalice claimed that, on her sister's suggestion, she'd gone to visit the dead woman for a psychic reading. Rather than learning of her future, she'd found Jeanne LaRoux swinging from the crossbeam of the hut.

Frightened out of her mind, Chalice had driven to the closest gas station and put a call into 911. That's where Deputy Tina Rounds had picked her up, called for backup, and met other deputies at the scene. Upon finding the body, they'd called it in, and that's when Reed was notified.

Chalice was put in the back of the police cruiser while her story was confirmed. Now, Reed tapped on the window of the cruiser, introduced himself and Sol, then asked if she would answer a few questions.

"I told the deputy everything I know," Chalice said in a rush, her eyes wide. "This is some scary shi—stuff. I mean it." She shuddered, but somehow pulled herself together as she slid across the seat. "If talking to you all will get me outta here faster, fine. Someone has to take me back to my sister's car," she added climbing out. "The Impala, it's back at that gas station with that little twerp of an attendant." Some of her fear was morphing into anger. "And I want my phone back. You find it?"

Reed nodded. "Forensics has it."

"And they're not giving it back?" she guessed, even more distraught. "Oh, Lord Jesus, I need my phone. And . . . and I need to get out of here. I should never have come. God knows, I shouldn't have come." Trying and failing to calm down, she began puffing frantically on an e-cigarette as she gave a personal account to Reed of how she'd come to visit Jeanne LaRoux, that she'd just wanted a quick glimpse into her future, and instead she'd gotten the fright of her life and had bolted from the scene as fast as she could. "I knew it was a mistake from the get-go, but I came anyway, and here I am. Now, I want my phone back and I need to pick up my sister's car! She's gonna be pissed as hell when she sees the condition it's in." And then she sighed. "Hell, she'll be more upset about that LaRoux woman. Dotty swears she is . . . she was the real deal, that she could predict the future." Chalice took a big hit, then blew out a cloud of scented vapor.

Reed tried a few more questions, but Chalice had said all that she could, so he ended the interview. "Deputy Rounds will drive you to the station, where you can give a formal statement; then someone from the department will drive you to your vehicle. And we'll see that you get back to your sister's. I assume Deputy Rounds contacted her."

"She let me use her cell phone. I called Dotty, and she's beyond upset." Chalice clicked off her e-cig. "Beyond!"

Reed didn't doubt it. "We'll need to talk to her as well. And anyone else who she might think of who knew Ms. LaRoux."

"If she knows any. From what Dotty told me, she was a bit of a recluse. She only was going to see me because of Dot." Chalice cast a wary glance down the lane, then rubbed the backs of her arms as if experiencing a sudden chill. "Weird shit going on here," she said with a shake of her head.

As Deputy Tina Rounds collected Chalice to drive her to the station, Reed's phone rang. He checked the screen.

Unsurprisingly, it was Nikki.

"Hey," he answered, walking away from the cluster of vehicles that was parked near the gate.

"Another one?" she asked.

"Maybe. Looks that way," he admitted.

"Jeanne LaRoux?"

"You know her?"

"Did a piece on her a few years back," she said. "Dear God in heaven."

"How did you find out?"

His question was met with silence, and he wasn't surprised. She never revealed her sources, including whatever leaks there were in the department.

"What do you know about her?" he asked.

"Just what I wrote. She's a widow who practices a unique kind of religion, part voodoo, part witchcraft, pagan stuff, but it also has a Christian bent to it. She reads fortunes and predicts the future, that sort of thing. I'll tell you all about it when I get there."

"You're not . . . Nikki, don't."

But she'd already disconnected.

Swearing under his breath, Reed started to call her back when headlights cut through the night. He looked up to see an older-model Ford Bronco grind to a stop on the gravel shoulder. The driver, a big, bearded man, jumped from behind the wheel. He was wearing jeans, a navy blue jacket that stretched over his large belly, and thick rubber boots. He slammed the door of his Bronco shut and, ignoring the cops and vehicles and flashing lights, strode straight toward the gate.

"Wait!" Reed caught up with him.

"I'm looking for my mother," the guy said and kept walking without so much as pausing, his big eyes wild beneath a fringe of dark hair and a baseball cap jammed onto his head.

"Your mother?" Reed repeated, then caught the guy by his elbow. "Stop," he commanded.

At that, the man finally halted and glared down at Reed.

"You said you were looking for your mother?"

"Yeah. That's right. She lives here." The big man was glowering down at Reed, but his eyes finally lifted enough for him to assess the other officers. "Wait a second. Wait a fucking second. What the hell is going on? Is she in some kind of trouble? I told her to knock off all that looking into the future voodoo shit." His eyes were on all of the police vehicles parked near the gate, the light bars strobing the night.

Reed took the opportunity to introduce himself. "Detective Pierce Reed."

"Detective?"

The guy blanched.

"I'm afraid I have some bad news—"

"Oh, shit . . . oh . . . God, no! No, no, no!" Shaking his head, he started for the gate again.

"Stop!" Reed's command rang out.

The man rounded on Reed. "Tell me she's okay! Tell me my mom is okay!"

"I'm sorry to inform you that—"

"Noooo!" The big man wailed, shaking his head as he fell to his knees in the ruts of the lane. He grabbed at his cap, ripping it from his head, digging his hands into his hair. "No! No! No!"

Reed waited, letting this man, Granger LaRoux, he assumed, let out his shock and anger and grief. A meaty fist hit the ground. Once. Twice. Then in rapid succession until, breathing hard, he raised it only to let it fall to his side. His burst of fury spent, he exhaled a long, shuddering breath. "I knew something would happen." Replacing his cap, he rolled onto his butt and sat on the ground, looking up at Reed from beneath the brim of the cap with a marlin stitched across the front.

"You need some help here?" One of the deputies stepped forward.

Keeping his eyes on Granger, Reed held up a hand. "I've got this."

He'd been in this awkward, painful position more times than he wanted to count, had dealt with grieving spouses, wives or husbands in denial, children who were frightened. Friends and neighbors who were shocked. Bereaved relatives who had accused him of lying, one heartsick mother who had crumpled in his arms only to stiffen suddenly and slap him across the face.

Grief came in many forms.

None of them pretty.

And sometimes it was a lie. But not, he thought, in this case.

Aware that a firefighter and two deputies were watching him, Reed crouched next to the guy. "Let's start over."

"I told you. I'm her son."

"Your name." Reed prodded, wanting him to self-identify.

"What? Uh, Granger LaRoux. My mom lives . . . oh, God."

"Just to confirm, who is your mother?" Reed asked, though this was just a technicality.

"Jeanne. Or, uh, Madam Jeanne, whatever she goes by. Don't you know that already? Jesus Christ, her name is Jeanne LaRoux, and she lives, er, lived, right down there!" Still distressed, he jabbed a finger toward the gate and the dark lane beyond. "The neighbor called and said there were cops all over this place. What happened?" In the eerie glow of the headlights and light bars, he stared at Reed as a car passed slowly by, rubberneckers gawking, a deputy waving them on.

"I'm sorry," Reed said, and he meant it. He stood and offered the big man his hand.

"Yeah. Okay." He sniffed. "You—you got a smoke?" he asked, wiping his eyes with the back of his hands.

"No, but . . ." Reed motioned to the deputy at the gate, who scrounged into a jacket pocket, then offered up a crumpled pack of Camels. Granger already had retrieved a lighter from his pocket, shook out a cigarette, and lit up with shaking fingers.

After a long drag, he cleared his throat and said. "So she's gone."

"Afraid so."

"Jesus." Another pull on his cigarette. "You know, when Dad died, I told her over and over again to move out of here." Another long hit of nicotine. And finally, in a cloud of smoke he asked, "So what happened? This," he made a gesture with one arm to include all the official vehicles collected at the end of the lane, "says to me that she didn't just die of a damned heart attack." Eyes narrowed, he stared at the array of police cars. "Holy shit." He sighed through his nose, smoke curling from his nostrils. "I told her it wasn't safe here."

"Why would you say that?"

"Why do you think? Hell, she's an old lady, living here in the middle of the fuckin' swamp, having all sorts of clients or whatever the hell you call them. Strangers. Weirdos, if you ask me. People who come looking for answers to their messed-up lives. They come out here, and she reads their fortunes? Sometimes at night? Some of 'em are just fuckin' crazy." He threw his cigarette onto the road and ground the butt out with the heel of his boot. "But would she listen?" He blinked rapidly, looked up at the night sky, and his lips folded in on themselves as he tried to compose himself.

"We'll need a list of the people she saw, especially anyone who would want to do her harm."

"Yeah, yeah." Granger nodded. "I know the drill. But I don't know who she saw. I mean the people who came out here looking for answers? It's not like they registered online and were on some kind of appointment chart or client list or anything. Most of 'em heard of her through other 'clients.' Locals. Word of mouth." He sniffed loudly and looked away, down the road, but was lost in his own thoughts. "Look, I want to see her."

"It's not a good idea." Not like this, not when she'd been found hanging from a crossbeam, blood staining her clothes, her eyes bulged, her neck broken.

Now, she'd been cut down and moved, zipped into a body bag, but it was still bad. Worse than viewing a cleaned body on a cold slab beneath a sheet.

"Don't you need someone to confirm that it's her?" Granger demanded. "Y'know, ID the body or whatever."

"In the morgue."

"No, man. No way." Granger shook his head. "I don't like morgues," he said. "They give me the heebie-jeebies."

Reed couldn't help but ask, "You grew up here, with your mom and her, um, 'clients' and all, but morgues make you anxious?"

"Morgues and hospitals and cops!" he said pointedly. "Mom was eccentric, or odd, and people thought she did some occult shit, but this was normal to me. What I knew. Morgues? Where they keep dead people on ice? That's not." He seemed to stiffen his spine as he gathered in a breath. "So—are you gonna let me see her, or not?"

Normally, Reed would have denied the man until the body had been taken to the morgue, but Granger seemed determined. He was reluctantly explaining how she was found just as the ambulance was pulling out of the lane. Reed flagged it down and watched as the EMTs stopped and allowed Granger inside. They unzipped the body bag. Through the open door Reed watched Jeanne LaRoux's son brace himself. He visibly paled and took in a swift breath before, beneath his scruff of a beard, his chin wobbled, and again he blinked against tears before stumbling out of the back of the ambulance and leaning against the front panel of Reed's Jeep.

"Who did this to her?" he said and fumbled into his pocket for the pack of cigarettes. "What motherfucker would stab her in the neck and . . . Fuck!" He lit the filter tip with shaking fingers, cupping the cigarette with his free hand as he drew in hard. "Son of a . . . goddamn!" Another drag and, a bit calmer, he asked, "Who? Who did that to her?"

"We were hoping you could help us with that. Give us a list of the people who might have held a grudge against her."

"Maybe one of those religious nuts around here. You know, the go-to-church-on-Sunday, holier-than-thou hypocrites who preach about loving thy neighbor and all that shit, but do anything they can against anyone who don't believe like them."

"Anyone in particular?"

"Nah."

"Who was it that let you know about the police here?"

"The neighbor."

Reed glanced up and down the narrow road and didn't see lights from a house anywhere near in this lowland filled with brush and trees. "What neighbor?"

"Childers. The guy who lives on the other road. To the west. He uses this one sometimes because his land backs up to here." Granger motioned to the woods on the far side of the road. "I went to school with his kid."

"Otis Childers?"

A neighbor of Billy Huber. Reed hadn't thought about it until now, but obviously the acres of the Childers' property sat between the two roads that ran somewhat parallel to each other, at least in this part of the county. The Hubers' place as well, and possibly the Wheelans'. Their parcels backed up to this road and though they sat shoulder-to-shoulder on the next road over, only scrub pine and weeds ran along the fence line on this road as the houses and outbuildings weren't visible. Scrub pine, weeds, and berry vines blocked any view of the houses and outbuildings that were accessed by the next road over. And yet they were all neighbors and lived in close proximity.

"He drove past, I guess. I don't know." He swiped at his eyes with the arm of his jacket.

"I could drive you to the station for a statement."

"Fuck, no." He sniffed loudly. "I can make it on my own." Frowning deeply, he glowered at the ambulance as it drove away, toward the distant glow of the city. "This is fucked."

With that, he jammed his Camel into the side of his mouth and headed toward his truck.

* * *

Nikki arrived at the scene just as the ambulance was leaving—and, with it, Jeanne LaRoux's body.

She spied the forensic team's van partially hidden by brush and parked on the other side of the gate. Had it not been for the temporary floodlights that had been brought to the scene, she wouldn't have seen it.

"Don't even think about it," Pierce said when she approached him as he stood with two of the deputies assigned to secure the area.

"About what?"

"Going down there." He hitched a thumb toward the overgrown lane that had already been cordoned off with crime-scene tape. She stopped but peered into the shrubbery, hoping for more than a glimpse.

"If I could just look around."

"And what? Come home with some rescue chickens and hogs?"

The joke fell flat. She was in no mood for any attempt at humor. She'd left the house as quickly as she could, right in the middle of Chloe's bath, when she'd heard the news from her contact in the department. She'd plucked her daughter from the tub, still filled with bits of foam from the bubble bath and a flotilla of toys that swirled slowly as she'd drained the tub.

She'd dried Chloe, put her in a fresh pair of PJs, and even run a comb through her wet curls before dumping her unceremoniously in Lily's room. "Do you mind putting her to bed in an hour if I'm not home?" she'd asked her sister.

"Where're you going?"

"Just out for a while. I'll owe you."

Lily had arched a disbelieving brow. "I'll add it to your tab. I take it there's another murderer you have to chase down."

"Shhh," Nikki admonished, glancing at her daughter, but Chloe wasn't interested in their conversation, not when there was Ophelia's unattended makeup vanity with its interesting bottles of nail polish and tubes of lip gloss shining beneath the glowing bulbs of the vanity's Hollywood lights.

"She's not paying attention."

"Good." She wasn't ready to explain to her toddler that both Mommy and Daddy were involved with solving murders or even what a homicide was. Nikki didn't even know when that day would come, but she hoped not for a long, long while and certainly not tonight. "Thanks. I'll be back as soon as I can."

"Sure. Oh, no, you don't," Lily said and shot out of her chair and grabbed Chloe as she was climbing onto the vanity's tufted stool.

Phee, who had been downstairs rifling through the pantry for a snack, climbed up the stairs and, spying the action through the open door to her bedroom, let out a squeal. "Don't let her!" she yelled. "Mom, don't let her get into my stuff! Chloe, don't you dare!"

Nikki raced down the stairs and out of the house before she could be pulled back into the drama.

And still, she'd gotten to the crime scene later than she'd hoped—so late, in fact, that, as she watched, a white news van emblazoned with the logo of a local station across its side, satellite dish visible, rolled to a stop as close as possible.

So much for exclusivity.

"Let's get out of here," Pierce said, eyeing the van as a reporter stepped from the passenger side.

"But—"

"I'll fill you in later."

"Promise."

"As long as you stick to our deal." His eyes met hers, and she nodded. "I'll be home in a couple of hours."

"Me, too," she said, and when she saw the questions in his gaze, she didn't elaborate, just climbed into her Subaru and drove into town. She wasn't going to let this moment pass. Lily had control of the house, and she had some research to take care of.

Let Pierce guess what she was up to

Chapter 26

Granger LaRoux was no hero.

He'd had more than his share of problems with the law.

As Nikki sat at her favorite desk in the darkened newspaper office, the computer monitor serving as her main light source, she went through his rap sheet to discover offenses including poaching and getting into bar brawls. The most significant charge was one filed by a girlfriend; however, it was eventually dropped. From what Nikki could piece together, the girlfriend had been the attacker, with a weapon—a screwdriver—that she'd managed to put through Granger's left hand.

As far as she could tell, Granger had no connection to Billy Huber or Mavis Greenlee, nor did they with his mother. Granger had some social media accounts, but the victims, oddly, did not.

Nor did Jeanne LaRoux have a criminal record. She'd been a recluse and had practiced some kind of mixture of religions, pagan and Christian, but hadn't been in trouble with the law or even been in a spat with any of her neighbors. Nikki had done a story on her in the past, and since that time, Jeanne LaRoux hadn't been in the news.

But someone had known about her.

And targeted her.

And murdered her.

"Who?" she said aloud, drumming her fingers on the desk as she thought. The newsroom was quiet at this time of night—just two techies, who manned the incoming feed from the Internet, making certain that the *Sentinel*'s website and social-media accounts were up to the minute—but everyone else was gone. She glanced at Fink's office, now dark, then turned her attention back to her screen.

What did a lone hoarder, a Savannah socialite, and an isolated woman who claimed to be a sorceress have in common? Why would someone target them? For a second, she considered the fact that their deaths might be random, but it seemed unlikely. The stones with their numbers were the connection.

But how?

And why would they be polished and etched on two sides with numbers in Arabic and Hebrew? What was the point of that . . . if there was one. She leaned back in her desk chair, ignoring the headache building at the base of her skull. She knew she was missing something, something vital, but then she didn't have all the evidence; she was driving somewhat blind. The police had more information, of course, and though she'd gotten more info than some other reporters, she felt hamstrung. And frustrated.

She was getting nowhere fast.

Shutting down her station, she dropped by the website area, where Effie Savoy was sipping from a giant-size coffee drink.

Effie, a sourpuss with ever-changing hair color, didn't bother to smile as Nikki approached. No surprise there; they'd never gotten along. They tolerated each other. Coworkers? Yes. Friends? Never.

"Anything new on the murders?"

Effie peered up at Nikki over the tops of her new glasses; the frames were pale green, almost the same shade as her hair.

"Couldn't you look it up yourself?"

"You get it first."

"What do you want?"

"Anything on the Jeanne LaRoux homicide."

Sighing, Effie set down her drink, her fingers flying over her keyboard. "Isn't your husband investigating? Why don't you ask him?"

"He's not here. You are."

"Fine." Effie typed in some information, and a news clip from the local station showed on the screen. A woman reporter in her late twenties was standing near the cordoned-off area of Jeanne's property and staring into the camera to report on "another local murder," saying that police hadn't discounted the possibility of a serial killer stalking the streets and the area around Savannah. Nikki noted that police were asking for the community's help, that if anyone had seen anything suspicious, they should call the authorities.

And blah, blah, blah.

"You could have found this yourself," Effie pointed out. "Oh, wait . . . looks like the story's been picked up in Atlanta." She paused, brought the information up on the screen. "They're calling the killer the Savannah Slasher. That's new."

Nikki read the data over her shoulder, and Effie, after a few more quick searches, said, "That's it. So far." She picked up her drink again.

"Thanks." Nikki headed outside, where the night was just starting to cool, a soft April breeze floating through the quiet streets. A few cars drove past the old brick warehouse where the *Sentinel* was located, headlights offering passing illumination, while crickets chirped from the steps and shrubbery.

Walking across the parking lot, she sensed, rather than saw, someone nearby.

And yet, at first glance, there was no one.

She glanced around, searching the area. Nothing.

Just your nerves, she told herself. *That's what you get for spending your days investigating murders and—*

Was that a footstep?

She whirled.

Reached into her purse.

Scrabbled.

Her fingers located her keys.

But she saw no one.

The parking lot was empty.

Still . . .

Nerves strung tight, she kept walking, her gaze moving around her. The brick building where the newspaper office was located loomed upward, some windows lit and a streetlamp on the corner offered soft, ethereal light. A few cars drove past.

The city was quiet.

Nerve-rackingly so.

All in your head.

No one else around. And yet, she felt eyes upon her. Unseen eyes.

Hairs on the back of her arms lifted.

The back of her neck tingled.

She started for her car again. Faster. Across the lot.

A footstep.

Crap!

She was almost to the Subaru.

More footsteps.

Faster.

Running!

A flash of movement in the corner of her eye.

A dark figure was racing toward her.

All in black. Head to toe.

Running fast!

She hit the door-unlock button.

The car beeped, and its lights blinked on, and in the darkness, she saw that the Subaru was already damaged, something scratched into the driver's side.

The rush of footsteps stopped.

She yanked on the door handle.

Saw her assailant haul back.

Something hurled through the air.

She ducked.

A rock the size of a baseball whizzed past her head.

Crash!

The rock hit the windshield hard and bounced back.

A thick web of jagged cracks sizzled through the glass.

"Hey!" Nikki yelled, her heart jumping.

The dark figure took off.

Fast.

No longer running at her, but away.

"Hey!" she shouted again, moving forward, telling herself that if he had a gun, he would have already shot at her. "You! Stop!"

Too late.

Whoever it was darted through the row of untended shrubbery

separating the parking area from the street. She followed, running, hurrying to catch up, her eyes on the spot where he'd disappeared between a copse of live oaks and crepe myrtles.

Be careful, she warned herself, heart pounding, her gaze scouring the thicket, but coming up empty.

A car rolled past, and she caught the glint of metal as light swept across the building face and shrubbery.

In that second, she saw movement, something glinting. Instinctively she crouched. Her attacker appeared on the far side of the hedgerow.

On a bike.

She raced forward, but it wheeled away, furious pedaling giving way to the smooth hum of an engine as the attacker engaged the electric bike, sped up, and disappeared around a corner. "Damn." She ran back to her car, hopped in, and took off after him. Visibility was inhibited by her ruined windshield, but she drove fast, into the street and down the alley into which he'd disappeared. At the far end, past the dumpsters and parked cars, she came to a cross street. One way. Not that her attacker would have cared.

But she saw no hint of the bike in either direction.

She drove carefully along the street, but saw nothing out of the ordinary. No one riding a motorized bike through the historic district, no bike left unattended.

What she did see, as she passed by a glass storefront that reflected weakly from a streetlamp, was an ugly message gouged into her passenger door in huge letters:

COP KILLER

Her heart froze.

Guilt cut through her soul.

The letters were jagged and uneven.

But the meaning was clear.

This wasn't a random act of violence.

Whoever had done this was targeting her.

Just as was done in the parking lot.

For Sylvie Morrisette's death.

"Got it," she said under her breath as she turned a corner and drove home.

Once home, she showed Pierce the damage, and he swore under his breath. "It's Toby."

"Toby Yelkis?" A hard knot formed in the pit of her stomach as they stood in the garage beneath the harsh fluorescent lights. The gouged paint looked far worse here than it had when she'd caught just a glimpse of it in the reflection of the storefront.

"Who else?"

"I don't know, but there are tons of other people," she argued. "Anyone in the department, for starters." She didn't want to believe that Sylvie Morrisette's son was behind the damage, that he was so broken, so angry that he would take a knife or key or screwdriver to her car. Her heart ached for the kid, and she argued in his defense, even though, deep down, she conceded Pierce was probably correct.

"Doesn't look like the kind of thing someone I work with would do." He looked at her with a "Come-on, Nikki, get real" expression.

"Well then, how about friends of Morrisette or other family members?"

"Priscilla? She's in college. Lives downtown."

"No, no, not her daughter," she said, knowing he was baiting her. "But—think about this—what about her sister? You said she had a sister."

"And two brothers, all who live far away." His troubled gaze held hers. "They wouldn't."

"Well, then maybe one of her ex-husbands? How about Bart, the father of her kids? She thought he was the worst."

"Too juvenile, even for him. For any of them. And they all are in Texas, just like that song. Except for Bart. But why would Bart take the risk?"

"Because he's unhinged," she argued, though it was a losing battle. She was arguing against herself.

Pierce shook his head, his dark hair glinting in the overhead lights. "Believe me, there was no love lost between Sylvie and her ex. They fought all the time. He wanted custody, and now he has it. Along with the death benefits. When she died in the line of duty, he lost a thorn in his side, gained his kids, and made out like a bandit.

Win. Win. Win. Nope, not Bart. You and I both know it has to be Toby."

"I don't want to think it," she finally admitted, not wanting to dwell on the pain the boy had endured, pain she'd caused.

Crouching down, Pierce touched the offensive letters, studying them, then looked up at her. "I've been reaching out to him, trying to help. To say he's rejected me would be an understatement. I even offered for him to live up there." He motioned toward the ceiling, above which was the attic over the garage that they'd been converting to office space bit by bit.

"What?" she asked, more than a little taken aback. "You didn't want another dog, but you'd take in an angry teenager with a serious grudge against us—or at least me?"

"Don't worry. He wasn't interested. But you're right. Toby's angry. Really angry. With you. With me. With the whole damned world. Ten to one, he did this."

She still didn't want to buy it. "But Tom Fink's car was vandalized just recently, too. Someone scratched MAN-WHORE into his Corvette. Would Toby do that? Why?"

"Don't know."

"But . . . it's reaching to think that there are two vandals out there doing the same thing at the same time."

"Both messages are personal," Pierce pointed out, straightening, but still eyeing the car and its damage. "Not just obscure or random graffiti like you'd expect from a gang or a bunch of kids out for some kind of thrill. I don't like it, Nikki. You could have been killed or seriously hurt."

"I don't like it, either, but I don't think he was aiming for me." She'd replayed the scene over and over in her head. "I assume he was aiming for the car. It seemed that way. And the reason I'm calling him a male is because of the way he threw the rock. He looked like he knew what he was doing. Like he'd practiced a lot."

"Like maybe a kid who played baseball?"

"Yeah . . . It was hard to see, but that was the feeling I got. Growing up, I played catch with my brothers, and they'd always throw the ball hard, trying to knock me over. That's what it felt like."

"Don't suppose you kept the rock or whatever it was that hit the car?"

"Didn't think about it."

"Could have had fingerprints."

"Maybe," she said aloud, but thought back to the fleeing figure dressed in black. "I think he was wearing a ski mask and gloves." She paused. "He threw left-handed."

"Did he?" Pierce's face darkened, and he swore under his breath. "Toby was a pitcher for the JV team. Ambidextrous. Could throw left-handed."

"He didn't play varsity?"

"Quit." His eyes held hers.

"Because of his mother's death," she said and felt terrible all over again.

Pierce exhaled a long breath, stared up at the ceiling and ran stiff fingers through his hair. "I made a promise to Morrisette," he admitted, then added, "but there's nothing we can do tonight." Once more, he surveyed the damage to her Outback, which looked ready for the junkyard parked next to Pierce's gleaming Cadillac. "I don't want you driving around in it."

She let out a laugh without any humor. "So you're going to let me drive the Caddy?" she said, tapping his vintage car's hood.

"We'll see."

"No—just kidding." She couldn't imagine driving around in the huge vehicle. It would draw more attention than her vandalized Subaru. And she needed stealth and anonymity, to blend into the woodwork for what she planned on doing in the next few days. "I'll get a rental." Something innocuous. A vehicle that no one, not even her husband, would notice.

She caught Pierce's eye and imagined he could read her mind, so she determinedly shrugged off all her concerns about the car, at least for now. Heading into the house, she was immediately greeted by Mikado and Arlo, both dogs acting as if they hadn't seen her in days as they wriggled and twisted, demanding attention and generally getting in her way.

Chloe was seated on the floor in the middle of the family room, where the TV was on mute, Lily on the couch with a book. Chloe looked up from surreptitiously playing with Phee's forgotten Barbie dolls, then quickly clambered to her feet and ran across the room.

"I thought you'd be in bed, fast asleep," Nikki said, sweeping her daughter off her feet, only to be ignored. Chloe leaned away and stuck out her arms to Pierce as he came inside.

"Daddy!" she cried, excitedly.

Nikki grumbled, "Traitor," as she passed the toddler off to Pierce, who twirled her around. Chloe giggled wildly, while Arlo, thinking it was a game, spun in circles beneath her, his tail wagging wildly above his rear end, where his fur was trying to grow back over his wounds.

"She had a fit about going to bed tonight," Lily explained. "Trust me, I tried. *Everything*."

"So you just let her stay up?" Nikki asked.

"I can only take her crying so long. Besides it's only been a couple of hours."

And we'll pay for it tomorrow, Nikki thought, noting that the TV was tuned to the news and a reporter was standing in front of Jeanne LaRoux's lane, inaudibly giving off the few details about the homicide, all of which were showing in closed captions, all of which Nikki already knew. Lily pointed the remote at the television. "I assume this is what kept you both." The screen flipped to a picture of Jeanne LaRoux, larger than the two other photographs that flanked hers. One was a very unflattering mug shot of Billy Huber, the other a posed headshot of Mavis Greenlee.

"Still trying to piece it together," Pierce said, as he set his daughter onto the floor.

"You, too?" Lily asked her sister, then, before Nikki could respond, added, "I don't know why I even asked; of course you are." She stretched to her feet. "Phee's already upstairs, finishing homework, I hope, but probably on her phone. I'm going up to play the role of drill sergeant." Motioning to Chloe, still in Pierce's arms, she added, "You can try to get little Miss Fussy Pants up to bed."

"Am *not* fussy pants!" Chloe said petulantly.

Lily smothered a smile. To Nikki, she said, "She's all yours."

"And I love it." Nikki snagged Chloe from her husband, then nuzzled the little girl's neck, while Pierce quietly explained about the vandalism and Lily took a quick trip into the garage to see for herself.

Upon returning, she looked at her sister. "Someone doesn't like you very much."

"Whoever it is, they can join the club. It's not all that exclusive." Nikki had made more than her share of enemies while investigating some of the most heinous crimes in the area, but she couldn't dwell on that now. She touched her daughter on the tip of her nose. "Come on, let's take these Barbies up to bed."

Once upstairs, she sat in the rocker, cuddling with Chloe and a blond Fashionista Barbie, a Black Barbie with an Afro, and a half-naked redheaded Barbie in pigtails. As Nikki read *Goodnight Moon* for the kazillionth time, Chloe started drifting off, and the redheaded doll fell out of her arms. By the time Pierce walked into the room and told her there was cold pizza in the fridge, their daughter was fast asleep.

The transfer of Chloe from her arms to Pierce's didn't quite go as planned as the little girl, groggy, half woke and started crying about the doll that had fallen, that she couldn't reach it.

Nikki headed downstairs, where she warmed up a couple of slices of pepperoni, added tomato, then carried the makeshift pizza dinner, along with a bottle of Dr Pepper, to her office. She paused on the second floor to hear her husband trying to cajole their stubborn daughter back to sleep.

Good luck, she thought, as there were nights when Chloe, exhausted as she obviously was, refused to settle down. Tonight, it was Pierce's problem, she reminded herself, as she climbed the spiral stairs to her office.

Once in her chair, she alternately took bites from the pizza and read through her notes. Arlo had followed after her and spent a couple of minutes adjusting the toys and blanket in his dog bed before he tucked in, nose to tail, and began to softly snore.

Fink wanted another story, so she pulled up the article she'd written about Jeanne LaRoux from years before and tried to figure out how to bring it back to life, a new angle, with updated information, if she could find it.

Maybe an interview with whoever had found her?

A client—if she could find one.

Or possibly something more in-depth from Granger?

Or what about Archer Greenlee? No, scratch that. He wasn't exactly the grieving widower. He wouldn't talk to her. Nor would Annabelle. Archer had seen to that.

She came back to the simple question: Who gained from the deaths?

Billy Huber's daughter, Janelle McGowan, possibly, if there was any value to his estate. Or possibly his brother, Robert, in payment of the loan Billy had reneged on. But his property was mortgaged and not worth much at that.

With Mavis Greenlee's death, Archer was the big winner. No divorce; he would probably inherit all of her estate, and he was free to be with Annabelle.

She tapped her fingers on the desk and thought.

Though it was unknown about Jeanne LaRoux, it seemed likely that her only son would inherit. But unless there was life insurance, her estate wouldn't be worth much.

Not enough to kill for.

Or was it?

But, even so, that didn't explain why they all were murdered. There wasn't one single person or entity who would benefit from the three deaths. At least not one she'd uncovered.

Yet.

Leaning back in her chair, she considered the All Christian Church connection, but it was thin. Too thin. Mavis had been a parishioner and active in the church, but Billy Huber was far from churchgoing. So he had a collection of Bibles. So what? He had a collection of everything. It was true, Linda-Sue, his wife had been a member, but that had been years ago.

As for Jeanne LaRoux, she'd been raised as a Catholic, but practiced a weird blend of voodoo, paganism, and Christianity that seemed unrelated to the other victims. And it didn't connect her to All Christian and Westin Stark.

So, another dead end.

She finished the pizza and wiped her hands on a napkin. Arlo raised his head, as if hoping for the last scrap of pepperoni, but she'd eaten it all. Leaning back in her chair, she glanced out at the moonlit night; then her gaze landed on a map of Savannah and the surrounding area. On a whim, she brought a similar map up on her computer, one from the county, and enhanced it by adding in the victim's houses, where each had been murdered.

It would have been easy enough to find Billy Huber alone. He had no friends or family nearby.

As for Jeanne LaRoux, she, too, was a loner.

Not so, though, Mavis Greenlee, who lived within the city limits of Savannah. Yes, her house had been protected from view from the street, and the neighbors, too, were at a distance, separated by thick foliage. But she didn't live alone. At least not all the time. Archer might have had his lover tucked away on Tybee, but he ostensibly had lived with his wife, though, of course, who really knew?

The thing she did notice on the map was that Jeanne LaRoux's property was not far from the acreage belonging to Billy Huber—it was just across the road, in fact—though Huber's property was accessed by another road, parallel to the one that ran past the LaRoux acreage. The Huber farm was only buffered from the LaRoux place by a strip of land owned by Otis Childers, a piece that ran the width of the Hubers' place and butted up against the Wheelan property.

Was that something?

She dug through the county records and discovered that, eight years earlier, Childers had bought the parcel from Huber, the reason having to do with water rights, as far as she could determine.

She thought about Otis Childers and his wife, Daria, and wondered if the sale of the property was before or after Billy had ogled the wife and Childers had come at him with his grandfather's shotgun.

Did it matter?

Probably not. She was grasping at straws, and it was nearly midnight.

Aside from Arlo softly snoring, the house was quiet as she carried her plate and glass to the kitchen and left them in the sink. Passing by Pierce's study near the bottom of the stairs, she heard the muted click of computer keys. She knocked softly on the door and poked her head inside.

His back was to her, but he said, "I'll be up in a minute."

"I just have a couple of questions."

"Wife questions or reporter questions? No, wait, let me guess."

"We haven't discussed what happened to Jeanne LaRoux."

His shoulders stiffened.

She reminded him, "We have a deal."

He clicked off his computer and turned to face her. She thought he might argue with her, but his face relaxed. "Okay. But what I've got is strictly off the record." His gaze met hers. Held. "Right?"

Holding up a hand as if she were taking an oath, she nodded. "Right."

"Victim of homicide," he said and went on to explain that LaRoux had been found by a would-be client and that she was hung from the crossbeam over a fire pit in her own sanctuary, clutching a polished stone with the number 1 carved into it. Like the others. Hebrew on one side, Arabic on the other. "The numbers are significant," he told her. "We just need to find out why."

"Did you know that the back of the Childers's property abuts the road leading past the LaRoux place?"

"Granger told me," he said, nodding, and then once more stated that everything they'd exchanged was off the record.

Nikki tried to learn more about Jeanne LaRoux's death, but Pierce had limited answers.

"You're holding out on me," she charged when it was evident she was getting no more information.

"I'm telling you what we know for certain. No hypotheticals. No guessing."

"You don't trust me!"

His eyes narrowed a bit. "Put yourself in my position for a minute, would you? I know where you're coming from. You've got a pushy editor to report to as well as an agent who seems to be salivating for your next book. That's it. But I have protocol. And a chain of command to report to, as well as an investigation I can't compromise.

"Now the Feds are involved. It's looking very much like there's a serial killer here in Savannah again. So the FBI is taking over."

"But you'll still be investigating."

"Yes. In conjunction with the Bureau. You know how it works, Nikki. Everything has to be done by the book. I can't be confiding in my wife, the journalist, no matter how much I trust her."

"I can help!"

He shook his head. "Just think how it looks."

"It doesn't matter. If I can help."

"After what happened last time?"

Morrisette. She closed her eyes. Remembered that horrid day on the river.

"I'm sorry," he said and stood, folding his arms around her. "But this is the way it has to be. The way we play it."

Though a part of her itched to escalate the fight, to make him see her perspective, to force him to understand that she was just trying to help, she bit her tongue. She would have to run her own investigation around him. It wouldn't be easy, but it could be done, and breaking off his embrace, she said, "Fine," but didn't mean it.

Leaving him watching her, she headed back upstairs, not to their bedroom, but again to her office, where Arlo was still dozing. She plopped down in her chair with enough force to cause it to roll back and hit the edge of the dog bed.

The shepherd was instantly awake, on his feet, hackles raised. He emitted a sharp, low growl. A warning.

"Shhh. No, no, no! It's okay," she whispered and patted his head, calming him. "No barking." The last thing she wanted was to wake up "Fussy Pants." He turned dark eyes up to look at her as she stroked him. "That's better. Go back to bed." With a slow wag of his tail, he curled up again, and Nikki was left stewing over the same questions that had plagued her for the past three weeks:

Who would commit these heinous murders and why?

If Pierce wouldn't help her figure it out, she'd damn well do it herself.

Chapter 27

The call came in at 5:47, according to the digital clock glowing on the bedside table. Jamison Kittle's voice was rough, stretched thin. "I need you to come to the house," he said as Pierce, half-asleep, levered himself up on one elbow. It was still dark outside, and Nikki was breathing deeply next him, her hair falling out of the high ponytail she often wore to bed, one of her arms thrown across his chest.

"Now?" he whispered, carefully removing his wife's arm with his free hand. She sighed in her sleep and rolled away.

"As soon as you can get here."

"What's wrong?" Pierce slipped out from under the covers.

With his phone pressed to his ear, he padded barefoot down the stairs to his office, where he quietly shut the door.

"It's Naomi," Jamison said. "She's missing. Didn't come home last night."

"What?" Pierce was finally awake. "What do you mean, 'didn't come home'? Where was she?"

"I don't really know. Out with friends, I guess. Anyway, that's what she said." He sounded distressed. Worried. "Look, just get here. Okay?"

Pierce blinked. Rubbed a hand over his eyes. "I'll be there in half an hour."

He cut the connection, hurried upstairs. Took a quick shower to clear the cobwebs. He didn't bother shaving, just toweled off and, in the bedroom, threw on a pair of jeans, a long-sleeved T-shirt, and socks.

Nikki was awake and had scooted up to the headboard, removing the scrunchie holding her hair away from her face.

"What's going on?" she asked, eyeing his clothes and, he guessed, noting he wasn't wearing his usual running gear.

"I'm going out to Jamison's." Sitting on the foot of the bed, he started putting on a pair of running shoes and noticed a striped paw reach from under the bed to try and snag a lace. Jennings, who seemed to have finally accepted the new interloper and was back to his old tricks. Pierce yanked the shoe away.

"Why?" Nikki asked.

"Not sure, but he asked me to come over," he lied, thinking it better not to pique her overactive interest. "I'll let you know when I get back."

"But—?"

"I'll fill you in," he promised, though he'd only tell her what he could, once he found out what was going on. No reason to worry her unnecessarily. Though Naomi and Nikki weren't really close, she would still be concerned, and before he said anything to anyone, he'd hear what Jamison had to say.

"Wait a minute."

"I'll call. Promise," he said, as she threw back the covers, causing Arlo to lift his head from his dog bed under the window, then clamber to his feet.

Pierce was already out the door, unwilling to lie any further or get into it with her. They'd had an uneasy truce for the last couple of days, ever since they'd argued in his office about how much he would divulge to her.

He backed the Jeep past his Cadillac and the rental Nikki had procured two days ago, a white Nissan Rogue, and nearly hit Lily's Toyota, as she'd parked a little too close in the driveway.

Swearing beneath his breath, he drove out of the city limits. Naomi just hadn't come home when expected. That wasn't cause for extreme alarm. She could have gotten hung up somewhere, and maybe her cell phone wasn't charged.

Maybe.

Except that Jamison wasn't one to overreact.

Pierce only hoped there was an easy explanation for Naomi not showing up. Better yet, he thought, if she'd already returned after Jamison had called.

Dawn was just streaking the sky as he turned into the Kittles' long lane. Shades of magenta and lavender streaked across the fields and forests of the Kittle acreage. Jamison, the oldest of the five brothers, was considered the patriarch of a family that had been at the forefront of Georgia politics for generations. Like his father and grandfather, Jamison had his eye on a judgeship and then, potentially, running for governor, though, as a matter of record, he'd never admitted as much to the press.

It was just common knowledge.

And now his wife, a beauty queen, once-upon-a-time runner-up for Miss Georgia, and daughter of another grand old Georgia family, was missing.

Maybe.

Pierce still wasn't convinced as he drove over a slight rise to view the Kittle complex, dominated by a two-storied home, painted white, black shutters framing tall windows and French doors that opened to a wide, wraparound porch. The white siding reflected the colors of the sky as the sun peaked over the eastern ridge.

He'd been here often, of course, usually either at the Kittles' annual Fourth-of-July barbecue or Christmas Open House, where Naomi insisted everyone wear "holiday attire." She, if nothing else, was the consummate Southern hospitality hostess.

And now she was missing.

He drove around the house to the parking area in front of a six-bay garage and cut the engine. Before he got out, the garage side door swung open, and Jamison called, "Come on in this way," waving him in to a spotless kitchen where a bouquet of cut flowers dominated the island and a coffeepot was gurgling on a side counter.

The house was quiet. Not a sound other than the final hiss from the coffeemaker and the soft hum of the refrigerator. It seemed odd, out of sync, but then Pierce realized he'd never been here when the home hadn't been swarming with activity.

"Coffee?" Jamison asked, already pouring Pierce a cup.

"Sure."

Jamison looked like hell, something else that was out of the ordinary. His hair was uncombed, he hadn't yet shaved, and he was wearing pajama bottoms and a T-shirt. Noticing Pierce surveying him, he admitted, "I haven't slept all night. I've been up, waiting. Calling. Not just her phone, but all of her friends." He handed Pierce the mug. Dark circles were visible under eyes that weren't as clear as usual.

"Are the girls still in bed?"

Jamison shook his head. "They're with Roxanne, Naomi's sister. They're staying with her for the weekend. Thank God. I'd hate for them to come bouncing down the stairs and ask about her." He glanced toward the staircase, visible through an archway. "Come on," he suggested after filling his own cup with coffee. "Let's go into the den."

He was already through a broad archway and down the two steps to the expansive game room with its high ceilings, oversize television, and huge leather sectional. The pool table was to one side of the room, a poker table in the corner. The last time Pierce had been here, the room had been filled with teenagers for Lara's sweet-sixteen party, a few weeks earlier. Hip-hop music had blasted from the speakers, barely audible over the din of kids talking and laughing and pool balls clicking.

Now it was quiet as a tomb.

Two pool cues lay crossed on the green felt, the balls racked on the table.

The poker table was polished, a carousel of chips at its center, each sleeve-like compartment holding a separate color of poker chips.

Covering two walls, the weaponry stood in place, polished and locked behind spotless glass doors in lighted display cases. Neat racks of hunting rifles, bows and arrows, and shotguns shined from their racks, while the heads of trophy kills were mounted high overhead.

Everything was neat, including the perfect stacks of coasters on the end tables.

Tidy.

Nothing out of place.

Except for Jamison's missing wife.

"Tell me," he said, as Jamison waved him onto the sectional. "What happened?"

Jamison sank heavily into the cushions on the other end. "I wish I knew. This was supposed to be a weekend alone for Naomi and me. Our anniversary is next week, so we shuffled the girls off to her sister's house—well, actually Naomi took them up to Charleston last night. It's a three-day weekend for the kids—some kind of teacher in-service or something. I don't really know. Naomi keeps track of all of that, the kids' schedules and all."

Pierce believed that. Jamison was nothing if not a workaholic. Many times when Pierce had worked late, he'd seen lights in Jamison's office, and often, in the morning, Jamison was the first one in the department, after going for a morning run or hitting the gym.

Type A didn't begin to describe Jamison Kittle.

But not this morning.

Today he was a mess, unshaven, his face drawn, dark circles under his eyes.

"Anyway," he said after taking a swallow of coffee, "even with everything going on with the homicides, I agreed that we should spend time alone together. I suggested we go somewhere. Like, Bermuda or the Bahamas, really get away, but she didn't want to do that." He stared into his cup as if he could find answers in the dark liquid. "She said if we went away, we should take the girls, that we didn't have that much time with them, as Lara would . . . Lara would graduate in a couple of years." He thought for a second, lost in thought.

"So?" Pierce encouraged.

"So we decided to have a 'staycation.' Just stay home. I guess it's a thing now." He paused and sighed. "And, if I'm being completely honest, the time alone was for another reason. We wanted the privacy. The fact is that we're trying for another baby." His smile was without humor. "Hoping for a boy. An heir, I guess."

When he saw Pierce's raised eyebrow, he nodded. "Yeah, I know. It's old school. Out of favor. I know it. Still, it's the way my family has worked for generations. Don't get me wrong. I love my daughters. I'd do anything for those girls. Anything. You know that. They're the best. So don't give me any grief about being a misogynist. It's just my family tradition, and, the truth is, I'd really like a son. A boy. You know, someone I could toss a ball around with or take hunting and fishing."

Pierce was about to argue that he could do just about anything with a girl that he could do with a boy, but he held his tongue, deciding to let the man talk and see where the conversation would lead.

There was a pause.

Pierce waited.

"There's something else," Jamison admitted, and by his tone, Pierce sensed something bad was coming.

"Yeah?"

"Naomi and I . . . have been struggling a bit. In the marriage. The usual midlife stuff, you know. She accused me of working too many hours, that it took away time from the family, and really, she's right. So the baby was meant to fix things, put everything back on the right track." His gaze met Pierce's. "I know what it sounds like, but we both wanted it, so . . ." He got to his feet again and strode restlessly toward the windows. "So this weekend was supposed to be kind of a reset, I suppose. Anyway, I agreed that we would stay here, even though I figured she might have a honey-do list. I'm pretty sure she wanted me to tackle some of the projects I'd been ignoring . . ." His voice trailed off as he watched the sun inch upward, sending rays through the forest and over the grassland where cattle grazed. "She took the girls to her sister's place in Charleston around six, and that was the last I heard from her. I called, of course, and talked to Roxanne."

Roxanne, Pierce knew, was Naomi's older sister, but he didn't like this turn in the conversation.

Jamison went on, "Roxie told me Naomi had dropped them off just as planned. Around six. She stuck around for about half an hour, had a glass of wine, then left."

"And then she was supposed to come back here?"

He glanced back at Pierce. "Eventually. She said something to me about meeting friends for a drink . . . I don't really know. I was working late, and she was a little pissed about that but got over it."

"What time did you get home?"

"Around ten."

"And she wasn't here."

"Right. And didn't check in." He returned his gaze to the windows, his gaze seeming to hover over the tree line. "I waited until about ten-thirty or so and tried calling. But she didn't pick up. Never responded."

"Is that unusual?"

"If she's busy, it might take an hour or two, but she always gets back to me." He was still staring out the window, past the pool area. "Once in a while, it's been overnight, just a couple of times, but that was because her phone wasn't charged or she left the phone somewhere or somehow she missed the message."

"Has this ever happened before? When she didn't show up to where she was supposed to be?"

A beat.

Just a slight hesitation.

"No," he said, but there was something in his tone that didn't convince Pierce. And he'd just admitted that he and his wife were going through a tough time. Then again, why would Jamison call Pierce out here, if he wasn't going to be completely honest, if he didn't want his help?

Jamison knew as well as Pierce that spouses were always "persons of interest," if not actual suspects, until they were cleared.

As if reading Pierce's mind, Jamison said, "I know how this looks. That's why I contacted you. As a friend, yeah, but as an investigator. If something's happened to her . . . if she's a *victim* . . . they'll look at me."

Fair enough. "Just don't hold back on me."

"I won't," Jamison assured him.

"Has Naomi contacted Roxanne, or the girls, since she dropped them off?"

"Texted them all good night, around ten, I think. You know, they all have phones, so I think she texted each of them, individually. As I told you, that's what Roxie said when I called her around midnight, that Naomi had dropped the kids off about six or maybe six-fifteen, hung out for a bit, then she took off. She told Roxie she was meeting me later.

"I texted Roxie again this morning, and she called me right back. Said she hadn't heard a word, so now she's worried sick. That's when I called you." He ran tense fingers around the back of his neck.

"Have you called the hospitals between here and Charleston?"

"Yeah. Around three this morning. Before I called you." He exhaled heavily. "No one matching her description came into any of the ERs."

"What about her friends?"

Checking his watch, he said, "I haven't called them yet. It's still early. But I will, and if anyone's heard anything, I'll let you know."

"I'll want their names and numbers. She drives a white Mercedes?"

"E-Class 350. Hybrid."

"I'll need the plate number."

"I should know it, but I don't," he said. "I've got it in some paperwork in my office." He left the room for a few minutes, leaving Pierce in the huge room alone. He stood and walked to the one wall near the bar where pictures were hung. Mostly they were glimpses of Jamison's life as a football quarterback in high school. Wearing a cap and gown when he'd graduated, his father at his side. With his father and brothers on a hunting trip, a dead buck in the foreground. Holding hands with Naomi and laughing, newlyweds running down the steps of the local church where they'd gotten married. She in a lacy white gown, he in a tux, as they were showered with rice and birdseed as they fled through a gauntlet of friends and family. The people surrounding them were blurred, but Pierce remembered the day and knew he had been standing at the top of the steps. The day had been filled with sunshine and promise.

They had moved here soon after the wedding, taken over the house from his parents, who had moved to Florida. Then, somehow, when his father had passed years later, Jamison had inherited the place.

He stared at the picture of the joyous couple.

They'd had such big plans, and their future had seemed bright.

And now Naomi was missing . . . Had she disappeared of her own accord, or had something happened to her?

He heard Jamison's footsteps and turned as his friend walked down the steps into the room. "Here you go." He handed Pierce a sheet of paper with the car information on it and the names and phone numbers of Naomi's closest friends. "For now, keep it on the down-low. I don't want this to get out of hand in case she shows up with some plausible excuse. Like maybe the car broke down and her phone was out of juice or she had too much to drink and stayed with a friend . . ." His voice trailed off, and they both knew he was likely grasping at straws, hoping against hope.

"I'll try and call again," he said as he yanked his phone from his pocket and punched a speed-dial number. A few seconds passed and from across the room, Pierce heard a soft female voice answer. Naomi. But a recording.

Jamison's gaze met Pierce's as he said at the beep, "Hi, hon. It's me again. Gettin' worried. Give me a call." He clicked off, and he stuffed the phone back into his pocket.

"I'll work on it," Pierce said. "Make some inquiries. Put out a BOLO on her car."

Jamison nodded. "Right. But keep it as quiet as you can. It's still . . . there's still time." He grimaced. "There's a chance she might still show up." But he didn't look like he believed it. His expression was taut, and though he was keeping his cool, he was tense. Worried.

"I'll double-check with the hospitals. See if there's anything, but you should probably call her friends before I do."

Jamison nodded absently, again looked through the windows. A slight mist was rising over the fields, where cattle and horses grazed. "I will . . . Yeah. This morning."

"So do you know anything about someone who might want to harm her?"

"Of course not." His head whipped around. "You know Naomi. Everybody loves her."

Pierce wondered about that, but held his tongue. "If you think of anyone she might have pissed off, let me know."

"There's no one. Holy Christ, she does volunteer work at two schools and the church. She helps with the Birds of Paradise at All Christian, and most of those women are her friends."

"Including Mavis Greenlee?"

Jamison's head snapped up. He held up a hand as if to stop Pierce's train of thought. "Jesus, where are you going with this?" he demanded, but he was following the same dark path of Pierce's thoughts himself. "No . . . Oh, God, let's not even go there. Okay? This is just a simple case of Naomi . . . my wife being waylaid . . . or in an accident or . . ." His voice broke, but he cleared his throat and visibly pulled himself together. "She's just missing, and it hasn't been that long . . . so don't go off the deep end on me." But he'd paled, his concern that something deadly had occurred written all over him.

A dog barked from the distance, and another joined in. Jamison glanced out the window again, to a spot lower on the hill, where behind a copse of pine, a building was visible. The kennels.

"Hell. I forgot to feed them," he said, glancing at his watch. "Naomi usually does it. Takes her morning walk and feeds and lets out the dogs before she gets the girls ready for school. They're on a schedule, and they know when breakfast is late. I'd better go down there." He turned back to Pierce. "Thanks for checking this out," he said. "And keeping it between us. I appreciate it."

"No worries."

"I just . . . I just hope . . . that she shows up. Soon."

"Me, too," Pierce said, and he meant it. Boy, did he mean it.

But he had a bad feeling. A very bad feeling.

Chapter 28

"So what did you learn from Jamison?" Nikki asked. She was upstairs, getting ready for the day, two dogs lying near her feet, Chloe, still in pajamas, in their bed, with toys and books spread over the rumpled duvet. The little girl looked up at the sight of her dad and lifted her arms.

"Can't talk about it now," Pierce said to Nikki before picking up Chloe and then, as she laughed, tossing her back onto the bed.

"Again!" she ordered.

He snatched her up, then gently flipped her onto the bed again.

"Again!" Giggling, she was on her feet, bouncing atop the mattress.

"You've started something now," Nikki observed. Her hair was wet, her reddish curls untamed.

"One more time." He obliged his daughter, then before she could make any further demands, he headed into the bathroom.

Nikki followed. "Something's up."

"I have to go into the station." He began stripping off his clothes.

"More, Daddy!" came the command from the bedroom.

"I'll fill you in later," he said to Nikki, kicking his jeans toward the closet and reaching into the shower. The spray was still cool.

"You were called at home."

"Later," he repeated, stepping under the water, sucking in his breath as the cold needles hit his chest.

On the way home, he'd phoned the major hospitals again, but no one matching Naomi's description had been admitted or come through the ER. He'd also checked with the station as well as the state police. There were no reports of crashed vehicles.

"Why did Jamison call you and what did he say when you got to his house?" she asked again, more insistently. He'd have to talk to her, but just couldn't. Not yet. She'd have too many questions and he didn't have answers. Nonetheless he couldn't put her off forever. She wouldn't stand for it. Torn, he adjusted the water temperature and rinsed off. "What was so important that he called you at home and you raced over to his place?"

"Can't talk about it now. Potentially a missing person."

"And it couldn't wait. Why?"

"Personal connection." He inwardly cringed. Him being enigmatic would only fire her curiosity. Finally the water was hot and steam was beginning to rise, obscuring Nikki's image.

"How personal?"

"I said I'd explain later." He reached for the shampoo bottle, unscrewed the lid, and had to pound the top of the bottle into his fist for the last dab to drop into his hand.

"Does this have anything to do with the homicides?" she asked from the other side of the glass door as he quickly washed his hair. "Was there another one?"

"No."

"Then what?"

"Business. But not the murders."

"You're a homicide detective."

"Nikki, please, I'm trying to shower."

"I see that!" She didn't like being put off. He didn't blame her, but he wasn't about to break his friend's confidence. Not until he knew something more. He saw movement through the glass, small and pink.

"Daddy!" Chloe cried happily.

Nikki said, "She wants to shower with you."

"Not today." He rinsed his hair, blinked against a bit of soap in his eyes, and saw the blurry image of his wife picking up their daughter. Chloe pressed her hand against the glass. "Daddy!"

More movement. A brown blur. Oh, for the love of God, the new dog was in the bathroom, too.

"Hey, a little privacy!" he yelled as the water, now almost scalding, ran down his back.

"Daddy will be out in a minute, sweetheart," he heard his wife say, her voice raised to ensure that he could hear over the running water. "And when he is, he's going to tell us where he's been and what he's been up to so early in the morning. Come on, you." He didn't know if she was talking to Chloe or the shepherd, but she did carry Chloe out of the room, all the while shooing the dog.

Finally, he was left alone with the hot water and his thoughts about Naomi Kittle. He couldn't put his finger on it, but something was very wrong there, and it ran deeper than Naomi not coming home when expected. It had been obvious that Jamison was extremely agitated. Worried sick. Pierce had been an investigator too long not to pay attention to his instincts and something about Jamison's explanation about having a second honeymoon to bring another kid into the world seemed off. Their youngest daughter was eleven, their oldest sixteen. It seemed odd to want to start out with a new baby now. Not that it was unheard of, but Naomi worked hard to maintain her home, her children, and her figure. Pierce knew that she went to the gym often and had already opted for plastic surgery, at least once, maybe twice, and had never shown interest in starting over with an infant

Would she give all that hard work up to get pregnant and have another child?

Stranger things had happened, but Naomi?

Maybe he was making more of it than there was, but he couldn't shake the feeling that he wasn't getting the full story.

He finished with the shower, toweled off, shaved, then quickly dressed and headed down to the kitchen, where his wife was waiting, arms crossed, hips leaning against the counter. "Well?" she said as he found his jacket on a hook by the back door, then returned to the family room to pick up Chloe from the floor where she sat between the two dogs. He kissed her mop of curls and said, "I'll see you later, Princess."

"Work?" Nikki asked.

"Yep. But I'll be back."

"When?"

"Don't know." He saw Nikki's suspicion in the arch of one eyebrow. "After work. It could be a while."

He gave Chloe a raspberry on her belly, and she chortled. "Daddy, no!"

"Okay. Later." He set her down and glanced up at Nikki. The look she gave him said more clearly than words: *You're so full of BS.*

He started for the door again. "I've gotta run."

"No coffee?"

They always had coffee together. It was their morning ritual and, once in a while, the only time they talked during the day, or at least until late in the evening. Not today. "I'll grab a cup at the station."

"You'd tell me if there was a break in the case." It wasn't a question.

"We have a deal," he said.

"I was just going to remind you of that."

"It's still on." He slid one arm through his jacket. "Tonight," he promised. "We'll talk tonight."

"I'm holding you to it, Detective."

He thought she might be teasing, but the look on her face convinced him that she was just this side of being really pissed and calling him out.

At the station, Reed stopped for a cup of coffee in the break room. Several cops had gathered, talking, laughing, grabbing coffee, and getting ready for their shifts. As quiet as the station could be at night, at this time in the morning, it was alive with the thud of boots, the clang of lockers being closed, and the ever-present hum of conversation. Cell phones jangled their individual tunes, while the distinctive ring of desk phones punctuated the air.

He checked Jamison's office, but the door was closed, inside dark.

Once at his desk, Reed scrolled through his e-mails and stopped short when he saw the lab report he'd been waiting for: blood analysis on the stones left at the murder scenes. And not just the blood from the Huber homicide, but from the Greenlee and LaRoux scenes as well. There was a short note from the technician explaining about the delay due to a problem with equipment, but now that it had been fixed, she had processed the blood from all the rocks found at the three scenes. The blood in each case was identical. Not from the victims. And only partially human.

"Partially?" he said aloud. Someone had made a concoction of equal parts human, caprine, and bovine blood.

And the human blood came from an unknown female.

His stomach knotted.

Another victim?

One they had not yet discovered?

He and the department had worked on the premise that Billy Huber was the first victim, though there had been conjecture that there could be others, but, until this report, there was no real evidence or indication that there had been others.

As he was looking at the report, Sol pushed open the door. "Mornin'," she said, dropping her backpack onto the file cabinet.

"Morning. Report on the blood came in."

"Finally."

"Take a look."

She peered over his shoulder. "A mixture. Human. Goat. Cow."

"Yeah."

"What's that mean?" she wondered aloud as she read the rest of the information.

"Don't know. What do you think?"

She settled into her desk chair, and he expected her to type in the information and do some sort of Internet search. Instead she said, "Sacrifice."

He looked at her.

"Animals used for sacrifice," she elucidated.

"And human," he reminded her.

"I'm just sayin'."

He thought about it. "So you think the numbers carved onto the rocks have something to do with . . . what? Some kind of satanic ritual?"

"Not necessarily satanic, but maybe." She shrugged. "I'm just spitballin' here, but what else you got?"

"Not much," he admitted, as his phone rang and Jamison Kittle's name and number appeared on the screen. "Yeah?" he answered, hoping beyond hope that his friend was calling to say that Naomi had come home or been located. "You hear from her?"

"No." A long pause. "I'm going quietly out of my mind."

"I bet."

"I think . . . shit. I think I have to, we have to make it official. Start looking. I mean. Jesus," he whispered, and it was somewhere between a prayer and a curse. "I don't know what to think," he admitted. "Don't know what to do." He sounded befuddled. Worried. So unlike the confident, ambitious Jamison Kittle that Reed knew.

"I'll do whatever you think best," Reed said, but he was already forming a plan.

"Give me an hour to pull myself together. The girls . . . they're okay. I talked to Roxanne, and she knows that Naomi's missing, but she's keeping it from the kids. For now. I, um, I just don't want to worry them unnecessarily, you know."

"Right."

"If we could keep this within the department, away from the press?"

"I'll try." But, of course, it would be impossible. Sometimes he thought the station was a sieve of leaks.

Jamison said, "Your wife . . ."

"Doesn't know anything. Not from me."

"Good. I mean, I didn't think so. But . . ."

"It's gonna come out," Reed warned. Not only were there leaks, but once the police started looking for Naomi, the media would know it. They would have to. They had their own resources and could get information to the public.

"Yeah, yeah, I know. Just not yet."

"Okay." He hung up, but felt the weight of responsibility settle on his shoulders.

"What was that all about?" Sol asked, her dark eyes concerned.

"Nothing I can discuss. At least not yet. And it has nothing to do with our cases."

"If you say so." But her eyes belied her words. That was the trouble with her, she was intuitive, seemed to sense things that others didn't. He'd told himself that her perception was a good thing, that she might catch things he didn't, but when her concentration was tuned in to him and what he might need to keep close to the vest, it was uncomfortable.

"What else do we know?" he asked, leaning back in his chair and drinking his coffee as they discussed the facts of the case. Jeanne LaRoux's preliminary autopsy had come through. The murderer's MO seemed to rely on a brain injury to kill his victims, and he seemed to use whatever was handy. The tiller, in Billy Huber's case, the marble floor for Mavis Greenlee, and some kind of jagged implement, most likely a rock, for Jeanne LaRoux. But then the killer would add a personal touch by cutting them with what seemed to be a serrated knife of some kind, though no weapon had been found at any of the crime scenes. The stones, with their cryptic numbers engraved on them, had been left on or near the bodies, each with a different digit engraved, then enhanced with the blood of a female human, a goat, and a cow.

This, apparently, was the killer's calling card. Significant. He/she wanted to make a statement to the police and whoever found the victims.

Was Billy Huber the first victim?

Or were there more, perhaps the woman whose blood had been mixed into the macabre paint.

"So far, all the victims were found in or around their home, the bodies not transported. Killed on the spot," Sol pointed out. "Easy enough to do with Huber and LaRoux; they lived alone and kept to themselves. But Mavis Greenlee is the odd one out." She pointed to the map of the area that showed where the victims were found. "She lived in town, with her husband. At least part-time, as we now know; he spent a lot of days and nights with his girlfriend, Annabelle Van Camp, out on Tybee. So the killer had to have known her schedule and his, or else just got lucky, but that's a stretch, I think."

"Agreed." He examined the map. "And LaRoux and Huber live not far from each other, at least as the crow flies," he pointed out.

"But Greenlee is in town." She frowned at the map and tapped her fingers on her desk as she thought aloud, "In a way, they were alike, in that all the victims were isolated." He was about to argue that Mavis Greenlee lived close to her neighbors, but Sol went on. "I'm not talking about physical location, I'm saying emotionally. Both LaRoux and Huber were loners, keeping to themselves for the most part. I can't find anyone who had a kind word to say about Billy Huber, and that includes his kid and brothers. The same with Mavis Greenlee. She had three husbands and no real friends. Even the women in that church's ladies'-aid society, the Birds of Paradise, didn't sing her praises. All in all, I get the impression that she didn't have anyone close, and that includes her brother and mother."

What she was saying was true. In the interviews they'd conducted, most people thought Billy Huber was a cheat and a grifter, that Jeanne LaRoux was weird as hell, some psychic who practiced the dark arts, someone to avoid. And Mavis Greenlee, despite all her work with the church and her societal connections, was a self-centered snob.

"So, what're you saying?" he asked.

Sol frowned and reached into her backpack for a Red Bull. "I don't know yet, but I'm getting kind of a vibe about them."

When he didn't respond, she flashed him a smile, showing off a dimple. She cracked the energy drink. "Call it women's intuition."

He snorted.

"Y'all would call it a 'hunch,' right? Cops are supposed to have 'hunches' or gut instincts. I'll go with that." She laughed a little, and it was refreshing to see a humorous glint in her gold eyes. "Oh, by the way, thought you should know that I've got dibs on the cat."

"What?"

"Princess," she clarified. "Mavis Greenlee's Persian. I talked to animal control and the shelter. Since Archer gave her up, I'm adopting her. Kinda like you did with Billy Huber's dog."

"We could start our own rescue," he groused.

"How're you getting along with . . . what was his name? Arnold?"

"Arlo. And it's been okay," he admitted, as he liked the shepherd. Surprisingly. "But if we find any others, we're out."

"I heard Jeanne LaRoux kept chickens. And maybe pigs."

"Forget it." He really had no time for small talk. Not with the three homicides and Naomi Kittle being MIA. Glancing down at the autopsy reports again, he asked, "So where does a killer get a goat, a pig, and a female human so he can drain off their blood?"

She took a pull from her energy drink and scrutinized the map again. "Probably not in the city." What she didn't add was that she knew more than her partner.

Reed's cell interrupted her thoughts.

He answered abruptly, then without explanation, he left the office quickly. He didn't bother with his jacket. Which meant he probably wouldn't be gone long and wasn't leaving the building.

Right now, she couldn't tell him what she knew, because he wouldn't want to know and wouldn't believe her.

Last night, with the moon and stars to guide her, she'd driven to Jeanne LaRoux's swampy patch of land. Sol had been careful and parked her truck a mile down the road at what appeared to be a fisherman's turnout near the river. Using her flashlight sparingly, she'd hiked back to the property, feeling the moist air, smelling the heavy scent of the swamp. She'd wandered through the live oaks, with their gauzy, ghostly veils of Spanish moss moving with the breeze, and eyed the darkened cabin and sheds in the clearing where Jeanne LaRoux had lived and practiced what many considered the dark arts.

Sol understood.

She felt the older woman's presence in the ramshackle buildings as she tuned her senses in to the still night air. She heard mosquitoes and bullfrogs, crickets and bats as they swooped overhead and noticed the leftover scent of ash in the air. The water was dark as she crossed the rotting bridge to the sanctuary, a hut of bleached wood. Inside, she'd caught the aromas of eucalyptus and something else—patchouli, she thought—along with the odor of charred wood.

And blood.

She recognized the metallic scent of blood in this sanctuary of sorts, its altar having been desecrated, violated by those who had been here before her.

Quietly, she slid out of her clothes and laid them carefully near the door. Then she stepped into the center of the fire pit, her bare feet sinking into the ash, the bits of blackened wood rubbing against her ankles.

She felt nothing.

No restless soul stirring.

"Come to me," she whispered and, balancing on one foot, placed the other on a rock rimming the cold embers, a rock stained with Jeanne LaRoux's blood. "Please, come to me."

The night seemed to close in on her.

The crickets and frogs and bats grew silent.

She felt a breath of wind as it slipped through the open doorway.

It seemed to swirl around her in a gentle cocoon.

"Jeanne," she said under her breath.

She sensed a movement, just a whisper, deep in her soul.

Closing her eyes, she murmured, "Who did this to you?"

The movement, a tingling breeze within her, curled around her heart.

"Who?" she demanded.

"*Le fils de Satan*," was the answer. The son of Satan.

"*Il m'a pris la vie*."

He took my life.

And then she was gone, swept up in a midnight breeze, her soul rising upward into the night.

And Sol had been left to find out who this beast was, a mortal man infused by the devil.

Chapter 29

The last person Nikki expected to show up on her doorstep was her brother, but there he was, big as life, holding his baseball cap in his hands on the front porch. "Kyle?" she said, surprised. "What're you doing here?"

"Glad to see you, too," he said, as both dogs, barking, came to the door to check out who had rung the bell.

"Well, yeah, of course, I'm glad but . . . Wow. This is a surprise." To the dogs she added, "You two! Hush!"

"Can I come in?"

"Sure. Sure. Of course!" She stepped out of the way, just as Chloe, who had been playing in the family room, toddled into the entryway. She took one look at Kyle, scowled, and stepped back to hide behind Nikki and peek around her legs.

"This is—?" Kyle asked, and crouched down to be at eye level with the girl.

"Chloe. My daughter. Chloe, this is your Uncle Kyle." She yelled up the stairs as she picked up the suddenly shy Chloe, "Lily! Kyle's here!"

"What?" Her sister flew out of her room to pause at the landing and look down. "Seriously?" She was down the stairs in an instant. "What's going on?" she demanded, barefoot, but in jeans and a blouse, her hair pulled back in a ponytail, her face devoid of makeup. "Oh, shit! Is it Mom?"

"No, no," he assured her. "She's fine. I was . . . I'm just dropping by." He actually blushed a little.

Lily skewered her brother with an "I don't believe you for an instant" glare. "Oookay," she said, then yelled up the stairs. "Phee?" When nothing happened, she said, "I'll be just a sec" and raced up the steps once more.

"You want something to drink?" Nikki asked over her shoulder as she led him into the kitchen, all the while wondering what his visit was all about.

"You got Dr Pepper?"

"Yeah, but are you sure you want to start this early," she teased, leading him and the dogs toward the back of the house. "It's before noon." It was a joke they'd shared as children, always hearing their father remarking that any time after noon was time for a drink, usually whiskey.

As she opened the refrigerator door, she caught his grin. She snapped a can from the six-pack, then tossed it to him. "Careful. Don't let it get all over the kitchen."

As a kid, he'd loved to shake up a can and have it geyser out in a thick spray.

"Gotcha." He opened the can over the sink, while Jennings, hiding under one of the barstools, scooted out of the way. In that second, Lily returned with a groggy Ophelia in tow. Phee, still in pajamas, her hair a tangled mess, couldn't scratch up a smile, as if her face was set in a permanent scowl.

Lily made quick introductions as they settled into the family room, but Phee wasn't about to make any kind of small talk or overture to her newfound uncle. She jammed earbuds into her ears and lay on the couch, clearly blocking out the family as if she found whatever it was on her phone absolutely intriguing. Chloe was no more friendly. She studied Kyle suspiciously while cuddled up against Nikki in an oversize chair.

"Mom wants us all to reconnect," Kyle said. "You know, before she . . . Before she passes."

"Is she—is she sick? I haven't heard that, and I usually take her to all of her appointments," Lily said, worry lines appearing on her forehead. For all of her talking about how their mother was a pain, Lily was still close to Charlene.

"No, I don't think so." From the leather chair where Pierce usually sat, he shook his head. "She's feisty enough to outlive us all, but several of her friends have passed, and she's seen how some families never do get it together, so she asked me to reach out. To, you know, start mending fences." Leaning back against the worn leather, he added, "So here I am."

"Well, I, for one, think it's a good idea," Lily pronounced. "Let's start mending."

"You know, I think Mavis Greenlee really sent her over the edge," Kyle said. "Maybe because she was murdered, but as much as she resented Mavis for the whole Dad thing . . ." He raised his eyebrows as if to question if both of his sisters knew of Mavis's affair with their father.

"Yeah," Nikki said, while Lily, lips turned downward, nodded.

"She thought it was a damned shame how that family had fallen apart. Mavis, with all of those husbands and no children of her own, and then Archer taking up with a new girlfriend so much younger and all. She just doesn't want our family to, you know, be disjointed, I guess." He held up a hand as if to stave off the arguments he saw brewing in his sisters' eyes. "Before you say anything, I know it's been my fault. I own it, all right? But it goes both ways, and Mom saw how Mavis treated her parents, and she doesn't want that to happen to us."

"You mean, to her," Lily corrected as she stood by the back door, staring out at the yard, where a bird was splashing in the birdbath. "Mother doesn't want us to ignore her or stuff her into some awful spot without good care. I already heard all about that when I visited her, how shameful it was the way Mavis treated Norton and especially Blanche."

"She's not wrong. I saw it for myself. So did you," Nikki said to Kyle.

"Yeah." He took a long drink from his can.

"So, wait a minute," Nikki said, "so you knew Archer was having an affair?" she asked, seeing him blush again and turn his attention to the windows that looked into the backyard.

"I suspected. I take care of the yard out there, too, and yeah, I'd seen the girl in the pool."

Nikki asked, "And you didn't say anything to Mavis?"

"Nope. My lips are sealed for all of my clients." He turned his drink nervously in his hands. "There is one more thing."

"What?" Lily asked, instantly suspicious.

"Mom wants us to go to the funeral as a family."

"Mavis Greenlee's funeral?" Nikki said in disbelief. "Wait a minute. Mom sent you over here so that you would sweet-talk us into going together?"

Lily rolled her eyes. "She wants to make a statement. About the solidarity in her family, or something. At her old friend or frenemy's funeral. Because of Dad or whatever." She threw up a hand and stared at her brother. "It's all about appearances with Charlene. Wow. I can't believe she talked you into it, though."

He shrugged. "I figured why not?"

"Because it's so fake, that's why not. She just wants to make it look like we're such a tight-knit perfect little family! Seriously?" Lily found a glass in a cupboard, then turned on the tap and filled the tumbler. "That's why you're here, Kyle? To do Mom's dirty work?" She took a gulp from her glass. "Oh, I get it. She thought you could weasel your way in with us and she wouldn't have to have the argument."

"Mom isn't the kind to back down from a fight," he pointed out.

That much was true.

"The funeral is tomorrow."

"Tomorrow?" Lily repeated.

Nikki had seen the notice. "Eleven in the morning. At All Christian." She was definitely going.

"Well, I'm not doing it," Lily said emphatically. "And I'm certainly not taking my daughter. Mavis Greenlee was a snob. A horrible person. Mom *hated* her. For God's sake, she carried on with Dad. Nope. Not doing it. I have no reason to go and pretend to be all sad."

"I'll go," Nikki said.

"Of course you will!" Lily set her glass onto the counter so hard the water sloshed over the rim. "But it's not because of any love for Mavis. We all know that. It's because you're a snoop. Always poking around. You don't even care if you have to fake it and act like you're at the funeral for Mavis or our mother, just so you can check things out. Well, it's all sick, if you ask me."

"Calm as ever, I see," Kyle observed.

"I'm trying," Lily said through gritted teeth, "but this, this hypocrisy is too much. I can't imagine sitting in the church listening to Father Stark—that's Westin Stark, by the way. Kyle, you remember what a jerk-wad he was when you were in school. He's gonna be up on the altar in all of his robes and clerical collar or whatever and ask us to pray for Mavis's soul. And he and the rest of the damned flock will listen while Mavis is made to look like a goddamned angel, when we all know she wasn't. Worse yet, we'll probably have to watch Archer blubber and wipe his eyes in the front pew, while he's just itching to get out of there and back to his teenager of a girlfriend."

Lily's face was turning red with her rant. "And you want to know the worst part of it? The very worst? Charlene wants us to go, and we all know that she hated Mavis and has never forgiven her for having a damned affair with our father. So, no, Kyle, I'm not going to be a part of the charade, and if I'm not calm? Tough! So be it."

With that, she stormed out of the room. "I'm late," she tossed over her shoulder to Nikki. "You've got her, right?" she said, motioning to the still-sulking Phee. "You'll see that she gets to her lesson?" Though there was no school today, the riding academy was open, lessons ongoing.

"Yep," Nikki said and noticed that Ophelia, caught in her own world, hadn't looked up from her screen once, not even when her mother was reading them all the riot act.

"Wow." Kyle walked to the glass door leading outside. "I'd forgotten how volatile she could be. Beneath all her peace/love/dove/kumbaya vibe, she can go from zero to a hundred in a second."

"I could say something about apples not falling far from the tree."

"There was a reason or two or fifty that I backed away from the family," he admitted, then changed the subject. "You've got a nice place here."

It was the first time he'd been in her home. Nikki could well imagine he might have driven by the house a number of times, but she couldn't remember him ever walking over the threshold. "You want to see outside? You know, since you're the landscape guy and all."

He lifted a shoulder. "Sure."

As she opened the door, Arlo, nails clicking frantically, sped past her to bound across the patio and send a robin into panicked flight. Mikado was a step or two behind, but he'd noticed a squirrel on the fence; it ran across the top and leapt into the air to land upon the overhanging branches of a magnolia tree. Both dogs went wild, scrambling and circling while whining and barking, the squirrel scolding from the safety of the blossom-laden branches.

"Welcome to my world," she said, and for the next half hour they sat on the patio, Chloe coming out to play in the sandbox that Pierce had constructed near a planter overflowing with brilliantly colored azaleas. Nikki checked her phone several times, hoping Pierce had texted, but so far, her husband had been radio silent.

"Expecting someone?" Kyle asked.

"Just hoping to hear from Pierce."

"Ah. Checking up on him?"

"No. We're, um, we're working on something together." That was stretching the truth a bit, but not a complete lie.

"The Mavis Greenlee murder," he guessed.

She nodded. "Kind of. How well do you know Archer?"

"Well enough to know he's a lousy poker player."

"You play cards with him?" She was surprised, but she shouldn't be. Other than where Kyle lived and that he wasn't and had never been married, she didn't know much about him and certainly not about his social life.

"Once in a while." He chuckled at her expression. "Don't be so surprised. It's kind of a ragtag group of guys that has evolved over the years. You know somebody who knows somebody who wants to play. That sort of thing."

"Where?"

"Oh, usually at someone's house, because, you know, it's not exactly legal." His eyes twinkled a bit.

"Right."

"It's the same group that meets on Friday nights for a couple of beers. Mostly guys from high school, you know, from way back when. Some of 'em belong to a rifle club and go shooting before we meet at the Stag and Boar," he said. The bar, just off the river, was in the historic district, not far from the newspaper offices. It was also the site of Archer Greenlee's alibi.

"You meet weekly?"

"Around seven thirty on Fridays, give or take. Sometimes other nights, but Friday is a standard."

"Like tonight?"

"Yeah."

"And you were there, with Archer, the night his wife was murdered?"

"What? No." He shook his head. "I missed that game."

"Why?" she asked, suddenly more interested.

"I'd spent the day laying pipe for a new irrigation system for a client. A main burst, and it was a real mess. Took forever. By the time I got home and cleaned up, I decided I didn't want to go out again. Instead, I ordered a pizza, had a couple of beers, and watched the Braves on TV." He added, "They won. Extra innings." He couldn't help smother a smile. "So are you asking if I have an alibi for that night?"

"No." Well, not really. Kyle had no reason to kill Mavis, and he certainly wasn't some kind of paid assassin. "But who's in the group?"

"It's kind of fluid. Different guys, depending on their schedules. And, as I said, someone might bring a friend along. But I heard Archer was there on the night his wife was killed, even though he hasn't been there often lately."

"Since he started seeing Annabelle?"

"I guess." Kyle shrugged. "He was kind of on a tightwire, balancing a wife and a mistress. Hard to keep 'em both happy," Kyle pointed out. "So not much time for a night out with the guys."

"What about the other guys? Who usually shows up?"

"Besides me? There's Stoney, Otis—"

"Wait. Stoney Tripp? Isn't his real name Stanley?" She'd already checked, just wanted to confirm.

"Yeah, Stoney's a nickname from grade school. He's a science nerd. Geologist. Into rocks when other kids were into football and slingshots and stuff."

"He still a rock hound?"

"Don't know. Maybe."

"Okay, and you said there were others."

"Well, yeah. Knox and, you'll love this, your buddy Wes, once in a while."

"Wes? You mean Westin Stark? The preacher?"

"He's not a regular. But, yeah, he's been there a couple of times."

"Was he there the night Mavis died?"

"Dunno. I wasn't there that night, remember?"

"Right." When she'd checked Archer's alibi with the bartender, he hadn't mentioned the preacher. Still, she couldn't help feeling she was finally getting somewhere, that a few of the loose ends surrounding the recent murders might be starting to connect. "And you said 'Otis'?"

"Right. Otis Childers."

As in Billy Huber's neighbor. "He's always part of the group?"

"Always? Not really. But I guess he shows up as much as anyone. He and Knox and Stoney don't often miss."

"Knox Quinlan."

"Yep. Now, if the inquisition is over . . ." He finished his drink and stood. "I've really got to run. Tell Lily it was great seeing her." His smile was ironic.

"I will," she said, before she, with Chloe and the dogs tagging after, walked him to the front door.

"You know," he said, pausing on the porch, "Mom has a point. We shouldn't let time get in the way. Or away from us. That's been my fault, I know. But we live in the same town, so . . ."

"So." She agreed, nodding. "We'll try."

He managed a grin, and once again she remembered the boy she'd once known, the kid with freckles, a gap-toothed smile. More often than not, Kyle had sported a raspberry on his knee or a scraped elbow or a black eye or some other injury he'd sustained by being totally reckless, and according to their father, "having more balls than brains." But that was the nature of their family, each of them daredevils in their own way, each super competitive.

As a child, Kyle had been her best friend.

And then, later, he was gone.

Maybe that could change.

Then again, she thought as he drove away, maybe not.

Chapter 30

Pierce took the call from Jamison.

"I'm in my office. Come on down."

"On my way." Pierce cast a glance at his partner and told her where he'd be.

"How long will it take?" Sol asked, her gold eyes assessing. As if she knew something serious was up, something even more out of the ordinary than usual.

"I'll fill you in once I know." He left in a hurry and made his way through the crowded hallway to Jamison's office.

"Close the door," Jamison instructed, waving Pierce into one of the visitor's chairs in front of his desk.

"I don't know anything new," he admitted, as Pierce took a seat. "I called all of Naomi's friends, checked with Roxie, even called the hospitals again, but . . . nothing. No one's heard or seen anything. It's like she just vanished." Despite the dark circles under his eyes and the tension evident in his tight jaw, Jamison looked every bit the lawyer he was. His still-damp hair was slicked back, and he'd shaved and donned a suit and tie. His shirt was crisp, the knot of his tie precise, his suit pressed. Somehow he'd managed to pull himself together. At least on the surface. "Whatever it takes, we have to find out what happened to her."

"We'll find her."

"God, I hope. But—oh, hell, I can't even think it."

"What?" Pierce asked.

Jamison's eyes squeezed shut, and he gave a slight shake of his head. "We've got a real psycho out there right now," he admitted. "What if . . ."

"Don't go there," Pierce said and noted, along with the thick tomes of case studies and statutes, the display of Jamison's accomplishments. Multiple framed diplomas and awards hung on the wall behind him. Framed pictures of his daughters and wife sat on his desk near a military-service award.

He said, "No one has heard from her for a couple of days. No one met her yesterday. I thought she told me she was meeting friends. But who? Or was it all a lie? God, I don't know!" He rubbed his jaw in frustration. "And Roxanne hasn't heard anything, either. She even called her folks, just asking if they'd contacted Naomi." He shook his head. "Again: nothing. So now they're probably worried sick, too." He sat down behind his desk, seemingly lost in thought for a minute.

Pierce waited.

"So I guess I'm giving you the green light." Jamison pulled his attention back to Pierce. "I'll tell the brass, then I'll have to go to Charleston to pick up the girls." He winced at the thought. "I'll probably work remotely as much as possible for the next couple of days or so. If I can. It's already a zoo around here, and this will only make it worse."

"Okay. I'm on it," Pierce assured him and stood.

"Good." He shook his head. "Somehow I have to hold it together. I have to. For the kids." He let out a long breath and paused, seeming to fight some inner battle, as he stared down at the desk. Finally, he met Pierce's gaze again. "But I am going out of my mind."

Pierce wanted to say, "I imagine" or "I understand," as he, too, had been in tight, worrisome situations with his wife. Nikki had been missing in the past. He had feared for her life more times than he wanted to count, but telling Jamison that he understood what his friend was going through would only come out as a platitude.

"I really need your help on this one, Pierce."

"I'll do everything I can. But you will have to go through all the regular channels."

"I *know*," Jamison snapped, his calm finally breaking. He took a deep, measured breath and added, "Sorry. I'm . . . well, you know."

Pierce nodded. "I'll talk to Missing Persons and file a report."

"For now, I'd still like to keep the press out of it as much as possible."

"Publicity might help. Someone might have seen her, or her car. If we could get Naomi's picture out there, with the help of the press, there's a good chance we might find her faster."

Jamison grimaced at the thought of the ensuing media circus and scandal, but he couldn't deny the bald-faced truth. "Okay." He thought a moment. "Just give me a couple of hours to get my kids before all of this breaks wide open."

"You got it."

Jamison's phone rang. He looked at it and frowned. "I've got to take this," he said, and with that, the meeting was over.

However, Pierce knew his nightmare was just beginning.

Nikki checked her phone for the millionth time.

Nothing.

Damn that Pierce.

Why wasn't he responding?

She'd called him once, and his voice mail had answered.

She'd texted twice since Lily had stormed out and Kyle had left.

Still, no response.

He'd acted weird this morning after getting the phone call from Jamison and leaving for about an hour or so. Secretive. Unlike him. And he'd been evasive when she'd tried to talk to him in the bathroom, which probably wasn't the best idea. Still, the fact that he wasn't answering pissed her off. Sure, he was a cop, a detective no less, and he had to keep things regarding his profession close to his vest, not do anything to compromise the investigation.

But she was his wife, and they had a deal, and now he wasn't responding, so she had no option but to go around him.

So thinking, she fed the girls a quick lunch of grilled cheese, put Chloe down for a nap, then retreated to her den, where she put in a quick call to Jill at the station, but was forced to leave another voice mail.

She was being stonewalled.

Something important was up.

Had there been another murder?

Had the police and the FBI found a link between the victims?

Had the killer been identified?

A dozen questions chased after her, and she could get no answers.

In the late afternoon, the heat of the day lingering over the city, Nikki still had had no response from Pierce or anyone in the department. She drove Phee to her lesson at the riding academy. Maybe she could wangle some more information from Annabelle Van Camp. It was a long shot, but Nikki decided it was worth a try.

Except today Annabelle wasn't Phee's instructor.

Instead, another twentysomething woman greeted Phee in the riding area that smelled of horses and dust. And the ceiling fans mounted high in the rafters were unable to cool the building on a day that promised an early summer.

With short, near-black hair, a smattering of freckles, and an effervescent smile, the replacement instructor introduced herself as Gia, then immediately went all googly-eyed over Chloe. "You know, you're never too young to ride. I started when I was three." She crouched down to Chloe's level and added, "I bet you'd love to ride a pony, wouldn't you?"

"Yes!" Chloe declared. "Pony."

"Maybe later, Chloe," Nikki interjected swiftly, watching as Phee mounted a rangy palomino mare.

"So what happened to Annabelle?" Nikki asked Gia, who was adjusting the stirrups to fit Phee's legs.

She shrugged. "I was just called in to sub for her at the last minute, and believe me, I take any chance I can get to work with kids. I think they can have a really special bond to the horses, you know?"

"Sure," Nikki said, just to agree.

Gia patted the palomino fondly, then looked up at Phee and said, "Come on, let's see what Daisy here can do. Or what you can get her to do." Clicking her tongue, Gia led the horse and rider to the dusty arena just as Nikki spied the same stern-faced woman she'd come across during Phee's previous lesson.

She appeared as dour and taciturn as ever, her expression severe, her hair pulled back in that no-nonsense gray bun at her nape. Pinned to her shirt was a name tag that read simply: Miss Stacy. She sent Nikki a hard glare.

So she remembers me, too.

Great.

Oh, well.

Nothing ventured, nothing gained.

Chloe was entertaining herself by feeding handfuls of straw through a wire enclosure, where a couple of pygmy goats were eagerly nibbling the bits offered.

Nikki turned her attention to Miss Stacy and extended her hand. "I'm Nikki Gillette, Ophelia's aunt."

"I remember you." Miss Stacy's eyes were positively glacial. Pointedly, she ignored Nikki's outstretched arm.

So much for civility. "I'm looking for Annabelle." She dropped her arm.

"She's not here."

"I see that. But she was supposed to give my niece a riding lesson."

"I'm sure Gia can teach a beginner." She gave a nod to the arena, where the dark-haired girl was offering advice and encouragement while Phee rode the big mare around the ring.

"Do you know why Annabelle didn't come in today?"

The steely eyes moved over Nikki's features with unconcealed disdain. "It's company policy and my own personal code of ethics to never discuss the private lives of my staff."

"It's just that Ophelia has developed a personal relationship with Annabelle," Nikki persisted.

"Has she?" Miss Stacy asked. "Hmm. Well, I'm sure she'll do just fine with Gia." She eyed Chloe, who was happily talking to the two little goats. "And, you should know, this is really no place for a toddler."

"Really?" Nikki said, unable to hide her irritation. The woman was just plain rude. "Gia told me she took up riding when she was just three."

"Not here, she didn't." With that, Miss Stacy stiffly headed up the short flight of stairs to the office.

Nikki was left doing a slow, steady burn. People in authority had tried to dominate her all of her life, but she wasn't intimidated. You didn't grow up as the offspring of Big Ron and Charlene Gillette without growing a backbone.

But for now, she backed off and tried to pay attention as Phee guided the horse around the arena, riding over low jumps and encouraging Daisy through multiple obstacles. As she watched horse and rider, she kept an eye out for Annabelle, should she decide to show up, and also for Shana Kittle, whose lesson usually followed Phee's. But Annabelle was a no-show, and Shana, too, didn't arrive.

No big deal, she told herself, but she noticed the instructor she'd seen with Shana the week before waiting and pacing impatiently by the main door, now wide open, the view of the surrounding fields and lane visible. Tan, lean, and obviously irritated, she alternately stared down at the entrance to the academy and looked down at her cell's screen, finally stuffing the phone into the back pocket of her jeans.

"Waiting for someone?" Nikki asked.

"What?" She seemed startled out of her own thoughts. "Well, yeah, I guess." Lips pursed, she shaded her eyes with a hand and squinted into the lowering sun hanging just above the horizon.

"No one called and canceled?"

"Right."

"Maybe they're just caught in traffic or something."

"Maybe. But she's never late. Never. If something happened, you'd think she could call or shoot me a text." Hands on her slim hips, she scowled. "I've got a life, too, you know. I gave up a babysitting gig, a really good one, for this lesson!" She started to turn away, but Nikki caught her by the elbow.

"Hey!" She glared pointedly at Nikki's hand.

"Sorry." Nikki let go, just as the girl yanked her arm back. "I'm waiting for Shana's mom," she lied. "Usually she drops Shana off, right?" Nikki was just guessing. There could be other riders needing instruction at the same time, but she gambled.

"Yeah." The girl backed up a step to allow Ophelia, leading Daisy, to pass by on her way to the stable area, the mare's steel-shod hoofs ringing against the asphalt, her flaxen tail swishing against flies.

Nikki pressed, "And Naomi—I mean, her mom—waits for Shana?"

"Well . . . sometimes she waits, but usually she, you know, doesn't stick around."

"Where does she go?"

"God, how would I know?" she asked a little suspiciously. "*You're* her friend."

"Does she meet someone?" Nikki pressed.

The instructor hesitated. "Sometimes, yeah." She glanced through the open door to the lane, and Nikki followed her gaze. A black pickup was rolling up the tree-lined drive, the same black Ram crew cab Nikki had seen the week before. "Huh. I guess Knox didn't get the memo, either."

"Knox?" Nikki repeated, remembering the name. Kyle had mentioned that Knox Quinlan was part of the group that met at the Stag and Boar.

"Yeah. He's the guy she meets here," the blonde said, then turned her narrowed gaze on Nikki. "Why are you asking all of these questions?"

Before Nikki could come up with a plausible lie, the door to the office burst open, and Miss Stacy bustled down the steps. She shot an irritated look Nikki's way and said, "Brittany, I need to talk to you."

"About what the eff happened to my lesson?"

Miss Stacy bristled slightly. "There's been a slight mix-up," she admitted, obviously flustered. She angled a shoulder between Nikki and Brittany, and tried to keep their conversation more private by lowering her voice. "Apparently, Mrs. Kittle called after hours yesterday and canceled. We, um, didn't get the message until just now."

"Well, great," Brittany said, throwing up her hands as if it were the end of the world. "I turned down another job for this!"

"I'm sorry, but Mrs. Kittle left the message on the office answering machine, and we didn't get it until now. Annabelle usually deals with any messages that come in on the machine, but she's not here and so, well, no one noticed."

"Awesome." Brittany didn't bother to hide her sarcasm. "Just frickin' awesome."

"If you can stay another half hour," Miss Stacy suggested, "we have a new student that you could teach." She offered Brittany a plastic smile. "See, all is not lost."

Brittany glowered for a second, then finally muttered, "Fine," and stormed up the steps to the office. Miss Stacy sent a quick, disapproving glance at Chloe, who was still happily plying the goats with straw. Then she turned to follow Brittany into the office.

"Drama at the horse barns," Nikki muttered. For a fleeting second, she considered complaining about the rude woman. She, or at least Lily, was a paying customer and—

Her phone buzzed in her pocket.

Retrieving it, she saw Pierce's name and face appear. "About time," she declared, then clicked on. "I was beginning to think you were ghosting me!"

"Just busy."

"Yeah? I've been calling and texting all day."

"I know." He was serious. Dead serious. "This is the first chance I've had to call."

So something was up. "Has there been a break in the case?" she asked. Damn it, why hadn't she paid more attention to the news cycle on her phone?

"No. It's something else," he said and despite the heat settling in the building, she felt a chill run down her spine.

"Okay. I'm listening."

"It's Naomi Kittle. She's missing."

"What do you mean, 'missing'?"

"Just that," he said, and her gaze moved from Chloe and the small goat, through the door to the black crew cab parked in the lot. Knox Quinlan, in low-slung battered jeans, an open-collar shirt, and scuffed cowboy boots, stood near his big rig, his gaze fastened on the empty lane.

"After Jamison called this morning," Pierce said, "and I went over to his house, he told me she didn't come home last night."

Nikki watched as Knox paced and squinted down the road, while Pierce explained Jamison's story about how Naomi had dropped off her daughters with her sister in Charleston and then never returned. The police in both South Carolina and Georgia were looking for her or her car, and so far nothing. No friends knew where she was, and she hadn't ended up in a hospital ER. Jamison was currently picking up his daughters from Naomi's sister.

"Has anyone talked to Quinlan?" Nikki asked, watching as the tall man was now talking on his phone. But the conversation was short. Maybe just leaving a message?

"No. Why?"

In obvious frustration, Quinlan jammed the phone into a worn back pocket and kicked at a stone on the asphalt to send it flying.

"I'm here at the riding academy picking up Phee, and Quinlan is, too, and it looks like he's waiting for someone who isn't showing. I'm guessing it's Naomi Kittle."

"What?" If possible, Pierce's voice became tenser.

"I guess they meet here," she said and, from the corner of her eye saw Phee, lugging her bag and helmet, walking from the stable area toward the main entrance. Nikki waved to her niece and said into the phone, "I saw them talking the other day and, like I said, he's here now, and it looks like he's waiting for her. Is that a big deal?"

"I don't know," Pierce admitted. "Maybe. Remember I told you once that Jamison came back to Savannah and swept Naomi off her feet? That she was engaged to someone else?"

"Right."

"That guy was Knox Quinlan."

"Oh."

"And he's got a record," he added grimly.

Chapter 31

"Knox Quinlan?" Nikki repeated, remembering that he was part of the good ol' boys club of the elders of All Christian Church.

"Mainly misdemeanors, but he's definitely not a stand-up guy. Or at least he wasn't," Pierce told her.

"He do time?" Phone pressed to her ear, she watched as Quinlan climbed into his large pickup.

"Community service. Got into it with his neighbor. Flashed a gun. Neighbor said he was threatened. Quinlan got off easy, if you ask me."

"When I saw Naomi with him last week, I didn't know who he was." She started down the path to the parking area. "I'll talk to him."

"No! Wait!" Pierce ordered, but she was already walking down the path, halfway to the lot.

"I'll call you back." She hung up and called over her shoulder to Phee. "Give me a few minutes" and, pointing to Chloe, added, "Watch her. Stay there."

"Why?" Phee asked, stopping at the door near the goat pen and dropping her bag.

"Just do it." Nikki said, then, meeting Gia's curious gaze, pointed from Phee to Chloe and ordered, "Stay with them." She didn't expect any trouble from Knox, but if there was, she wanted to make sure the kids were out of it.

"But—" Phee started to complain, but Nikki had already reached the edge of the parking area just as she heard the big truck's engine roar to life and saw its backup lights come on. "Hey!" she shouted, running to reach the driver's side before he could leave. "Hey! Knox!"

He hit the brakes and rolled down his window. "What?" he asked, thick eyebrows knitting over intense, deep-set eyes. He was handsome, she thought, in that rugged cowboy way. Uncombed hair, three-day's worth of beard shadow over a granite-like jaw.

A little reckless, a bit dangerous.

And staring at her.

Hard.

With no plan, she plunged right in. "I saw you here the other day, talking to Naomi Kittle, and you're here now, so I was wondering if you were waiting for her."

"Who are you?" he demanded, then the light dawned. "You're that reporter who writes books. I've seen you being interviewed on TV. And you write for the *Sentinel.*"

"Right," she agreed and noticed that behind the back seat was a rifle. Not unusual for men around here, but still, because of Pierce's warning, she was wary. "Nikki Gillette," she added.

"I have nothing to say to you." Knox reached for the gearshift.

"You know that Naomi's missing?"

He froze. "What?"

"I just heard that the police are looking for her." Nikki wasn't going to go into too many details, but she had to tell him enough to get him to talk. "I thought you might have an idea where she is."

"Why would I?"

"Because you're waiting for her, and you and she are—?"

"What?" he demanded and swatted at a horsefly that had flown through the open window.

"Close," she guessed. "I know that you were engaged once."

He muttered something under his breath. "Son of a . . ."

"So, if you're close," Nikki barreled on, "you might know where she went. Where she is."

"Well, I don't."

"You were supposed to meet her here today?"

Knox hesitated, but his eyes held worry. "I got nothing to say to you." He seemed about to leave again.

"I thought you could help find her."

"Are you with the police?" he asked. "Or lookin' for a story?"

"I just want to locate her. We're friends," she added, even though that was a bit of a stretch.

"She never mentioned you." He was dismissing her, ready to leave.

"There's a killer in Savannah," Nikki said.

That caught his attention.

"You think that . . ." He glanced to the front of the truck, through the bug-spattered windshield. "Oh, hell." His voice trailed off, and his expression grew grim, and his eyes thinned suspiciously. "Look, lady, I don't know what your game is, and I don't really give a rat's ass, okay? But it has nothing to do with me!"

"I'm not with the police, but they'll uncover whatever your relationship is."

"We know each other, okay? That's it. That's all there is. Leave it alone!" Before she could say anything else, Knox reversed out of the parking slot, jammed his truck into drive, and roared off. She watched as the black truck sped down the long lane, sunlight bouncing brightly off the pickup's chrome and glass. He was somehow involved with Naomi Kittle, and he was part of the Friday night group Kyle had mentioned and had a rap sheet. Huh.

But as she watched the truck disappear, she couldn't quite see Knox Quinlan having anything to do with Naomi's disappearance. Maybe he was capable of petty crimes; however, homicide seemed far-fetched.

But then, you never knew, she thought, returning to the stables to collect Phee and Chloe. Murderers came in various shapes and sizes.

But still she was bothered. Her skin prickled. As if someone were watching. She cast a glance to the thickets of pine, live oak, and mulberry, studying the shadows, telling herself that too many thoughts about serial killers were affecting her. Returning to the stables to collect the girls, she attempted to push her fears aside. Yet, as she strapped her daughter into her car seat, she sensed again that someone was watching.

Hiding in the umbra.

Stealthily observing.

Sweeping her gaze around the surrounding acres, she found no one silently staring, no one harboring malicious intent.

But she was unnerved.

Glancing back at Chloe—so innocent and trusting, so full of vim and vigor, laughter and chaos, shy charm and brash defiance—Nikki felt a fear worse than death to think that anything bad could happen to her child. From the second Chloe had entered the world, she'd bored a spot deep inside her mother's heart.

Castigating herself for her fears, Nikki started the engine and squinted as she drove past the edge of the forest. Was that movement?

No, a shadow.

Possibly a hunter.

Or a bird-watcher.

Nothing . . . evil.

Nevertheless, she hit the gas. *It's nothing*, she told herself.

But she didn't believe it for a second.

Her mind racing faster than the wheels on her rental car, she drove home, ignoring the pleas from both girls to stop for ice cream or some other treat again. "Not today."

"Please," Phee begged from the passenger seat. "I'm starving."

"I'll let your mom know." But her mind was elsewhere. On Naomi Kittle. On Knox Quinlan. On the murders. On the shadowy figure she was certain she'd seen.

Phee rolled her eyes and pouted, while Chloe fell asleep just before they pulled into the drive. "Perfect," Nikki murmured cynically as she saw Chloe's relaxed features in the rearview and the garage door rolled up. She parked, still trying to convince herself she'd overreacted as Phee, still sulking, put away her gear.

"Good boys," Nikki shushed the dogs, who had converged on her as she hauled "rag doll" Chloe into the house.

Lily was standing transfixed in front of the television, the remote in her hand. She turned at the commotion and asked, "Did you know about this?"

Nikki took in the screen where Vivian Johnson, the public information officer, was standing in front of the brick facade of the police station, flanked by several officers. She was a tall, thin woman with even features, near-black eyes, a short Afro, and a no-nonsense demeanor. She was staring straight into the camera and was wrapping up her official statement. "If anyone has seen this woman or has any information about her, please call the department." A phone number appeared on the screen below a recent picture of Naomi Kittle, a professional photograph of Naomi in the same dress she'd been wearing on the night of her daughter's sweet-sixteen party. It seemed the picture had been taken on that same April night just a few weeks earlier.

Lily looked at her sister. "Did you know about this?"

"Pierce called as I was leaving the academy," she said, irritated that the story had somehow been leaked to the press before she'd even heard. "I need to get on this. Do you think you could watch the girls for a while?" Chloe stirred in her arms but didn't wake.

"Sure. It's Friday night and with my busy social schedule, I'll try to fit it in." Lily didn't bother to hide her sarcasm as she stared at the screen. The image faded to two in-studio anchors at a wide desk. They began discussing Naomi Kittle's disappearance and then slid into the next story, the ongoing investigation into the homicides of Billy Huber, Mavis Greenlee, and Jeanne LaRoux, all their pictures flashing onto the screen.

She watched the TV, but there was no more information offered, just a warning for citizens to stay wary and report any suspicious activity to the police.

Lily said, "You know, the way the stories were reported, they were almost linked."

"I got that." The anchors hadn't actually said it, but the hint was there, that Naomi could be the next victim. Even worse, the anchors kept referring to the unknown killer as the Savannah Slasher. The name had caught on. Someone in the television world, and probably the podcast and social-media worlds, had coined the phrase, and all of a sudden the murderer had a name.

Lily grimaced. "Does the killer actually slash the victims' throats?"

Pierce had confided in Nikki that a knife was used in the homicides. "I'm not sure," she hedged, still sticking to her part of the deal with her husband, even though the wounds to the carotid artery and jugular veins seemed to have suddenly become common knowledge. "That's a really big leap." Nikki dropped her purse on the kitchen table as she watched the report, which had turned the subject back to the connection between Naomi's disappearance and the ongoing homicide investigations. "She's missing, and they're already speculating . . ." she muttered.

"Do you think—" Lily started.

"What are you talking about?" Ophelia interrupted. "Why is Shana's mom on the news?" She'd looked up from her phone long enough to zero in on the television, where, once again, Naomi's picture was on the screen, this time a photograph that looked as if it had come from the DMV.

Lily quickly switched off the TV with the remote. "We're really not sure."

Ophelia's eyebrows lifted. "Did something happen to her?"

"No one knows." Lily gave an exaggerated shrug, but didn't lie. "It's just that the police are looking for her."

"Why? Did she do something wrong?" For once, Phee was engaged.

"I don't know, but I doubt it."

Somewhat mollified, Phee said, "Uncle Pierce will find her." But she glanced over at Nikki for confirmation.

"Of course he will," she said. "I'm going to go check with him now." She handed the still-sleeping Chloe over to Lily. "Good luck with this one."

"Oh, I think I can handle Little Miss Groggy." She kissed the little girl's forehead. "You wake up now, okay, sweetie, so you will go to bed for Aunt Lily at a decent time tonight."

Chloe's eyelids didn't so much as flutter.

"Maybe not," Lily said. "Hmm."

"I'll call," Nikki promised and started for the back door.

Arlo followed her.

Lately, the shepherd had begun tracking her out to the car, even hopping inside when she opened the car's door. "Not now," she told him. "Another time." He whimpered, but she couldn't deal with the dog right now.

She drove past Forsyth Park and deeper into the city. Dusk was creeping through the streets, headlights and streetlamps beginning to glow. Her phone buzzed, and she saw that Tom Fink was calling.

Great. She ignored the call and tried to phone Pierce. Her call, of course, went to voice mail. She texted him and said she was on the way to the station. Next up, she dialed Jill's cell phone, and again, no answer.

"Son of a . . ."

Reaching the police station, she had trouble finding a parking space. Two news crews were already parked, set up, camera operators focused on reporters planted in front of the building. When she finally found a spot for the rental car and tried to enter the building, she, like the rest of the media, was kept herded in the lobby.

She tried the back door, but, of course, a deputy was posted, and no amount of cajoling or talking gained her access. "I'll let your husband know you were here," Deputy Marlin Freeman told her as he blocked the doorway.

"Why don't you tell him now?" she suggested, but the big man wouldn't budge.

"Maybe you can call him and tell him you're here," he suggested.

"I've tried."

"Then I suggest—"

"I've got this," Pierce said, from inside the doorway.

Freeman moved aside, but before Nikki could step into the building, Pierce, his jacket slung over one shoulder, strode out, took her arm, and started walking toward the parking lot. "It's a madhouse in there. I need a break. Missed lunch." He unlocked his Jeep.

"And breakfast," she reminded him.

"I told you not to follow after Quinlan, but you did."

Nikki had left a brief message to that effect. "You didn't answer," she accused. "So I left messages."

"What did Quinlan say?"

"Nothing, really. Apparently, he and Naomi meet there sometimes when her daughter's taking a riding lesson. He seemed genuinely surprised she was missing."

They both climbed inside his car, the passenger seat hot, the interior stifling. "No word on Naomi?" she asked, rolling down the window as he drove out of the lot, merging into the thickening traffic of Habersham Street.

"None yet. She was supposed to have a weekend alone with Jamison, what they're calling a staycation, and she dropped off the girls at her sister's house in Charleston and never showed up back here. That's about all we know so far. So Quinlan was waiting for her. Could have been covering up." He slowed for a stoplight as a group of teenagers dashed across the street, laughing and talking.

"He wasn't really interested in talking to me."

"No surprise there."

"Yeah, I get it a lot, and by the way, why was I the last to know about what happened? I get home, and Naomi's picture is all over the TV."

He scowled. "The department leaks like a damned sieve sometimes."

She thought about Jill and held her tongue. "And now they're calling the serial killer the Savannah Slasher? How did that happen?"

"Don't know. Again, a leak. No one's supposed to know about the knife wounds, but," he admitted, "it was going to come out anyway from the autopsy reports." He slid a glance her way. "You're just mad because you didn't come up with the name."

"Oh, give me a break." But there was more than a little truth to the comment. "On the news, they speculated that Naomi being missing might be linked to the serial killer."

His jaw hardened, and his fingers tightened over the wheel. "She's not dead, hasn't been killed. She's just missing. That kind of irresponsible reporting is what gives the media a bad name."

She couldn't deny it. Both of them were feeling testy and anxious.

"What do you want to eat?" he asked.

"Whatever. I had half a toasted cheese and tomato for lunch. Hours ago." She glanced at her watch. "How about the Stag and Boar?"

"Archer Greenlee's alibi." He slid a glance her way.

"I'd like to have a look at the group that meets there," she said. "Kind of an eclectic group that Kyle told me about."

"When did you talk to Kyle?" Pierce nosed the Jeep into a parking spot on the street three blocks from the pub and close to Riverview Towers.

"Earlier today. I told you I saw him the day I caught Blanche Crawford being moved by her son into Riverview Towers, remember? Then today he came by unannounced and asked us to go to Mavis Greenlee's funeral as a family. Lily went ballistic. Refuses to go, even for Mom's sake, as she thinks she'd be seen as a hypocrite."

"And your mom won't?"

"Let's not start with all that," Nikki suggested.

"I assume you're going to attend?" He cut the engine.

"A service at All Christian? To watch Reverend Westin Stark wax on about the virtues of one of Savannah's finest?" she mocked. "You bet I'm going. I wouldn't miss it for the world."

He cut the engine.

"Sometimes this group meets at the rifle range; other times they play cards or end up here on Friday nights. The interesting thing is some of them have ties to the victims of the Savannah Slasher." She snorted and said, "I want to take a look at them," as they reached the pub with its curved plank door and worn brick exterior.

"They might not appreciate being spied on."

"They won't even know I'm there," she promised.

Inside, the ceilings were low and open-beamed above a warren of rooms that comprised the dining area. Up a winding staircase was the bar, where she assumed the group usually gathered.

Luckily, they were shown upstairs to a table for two in an alcove with a view of the river. More importantly, from her seat, Nikki could see the top of the staircase and view customers as they arrived. She didn't have to wait long. She had barely dipped a spoon into her roasted corn chowder before she noticed Otis Childers and Westin Stark enter. Stark was wearing black, his clerical collar visible as they made their way to a table across a hallway. A third man joined them, though Nikki didn't recognize him. He was possibly Stanley "Stoney" Tripp, the geologist Kyle had mentioned. No one else showed up. Though she kept an eye on the room across the hall, she didn't see Archer Greenlee or Knox Quinlan nor, as it turned out, her brother Kyle. The threesome were partially hidden by a wall, but as she finished her soup and salad, she made a note that no one else had joined their table.

"Tell me more about Knox Quinlan," she said.

Pierce was halfway through his hamburger and fries. "He's a hometown boy. Played on the same school football team as Jamison—tight end, I think. Don't really know. But they were kind of rivals, I think, and Naomi was engaged to Quinlan, or almost, when Jamison came back to Savannah, started working for his family law firm, and stole her away. They got married, and Quinlan went downhill." He shrugged. "Anyway, that's the way I heard it."

"What does he do?"

"Construction. But he's got a ranch that he inherited a few years back. As I said, he got into some trouble, did some time, but has walked the straight and narrow for a few years now."

"You checked."

"You bet I did. He found the Lord."

"And now attends All Christian and pals around with the reverend."

Why did that seem phony? She couldn't square his reckless, seemingly irreverent cowboy attitude with someone pious, but that was her own prejudice talking; the two were not mutually exclusive. She took a bit of bread from the basket on the table. So Quinlan was a sexy rancher type who seemed to be romantically involved with a married woman. It happened. All the time. Sometimes to the most faithful of believers.

"Naomi and Jamison were good, though, right?" she asked. "They were going to have a romantic stay-at-home weekend?"

"That was the plan, according to Jamison. And this is strictly off the record," he said, pausing, waiting for her to agree.

"Sure. Of course. What?"

"They're hoping for another baby."

"What? A baby? But Shana's . . . eleven. That's a gap."

"They want a boy, at least Jamison does. You know, a male heir to carry on the family name and all that. A kid he can throw a ball to and take hunting. Do all the dad/son things."

"You're kidding. And they could get another girl," Nikki pointed out.

"I'm just telling you what he said."

She sat back in her chair. "And yet Naomi is involved with Knox Quinlan? It doesn't make sense. I mean, I don't really know Naomi that well, but I was at a party, and she was talking to some friends. I overheard her complain about pregnancy, how awful she felt, really bad morning sickness, I guess. And she mentioned she'd had a couple of miscarriages between the girls." Nikki paused and set down her spoon, remembering the conversation. "She was talking to Janey Cartwright, someone we all went to school with. Janey was complaining about getting her body back in shape, and I swear Naomi said something along the lines of, 'Thank the good Lord I don't have to go through that all again!' Actually that might be a direct quote."

"She must've changed her mind," Pierce said, but he was holding back, she could feel it.

"What?" she said, and when he didn't answer, she added, "You didn't buy it either, when Jamison told you."

"No, that isn't it. He just said they'd hit kind of a rough patch and were trying to put some spark back in their marriage."

"By having a midlife baby?" She didn't hide her skepticism.

His phone rang.

"Hold on a sec." He wiped his hands, then pulled it from his pocket and answered, "Reed . . . yeah . . . okay. I'll be right there." He clicked off and threw his napkin on the table. "Gotta go."

"Did they locate Naomi?" Or was it to do with the Savannah Slasher? Dear God, was there another victim? Or has the killer been found?

He was already motioning to the waiter for the bill and scraping his chair back.

"Pierce, what?"

He gave a short shake of his head. "Give me a sec," he said, as the waiter returned. Quickly, he paid the bill. "Let's go."

They hurried down the stairs and outside, where darkness had fallen, night folding over the city. The riverfront was alive with tourists and locals walking in the cool of the evening, while streetlamps reflected on the dark water and the riverboats, all tiers glowing, docked near the shoreline.

"What's going on?" she asked, hurrying to keep up with his longer strides.

"Video has come in from cameras at the state line." He unlocked his Jeep remotely while they were still half a block away. "It looks like they've got images of Naomi's Mercedes going north to Charleston yesterday, and then, a few hours later, there's film of her returning to Georgia."

"So, she's back. But they haven't located the Mercedes?" she guessed as they reached the Jeep. "Or Naomi."

"Right. But this is the first confirmation that she returned."

"So where is she?" she asked as she climbed inside and he slid behind the wheel.

"That's the question, isn't it? We don't know. At least not yet." He started the engine and pulled into traffic. "But we're sure as hell gonna find out."

Chapter 32

Promising to tell her any information the second it came in, Pierce dropped Nikki off at her rental car.

As she climbed into the Nissan, she noted that more camera crews had arrived at the station. More reporters talking into microphones. More trucks with satellites. More general chaos.

Before she pulled onto the street, she checked with Lily, found out that Chloe had actually gone to bed without much of a fuss, then drove to the newspaper office, again, near the river. She parked the Nissan under a streetlamp that was in clear view of the building, then made her way upstairs, only to find Celeste cleaning out her desk. Though there had been temporary receptionists who had filled in over the years, the reception area had been primarily Celeste's domain.

Red-faced, almost shivering with anger, she was stuffing personal things into two boxes. As Nikki stepped through the door, she glanced up and glared. "Satisfied?" she asked.

"What?"

"Are you satisfied?" Celeste clarified, sniffing loudly. Her face was red, her usually neat hair uncombed, and she'd given up her pencil skirts, boots, and wide belts for leggings and an oversize Texas A&M sweatshirt, though she was still wearing the gold chain necklace with its teardrop-shaped diamond, the one she'd been wearing since last Christmas. "I'm leaving," she announced.

"Why would I be satisfied?"

"Oh, just shut up, Gillette! He fired me, all right? That son of a bitch fired me!"

"Fink?" Nikki asked.

"Yeah, Fink! Who the hell else? After I gave him the best goddamned years of my life!" She slammed a small pink stuffed dinosaur into a box next to a potted Christmas cactus.

"I'm sorry."

"Are you?" Celeste challenged, digging into a drawer and tossing pens and pencils into the box. "Give me a break! You've hated me from the first day I was hired."

"Wait. What? That's not true."

"I know. Okay? You never liked me. Never thought I was doing a good job. Never even tried to get to know me."

"Whoa, I never—"

"Don't!" Celeste snapped, straightening, the fire in her eyes directed right at Nikki. "Don't even try to explain. There you are, the daughter of a goddamned judge, a big whoop-de-do author with a silver spoon rammed down her throat. And you look down your nose at me and everyone else! You think I'm a fool. Isn't that right?" she demanded, tilting up her chin and setting her jaw. "And you know what? I figured it was you who told him that I keyed his car."

"What?" This was crazy. "*You* keyed his car?" Hadn't Roy guessed as much? "Seriously, Celeste, I didn't know. And even if I had, I wouldn't have ratted you out."

"Sure." Celeste spat out the word as if it tasted bad as she threw a couple of books into the second box and looked around the reception area, searching, it seemed, for any forgotten personal items. "Go ahead and deny it, but I know!" She jabbed her finger at her own chest. "I know, damn it. And kudos to you. It worked, damn it. It worked! I'm done here."

"You've got it all wrong," Nikki said, started to get angry. "Why would I want you to leave? I didn't—"

"Oh, save it, Gillette!" She found her keys in her oversize purse and slung the strap over her shoulder.

"Did you key my car, too?" Nikki demanded.

"No!" Celeste stared at Nikki as if she'd lost her mind. She let out a disgusted huff. "Why would I do that?"

"Out of spite."

"Oh, for the love of God. Of course not. Are you kidding me? Hell, no I didn't do anything to your damned car!"

"But Fink's Corvette?"

Celeste snorted. As if she thought Nikki were an idiot. "*You* didn't lie to me and tell me that you were getting a divorce so you could marry me, so no, I repeat, I didn't key your car."

"Oh."

"Yeah, he lied to me. Over and over again. Every time we broke up and got back together. That lying motherfu—He promised me he would get a divorce, and I believed him. I believed that fucker!" She was nearly hyperventilating. "So I guess you're right. I am a fool! But no more. I'm outta here."

Though, deep down, Nikki thought the newspaper office would be better off without all the drama Celeste brought, she couldn't help feeling sorry for her. She also believed Celeste would be far better off without being romantically involved with a slimy two-timer like Fink. "Look, I'm sorry about all this."

"Save it! I don't want your sympathy. Or your pity. Or your platitudes."

Fine. Nikki had tried. "Okay. But my car was keyed, too."

"Well, I didn't do it." Celeste placed one box on the other, and as she did, a tension ball popped out and rolled onto the floor. "I can't imagine anyone keying *your* car. It's not like you pissed off anyone." She picked up both boxes. "Why don't you start with the police department? You know the one. The place where your husband works? I hear they hate you over there! I mean, you're so goddamned careless and egotistical, you put your own husband's partner at risk, and she ended up dead, now didn't she?"

"Low blow," Nikki whispered, still heartsick at the thought.

"The truth hurts, doesn't it? So, suck it, Gillette! Just . . . suck it! Now, get out of my way!" She came around the desk and started for the door, but to avoid Nikki, she shifted too fast and tripped over the stress ball.

The boxes flew out of her hands.

And Celeste went down.

Hard.

Face first.

Onto the tile floor.

The boxes landed upside down, spilling their contents.

Nikki was on her knees in an instant. "Celeste!"

"God*damn* it!" Celeste cried.

"Are you okay?"

Celeste rolled over and glared at her. Blood was dripping from her nose. "No! No, I'm not!" she said, fighting tears and reaching for a tissue from the Kleenex box that had tumbled onto the floor. "And I probably won't be for the rest of my life." She broke down then, sobbing uncontrollably and dabbing at her face with the tissue.

"Let me help. If you need a ride or to see a doctor, I can drive you." Nikki reached out, but Celeste slapped her hand away.

"No!" she said angrily. "No one can help me. I'll be . . ." She swallowed hard. "I'll be fine. Just leave me alone!" She swiped the tears from her eyes, stuffed the tissue into her bleeding nostril and began crawling over the reception area and throwing her items into the boxes.

"I'm sorry," Nikki said.

"For what? For me fucking up my life?" she said, scooping up the stuffed animal and stuffing it into a box. "Well, don't be!"

Nikki managed to gather the books and put them into the box with the pink T-rex, and Celeste finally didn't argue. Instead, she gave out a little groan as she spied the spilled dirt and cracked pot of the Christmas cactus. "Perfect," she muttered, her voice muffled due to the tissue. "Just . . . fucking . . . awesome." Without Nikki's help, she struggled to her feet. Then, as if suddenly remembering something, she yanked the chain on her necklace, breaking it, and let it drop onto the floor, its small diamond winking under the overhead lights. Celeste gave it an angry kick, and it scraped its way under her desk. "Good riddance!" To Nikki, she added, "You can tell Fink where that is, and if he wants to, he can give it to his wife." Clearing her throat, she twisted on her heel, and with the white tissue hanging from her nose and her spine ramrod stiff, she walked out the door to the elevator.

"Wow," Nikki said under her breath. It was true, she'd never been close to Celeste and had found her cold at times and thought she was foolish to be so entangled with a married jerk like Fink, but never would she have expected the vitriol that the receptionist directed at her.

It really was time for Nikki herself to move on and away from the *Sentinel*, she thought, peering out the window to the lot, where she spied Celeste loading the boxes into her hatchback. Then, without even looking up at the third story of the old building where she'd spent so many years, Celeste drove off and maybe, this time, away from Tom Fink for good.

Nikki wasn't betting on it, though.

Old habits died way too hard, she thought while scanning the parking lot and noting that her rented Nissan was still safely parked in the glow of the solitary security lamp. With that reassurance, she walked into the warren of empty cubicles.

The only person inside was Effie, stationed in front of her computer, sipping from a massive drink cup as she stared at the screen. As Nikki passed, she didn't even look up, but said, "Still making friends and influencing people, I see."

Why did Nikki even come here?

Yes, the newspaper's resources were far better than her own, but did she really need the grief? "No," she said aloud, but sat down in her favorite chair and looked up anything she could find on Naomi Kittle, Knox Quinlan, Stanley "Stoney" Tripp, and Westin Stark. The one connection she found was that Westin Stark had been the minister for the corrections facility where Knox Quinlan had spent six months of a reduced sentence for stealing livestock—actually, what was once called cattle rustling. Upon further research, it seemed there was a dispute between Knox and Duke Wheelan when Quinlan's prize bull had broken through the fence and impregnated two of Wheelan's cows, and Quinlan had wanted payment. When he didn't get it, he stole one of the calves.

Duke Wheelan again, she thought.

Wheelan wasn't one of the men who met at the Stag and Boar. But that made sense, as the neighbors were far from neighborly.

But Wheelan was an elder of the church, as were some of the regulars of the Friday-night group.

Nikki sat back and thought about that, then brought up the map of the area again, noting that Knox Quinlan's property abutted

Wheelan's ranch on the opposite side from Otis Childers. And the parcels were all close to Jeanne LaRoux's small acreage, all close to the swamp.

But far from Mavis Greenlee's home in the city. Or even the beach house on Tybee.

Was there some other land connection with the Greenlees? she wondered. She pored through county records, but neither Mavis nor Archer, nor the Crawford family or any of Mavis's ex-husbands owned property out there.

But they all had a link, thin though it may be, to the All Christian Church. She checked all their names against social-media accounts but found nothing of interest. Nothing that would blow the case wide open. And as she went through information on the All Christian Church, she didn't discover anything out of the ordinary, just the mention of the usual church activities like fundraisers, obituaries, bake sales, and meeting times. Reverend Stark was forming a grief support group, and the Birds of Paradise were holding a prayer vigil for Naomi Kittle. The funeral service for Mavis Greenlee was listed, with the time and date. In lieu of flowers, donations should be sent to the parish.

Nikki wondered how many people would show up to the funeral.

Then she mentally berated herself.

There was no connection, no serious connection between these people who attended All Christian and the murders. She could be completely barking up the wrong tree. For that matter, she could be in the wrong damned forest.

She studied the map of the area again, zeroing in on the location of Billy Huber's patch of ground. So close to the LaRoux property, and yet Granger claimed he really didn't know Huber all that well. Even though he'd grown up next to him.

Nikki wondered. She dug through news stories and old police reports that had been covered by the paper. At first glance, there was nothing, but when she probed a little deeper, she found a story that connected Billy Huber to Granger LaRoux, who had been accused of poaching black bears from a nature reserve. "Really?" she said aloud, taking notice and trying to locate more information.

There was none.

No charges had ever been filed.

It had all happened years before, when Granger had been barely out of his teens, and she could find no other mention of it. Still . . . there might be something there, something Granger LaRoux had lied about.

She leaned back in her desk chair. Billy Huber's daughter might know about it, she thought. On a whim, she dialed Janelle McGowan in Florida. The phone rang two times, then three. "Come on, come on," Nikki whispered, and before a monotone voice could finish telling her that the person she was calling was unavailable, Janelle picked up the phone.

"Hello?" she answered cautiously.

"Hi, this is Nikki—"

"I know who you are. I took down your number."

Just as sweet as ever.

"And if you want to go back onto the property, the answer is no. I've finally found a company that'll come and clean it up. I'm just waiting for the cops to give me the green light. Hey—I checked; you're married to a cop, aren't you? Maybe you could put in a good word, let them know they're holding me up!"

"I'll see what I can do," Nikki lied. The police worked on their own schedule. "The reason I'm calling is about an article I read about your dad and Granger LaRoux."

"That little hoodlum? What's he got to do with anything? Sheeit, that little bugger was always comin' over to Dad's place, lookin' through his stuff, and Billy, he let him, kinda acted like the kid was the grandson he never had—well, more likely it was because of Caleb, a replacement son or whatever some *psychologist* would call him," she said acidly, then a little more softly, "Billy, well, he never did get over losing him." She cleared her throat, coughed, then, her voice growing dimmer, as if she'd turned away from the phone, yelled, "Hey! Al, bring me a fresh pack, would ya? I got that reporter from Savannah on the phone and I could use a—what?" There was a muffled reply. "Yeah, the girl reporter, well, hell, she's a woman, and yeah, she has more questions . . . oh, for the love of Saint Pete, just toss me a pack." Her voice became louder as she said, "Excuse me a sec." Then Nikki heard some muffled conversation, and she imagined Janelle's big partner lumbering off to do his wife's bidding.

"There ya go, hon," a male voice said. "Got one out for ya."

Seconds later, Nikki recognized the sound of a lighter clicking and a deep inhale of breath. "I should never have started up again," Janelle said into the phone. "That's what dealing with Billy's estate's done to me. Sent me right back to smokin' and drinkin' too much. Now what was it you wanted? It's not about that damned dog is it, cuz, I'm tellin' ya, we got no use for him."

"No, Arlo's fine."

"Oh, God, that's right. Arlo. What a name for a dog." Another audible drag. "So what was it you wanted, something about that LaRoux kid? Hell, he was trouble. And could you blame him? With a whack-a-doodle mother like that? Always conjurin' up the dead, and talkin' to spirits, and leveling curses? No wonder he's the way he is."

"I read a story about Granger poaching black bears," Nikki put in. She knew now that the two men knew each other and that Granger had lied.

"Oh, that," she said. "I remember. Kind of a big deal at the time, but to tell you the truth, Billy didn't pay much attention to hunting laws or getting tags or whatever. He just did his own thing. He probably suckered that kid into it, but then, that boy was already on the wrong path."

"But nothing came of it."

"Couldn't be proved, I guess. I was already out of the house by then, but yeah, I heard about it. And I think that was kind of the end of their relationship. Granger's nutso mother really came down hard on him and Billy, even swore she would curse his soul or some such shit." She inhaled again and added, "I mean, I wasn't close to Billy, you know that, but when I did talk to him after, he never mentioned the kid again."

"Did Granger have a problem with your dad?"

"Didn't everybody who knew Billy?" she asked. "Look, that's all I know."

Nikki tried a few more questions but got no more answers, so she hung up and tried to figure out what it meant. If anything. For some reason, Granger LaRoux had lied about knowing Billy Huber as well as he did.

Why?

Did it even matter?

"Probably not," she said aloud, but she would definitely talk to Granger.

Skimming her e-mail, she saw that Fink was demanding a new story. There was also a friendly little reminder from Ina that a new book on the Savannah Slasher would be an "interesting" premise.

"Yeah," Nikki said aloud, "if we knew who he was."

What was she missing? The rocks, she thought, the clue left by the killer at each scene. Significant somehow. And information only she, married to the killer, knew about, information she couldn't use.

So far.

She wrote the victims and the numbers down.

Billy Huber, #9

Mavis Greenlee, #5

Jeanne LaRoux, #1

The carvings didn't seem to be in any kind of order, though they were all odd numbers, etched in blood, written in both Arabic and Hebrew. Only missing the three and seven between and counting backward.

So what?

What was the killer trying to convey? Was he just taunting the police, or was there some secret code known only to him, a clue?

If so, she was lost.

She texted Pierce, asking about updates on Naomi Kittle, and waited, tapping her fingers on the desk. But, of course, he didn't respond.

Looking up, she noticed Effie abandoning her post to go to the restroom.

Once she was out of sight, Nikki pushed back her chair and wandered over to Effie's station, where the ice in her oversize Diet Pepsi was melting. The screen showed news across the country and the world, with one window open to the page on all things Georgia, from weather to traffic reports.

The headlines for the Savannah area were all about the Savannah Slasher, but as she skimmed the reports and listened to the news, she heard nothing new. Nor was there any information on Naomi Kittle.

"Hey! Get away from there!" Effie said, returning, her face pulled into a frown as she grabbed her stool and eyed her keyboard and screen. "You didn't do anything, did you?"

"Wouldn't dream of it," Nikki said and gathered her things.

Tonight, she thought, had turned out to be a bust.

She called Pierce on the way home and was surprised that he actually picked up.

"Anything new?" she asked.

"No. We're tracking Naomi's car now. All we know is that it crossed the state line and was caught on camera heading into Georgia, toward Savannah, but then we lost contact."

"You don't know where she was heading?"

"She was on the road leading to their home," he said, as Nikki slowed for a corner and thought about the map she'd just viewed. Naomi, on her way back, would pass right by Knox Quinlan's place.

But she really believed Knox had no idea that Naomi had gone missing when he'd shown up at the riding school.

As she drove, she caught a glimpse of a car behind her in the rearview, then noticed that when she turned, it followed, taking the same route. No big deal. Savannah was a good-sized city, and there was a lot of traffic on this Friday night. She took another corner and saw the car, a silver SUV, take the same turn seconds later.

Don't let your imagination get the better of you.

Two more turns, and she seemed to have lost the tail, or, more likely, the silver vehicle hadn't been following her. Still, her nerves were a little jangled. After all, there was a serial killer out there somewhere, some sicko who killed his victims by smashing their skulls, cutting their throats, and leaving a polished stone as his mark.

Who? she wondered.

But more importantly, why?

That was the question. Assuming the victims were not random, that they'd ticked off the killer somehow, there had to be a connection. By no conscious thought, she drove away from Forsyth Park and her home and past Whitefield Square, where, even in the darkness, she spied the live oaks and blooming azaleas surrounding the square's intricate Victorian gazebo.

She kept driving, toward the outskirts of town, where she found herself face-to-face with the All Christian Church complex, the place where the bully/pastor Westin Stark held services. The church itself looked as if it had existed for two hundred years. White, with a tall steeple, sharply pitched roof, tracery windows, and wide double doors, it stood on one side of an expansive parking area. Across the lot, a large, low fellowship hall had been constructed more recently.

She drove past slowly and observed the parsonage, a cozy cottage connected to the back of the church by a covered breezeway. While a porch light had been left on, only a single lamp glowed from within the small house.

Though she had no real reason to snoop around the place, she couldn't resist. Parking down the street a bit, she locked the car and walked back to the church and parsonage.

All the while, she had the uneasy feeling that she was being watched.

The little whispery sensation felt like insect legs tiptoeing across her shoulders.

Your imagination.

That's all. First, you thought you were being followed, and now you think someone's watching you. But there's no one here. No car parked in the carport or driveway, only one light on in the house. And you know Westin Stark is at the pub.

But, a second voice in her mind argued, *does he live alone? Is he married? Have a live-in partner or even a housekeeper?*

She paused.

If so, though, no vehicle.

Unless they share a car.

She tried to talk herself out of her paranoia, for that's what it was, but she couldn't shake the feeling that hidden eyes were observing her. Silently. Almost stalking her. Edging around the house, she kept checking the windows, but no dark figure loomed, no ghostly apparition appeared.

Nothing.

And yet . . .

Just to make certain that no one was home, that she wouldn't be caught prying, she stepped onto the porch. While a moth beat itself against the weak porch light, she heard the dulcet tones of an old-fashioned doorbell sound melodically from inside.

Immediately, a cacophony of barking erupted.

Dogs.

Great.

Just what she didn't need.

"Quiet!" she yelled in her most authoritarian voice, and, miraculously, they stopped barking.

For the moment.

But who knew how long that would last?

Quickly, she walked to the side of the house where the one lamp was burning, visible through the window. A wooden desk was situated in front of open French doors and flanked by filled bookcases. Nothing out of the ordinary, she thought, but who knew what lay behind closed doors?

No sign of the dogs.

In one word, she'd managed to quiet them?

Weird, she thought, but she surveyed the perimeter, walking a few feet away from the house, hoping to keep the dogs from hearing or smelling her. There was nothing particularly out of the ordinary, other than an empty chicken coop and dog run behind the parsonage. The coop seemed to have been abandoned long before, as the grass was tall and no feathers littered the wire cage surrounding the henhouse. However, the matted grass, dirt trail, and half-filled water dish within the long, chain-link enclosure confirmed what she already knew.

As she walked around the back, she noticed an exterior entrance to a basement, now-locked doors that would open, she thought, to a staircase leading into some kind of storm cellar, and though there were a couple of window wells on this side of the house, the basement area was dark, like most of the house. Aside from the den and the front hallway, where some of the light spilled through the glass doors, the rooms inside the home were in shadow.

Well, what did she expect? Something linking Westin Stark to the Savannah Slasher? Bloodstains? Polished rocks?

She didn't have time to think about it.

At that moment, a car pulled into the short driveway, beams from headlights washing against the house. Nikki flattened against the siding, hiding behind a scrubby bush, and hoped beyond hope that Stark hadn't seen her. She wanted to talk to him, but she didn't want to be caught snooping.

Too late.

"Nikki?" he called, climbing out of his car, a blue sedan of some kind—an import, she thought. His keys jingled as he pocketed them. "Nicole Gillette?"

She shrank inside. How could she explain herself?

Deciding she couldn't hide or cower, she walked toward him.

"What're you doing here?" he asked, standing by the front walk, his face half in shadow, half-illuminated by the porch light.

"Waiting for you," she said.

"Hmm." He didn't hide his disbelief. He glanced around the darkened streets. "At this time of night? Don't tell me, Nikki, that you've had some existential crisis? Need some reaffirmation of your faith?" He was mocking her. Taunting her. Dressed in a black shirt and pants, the clerical collar white in the night, like a Cheshire cat's smile, he asked, "Is that it? You came here for spiritual guidance?"

"I just have some questions."

"For me?" he asked, placing a hand over his chest. "But you didn't call? Why am I not surprised?"

"I wanted to talk to you about Mavis Greenlee."

"You'll hear all I have to say about her tomorrow at the funeral." His smile was beatific. And false. Beneath his clerical collar and calm, patient veneer, he was still the same bully he'd always been.

"I don't think you'll be talking about her enemies."

His eyebrows shot up. "Well, no, that wouldn't be appropriate at the service."

"So tell me now."

"You want me to discuss the personal life of one of my parishioners? A woman so recently deceased? Taken from us so heinously?"

"It's not like you've got some kind of client-lawyer privilege."

"That's very much what it's like. In this case, client-clergy, and it would be highly unethical of me to discuss anything about Mrs. Greenlee or any other of my parishioners with you or anyone else. They trust me, Nikki. They know that their secrets are just between us—well, and God, of course."

"Of course." It was her turn to sound sarcastic, but she couldn't believe his convictions. From tough guy on the playground, Westin Stark? It seemed impossible.

People do change.

They grow up.

Some. But not all. She put Westin directly in the latter category.

"I see the look of skepticism on your face, and I guess I can't blame you. I wasn't very kind as a youth," he admitted, and for once, she almost believed him.

"No, you weren't."

"Well, yes, I did some very despicable things." Frowning, he glanced up at the sky, where a few stars were winking awake. "But I've atoned for them. Trust me. The Lord has shown me the way." He reached out and actually put a hand on her shoulder.

She took a step back.

He dropped his hand. "You know, I think you would find peace if you took Jesus into your heart."

"How do you know he's not there already?" she challenged and saw the smarmy little smile play at the corner of his mouth again.

"Oh, Nicole. I know you. Remember? I could have been kinder when we were kids, but you were no angel."

That much was true. She couldn't argue the point. "I was *not* a bully."

"You did your share of damage," he said. His eyes held hers. "And now you spend your time writing about man's brutality to man. You make your living off the pain of others."

"So do you."

"I offer peace. And solutions. I help people. I heal." His smile faded. "You, on the other hand, profit."

"You don't know anything about me."

"Just what I read in the papers," he said, cuttingly. "Under your by-line. Now, if you'll excuse me," he added, his false smile returning, "I have a eulogy to write." And with that, he was up the two steps and unlocking the door of the parsonage. As he did, three dogs scrambled onto the porch. Mutts, from the looks of them, a hound of some kind, a smaller terrier mix, and one that was part pit bull. They all started down the stairs, toward Nikki, but a sharp whistle from Stark and they stopped. "They're friendly," he said, but she suspected the gleam in his eyes was from more than the porch light. "But you should always be careful with animals you don't know. A friendly demeanor on the outside belies the animosity within."

"A wolf in sheep's clothing," she said, staring pointedly at his clerical collar, a white band in a dark night.

"Good night, Nicole. Be careful out there." He whistled again to the dogs, who shot into the house. Once at the threshold, he said, "May peace find you and always"—he paused, as if for dramatic effect—"may the Father be with you and Jesus bless your soul."

Chapter 33

Was she being followed?

Driving home from her meeting with Westin Stark, Nikki kept one eye on the rearview. Did she see the same silver SUV behind her, maybe two cars back? Her heartbeat accelerated as she saw it take the same series of corners she did. "It's nothing," she said aloud, but remembered how she'd thought she was being observed the other day at the horse barns, how she'd sensed an evil presence. Now, she made sure her phone was within easy reach. Fingers tight over the wheel, and telling herself that she was being paranoid, she changed course. Instead of her normal route, she followed a twisting, circuitous path through the historic district, turning back toward the river. With the silver vehicle still a few cars behind her, she drove out of Savannah proper entirely, heading toward the airport for several miles before doubling back.

She lost visual contact with the SUV.

Still nervous, she steadied her breath, took a few more unexpected corners.

No silver vehicle appeared in her rearview.

No SUV darted from an alley to track her.

Good.

She calmed a bit, but still took the back streets toward Forsyth Park before finally pulling into her driveway. Using an extra remote she'd scrounged from one of the junk drawers, she pulled into the garage and parked near Pierce's Caddy.

"Don't be crazy," she warned herself. She was probably just overreacting due to the recent homicides, Naomi Kittle's disappearance, and her own history of near-death experiences.

Tonight, she was safe.

Her family was safe.

She'd interviewed a preacher tonight, a man of God, not some master criminal, and yet she'd let her imagination run wild.

Pierce's Jeep was MIA, which, considering the current state of crime in Savannah, wasn't a surprise, but she was disappointed.

Once inside, she was greeted by the dogs, who were, she noted, not as obedient as those in Westin Stark's small pack. "Shhh. Babies are sleeping," she whispered to them, as she petted their eagerly wiggling bodies and made her way to the kitchen. An open bottle of wine stood on the counter. "Well, at least I hope the girls are down for the night."

"They are." Lily was curled on the couch with a book, a glass of red beside her, the TV on mute. She didn't bother rising, but smiled and picked up her nearly empty glass, wiggling it slightly in invitation, "Join me?"

"Not tonight."

"Don't tell me." She mock-pouted. "Work again?" One eyebrow cocked. "You know what they say about 'all work and no play,' don't you?"

"That it makes Nikki a dull boy? Or girl? Or woman? Or whatever?"

Lily grinned. "Close enough, but I was going to add that it's a sure way to end up on a psychiatrist's couch."

"As if I needed another reason," Nikki agreed, thinking of her near–panic attack that someone might be following her and how it had delayed her arrival home. She did need to unwind and chill out. "Okay, you convinced me." She poured herself a small glass, then carried the bottle around the island to the couch where Lily was cuddled. Adding a splash of wine to her sister's drink, she asked, "How did it go?"

"With the girls?" Lily shrugged. "Good."

"No trouble getting Chloe to bed?" Nikki sat on an ottoman, and Arlo settled down on the floor next to her.

"She wanted two more stories and umpteen glasses of water, which I cut off after three, but the truth was she was worn out. We hit the park today with the dogs, and she was beside herself, running all around." Lily continued on about the day, while Nikki picked up the remote and scanned the news. "Ah, ah, ah!" Wrestling the device from Nikki's fingers, Lily turned off the television. "Full attention. Mom tried to 'convince' me to attend the funeral tomorrow, but I declined. I told her that you'd meet Kyle and her at the . . . let's call them 'festivities.' I figured you'd want your own wheels. Or maybe go with Pierce. I didn't think you'd want to be yoked to Charlene and her need to socialize with the All Christian group."

"You're sounding like an atheist."

"If the halo fits," Lily said, taking a swallow. She then swirled the wine in her glass and stared at the dark liquid. "I *am* spiritual. Even believe in God, but not as the Judeo-Christian patriarchal manifestation that organized religion considers Her to be."

"Just how much of this," Nikki asked, lifting her glass, "have you had?"

"Definitely not enough." She thought for a second. "One glass . . . well, one and a half and then what you poured in. Just enough to relax. So. Don't go all teetotaler on me."

"I'm not." And to prove it, Nikki took a long sip. "But thanks for giving me an out tomorrow. I do want my own car."

"Thought so." Lily was obviously proud of herself. She set her glass on the side table. "Has anyone heard from Naomi yet? I watched a little of the local news and scrolled through the feed on my phone, but didn't see anything."

"Same here."

"How worried are you?"

"Pretty worried," Nikki admitted. "Because Pierce and Jamison are, and I haven't heard anything that suggests she's done this kind of thing before. She doesn't seem flighty, the type to leave the kids and hubby in a huff." Absently petting Arlo's head, she decided not to share what she knew about Knox Quinlan. "Naomi's pretty dedicated to her girls, wouldn't want to worry them."

"What about leaving her husband? If you ask me, Jamison Kittle is more than a little bit of a pompous ass. One of those sons who are suns, like in the solar system. You know the kind. A prince who thinks everyone orbits around them? Trust me, I've met more than my share, and Jamison has all the earmarks."

"He's an ADA."

"An ambitious ADA."

"So?"

"I'm just sayin'."

"Hmm." Nikki finished her drink and stood. "Now, since I've officially 'played,' I need to go upstairs."

"And work. I know. Booorrrring." Lily rolled her expressive eyes.

Nikki disagreed. Her work was frustrating, time-consuming, and oftentimes, she felt like she was spinning her wheels, but what she did was seldom boring.

With Arlo on her heels, she stopped by Chloe's room, where her daughter was fast asleep. Unaware of the dangers of the world. An innocent lamb.

The way it should be, Nikki thought, walking to the window to adjust the shades in her room. Looking outside to the front of the house, she spied a silver SUV drive slowly by.

Her heart stilled.

The same vehicle that she'd seen earlier?

It was big. Possibly American made? Like a Chevy Tahoe? Or Suburban? She caught a glimmer of the distinctive bow-tie shape on the rear and the license plate, which was local, but couldn't distinguish the lettering.

Don't freak.

The large vehicle turned at the corner and the edge of the park.

Nerves tight, she stood by the window, staring at the street while her baby slept soundly. Unaware of any danger.

Minutes passed.

Nikki didn't move.

Several more cars and one pickup drove by.

But no big, silver SUV.

Nothing nefarious.

Nothing out of the ordinary.

You're making villainous mountains out of innocuous mole-hills.

Finally, she lowered the shade. For a second, she considered calling Pierce, then thought better of it. He had a lot on his plate with the homicides and Naomi's disappearance. Nikki didn't want to add to his stress, nor did she want to come off as a woman jumping at shadows, easily panicked.

With a last glance at her sleeping daughter, she headed to her office and forced her thoughts to the article she needed to submit about Naomi Kittle's disappearance. Not that she had much to work with. But she wanted to give something to Fink that he could publish.

The room was hot, stuffy with the day's heat, so she cracked the window and listened to the sounds of the night. The soft rush of a breeze through the leaves of the magnolia and somewhere a frog croaking. So peaceful. So serene. So at odds with the chaos and near-panic that the city was feeling because of the Savannah Slasher.

She also wrote an update on the serial-killer case, but there was little new information that she could divulge. She was certain Fink would balk and demand more. "Too bad," she muttered under her breath. It wasn't as if she were holding back on purpose; she'd like nothing more than exposing the serial killer terrorizing the city. So far, she'd kept her agreement with Pierce, though when she saw her husband again, she was going to press him for more details on the homicides, ones she could report.

To date, her "exclusive" end of their bargain hadn't given her an edge over the new age of media. Even television news was beginning to appear old-school, with all of the podcasts and social media dominating the industry. "Reporters" were everywhere, and information hit the Internet almost before it happened. Print newspapers, including the *Sentinel*, were quickly becoming dinosaurs on the edge of extinction. Every day, Tom Fink was struggling to save the paper. No wonder he was always on edge.

"Adapt or die," she said and put the finishing touches on her article.

By the time she was finished and on her way to bed, she heard Lily in the hall bath and saw a text from Pierce that he was on his way home.

At last.

She couldn't help but smile when she heard the garage door rumble up and down, then the familiar jangle of his keys as he dropped them onto the table near the back door. His footsteps were soft against the stairs, and he stopped at Chloe's room before slipping inside their bedroom.

"Finally," she said from her pillow and reached to turn on the bedside lamp. "About damned time, Detective."

"Yeah, it's been a long one." He sat on the edge of the bed to take off his shoes.

"Anything new on Naomi?" she asked.

"No." He shook his head, his shoulders slumping a bit. "Nothing."

"Has anyone talked to Knox Quinlan?"

Nodding, he began unbuttoning his shirt. "He's as worried as anyone."

"You don't think he knows where she is?"

"Nope. Or if he does, he should get an Academy Award."

"What about Jamison?" she asked, thinking about how Lily didn't trust the ADA.

"He's still in Charlotte with Naomi's sister and the kids." The shirt came off, exposing the muscles in his shoulders and a little scar where he'd been grazed by a bullet years before.

Nikki asked, "How's he holding up?"

"About as well as you'd expect. Brave front for the girls." Pierce tossed his shirt onto a nearby chair, stood, and unzipped his slacks.

"You think it's an act?"

"He's destroyed, Nikki." Pierce kicked the pants toward the chair, then rolled into bed. "It's a nightmare."

"And you?" she asked.

He turned off the lamp. "I'm okay."

"But—?" she asked, as he wrapped his arms around her.

"But it's hell."

Then he kissed her. Warm, eager lips finding hers in the half light, the scent and feel of his skin surrounding her. "No more talking," he said, as he lifted his head.

"You got it, Detective." She pulled his head back to hers, her blood heating, her body responding.

And for the next few moments, the world, with all its sordid, painful problems, melted away.

The next day Nikki suffered through Mavis Greenlee's funeral.

Sitting on a hard pew and listening to Reverend Stark sing the deceased woman's praises was torturous, and observing Archer Greenlee fighting tears in the first row of the church was even worse. Thankfully, he'd had the good sense to leave Annabelle at home, probably keeping her under wraps until the reading of the will, or the solving of his wife's murder, or both.

Nikki sat at the end of a pew, with a view of the closed mahogany casket. Two immense sprays of lilies and white roses flanked the casket, while a large headshot of Mavis in her forties smiled on the congregation. Near the pulpit, a Christian flag stood proudly next to the Stars and Stripes while an enormous, intricately carved crucifix was suspended over the altar.

Prayers were offered, hymns sung, and Oliver Crawford spoke of the finer qualities of his sister, while Blanche dabbed at her eyes over the loss of her only daughter, the woman who had so obviously neglected her. Two of the elders delivered Bible quotes, Otis Childers reciting a quote from John 3:16 and Duke Wheelan providing a reference to the Ten Commandments. A solo artist sang "Amazing Grace," before Reverend Stark offered a eulogy of divine proportions, reminding everyone of Mavis's devotion to God and her fellow man.

At that remark, Charlene, seated beside Nikki, gave a quiet snort into her handkerchief. Dressed in black and white, a broad-brimmed hat angled over her newly coiffed hair, Charlene sat dry-eyed, her face pinched as if she were in physical pain.

Both of Mavis's ex-husbands showed. Radley Bowers, the golf pro, attended with his wife, Kelsey, and their kids, while Leonard Armstrong was flying solo and forever pulling at his too-tight collar as sweat collected on his bald pate.

Even Norm Metzger paid his respects, which surprised Nikki. After all the years of working with him at the newspaper, she'd never known Metzger to be the tiniest bit religious or pious, but there he sat in the pew with a couple of the other elders of the church: Duke Wheelan and Otis Childers. Both men lived in proximity to Jeanne

LaRoux and were neighbors of Billy Huber. Both disliked Billy intensely and, as far as Nikki could determine, were only linked to Mavis Greenlee through the church. Duke Wheelan was dressed in black, as was Frannie, who sat next to him, though not touching. Daria Childers, in a deep purple dress that showed a little cleavage, was squeezed into the pew next to her husband.

As for Norm, at the far end of the pew, he was alone and kept staring down at the funeral program they were all given upon entrance. She wondered about him. Was he Norm, the lazy man skating to retirement that she'd always thought? Could he be one of those Saturday-night sinners who became, overnight, Sunday-morning saints?

She realized that, for all the years she'd worked with him, she knew little about the man.

Lily, as promised, refused to be a hypocrite and did not attend. She kept the girls at home. Kyle looked like he'd rather be anywhere other than the hot church, wedged into a crowd of people he didn't know. He fidgeted, but stayed sitting in the pew. Pierce quietly observed the congregation from the back of the nave, in case he was called away. He'd confided to Nikki just before the service that a man out walking his dog might have seen Naomi Kittle's car, and deputies were currently checking the area.

After a final prayer, the mourners filed out, past Blanche, Oliver, and Westin Stark, who shook hands and accepted sympathy near the front doors. From the vestibule, the crowd moved into the fellowship hall, where the Birds of Paradise had set up tables for refreshments.

But she saw no one who appeared to be a serial killer in the throng of mourners, but then what had she expected? Someone wearing an evil leer or a sign that read: Watch out! I'm a murderer?

Well, she'd hoped for some kind of clue in the rows of mourners. However, no one looked the least bit suspicious or out of place.

She met Pierce inside and saw him checking his phone.

"Any news?" she whispered.

"Not yet. The guy who might've seen Naomi's car isn't exactly credible. Turns out he was out night hunting, and it wasn't for turkeys, which are about all that's in season now. But not at night and not with a rifle. Both illegal." He checked his phone again. "I'm waiting for a call." His phone buzzed in his hand. "Okay, here we go. Moment of truth." He turned and walked out of the door.

Nikki wasn't about to be left out. She made her excuses and left as soon as she could break away.

"You've got Mom," she said to Kyle, as Charlene, intent on talking to Blanche, was moving through the crowd more quickly than Nikki could have imagined.

"Fine," Kyle said. "We won't be here long."

"Don't count on it." Charlene was in her element, making small talk, mingling, putting on a sad face, even though she'd hated Mavis Greenlee in life. However, today, the stingy, adulterous, self-centered Mavis, who had neglected her parents, was an angel on her way to heaven. While some people seemed genuinely saddened by her passing, or even appeared to be taking heart in her rising to the pearly gates, others were quietly gossiping. Over the clink of silverware and glasses, Nikki heard, in the hum of conversation, Naomi's name mentioned more often than not, and some were even speculating on the other murders as well.

"I'll call you later," she promised her mother. "Kyle will take you home." She was rewarded by a dismissive wave of Charlene's gloved hand.

Good enough.

Nikki was out the door of the stuffy building. Spying Pierce waiting near his Jeep, in the shade of a magnolia tree near the edge of the parking lot, she hurried to where his Jeep was parked. As she reached him, he said, "I figured you would want to come out to the river."

"The river?" she repeated.

"At the bend near the old Cranston place . . . That's where a drone spotted a submerged car this morning."

"Oh." She felt a thrill of excitement, with a heavy measure of dread. "Naomi?" she asked.

"Unknown. But the car is white and looks like a Mercedes."

Her heart nose-dived. She'd hoped Naomi would reappear, but this sounded bad. "Oh, no. Do you think—?"

"No need to speculate." Then he heard his curt tone and cleared his throat. "It doesn't look good, but we don't know yet. Let's go. Divers are there now, the tow truck on its way."

"That point in the river is close to Knox Quinlan's place," she thought aloud and mentally calculated the distance, figuring it was less than a mile as the crow flew.

Pierce gave a curt nod, having apparently already reached the same conclusion. "Right." He opened the door of his Jeep. "Coming?"

"No. I've got my car here. I'll drive. Kyle's in charge of Mom."

"Bet he loves that."

"Right. But it's his turn." After all, Kyle had been virtually missing in action for years. "I'll call Lily and let her know that I might be late."

"Good." He turned to leave, but she caught him on the elbow.

"And this is my story, right?"

"That's what you're worried about?" he asked.

"No. But it's my job. You do yours, no matter what the circumstances, no matter how distasteful. And I'll do mine."

"Fair enough," he agreed, as she released her grip on his sleeve. "But I can't control the situation if other reporters are there. These days, information spreads like wildfire."

She couldn't argue that point. But she could get to the site on the river and watch the car being dredged and report it to their online content via her phone if she couldn't get a photographer out to the spot. Either way, she couldn't get a story to press ahead of what would be a flood of information over the Internet, but at least some of it would display under her byline for the *Sentinel.*

Pierce was already leaving by the time she climbed inside the warm interior of her rental and rolled down the windows and slipped on her sunglasses.

Before she left the lot, she turned on the air-conditioning and called her sister to sketch out what was happening. ". . . it's all on the down-low for now," she said.

"Oh, dear God. Naomi?"

"No one knows yet." Nikki put the car into reverse. "I could be a while."

"Okay. Got it," Lily said. "Don't worry about Chloe. I'll wear her out at the zoo today. She's into the animals. Big-time."

So true. Chloe loved their pets and the goats and horses at the riding academy, though lately her ardor for the llamas had cooled.

Ignoring the maternal pang of envy about Lily's outing with the girls, she said, "I'll keep you posted," and then hung up and backed out of the parking space. It was her decision to keep working once Chloe had come into the world, and she didn't regret it for the most part, but a little tiny voice in her head kept reminding her, *You're missing out on a unique time that is so precious and oh so fleeting.*

"It's a balancing act," she said aloud and noticed a big, silver SUV parked at the edge of the lot.

So what?

There were dozens of similar vehicles in the city.

And yet . . . She felt a chill deep in her bones and thought about sticking around, seeing who was behind the wheel.

But she couldn't. Not now. Not when Naomi Kittle might be found. She took a picture of the vehicle, including the license plate, then took off.

She drove out of the city limits and hit the gas, pushing the speed limit and rolling up the windows as the air-conditioning kicked in. Traffic waned, and the suburbs gave way to farmland. She was momentarily bottlenecked by a tractor chugging along under twenty miles an hour, but she was able to pass and keep moving.

Nikki had witnessed the river being dredged before, and once she'd watched as an escaped trailer stacked with hay was winched out of a pond. But this was different. This could be someone she knew; in fact, she had the cold, gnawing fear that the car being dragged from the river belonged to Naomi. Her insides tightened at the thought. If the car did turn out to be Naomi's, then most likely she was still inside.

Seeing a body pulled from the river would be difficult. Recognizing the dead person as someone she knew, worse. A vision that might haunt her the rest of her days.

Especially since Nikki herself had nearly drowned.

And Sylvie Morrisette had died in the water that same day.

"God help me," she whispered, taking a final turn and seeing the police cars and ambulance already parked near the river in a wide spot on the road that opened to a dusty track and a boat launch for small craft.

A tow truck was idling at the shoreline, its lights flashing, its cables already hooked to something beneath the water. Police and a fire crew swarmed along the bank, and a diver in a wet suit had pulled off his mask and stood dripping on the sunbaked rocks near the water's edge.

Nikki parked on the gravel shoulder and stepped outside, only to be stopped by a deputy in uniform and mirrored sunglasses, as she tried to walk closer to the river.

"I'm sorry, ma'am. This area is restricted."

"It's all right," she started to argue to get a closer look, but stopped short when she saw, from the distance, the white Mercedes, covered in mud as it was being winched from the river. Her heart stuttered. The car was identical to the Mercedes she'd seen at the riding academy. All hope that it belonged to someone other than Naomi vanished. Her throat grew tight as she watched water cascade down the sides of the vehicle in a noisy rush. The windshield was smashed, the windows rolled down.

Escape routes, she thought, hoping Naomi had somehow survived.

She saw there was no body strapped behind the steering wheel, thank God, nor did it appear as if anyone had been dragged from the river, as the ambulance was still waiting.

Had Naomi somehow escaped a watery death?

She swallowed back a swell of nausea that climbed up her throat. "Dear God," she whispered, imagining Naomi's panic.

If she'd been in the vehicle.

Nikki wondered if she'd been alone.

Or had there been someone with her?

The passenger side window was rolled down.

As were the windows of the back seat and even the rear.

How had that happened?

Again, Nikki scanned the slow-moving river and its narrow, brushy banks. A dozen questions swept through her mind.

What had happened here? Where the hell was Naomi? If, indeed, she had been in the muddy vehicle. Could someone else have been driving? Could she have been the victim of a carjacking? If so—why hadn't she called?

As the Mercedes was being pulled onto the flatbed, she caught Pierce's attention. With a wave, he walked her way, but, as if anticipating her first question, shook his head. "No body," he said, "But it's

Naomi's car. Registered to Jamison. The license plate matches, and divers found her purse and ID inside."

She was still staring at the wet, grimy vehicle, once sleek, now covered in sludge. "What about in the trunk?" she asked, fearing the answer.

"Empty."

Nikki felt a moment's relief. "So where is she?"

"That's the million-dollar question."

"How did the car end up in the river?" she asked, watching as the water lapped the shore. A snowy egret skimmed the surface as it flew away.

"Unknown."

"But you've seen the footage of her driving back into Georgia?"

He nodded grimly.

"And you're sure it was Naomi behind the wheel, when you said she crossed the state line?"

"We're enhancing the images from the cameras, but we think so."

"No one else in the car?" she asked.

"Looks like she was alone." He swatted at a mosquito hovering near his head and squinted up at the flatbed, where the car was being secured before it was taken to the forensic vehicle examination lab. "We should know more once we go through it."

"You've called Jamison?"

"Yeah." Pierce squinted against the afternoon sun. "He's on his way back from Charlotte."

"And the girls?" She just had to confirm that they were okay.

"Coming back on Monday, I think with Naomi's sister, Roxie. Her husband is going to handle their kids, to free her up so she can spend some time down here to support Jamison and the girls, at least until things settle down."

"And when will that be?"

Again he swatted at a bothersome mosquito, his eyes still on Naomi's car being strapped to the flatbed of the tow truck. "God only knows."

Sol didn't like it.

She stood on the edge of the river, just around the bend, alone, her gaze on the water, her senses attuned to the sounds, sights, and smells of this part of the lowlands. With the sun beating down on her scalp, she listened to the chirp of birds and the steady croak of a frog hidden in the cattails and dense foliage. The water lapped rhythmically, adding a quiet beat to the steady hum of insects, while the air smelled damp, of wet earth and running water.

She heard the voices of men shouting orders, the clank of the winch, and the grumbling of the drag of the car as it was hauled upward out of the river, but she closed out those unnatural noises and let her mind focus on the natural sounds while the slightest breeze whispered against her skin.

Something was off.

The balance of energy between what was real and what was perceived had been skewed somehow.

By someone.

Someone with malicious intent.

She went over what she knew about the missing woman, and it wasn't much, just what she'd witnessed when Naomi had come into the office, which was rarely, and then recently what Reed had divulged because of the case, that the ADA and his wife had scheduled a romantic weekend when she hadn't shown up. That they, with three stepping-stone daughters, were planning on another baby.

She doubted that would come to pass.

As a breeze cooled the beads of perspiration on her forehead, Sol didn't need anyone to tell her that the woman for whom they were searching wouldn't be found. Not here. Not in the water.

She stared at the sluggish river, the slow-moving current.

Naomi Kittle's energy wasn't lingering here, nor, she thought, had it ever been.

She felt no remaining aura.

Not even in the slightest.

No, she thought, bending down to pick up a little of the moist soil touched by the river, rubbing the fine grains between her fingers.

They wouldn't locate Naomi Kittle here.

No matter how long or deep they searched.

Chapter 34

Pierce watched as his friend emotionally collapsed.

"I just don't understand why we haven't found her!" Jamison said, pacing back and forth on the patio surrounding his pool. In running gear, he appeared haggard, his face more lined than Pierce recalled, his overall demeanor tense and agitated. Unshaven and with dark circles beneath his eyes, Jamison looked like he hadn't slept in days.

He probably hadn't.

Which was no surprise.

The news wasn't good.

Naomi was still missing, and as it was Monday, nearly two days had passed since her car had been dragged from the river.

Now the sun was sinking ever lower in the western sky, a few fading rays glinting off the waterfall that fed the deep end of the pool. Mockingbirds called from the nearby trees, a yellow jacket buzzed determinedly over the lip of the pool, and in the distance, a train was rumbling on its tracks.

Meanwhile, the effort to find Jamison's missing wife was ongoing.

Helicopters and dogs had been brought in, and a search team had been scouring the shoreline and forest around the bend in the river. More divers had delved into the water, only to come up empty, and

Jamison had arrived to pace the shoreline and stare, grim-faced, at the river.

Currently, the forensic team was still going over every inch of the Mercedes. Her phone had been located in her purse inside the vehicle, and Jamison had provided them with her password, so her texts, messages, scrolling history, and calls were being studied. More investigators had descended on Jamison's home, with his blessing, and he'd supplied access codes to all of the computers and electronic equipment in the house. The investigators had promptly unplugged the computers and taken them to be analyzed.

"We'll locate her," Pierce said. "But we could use the public's help."

"I know, I know. I've got a press conference scheduled," Jamison snapped, his nerves obviously strung to the breaking point. "In front of the station. I'm just waiting for Naomi's parents. They're settling into the condo they keep in town. They never sold it when they moved. They use it as an Airbnb and are going to stay there with the girls. Then all of us, as a family, will make a plea for her safety."

"Including your daughters?" Pierce asked, surprised. "You're going to have them there? In front of the cameras?" He'd heard that Jamison was making a statement to the media from Vivian Johnson, the public information officer, but he hadn't known that Naomi's daughters were going to be involved.

"They won't speak, of course. I wouldn't make them go through that. But I'll talk, and possibly Roxie or Naomi's mom will. I figure if someone's got her, if she's been kidnapped or something else has happened, and we make a public plea for her safety, it will help for the girls to be visible. Maybe the culprit or someone who knows what happened, but wasn't going to say anything, will come forward. An accomplice or confidante or someone who wasn't planning to get involved. Maybe they'll see my girls and have second thoughts and crack."

When Pierce didn't respond, Jamison threw up his hands as if giving up. "I really don't know what to do here," he admitted. "It's not like I've ever been on this end of a missing-person case." He exhaled in frustration and squeezed his eyes shut, as if trying to erase a painful image.

"Whatever you think is best," Pierce said.

"I wish I knew." His eyes opened, and he squinted into the setting sun. "I just wish I knew."

In the distance, beyond the tree line, the Kittles' dogs began to put up a ruckus. First one, then several of the dogs commenced barking.

"Those damned hounds!" Jamison said, his gaze swinging to the tree line. "I started out with one hunting dog, then another younger one, and Naomi, she went wild. Bred the two and started this . . . this family of hounds. She really got into it. Was all about their bloodlines or whatever." He glared at the thick copse of pine and live oak as if he could quiet the dogs by simply willing it. He was a powder keg, looking for an excuse to blow up. Not a good time to bring up a bad subject, but Pierce had a job to do.

"Was?" Pierce repeated, noting the past tense.

"Gave up on it. A few months back. Lost interest. She still takes care of them, but without the same passion, I guess you'd say. Maybe now . . . well, hell, who knows?"

Pierce decided to broach the subject that had been weighing on him. "You know that Naomi was seeing Knox Quinlan?"

Jamison's head whipped around. "What?" he snapped. "What do you mean, seeing him? Like she was running into him?"

"Like seeing him romantically."

Jamison barked out a laugh. "Oh, right." Then he caught Pierce's sober expression. "You're kidding, right? That's supposed to be funny. You can't be . . . I mean, you're not serious."

"Not kidding," Pierce assured him.

Jamison shook his head, his dark hair catching the lowering sun's rays. "No way. I mean there's just no way."

"Old boyfriend," Pierce pointed out.

"Oh, come on." Jamison snorted, then gave Pierce a long look. "Well . . . yeah, they were together a long time ago, but—" He held up both hands, palms out as if warding off any arguments. "No. *That* was over a long time ago. The guy's a loser. Was way back when and still is. She ditched Quinlan as soon as we got together."

"I remember. But old feelings die hard."

"Are you speaking from experience?"

"Just letting you know. When we talked a while back, you mentioned that you and Naomi had hit a rough patch in your marriage."

"Everyone has them," he said defensively, his back starting to go up. "It's natural and, you know, midlife. But it isn't a big deal. Just a communication problem. We were going to fix that this weekend."

"And try for another baby."

"Rrrighhht," Jamison said, but his thoughts were seemingly churning, his eyes growing dark. "Naomi wouldn't . . . I mean there's just no way she would . . ." His voice trailed off.

Pierce could only guess that Jamison was remembering. A feeling of unease? That something wasn't quite right? Dates that had been unexpectedly broken? Hours unaccounted for? Times when his wife was distracted, in her own world? Or had he found little clues that didn't add up and wondered about what secrets she kept?

Well, now Jamison knew.

And he didn't appreciate it.

"I find it hard to believe," he said tightly, his anger surmounting his fear.

"They've been seen together at the riding academy."

Jamison's expression hardened. "Naomi takes Shana there. Maybe they ran into each other. Knox, he's a rancher, probably supplies some of the livestock or . . ."

"Nikki talked to him. He didn't deny it."

"Nikki?" Jamison repeated, his face flushed, nostrils flaring. "Your wife? A reporter? He told her. But not the police?"

"Not yet. But he's coming in for questioning."

"He volunteered?" Jamison asked in obvious disbelief.

"No. He was reluctant but didn't argue about it. I'm on my way back to the station now."

"Fine." Jamison reached into his pocket for his car keys. "Let's go!"

"No. Just me."

"I'm the ADA," Jamison declared.

"You're the husband," Reed reminded him.

"Exactly! And I want answers."

"You know how this goes. Protocol."

"Fuck protocol!" Jamison was already striding along the edge of the pool toward the garage and his BMW.

"Hey! Stop!" Pierce caught up to him and grabbed his elbow.

Fists balled, Jamison whipped around. His eyes were bright, his teeth clenched, and he was itching to throw the first punch. Bruised male pride surfaced. "You're telling me that my *missing* wife is having an affair, cheating on me, risking everything we have for some ex-con boyfriend and then you expect me to what—just sit on my goddamned hands?" His fury was palpable, radiating off him, and every muscle in his body was tense, ready to explode.

Fine.

"That's exactly what I'm saying." Pierce braced himself, his own fists clenching. He couldn't remember the last time he'd had a fist-fight or who it was with, but he would bet his pension it was in a match with a younger, headstrong, winner-at-all-costs Jamison Kittle. One of those drunken, college tests of manhood when someone says the wrong thing, and all of a sudden you're in a wrestling match. Pierce had been in more than his share. Back in the day. Sometimes with his friend. And in those stupid, testosterone- and alcohol-infused matches against athletic, no-holds-barred Jamison, Pierce had invariably lost.

Kittle had claimed victory.

Always.

But not this time.

The sounds of the afternoon seemed to mute as he focused on his angry friend. The soft splashing of the waterfall faded, the chirps of mocking birds muted, even the drone of insects disappeared.

"Careful," Pierce warned his friend as Jamison, on the balls of his feet, started to circle him, looking for a soft spot to land the first, lightning-fast punch.

"Use your head, Jamison. If Knox has anything to do with Naomi's disappearance, we want to nail him. Legally. Don't do anything that would fuck it up." Pierce moved, keeping his eyes focused on his friend. He knew Jamison was a time bomb, ready to explode, needing to pound out his frustration in a burst of energy that would mean quick-fire jabs to Pierce's ribs.

If he let him.

Jamison glared at him, a muscle working overtime in his jaw. His lips barely moved as he said, "I just want to . . ."

"Beat the shit out of him," Pierce said and didn't shift his gaze away from Jamison's eyes. "I know. But this isn't the way. Be smart, Jamison. Brains over brawn. Let's nail him."

Jamison drew back. Pulsing with repressed fury. There was no changing his mind. A fight simmered in the air.

Pierce could smell it.

And he was ready.

He changed his tune. "Okay, then. Do it."

Jamison's eyes thinned, his color rising, his eyes glittering dangerously.

"Just try," Pierce goaded. "Hit me! Go ahead! See what happens."

That did it!

Jamison's control snapped.

He roared and rushed forward.

Pierce sidestepped onto the very edge of the pool.

Stuck out his foot.

Jamison feinted, but tripped.

Flailed.

Grabbed Pierce's leg as he went down.

Crack!

Jamison's face slammed against the cement. Blood spurted from his nose.

Pierce teetered and then landed hard. On his back. At the lip of the pool.

Pain radiated from his spine.

Still, they grappled. Swinging and breathing hard. In a tangle of curses and flying fists, they rolled near the water, Pierce trying to block the blows, Jamison spitting blood and punching wildly.

Wrestling near the pool's rim.

Landing punches.

Jabbing.

Swearing.

Pain jolting with each hit.

Pierce attempted to pin Jamison, but his opponent's fist shot upward, slamming into Pierce's cheek with a sickening crunch.

In a surge of strength, Jamison arched his back muscles, yelled, and flipped Pierce onto his back. Pain rattled Pierce's vertebrae. A sea of red blocked his vision as blood rained down from Jamison's wide nostrils.

"You sanctimonious son of a bitch!" Jamison cried, ready to strike again.

Despite the pain and weight pinning him down, Pierce twisted, every muscle in his body straining with the lift.

Jamison's legs tightened.

But his balance shifted.

One final push.

They toppled.

Entangled.

Over the edge.

Splashed into the water.

Jamison's legs loosened.

Pierce kicked.

With as much force as he could muster.

Then again as Jamison flailed, gulping water.

Quickly, Pierce swam underwater, putting as much distance as he could between him and Jamison, and surfacing near the waterfall, shaking the water from his hair, zeroing his gaze on Jamison as he bobbed to the surface fifteen feet away.

Blood from Jamison's nose ran into the water.

But the fight had been washed from him in the cold water.

"Oh, Christ," he muttered, blinking. He was in the shallower end, able to stand, his shoulders slumping. "Shit," he muttered, using two hands to scrape his hair from his face. "God! I'm—Oh, hell. What the fuck was I thinking?"

"You tell me." Pierce treaded water, his gaze fixed on the man who was either friend or foe, depending on his run of emotions.

Jamison swiped at the end of his nose with his arm. "I don't . . . Oh, fuck." He looked up at the sky as if searching for answers.

"You okay?" Pierce asked, easing toward the ladder.

"Hell, no. Would you be?" Jamison asked.

"No. But I sure as hell wouldn't try to kill my best friend."

Jamison barked out a humorless laugh. "If I tried to kill you," he said, "you'd be dead by now."

"Sure."

"Hey, man, I'm sorry." And he looked it, as he wiped snot and blood from the end of his nose again. "Jesus, you're in a suit."

"You'll get the dry-cleaning bill," Pierce said, reaching the ladder.

"I think I owe you a new suit."

"You do," Pierce agreed. "So make it an Armani."

"Okay. Fine." Jamison slogged through the water and crawled up the steps at the shallow end. He snagged a towel from the back of a chaise longue and wiped his face. "What do we do now?"

That was an easy one. "You take care of your girls and let me find your wife." Pierce climbed out of the pool, his clothes dripping all over the warm concrete.

"Deal?"

"Deal," Jamison said with a sigh. He tossed Pierce the towel, now damp and stained with some watery blood. "I don't like it, and I hate to admit you're right. You know that, but, in this case, damn it, you are. Now, just hold up your part and find Naomi."

The new stones were ready.

Polished and gleaming to a perfect sheen.

Each etched in blood.

Placed on his workbench in his private sanctuary.

While Perry Como sang "Ave Maria," he replaced the vial and worried that he might run out before his mission was accomplished. The goat's blood and calf blood were easily replaced, but the human blood was an issue.

Specific.

His source was no longer available.

He should have been more careful and thought ahead.

But how could he have known there were so many sinners who had to be exposed?

His list had grown.

Not that Nikki Gillette wouldn't have found her way onto the list, but she was an interruption, had altered his plan, because she'd forced herself to the forefront.

He read her latest article about the Savannah Slasher, and he scowled. It didn't reveal his identity. But he knew her, understood how dogged she was, what risks she would take. But he also realized that she now had a vulnerability. She was a mother. With a small child.

That was what he would use against her.

The curly-headed toddler.

Chloe.

He'd learned her name and where she went to preschool and that she was often left with Nikki's older sister. The blonde who snuck long, black cigarettes around the corner of the garage.

He'd watched as she'd left her young charge unattended for a few moments while she stole a smoke.

He would have to deal with Nikki Gillette.

And soon.

He picked up his vial of fast-depleting human blood.

Good for one, maybe two more applications.

He'd been foolish not to harvest more, and at that thought, his mother's voice came to him. Rough and low, but rising above Perry Como's smooth baritone.

"How could you be so foolish? So stupid? When your IQ is supposed to be so high. Near genius. Isn't that what the school tests showed? But here you are, useless as ever, playing with rocks." She tutted then, clicking her tongue in disgust. *"Such a disappointment. You could have been something, but you're not."* More tsking and shaking of her head as she reached for her pack of Marlboro Reds. *"Such a goddamned disappointment."*

And there she'd done it. Taken the Lord's name in vain. Not ever opening a Bible. Never stepping inside a church. Not once praying! If it had been up to her, she would have raised him as an atheist, but his father, often absent or lost in listening to his collection of precious records, had stepped in. With the aid of his paternal grandmother, God rest her soul, his father had seen to his Christian upbringing and his understanding of piety. Of atonement. Of retribution. Of the love and wrath of God.

His mother had never understood faith.

And so he'd taught her.

With her own knife.

That sharp little blade with its ram-horned hilt. Fashioned by her father, his grandfather, from the horns of a sheep the old man had slaughtered himself.

Now, he picked up the folding knife and caressed its worn handle. *Ahh, Mother*, he thought, with a prideful sense of satisfaction.

You were right.

I wouldn't be in this predicament if I'd thought ahead.

If I'd planned more carefully.

If I'd drained more of your blood when I'd had the chance.

Chapter 35

"You never told me about the funeral," Lily said from the family room as she muted the television.

"Nothing much to say." A lot had happened since Mavis Greenlee was put to rest. Nikki slammed the dishwasher closed and listened as the rush of water indicated the temperamental machine was running.

"No big 'aha' moments for you? You didn't root out the murderer?"

"Nope. It was all very standard fare." She thought about Westin Stark on the pulpit in his black robe and purple stole, hair neatly clipped. He had the look of a leader on him as he spoke of resurrection and everlasting life in heaven for Mavis Greenlee. For all who believed.

"So did the Partridge Family put on a big spread?"

"You mean the Birds of Paradise," Nikki corrected, though she knew Lily was just being sarcastic. As usual. "Yes, it was nice. All in all," Nikki had to admit, "the service was good."

"But not fruitful for you in chasing down a murderer?"

"Well, that wasn't exactly the intent of the funeral."

"No, I suppose not." Lily took a sip of wine. "I shouldn't be so judgmental."

"Amen to that."

Drying her hands on a towel, Nikki walked from the kitchen to stare at the television.

Lily was sprawled on the couch, the girls outside with the dogs, running in the yard, while the sky was streaked magenta and violet as the sun set. She caught a glimpse of Chloe running and giggling over the grass, Arlo bounding after her, even Phee giving chase, her hair flying, her grin infectious as she caught her much-younger cousin. Chloe screamed happily, laughing, while Phee spun her around and Arlo, tail whipping from his still-shorn backside, barked and galloped to join in.

The scene in the backyard was heartwarming.

And in direct opposition to what was being aired on the local news.

"I can't believe this is happening," Lily said somberly as she watched the TV and absently petted Jennings, who had deigned to curl up next to her. A half-full glass of red wine sat on the coffee table, where several magazines lay open.

On the screen a grim-faced Jamison Kittle was front and center, other officers nearby, and she caught a glimpse of Pierce, standing a few feet to one side.

An older couple were huddled next to Jamison. They were, Nikki guessed, Naomi's parents. The woman was petite, like Naomi, with the same arched brows and high cheekbones. She'd placed one manicured hand over the youngest girl's shoulder, while a stoic man in his early seventies stood close. Both parents looked devastated, their faces etched with shared fear. The Kittles' usually rambunctious daughters stood ashen-faced, like proverbial does in the headlights, while their father pleaded with anyone who had any knowledge of what had happened to his wife to come forward.

"We just want our Naomi back," Jamison said, staring straight into the camera, his voice cracking over his wife's name.

"What a nightmare," Lily whispered.

"I can't imagine." Nikki couldn't help but remember the night of Lara's sweet-sixteen party, where Naomi was in the kitchen, organizing the refreshments. Lara had been a little snappy and the center of attention, her two siblings dressed up in frothy silver dresses, but running through the house like the carefree kids they were.

Or had been.

No longer.

Now bone-chilling reality had destroyed the unfettered naivete and free spirits.

That much was evident in their haunted eyes.

Nikki's heart ached for what they'd lost. Could it be retrieved and nurtured, when their mother was found?

If she was found.

The night of the party, Naomi had been in control, organizing everything from food to music and the family photographs. But Nikki had also caught Knox leaving the Kittles' property after speaking with Naomi, outside the kitchen that night, and another time Nikki had seen them together at the riding school. Naomi was obviously involved with her ex-boyfriend again, most likely romantically. Sexually.

And yet the tired-looking man on the screen, one of Pierce's best friends, had confided that he and his wife had been planning to share their own romantic weekend. They were going to reconnect and create a new life, hopefully a son, to solidify their union and give Jamison the male heir that he so desperately longed for, so that he could claim his hereditary stake in the Kittle family tradition.

"Liar," she said under her breath.

"Who's a liar?" Lily stopped stroking the cat and picked up her wineglass. Still holding the stem, she pointed with her index finger at the newscast, where Jamison was just stepping away from the microphone. "Him? Well, you know what I think about Jamison Kittle, but I can't help but feel for him, and especially the kids."

"I know, I agree." Jamison Kittle appeared heartbroken. The camera panned on the three girls. "You know, he told Pierce that he and Naomi were trying to get pregnant, that they hoped for a boy."

"What if they got another girl?" Lily asked. "Maybe a basketball team of females. Then what? Even another one. And another?" She took a sip from her glass. "It happens. I know a family who had six boys before they got the girl."

"And how old was that mother?"

"She started young. Early twenties. Maybe was even still in her teens. I don't really know. But, to be fair, I have a friend who has four boys. Always wanted a girl, and now she's really cool with how it all turned out. Swears she can't imagine her life being any other way. So, you never know."

"Naomi's in her mid-forties," Nikki mused.

"Not too late," Lily said as a chyron ran along the bottom of the screen, displaying the number to call if anyone had information about Naomi's disappearance. "You weren't exactly a spring chicken when you had your first."

"And it wasn't easy," she said, remembering the emotional pain of her miscarriages as her phone buzzed in her pocket.

A text.

From Janelle McGowan, Billy Huber's daughter.

Janelle's message was to the point:

Got the police okay to clean up Billy's place.

Retrieved what I wanted (not much!) and found someone to clean it up.

The crew comes tomorrow to take all the crap away.

I went through most of it and left some of that dog's things on the porch. Toys. Leashes. A bed. Vet records and some dog food.

If you want anything, you can have it.

After tomorrow, it's gone.

Hope the mutt's okay.

Nikki wasn't interested in Arlo's things, aside from the vet records. But she wouldn't mind going through Billy Huber's place again. Before it was destroyed. And she was surprised that Janelle had even contacted her and said something kind about the dog.

Maybe she was mellowing.

But, thinking about Billy's only child, Nikki decided that Janelle's change of heart was unlikely.

At that moment, the door to the patio burst open.

Laughing and giggling, Chloe chasing Phee, the girls ran inside. Arlo sped after them, Mikado taking his time. "Shut the door!" Lily ordered, then added, "Please!" as Arlo began zooming around the room, circling in one spot, then making mad dashes from one end of the room to the other.

Phee closed the door with a bang.

Arlo sped around the coffee table, his tail whipping as fast as a striking snake. It hit Lily's glass, sending it flying.

"Stop!" she shrieked as wine sloshed from the glass to spill over the magazines and remote control. "Oh, God! Stop!"

Nikki retrieved the kitchen towel and tossed it to her sister as the dog streaked into the foyer and up the stairs.

"Get him out of here!" Lily was dabbing at the table, wiping up the spill. "Take him for a walk or, better yet, a run!" she said. "Oh, God!"

Arlo zipped back into the room.

"Open the door! Let him out!" Lily yelled.

Phee's fingers were still on the handle. "But you said to close—"

"I know! I changed my mind!"

"Okay. Geez, Mom, don't have a fit!" Phee opened the door, and Arlo shot through.

"Fine, I'll take him to the dog park for exercise," Nikki said, which was stretching the truth more than a little. She had no intention of going to the park and instead planned to return to Billy Huber's property at Janelle McGowan's invitation.

"Good!" Lily was frantically blotting up the dark liquid and shaking out the remote.

"I come, too!" Chloe had taken in all of the excitement.

"Not this time," Nikki said, picking up her daughter. "It's beddy-bye for you now."

"No!" Chloe stuck out her lower lip. "You're mean!"

Lily, her frantic fury expunged, actually laughed. "This from the most privileged princess in Savannah." She drank the few remaining drops of wine from her glass, then tossed the stained towel into the sink. "I'll take her," she said to Nikki and left her empty glass on the table to retrieve her niece. Sending a sidelong glance to the glass door, where Arlo was now whining and scratching, she added, "You deal with the devil dog."

Nikki drove directly to Billy Huber's place.

As Janelle had promised, all of Arlo's dog paraphernalia was on the porch, piled surprisingly neatly on a small table. The rest of the property, with its piles of junk, appeared the same as it had weeks before when Nikki had first viewed it.

While Arlo nosed around the place where he'd last lived, Nikki surveyed the place. She eyed the barn, where Billy had, it seemed, been repairing a gutter, and the area below it, where he'd met his maker, compliments of a killer still at large. The tiller that had been used to crush his skull had been removed, but pieces of old carnival rides were still piled near a shed, and vines still grew over the face of a clown with a light bulb for a nose. Furniture was broken and rotting, some with stuffing exposed and probably home for rats and other rodents. The rusting arm and carriage from an old octopus ride was rusting near the fence.

She studied the forested area that separated Billy's property from that of Duke Wheelan, and as dusk settled over the land, she thought she saw movement in the thickets. Someone or something watching.

A deer?

Stray cow?

Whatever it was, shadow or being, it remained in the depths of sycamore and pine.

Unmoving.

Watching.

Waiting.

A chill ran down her spine.

Did it move again?

Or was it the coming darkness, deepening the shadows?

"Come on," she called to the shepherd.

Night was swiftly approaching. "Let's go."

Eagerly, Arlo galloped past an old refrigerator and stove without a front door, then stopped at Nikki's rental car. She let him in, and as soon as he leaped into the Nissan, she slid behind the wheel and locked the doors before negotiating a tight turn and driving out of the lane, all the while trying to turn on the damned headlights, as the rental's dash configuration wasn't exactly like her Subaru's. At the end of the drive, she slowed, allowing a van to pass, then turned onto the road, driving through the lowland of darkening fields and forests. Almost by instinct, without serious conscious thought, she found the road leading to Jeanne LaRoux's plot of land, which backed to the Childers, Huber, and Wheelan properties.

Nikki had been denied access to the property on the night that the fortune-teller's body had been discovered, but now there was no one to stop her. It wouldn't take long, she figured; she just wanted to see for herself how Jeanne LaRoux lived, get a feel for the place and for the woman who'd been called everything from a charlatan to a modern-day witch. She was already developing an idea for an article as she turned into the lane. Of course, the gate was closed, with yellow crime-scene tape still attached to the top rail, flapping in the breeze. Darkness had fallen, the only natural illumination emanating from a pale, rising moon.

Despite her trepidation only minutes before at the Huber place, Nikki was determined to take this opportunity to view the LaRoux property and even take some pictures.

"Come on," she said to Arlo, as she grabbed her bag with her phone, camera, flashlight, and the canister of pepper spray that Pierce insisted she carry. The dog eagerly jumped from the back seat and tagged along after her as she pried open the gate. With his nose to the ground, Arlo sniffed the brush and weeds at the edge of the twin ruts comprising the drive.

She flipped on her flashlight, and the surrounding area was suddenly illuminated in an unearthly blue-white glow. She ran the beam through the buttonbush and winterberry, and up the trunks of live oaks, where gossamer folds of Spanish moss waved, ghostlike, from the thick branches.

Usually she wasn't prone to unsubstantiated fears, but lately, her nerves had been strung tight and tonight she was a little skittish about poking around the eccentric woman's place in the dark. She had lived in this area all of her life and had spent hours, in both day and night, exploring the woods and swampland. She felt at home outside, in nature. The soft hooting of an owl, hidden somewhere in the dark, and the flutter of bat wings didn't unnerve her. Tonight, though, she was tense. She breathed deeply of the earthy air, tried to calm herself, and didn't jump when eyes reflected in the lamplight for a brief second before the raccoon scooted away through the underbrush. Arlo caught the movement and gave chase, crashing through the underbrush.

"Careful," she warned, but kept walking. She wasn't afraid, but her nerves were a little on edge. It was good to be alert, and she didn't have a lot of extra time. Stepping into a clearing, she ran the flashlight's beam over a small cottage and outbuildings that seemed to include a pump house, a chicken coop, and a leaning garage. A few fallen trees, now rotting, were not far from the house, a forgotten axe wedged into an old stump.

She started with the house, walking onto the porch, and wasn't surprised to find the front door locked. Same with the single window, where the curtains were drawn and all she could see as she shined her flashlight inside was the reflection of its harsh beam and her own shadow behind. For the briefest of seconds, she considered breaking in, but thought it better to wait. She didn't want to have to explain to Pierce what she was doing, should she get caught.

Instead, she noticed the board path that wound across the marshy ground to a hut built on a small island of sorts, surrounded by swamp and cypress trees that stretched to the starlit heavens. The boards were decaying, adding to the moist, rotting scent, and her flashlight caught the eyes of alligators moving slowly just above the surface of the brackish water.

Keep moving.

She wasn't going to be intimidated now. Not when she'd come this far. But as she felt the slick, soft boards beneath her feet and the night closed in on her, her nerves were strung as tight as bowstrings. Screwing up her courage, she shined her light on the hut, built crudely, the graying boards warping, the entrance a large, cave-like gap.

Stepping forward, she felt a shift in the atmosphere.

A ripple of water moving as an alligator or a snake slithered by.

A warning.

The hairs at her nape stiffened.

She felt a moment's hesitation and had a fleeting thought of turning back, of quickly fleeing this night-drenched swamp, with its tales of spirits and hauntings and clairvoyance.

And murder.

Oh, get over it. Chastising herself for acting like a frightened ninny, she shined the light inside. The beam illuminated a fire pit, dark, sooty rocks encircling charred logs. On the far wall was what she assumed was an altar, or had been, some candles and crystals in evidence, though it seemed that items had been taken. By the police? By looters? Or the murderer?

She slipped inside.

Paused.

Something felt off.

Smelled rotten.

An odor, an *aura* that had changed the second she slid through the doorway.

She studied the altar.

Plop!

A thick drip from above. Cool. Sticky. Landing in her hair.

"What the—?"

Creak.

Old wood straining.

Plop!

Another heavy drip. She brushed at her hair and shined her light upward, tilting her face toward the hole in the roof.

A coagulated drop hit her in the forehead just as she saw the body.

A woman dangling upside down from a crossbeam that groaned with her weight.

Drips of dried blood dyed the blond hair falling over her face in ghastly, dark red streaks.

Nikki screamed and backed up toward the door, then noticed the woman's arms, stretched downward toward the pit, where she saw more blood had pooled and dried. One of the woman's hands was open, fingers splayed, as if in supplication. The other hand was fisted, fingers clutched around a smooth stone.

"No," Nikki whispered.

As the dead body swayed slightly, the overhead beam creaking, the blond hair shifted.

Nikki saw her face.

Upside down.

Gray.

Bloated.

The distinct profile of Naomi Kittle.

Chapter 36

Horrified, her heart trip-hammering, Nikki backed up a step. The back of her legs touched something furry.

She jumped.

A low growl erupted.

Panicked, she whirled, leveling her flashlight at the snarling beast.

Arlo.

Crouching in the doorway, ears flattened, eyes glittering, he stared up at the suspended woman.

"Let's go," she ordered. "Go, go, go!"

She couldn't stand another second in the grotesque death scene.

The dog took off.

Paws clicking, he raced effortlessly along the decaying wooden path.

Right behind him, Nikki, barely able to breathe, the image of Naomi's suspended body seared in her brain, scrambled after him. Slipping and sliding, clutching her flashlight, her bag bouncing against her, she ran. Her heart was knocking so wildly she thought it might burst. Frantically, she ran along the rotting boards, past the dark swamp to the solid ground of Jeanne LaRoux's yard.

Breathing hard, she stopped long enough to call for help, punching in the number with trembling fingers while still holding her flashlight. Her breathing was ragged as she fought panic, and her fingers trembled, but she connected.

A steady female voice answered. "911, what is the nature of your emergency?"

"This is Nikki Gillette," she chattered. "I'm at Jeanne LaRoux's house, and the address is . . . Oh, God, I don't know, but it's on a county road . . . and I . . . I've just discovered a dead body. It's Naomi Kittle, the woman the police are looking for."

"Hold on, Mrs. Gillette. I'm with you. Now, can you tell me your exact location?"

"I told you! I mean, I'm not sure . . ."

Think, Nikki, think. You saw the maps of the area. Studied them.

But her mind was all over the place. "The address is on . . . it's on McCallister Road—look, you've got it on file."

"If you'll just stay on the line—"

"Just send someone to get here!" She cut the connection and immediately hit the speed-dial number for Pierce's cell.

One ring

Pick up! Please, Pierce, pick up the damned phone!

Two.

Oh, come on! Answer!

She was breathing unevenly, heading to her car.

A third ring.

If voice mail answered, she'd have to leave a message and what? Call 911 again? Or Lily or—

"Nikki?" Pierce's voice was suddenly loud in her ear. Her knees threatened to give way in relief. "Where are you?"

"I'm at Jeanne—"

"Put down the phone!" a deep male voice commanded.

Nikki froze.

Where? Who?

A dark shadow appeared, stepping around the corner of the porch of the LaRoux cabin. A big man, pointing a double-barreled shotgun straight at her. Not twenty feet away. "Put it down!" he said again. "End the call! Now!"

Her insides turned to jelly.

"Nikki?" Pierce's strident voice was in her ear. "What's happening?"

"Drop it!"

Oh, Jesus.

He repeated. "I said put it down."

Eyes on the end of the long gun, she let go of her phone and prayed it wouldn't disconnect. *Please, Pierce, hear this!*

"Now put down the flashlight."

But she didn't. Mustering her courage, she asked. "Who are you?"

"Who the hell are you, and what the fuck are you doing here?" he shot back.

"Here?" she repeated, trying to keep the tremor from her voice. "At Jeanne LaRoux's place?" she said loudly.

Oh, God, let Pierce still be on the line.

"What the hell are you doing here!" the man shouted.

"Nikki?" Pierce's voice sounded far away. Tinny. Coming from the phone dropped into the weeds. "What's going on? Nikki?"

Please, please, Pierce, just come here! Come here now! Bring backup!

"Shit." The end of the shotgun moved, hitching toward the tuft of weeds, where the phone's illuminated screen was visible. "Turn it off!"

She couldn't rely on anyone else.

There was no time.

She had to figure out how to disarm him. How to get away.

Think, Nikki. You've been in tight places before. Think, think, think!

"I said, do it!" he ordered.

"Okay, okay!" Eyes focused on the end of the shotgun, she slowly lowered herself into a crouch, scooped up the phone as if to obey, but instead of disconnecting, she picked up the phone, then fell to the ground. In one swift movement, she shined her flashlight directly into the man's eyes with one hand and hurled the phone at his face with the other.

"Hey!"

He ducked.

Too late.

The phone smashed into the bearded face of Granger LaRoux.

"Ow!" he howled, stunned and backing up a step.

Before he could pull the trigger, she rolled toward a fallen tree.

"Stop!" he ordered. "You fuckin' bitch. Stop right there!"

She scrambled over the rough bole, to cringe, waiting for the shotgun blast to echo through the night and splinter the tree.

If she survived that, before he reloaded and aimed, she could sprint to her car.

Maybe.

She fumbled inside her bag, her fingers frantically searching for the keys.

As a deep growl erupted from the woods behind her.

She turned and saw a blur of motion in the flashlight's weird light. Running at full tilt, Arlo streaked from the shadows and leapt across the fallen log.

Granger turned slightly, aiming his weapon at the dog flying toward him.

"Arlo! No!" Nikki cried.

But there was no resonating blast from the shotgun.

Instead, the dog knocked Granger to his knees.

The gun went flying.

Long fangs clamped over Granger's arm.

"Oooww!" Shrieking in pain, he threw himself to and fro, trying to shake the dog off.

But Arlo clung burr-like, his canines exposed, clamped over the attacker's arm.

"Fuck! Get him off me! Get him off me!" He was screaming in pain, trying to grab Arlo by the throat with his free hand as dog and man wrestled on the dirt.

Nikki vaulted over the tree trunk.

She yanked the axe from where it had been slammed into the stump. Sharp weapon in hand, she dived for the shotgun, snagged it, and sprang to her feet.

"Get him off!" Granger shrieked.

Breathing hard, she carefully set down the axe and leveled the long gun at the wrestling dog and frantic, bearded man. "Arlo, stop!" she ordered.

Still the snarling shepherd wouldn't let go.

"ARLO, LEAVE IT!"

The dog froze.

"Leave it!" she repeated, and surprisingly, the shepherd obeyed, backing off, eyes still fixed on his target.

Granger, cradling his arm, gazed up at her from the ground, clearly shocked.

Blood had soaked through his sleeve.

"I need an ambulance," he said angrily. "What the fuck's the matter with your dog . . ." He glared at the barely restrained shepherd. "Oh, shit. Arlo? That's Billy's dog, isn't it? Billy Huber's. That goddamned mutt never did like me."

"Well, he wasn't too keen on me being held at gunpoint."

"I wasn't gonna shoot you," Granger grumbled, acting as if *he* were the injured party, and maybe, considering how he was holding his arm, he was. "I just wanted to scare you off. I mean I didn't even know who you were, couldn't see your face over that damned flashlight."

"But you do now?"

"Hell yeah, I do." He sounded defeated. Miserable. Already regretting what he'd done. "You're that writer, right? The wife of the cop. I've seen your books before. Seen your picture on the cover." He let out a long-suffering sigh and turned his eyes toward the starlit sky. "Oh, sweet Jesus." Still clutching his arm, he rolled onto his back. "I'm so screwed. I thought you were one of those kids that keep coming down here either to steal some of Mom's artifacts or because they've taken a dare. They do that. Challenge each other to go down to the witch's place and steal some kind of magic token. Like they're gonna find a voodoo doll stuck with a million pins or something." He let out another disgusted snort. "As if!"

She wasn't persuaded. She picked up the axe again and now was holding both weapons. "What do you know about Naomi Kittle?"

"Who? *What*?"

"The missing woman all of Savannah is looking for?" When that didn't seem to register, she hitched her chin in the direction of the boardwalk stretching over the black water and added, "The woman who's hanging over the fire pit in your mother's shack down in the swamp?"

"What?" he demanded. "Are you crazy?" Then he saw that she was dead serious. "Someone's hanging . . . down at Mom's sanctuary?"

"Naomi Kittle, the woman you killed and hung upside down like a deer being dressed—"

"Whoa!" His expression altered from confusion to suspicion. "What the fuck are you talking about?" He was sitting up again, still holding his arm, but staring at her as if she'd lost her mind.

"She's down there." Nikki pointed with the shotgun. "In the sanctuary, or whatever Jeanne called it."

He turned his head toward the shack and the swamp surrounding it as if he could see for himself. "You're lying."

"Why would I?"

"You tell me. You're the one who came here and trespassed."

She wasn't about to be derailed. "You don't know about her?"

"A woman hanging in Mom's shed? How the hell would I? And . . . and I don't believe it." He tried to struggle to his feet, then winced in pain, sucking air through his teeth. "I really need an ambulance. That damned dog near broke my arm. Maybe bit through an artery!"

"Listen, Granger. No matter what you say, the plain truth is that you've got a dead woman in your mom's hut, and you're here, threatening me with a damned shotgun. So, the way I see it, you've got a helluva lot of explaining to do."

Her attitude must have finally convinced him that she wasn't bluffing.

Even in the weird half light, she noticed that his eyes rounded. "No." He was shaking his head. "I mean . . . no! No. Jesus, I don't know what you're even talking about!"

The dawning awareness on his face and the fear that followed—fear because he was trying to save his own skin—convinced her that he might be telling the truth. But he was dangerous.

Nikki kept the shotgun trained on him, while Arlo, quivering to be let loose and attack again, sat at attention next to her. His unblinking gaze was fixed on Granger, as if he were waiting for the man to make one wrong move.

Or for Nikki to say, "Sic 'em."

"How do you know Naomi Kittle?" she demanded.

"I don't!"

"Then how did she end up here?"

"Are you serious? I don't know! Jesus, aren't you listening?"

The pulsing wail of distant sirens filled the night.

"Oh, yeah, Granger," she assured him. "I'm serious, all right. Serious as hell. And you'd better start telling me everything you know, because the cops are coming. You hear them, right? They're going to have a lot more questions, so you better start talking and fast because you're in big trouble, here. Really big."

Pierce didn't know whether to hug his wife or strangle her as he jogged into the clearing with Sol beside him, two other deputies on their heels.

What the hell was Nikki doing running around in the swamp after nightfall? And alone, to boot.

Even if, as she'd explained when she'd finally called him back, she was with the dog.

So what?

She was still putting her life at risk. But now she didn't have just herself to think about, or even him . . . now there was Chloe.

He reached the clearing where Nikki stood, shotgun and some kind of axe beside her, Arlo standing at attention while she was talking with—or interviewing?—Granger LaRoux. Possibly interfering with his investigation?

She needed to back off.

As angry as he'd been, as scared to death after her frantic call, all Pierce now felt was a major sense of relief that she was alive.

This time.

But if she were a cat, she'd be quickly running out of her nine lives. In fact, was probably at eleven or twelve already. Maybe more.

As if she'd read his thoughts, she held up a hand. Though her face showed how relieved and glad she was to see him, she still held Pierce at bay. "I don't want to hear it, okay? I know you're mad at me, but Granger here was just explaining to me why he thinks it's okay to threaten a reporter with a shotgun."

"I was going to say, 'Thank God, you're alive.'"

"Well, okay then." But she flicked him a look, as if she knew the mental frustration he was wrestling with.

"And what the hell were you thinking?" he admitted.

Granger interrupted them by explaining, "I had the gun because you're trespassing, and I didn't know you were a fu—an effin' reporter!" His gaze moved to Pierce and Sol and the two deputies, weapons drawn, accompanying them. "I own this place now, you know," he said, struggling to his feet while holding his arm. "Mom left the house and acreage to me, so I have the right to protect my property. And by the way, I need an ambulance. Did she tell you that, huh? That I was attacked by that friggin' dog." He motioned to Arlo.

Pierce ignored him. "Is it true?" he asked Nikki. "Is Naomi here?"

Nikki squeezed her eyes shut for a second, as if blocking out an image too horrible to contemplate. Her grim expression told him all he needed to know: There was no mistake. He'd phoned her on the way out here, and when she'd finally called him back, he had gotten a quick rundown of all the details, but it was still hard to believe. "In the shed out in the swamp," she said, glancing to the dark water and the shack beyond.

"I don't know nothin' about that," Granger insisted. He was holding his arm with one hand, blood staining his fingers. "First I heard of it was when she told me. I mean . . . Hell, I don't even know if it's true."

"Put him in cuffs." Pierce motioned to Deputy Rounds, and she stepped forward.

"What?" Granger threw out. "Hey. No! I just told you I own this property!" He started to back up. "I have the right to be here and to protect it!"

"It's your property with a dead woman on it," Pierce countered. Then to Deputy Rounds, "Take him to the station. I'll be there soon."

"But she's trespassing!" Granger repeated, "I didn't do nothin' wrong." But he didn't fight being handcuffed, and his big shoulders fell. "I could use a smoke."

"Later," the deputy told him, glancing at the hands now restrained behind his back. "When you can do it."

"Have a medic look at him," Pierce ordered.

Granger glared at Nikki. "You'll hear from my lawyer!"

"Can't wait," she replied.

"Move it." Tina Rounds escorted Granger toward the waiting police cruiser, giving him a soft nudge when he hesitated.

"Let's go," Pierce said to Sol, and when Nikki stepped forward, he shook his head. "Wait."

"But—"

"You've already seen enough. Take the dog and go home. I'll talk to you there, but then you'll have to go down to the station and make a formal statement." He didn't wait for her to argue. Using his high-beam flashlight as his guide, he started toward the hut with its altar.

Again.

To deal with *another* body.

Sol walked a step behind him along the narrow approach, their footsteps ringing through a night where insects hummed, fish jumped, and a still unidentified evil lurked. Sol was silent, as usual, but he knew she was taking in everything, her senses attuned to the crime scene and surroundings. He'd seen her in action, watched how she kept to herself, quietly observing, asking for and providing only the important information.

As he reached the hut, he steeled himself. Though he'd often witnessed death and had studied many grisly crime scenes, this one would be more difficult.

Because he knew the victim.

Because she was married to his friend.

His stomach lurched a little as he slipped into the decaying hut to shine the beam of his flashlight upward toward the rafters.

Bile rose up his throat, and he had to forcibly steady himself.

Hung by her heels, positioned over the fire pit, stretched Naomi Kittle's body. She appeared to be reaching out to him. Beckoning. She was wearing tight, hip-hugging leggings and a shirt that fell downward over her shoulders. Her bare abdomen was exposed, as was a lacy bra barely containing her full breasts. Her skin had grayed, her blond hair tumbling toward the floor and partially covering her face. Blood had run from an ugly gash in her neck and downward over her chin to drop into the fire pit, where several of the blackened stones were stained.

In her right hand, she seemed to clutch a polished stone.

The work of the Savannah Slasher. Again. In this same place.

Pierce felt the urge to cut her down.

As if in so doing, he could relieve her pain.

An emotional, irrational response.

And yet he wanted to somehow change the horrible spectacle.

But he had to wait.

For the forensics team.

For the medical examiner.

For science to help him locate her killer and bring the prick to justice.

As he stared at the dangling body, he hoped beyond hope that Jamison wouldn't want to see her this way, displayed like a prized buck, ready to be drained of the last of its blood before being butchered.

Beside him, Sol moved closer, training her flashlight on Naomi's bare abdomen. "Did you say—?"

Thunderous footsteps, rushing over the planks of the boardwalk, echoed through the night, cutting off whatever it was she was going to ask Pierce. He turned just as Jamison Kittle nearly skidded into the tight quarters.

"You shouldn't be here," Pierce said, but his friend was already staring upward at the crossbeam, at his dangling wife. "No!" he screamed, his knees buckling. "No, no, no!" He pounded the floor with his fist. "Not Naomi. Not my Naomi!"

Deputy Tina Rounds stuck her head inside.

"I tried to stop him," she said, "but—"

"No, oh, God, no!" Jamison wailed, his face twisted as if in pain.

"Jamison, let's get you out of here," Pierce said, leaning down, offering his hand. "You don't want to see her like this."

"Why?" he asked, his face twisted in revulsion. "Why would he do this?"

"Who?" Pierce demanded, helping his friend to his feet.

"The killer!" Jamison snapped. "The Savannah Slasher. What did Naomi do to him?"

Pierce said, "We don't know yet whether—"

"Isn't it obvious?" he cut in. "I mean, look at her! Oh, Jesus, just look at her *hand*. She's got a damned rock in it, doesn't she? Isn't that the freak's calling card?"

"Jamison, you know you need to leave."

But he wasn't listening. "Cut her down! Damn it, cut her down!" He was still pointing at his wife's dangling body. "For the love of God!"

Another deputy arrived and crowded into the small space, probably contaminating the scene. Hell, they all were.

"I'm sorry, sir," the deputy apologized. "We couldn't stop him."

"I know." To his friend, he said more sternly. "Jamison, you have to go. This is a crime scene."

"But, Naomi!"

"You don't want to mess this up," Pierce insisted. "Just go. Now."

Finally, it appeared he was getting through. Jamison's gaze moved from the body of his wife to Pierce, then back again to Naomi's suspended corpse. He swallowed hard, but gave a faint nod. "Okay, okay." He cleared his throat and visibly straightened. "Right."

Pierce motioned to the deputies, who helped Jamison out of the sanctuary and listened as the footsteps retreated. "I think I've seen enough," he said to Sol. "You?"

Her lips tightened, and she continued to stare at Naomi. "This isn't right."

"None of it is," he agreed, though he suspected she didn't just mean the obvious.

"It isn't the same."

"What isn't?" he asked, and she moved her gaze to his.

"Everything." She motioned to the interior of the hut, then to the doorway, her eyes narrowing. "Trust me, Pierce; this one's not like the rest."

Chapter 37

Driving home, Nikki tried to scrub the image of Naomi Kittle's dead body from her mind. But she couldn't. Nor could she erase the memory of Jamison's car screeching to a stop in the lane before he jumped out, leaving the BMW running while he ran headlong into the clearing. He'd ignored warnings from the deputies and sped to the sanctuary, where he'd viewed the horrible, gut-ripping scene of his wife's macabre death.

Even though she'd both secured an interview and Jamison's agreement that she could publish the story of the discovery of Naomi's body once he'd told his children, Nikki felt hollow inside. The old, pre-motherhood Nikki Gillette would have been elated at the prospect of an exclusive interview with Jamison Kittle, the husband of the latest victim of the Savannah Slasher. But the new, maternal Nikki was fighting a losing battle with empathy and grief for the loss of a wife and mother. As she drove toward the city, the lights of Savannah glowing in the distance, she couldn't help but remember the middle Kittle daughter Shana's pale, tortured face during Jamison's briefing with the press. Now the little girl and her sisters were motherless, and their unfettered joy of childhood, their feeling of safety within their family, was shattered forever.

"And now you spend your time writing about man's brutality to man. You make your living off the pain of others." Westin Stark's accusation still stung.

But tonight she had a job to do.

She pulled into the driveway, and Arlo whined to get out of the rental. "Okay, okay, I think I owe you a treat, or maybe a thousand," she said, thinking of how the dog had raced to her rescue. How far Arlo had come in the past few weeks. From a snarling, fearful beast who had threatened her to a snarling, brave animal ready to sacrifice himself for her. "Come on, now, hero dog," she said, once she'd parked.

Arlo bounded out of the car and ran to the back door, whining and scratching to get inside.

Lily hurried down the stairs as Nikki set her purse on the side counter, then found the pre-offered dog treat, not only for Arlo, but a patiently waiting Mikado as well.

"It's really Naomi?" Lily asked, swallowing.

"Unfortunately."

"God, what's happening around here?"

"That's what Pierce is trying to piece together." Nikki grabbed a glass and filled it with water at the sink. "How're the girls?"

"Asleep, thank God. But it's all over the news. Not Naomi's name, of course. I got that when Pierce called to check on Chloe. But . . . dear God."

"I know."

"You found her?"

"Yeah." Nikki took a long swallow from her glass. "Awful," she admitted, then filled Lily in on the details. "Look, I need to write this story and submit it, so we'll catch up later."

"Sure. But, oh, sweet Jesus." Lily collapsed on the couch and wrapped herself in a blanket. "This is . . . obscene."

"Amen." Nikki hurried up the stairs and took a minute to check on Chloe, who, as Lily had said, lay deep in slumber. In a onesie decorated with pink llamas, her hair a mop of curls, she looked peaceful, serene, and safe.

She pressed a kiss to her soft cheek as Mikado crept into the room and curled up next to Chloe's bed. "Sleep well, angel," Nikki whispered before heading up to her office and finding Arlo already in his bed, eyes trained on the door. His tail thumped as she gave him a quick pet, then settled into her chair.

She had a story to write and then a companion piece on Naomi.

Fink, she thought, would be satisfied, even if the articles would have her byline without any credit given to Metzger. As she wrote, she gave out the details she was allowed by the police, but thought of those she couldn't acknowledge. At least not yet.

She'd stayed at the scene long enough to hear that the stone held in Naomi's hand had been etched with the number 11, just like the other three rocks, in Arabic and Hebrew, the numbers darkened presumably by blood. But this was information she couldn't share with the public.

Yet.

Until it was her exclusive story.

Or was leaked, she thought sourly.

Even so, she didn't feel that same sense of accomplishment, that satisfaction of discovering something that turned the case around. Not for the first time, she wondered if she were losing her edge. If she should hang up her journalism degree before she became lackluster, uninspired, and lazy like Norm Metzger. Or maybe just write books about crimes others had solved.

Would that be enough?

What about podcasting? That seemed to be a thing, and she could do a twist on crime solving, here from the comfort of her own home.

For now, though, she sent her story digitally to Fink, who would look it over, approve it, most likely, and it would be on the *Sentinel*'s website before the actual newspaper was published. That way Fink was satisfied. They could break the story online, and other outlets would pick it up, but the *Sentinel* and Nikki would get the credit. Later, the actual print edition would land on subscribers' doorsteps.

The industry was changing.

Nikki should change with it. Again, she said, "Adapt or die." It seemed to be her mantra these days.

Once she submitted her story, she leaned back in her chair and stretched her arms over her head, but that reminded her of Naomi's outstretched arms and the stone clasped in her fingers, so she dropped her arms. But her mind was still spinning.

Eleven.

What was the significance of the number cut into the stone?

She scratched notes to herself on a legal pad.

Billy Huber, with the number nine.

Mavis Greenlee, a five.

Jeanne LaRoux, number one.

And now Naomi Kittle, eleven.

Obviously, the numbers were significant to the killer. They meant something, but what?

She scribbled them down in the order of the deaths: 5, 9, 1, 11.

Not in normal numerical order. All odd numbers.

Were they some kind of sequence?

A code?

She switched them around. Reversed the numbers and couldn't help but wonder if there were other victims, as yet unfound, who'd been assigned other digits.

Why in Arabic and Hebrew?

What was the significance of that?

Again she wrote the symbols on her notepad, this time in Hebrew.

But they meant nothing to her.

And yet, the killer had ensured that the Hebrew numbers were included. Why?

"Come on, Nikki, figure it out." She googled the numbers, switched them around, looked up sequences of odd numbers.

And came up with nothing.

"Damn it."

In frustration, she threw her pen onto the desk. It clattered on the desktop and rolled off and across the floor to the bookcase.

Startled, Arlo lifted his head and gave a soft "woof."

"It's all right, buddy," she said. She gave him a quick pat, then retrieved the pen and straightened, hearing her spine pop in the process. She noticed the Bible on the third shelf of the case, at eye level. Leather-bound and worn, it had once belonged to her grandmother. The old woman had spent a half an hour every morning, sipping tea on her veranda or in her living-room easy chair, reading verses aloud, her own way of meditation.

Nikki ran her fingers over the soft spine. "It wouldn't hurt you to spend some time with God's word," the older woman had told her.

Grannie had always smelled of perfume and cinnamon, and some of Nikki's most cherished memories were of standing on a stool in the kitchen at the counter and learning how to roll out the thinnest and flakiest of piecrusts. Grannie had always whistled softly under her breath as she'd constructed her incredible peach or pecan pies, while crimping the edges or creating a latticework top.

As she'd worked, she'd allowed Nikki and Lily to bake their own individual pies in tiny aluminum tins. The boys were invited to partake as well, but Andrew had never been interested, and Kyle gave up when he was around seven, when he discovered he'd rather play baseball or catch toads. At least, that's how Nikki remembered it now.

She also recalled that Grannie would never allow her to taste one bite of her concoction without a prayer of thanks or a Bible verse being whispered. That was the rule. No matter how good her pie smelled after it was removed from the oven, or how hungry Nikki claimed to be, Grannie insisted a thankful prayer be sent straight to heaven and to God.

"Remember, Nicole, always be thankful. And respectful. And remember your Bible verses," Grannie had told her time and time again. She recalled one time in her grandmother's kitchen when, waiting for the pies to cool, her grandmother had stared out the window to the pasture, where the horses were grazing. She'd been unhappy with Nikki that morning as she'd caught her taking Lily's favorite doll and hiding it in her room. Nikki had lied about taking the Barbie, and Grannie had caught her in the lie.

Grannie said, "You know, if you would just live by the Golden Rule, Nicole, or . . . wait, better yet, the Ten Commandments, because they're actually written in the Bible, you would be a better person and have a more fulfilling life."

Nikki hadn't responded, but Grannie had persisted. "Why don't you recite those commandments?"

Stubbornly, Nikki had jutted out her chin and refused. She'd hated being chastised by the grandmother she adored, and Grannie seemed to understand. Behind her rimless glasses, her blue eyes had twinkled a bit. "You know, honey, I was a lot like you when I was your age. Rambunctious. Daring. Always pestering my brothers. They got to do things I wanted to, but wasn't allowed. It wasn't 'ladylike,' as your great-grandma used to say. And I don't want that for you. Oh,

"We will," Pierce said, "but we want to get this right."

"He's the damned Savannah Slasher," Jamison insisted. "Two bodies were found on *his* property, including that of my wife! Arrest the fucker!"

"I said we will, but we need all our ducks in a row. We want to nail him."

"You've got enough evidence."

"And he's got alibis."

"Break them." Jamison jabbed a finger at the two-way mirror. "He's guilty as sin, so do your damned job."

"And you do yours," Pierce snapped. "We'll get the evidence, you build the case, but have someone else handle it. Like the DA. Okay?"

"Because you don't think I can be objective?"

"No one does, Jamison. You're the husband of one of the victims, and as such, you need to go home."

"But we've got him. We've got the damned Savannah Slasher! I want a rush on this! Gather all the evidence and—"

"Go home, Jamison," Pierce repeated sternly. He was unconvinced that Granger had killed anyone, including Naomi Kittle, and he needed to concentrate his energy on the Savannah Slasher. "Go home. Take care of your kids."

"They're with Naomi's mother." He sighed heavily, his face ashen and drawn, then closed his eyes and plowed his hands through his hair. "I still have to tell them. If they haven't heard already. With the Internet . . . shit."

"Someone else from the department can talk to Naomi's parents. Not your kids, but—"

"No, no. It's my responsibility." He cast another disparaging glance at the window, with its view of the interrogation room and Granger LaRoux. "You're right. I do need to talk to the girls and try to explain . . . Jesus, how do you do that?"

"I don't know," Pierce said honestly.

"Well, I'll figure it out. And I'll tell Naomi's folks and Roxie before I go home."

"You're not staying with them?"

"At the condo? No." He shook his head. "Not enough room, and I need to be at the house. I've got horses and cattle, and Naomi's dogs, of course."

"Do you need someone to stay with you? I mean, tonight was pretty brutal."

He gave a sharp shake of his head. "I'll be okay. I've been through rough times before. In Iraq."

True enough. Jamison Kittle was a decorated war veteran who had been in more than one battle.

"But this is your wife."

"I know. Boy, do I know. This is . . . I've lost men, but . . ." His voice trailed off, but he pulled himself together with an effort. "I'll be okay."

Pierce nodded. Jamison held his gaze for a brief second, and Pierce noticed the bruise under his eye, evidence of their earlier fight.

Jabbing his finger toward the observation window and the man beyond, Jamison said in a low, deadly voice, "You just nail this fucker."

Chapter 38

Another murder in Savannah?

Linked to the Savannah Slasher?

No, no, no!

He re-read the article again as the haunting notes of Roberta Flack's "Killing Me Softly with His Song" filled his private, cavernous space.

He'd always found the song to be thought-provoking and deeply emotional.

Now, it was just background noise that irritated him and really got under his already itchy skin. He scanned the online article again, recently posted to the *Savannah Sentinel*'s website and linked to its social-media outlets. Written by that horrid, nosy heathen Nikki Gillette.

He felt his blood begin to boil.

Naomi Kittle?

The missing woman whose car they dredged from the river?

They thought *she* was one of the chosen sinners that he'd so carefully picked.

Insane. That's what it was. He knew her. Of course. Had seen her in church.

Were the police that stupid?

Well, of course, he knew the answer to that.

Give me strength, he silently prayed, *Please, Father, help me.*

The song ended, and he found another old LP, one of his father's favorites and oh so appropriate. Carefully, he removed the one record from the stereo and replaced it. As the turntable spun, he waited for the first notes of "The Ten Commandments" and Johnny Cash's distinctive bass baritone to fill the chamber.

He cranked up the volume, and soon the song was nearly reverberating against the thick stone walls.

But it didn't help.

Because someone—an interloper—was ruining his plans!

Copying his style.

Using the very place he'd left that pagan Jeanne LaRoux to die.

He gnashed his teeth. He hated to give up his carefully planned game. It had taken him years of waiting for the right opportunity, and he'd spent hour upon hour planning.

Until now, he'd been able to work in his own, perfect time line.

But no longer.

He'd lost control of the situation.

The new stone wasn't ready. Although he'd meticulously etched the number 3 in Arabic and Hebrew into it, he hadn't doused it in blood and let it dry. Nor polished it to a perfect sheen. He could no longer admire his work or savor his deeds. Reaching over his shoulder, he scratched his back, where his wounds from his recent flogging were healing and itching to the point of distraction.

Scratching was a problem.

Because it was noticed.

In the house, when he'd absently reached over his shoulder and rubbed his back, the woman had taken note and commented. She'd asked if he had gotten into some poison ivy or had been bitten by the ever-present mosquitoes that abounded? Did he need her to apply some salve? He'd brushed off her suggestion, but, he knew, she was suspicious.

She had reason to be.

She knew him. Knew what he was capable of.

Had witnessed it herself, though she was young at the time and her memory had clouded. Because he'd altered it for her. Insisting that he, older, remembered what had happened more clearly.

He'd convinced her, yet she was still wary.

He had to tread carefully.

But move quickly.

There was no longer time for perfection.

And that was a worry.

He couldn't afford to make a mistake.

He usually planned his attacks with precision, but tonight he would have to rely on his own intuition and the Father's help.

"Remember the passage: I can do all this through Him who gives me strength. Philippians 4:13."

"Yes, yes," he told himself, and though this deed would be far from perfect, he would get it done. "Forgive me, Father." He knew he needed to atone for his failings, that another self-flagellation was in order, though he could not attain perfection. That alone was for the Lord. He was but a mere mortal.

One who had broken the sixth commandment: *Thou shalt not kill*.

Well . . . He'd studied the commandments. He knew the meaning of that particular passage, and of course, murder of an innocent was a sin. But none of the lives he'd taken were without sin. In fact, they were riddled with sin. So, he reasoned, he was doing God's work.

He would never take an innocent life.

Never.

But sinners beware.

Idly, he fondled the rock he'd fashioned with its bold number 3 carved in Arabic and Hebrew. *Thou shalt not take the word of thy Lord in vain.* How many times in her lifetime had Nikki Gillette uttered the Father's name as a curse?

Hundreds?

Thousands?

Enough!

He found himself scratching over his shoulder and forced himself to stop. Irritated, he went to the medicine cabinet, where he located some anti-itch cream next to the roll of surgical tape and scissors. He applied a little of the medication to his shoulders and hoped it would relieve the itch, though he was a little ashamed at having to deal with it. The initial pain and subsequent discomfort were all part of his atonement. He rubbed in the salve and considered what he'd already accomplished.

Billy Huber had borne false witness against his neighbor, breaking the ninth commandment.

Mavis Greenlee had never honored her father, nor her mother, blatantly breaking commandment number five.

And that witch Jeanne LaRoux had flaunted her weird mixture of any pagan religion she came across and probably made up some of her own. Brazenly, she continued to break the first commandment by putting all kinds of false, heathen spirits before the one true God.

They all had paid.

As for the copycat killer who had taken Naomi Kittle's life?

Well, killing for killing's sake was a sin. Murder without holy intent was very much a sin, and so far he'd not used the sixth commandment.

That would change when he unmasked the copycat.

Now, he reached for his keys.

Tonight, it was Nikki Gillette's turn.

Sol was right, Reed thought.

Naomi Kittle's homicide was different.

It didn't quite fit into the same mold as the other murders attributed to the Savannah Slasher.

As he drove through the dark, from the crime lab to the station house, Reed reviewed the differences.

For one thing, the murder hadn't occurred in Naomi's home. Unlike the previous victims, Naomi's body had been moved. She'd died somewhere else and been taken to the LaRoux property and hung upside down in that weird hut.

While examining the body at the hut, the medical examiner had pointed out that the lividity on Naomi's body, the blood pooling on her back, indicated that she'd died lying down, not suspended from the crossbeam at the crime scene. Also, although there was a wound on her throat, like the other victims, there was also bruising on her neck. And yet she hadn't been dead long before she'd been hung and Nikki had found her. Some partially coagulated blood had drained from her nose and mouth and onto Nikki as well at the rocks rimming the fire pit. There hadn't been much blood, and the ME decided what little had drained was the work of gravity rather than a beating heart.

But why would someone go to the trouble of taking her to the LaRoux property? What was the point of that? Why would someone try to make this homicide look like the others, try to camouflage it?

He didn't like the direction of his thoughts.

Hadn't liked where they'd taken him in these early-morning hours.

Had discovered some answers in the wee hours that took him down the dark, lonely road of truth.

He pulled into the station's lot and parked in his usual spot. As he climbed out of his Jeep, he felt a twinge in his back, a sharp pain that was a reminder of his fight with Jamison. At least now he better understood his friend's mercurial temperament.

But it didn't bode well.

Frowning, he pocketed his keys and went inside. Even though it was long before dawn, officers were on duty, a few milling through the station house, bits of conversation audible. He found a pot of still-warm coffee in the break room and took the time to pour himself a much-needed jolt of caffeine before heading to his office.

And facing the damned music.

Sol was at her desk, a cup of tea steaming near a stack of papers.

"You didn't go home?" he asked.

"Just to check on Princess."

Oh. Right. The cat. Once owned by Mavis Greenlee.

"She's doing fine," Sol added with a grin. "Thanks for asking."

"You're welcome," he said, but he couldn't scare up any humor tonight, and it must've been infectious, because she turned serious.

"I knew I wouldn't sleep, so I came back. Thought I'd check out a few things." She was staring at the computer screen again, split into four sections, each frame a picture of an etched rock discovered at a crime scene. "What about you?"

"I tried. Failed. Maybe dozed for a couple of hours." But he'd tossed and turned, the image of Naomi Kittle's body burning through his brain. The questions about her death, the disparities from the other murders, were like sharp needles burrowing into his subconscious.

Nikki, too, had been restless, unable to sleep. She'd been in and out of the bed, alternately trying to catch a few winks or throwing off the covers and going up to her office, the new dog tagging after her.

"I thought about what you said at the Kittle murder scene," Reed said, cradling his cooling coffee and taking a seat on the corner of his desk. "That it's different from the rest."

"It is."

"I know. I agree. Let's talk it out." Although he had come to the same conclusion, he wanted her insight, her take on things, as she invariably came at a crime from a different perspective, one he found insightful, if not in keeping with traditional detective work. A good thing, he decided.

"Okay, but it's not just the scene that's different," she clarified. "The entire homicide isn't like the others, or at least has a lot of disparities. You heard what the ME said last night."

"Right. We know the body was moved."

"Uh-huh. And the rocks are different. Take a look." She showed him images of the stones found at all of the crime scenes. All polished to a shine, all about the same size.

"What am I looking for?" he asked.

"It's subtle, but the last stone is slightly different in tone and texture, and look closely—the engraving is a bit different. The first three we found are virtually the same, but this last one"—she pointed to the image in the lower-right corner—"the one found in Naomi's hand, seems to have been engraved with a different tool. Whatever they use in rock carving. Probably a diamond-tipped bit or some sort of a laser? Don't know. I haven't figured that out yet."

"That's not the only thing about the rocks," he admitted, taking a sip, but staring over her shoulder at the images on the screen. "I was just at the lab."

"They were working?" She pulled a face. "It's not even four in the damned morning."

"I know, but I pulled in a favor. One of the techs owes me. He wasn't happy, but I met him there and got a rush job on blood analysis on the stone found in Naomi's hand last night. It's different from the others."

"Not the same concoction of goat, cow, and human?"

"Not a combination at all," he said. "The blood on the stone Naomi held in her hand was from a chicken."

She arched a brow.

Not surprised.

"Lots easier to procure than human."

"Unless you self-harvest," he said. "Take your own blood."

"Nah. Don't think so. The blood we found on the other three stones? The human portion is female, according to the lab," she reminded him. "And we think our killer is male."

"It seems that way." He couldn't imagine a woman as the killer.

She added. "Not many people know that the blood we found on the stones from the previous homicides is a mixture," she said. "We just found out ourselves, so even people in the department aren't aware that our killer likes playing with platelets."

Reed nodded. "And we've kept the stones out of the press."

"Right. The public doesn't know about them, nor the blood." She said, "I think the concoction of blood is significant."

"Me, too."

"And the fact that the numbers on the rocks are soaked in it. Arabic numbers and Hebrew numbers. Like the Old Testament."

"Where goats and calves and sometimes humans were sacrificed?" he asked, following her line of reasoning, one that had toyed with the fringes of his mind.

"Bingo." Sol took a long sip from her cup, finishing her tea and nodding to herself. "But why go to all that trouble of procuring the blood and mixing it, leaving it at the scenes where he knew we would find it and analyze it, then all of a sudden use chicken blood?"

"Easier to procure."

"And a lot lazier. Our killer, he's precise. Pays attention to detail. Leaves us enigmatic clues. Goes to all the trouble of mixing up different blood and using the same etching tool, then thinks, 'fuck it. I'm just gonna kill a chicken and use whatever tool I've got. And pick up a rock from the damned driveway.' Does that make sense?"

"Does any of it?" he asked. "It's not like we're dealing with a rational person."

"No, he's def cray-cray. But precise cray-cray."

Reed said, "Most likely some kind of religious nut. If we're still going with the Old Testament theory."

Again the arch of her brow, but she bit the edge of her lip.

"What?" he asked, then said, "You've got something else."

He'd seen that look on her face before, when she was tossing an unsavory theory around in her head, one she couldn't avoid.

He knew the feeling.

"Yeah. I do have something." She finished her tea and set the cup down. "I was waiting for the autopsy report on Naomi Kittle, but it'll be a while."

"I've put a rush on it."

She let out a sigh. "I know. But everything about these cases has a rush on it. Hell, the FBI is working it, so of course," she said.

"Yeah."

"And even with a rush, the preliminary might not get here today," she said. "Maybe not even tomorrow."

"I know. I'm assuming you want to check on the bruises on her neck," he guessed. "To see if she was strangled."

"She was." Sol was certain. "The bruising and petechial hemorrhaging in the report will substantiate it, but no, that's not what I'm talking about."

"What, then?"

"You're not gonna like it."

He already knew that much. He wasn't liking his own wayward thoughts. "What've you got, Augustin?"

Her eyes grew dark, and he felt a second's trepidation.

Turning back to her computer, she said, "It's easiest to show you." Her fingers clicked over the keyboard, and as they did, the image on her computer screen changed from the four frames of etched rocks to Naomi Kittle's dead body hanging from the rafter at Jeanne LaRoux's hut in the swamp.

Reed involuntarily cringed. She was right, he didn't like where this was heading. And the bad feeling, which had been with him all night and kept him awake, loomed larger.

"Take a look," she instructed.

He stood and peered over her shoulder as Sol enlarged the picture, zeroing in on the dead woman's abdomen. "See those little marks there? Those tiny scars?" She pointed to a couple of small discolorations visible on Naomi's skin just above the top of her tight-fitting low-waisted pants.

"Yeah?"

"And this one here." Her finger moved to Naomi's navel.

His gut tightened. He knew what was coming.

"Looks like scars from a tubal ligation." She glanced over her shoulder to look him directly in the eyes. "Didn't you say that Kittle and his wife were planning a romantic weekend together when she went missing? That they were hoping to have another baby?"

"That's what he told me."

"Wasn't going to happen," she said flatly. "Unless I miss my guess, Naomi Kittle had already had her tubes tied. No more babies. No male heir for Jamison," she said. "The autopsy will confirm."

The evidence was damning.

Reed's fears that had kept him up all night were substantiated.

"He lied to you," Sol said.

"Yeah." Reed straightened and looked away from the damning image.

The truth was obvious.

Jamison Kittle had just become the number-one suspect in his wife's murder.

Chapter 39

Nikki couldn't sleep.

Every time she closed her eyes, she saw Naomi Kittle's body hanging from a crossbeam, blood crusted at her nostrils, her skin a sickly shade of gray. And when her eyes were open, her mind was racing with thoughts of stones, and odd numerals, and the silver SUVs.

Pierce, too, had been restless. When he'd given up on sleep, thrown on his clothes, and gone back to the station, she, too, had gotten up and climbed up to her office. Sometimes in the wee morning hours, when she was all alone and the house was quiet, the outside dark and still, she found that she could think more clearly.

Usually, she'd nurse a cup of coffee and let the caffeine help clear the cobwebs from her mind, but it was way too early for that. She was still holding out a slim hope that she might catch a few winks later, and she didn't want a jolt of caffeine fouling up any chance of sleep.

Once in her desk chair, she skimmed her e-mail and found the report she'd gotten from Jill at the station, a copy of the registration for the silver SUV she'd viewed in the church lot on the day of Mavis Greenlee's funeral. The owner of record was the All Christian Church, and the person who'd signed for it was none other than Reverend Westin Stark.

But she hadn't noticed the vehicle being parked in the lot on the night she'd visited Westin. She'd looked. He'd driven something else. What was it? A blue sedan—like a Toyota, maybe, or a Honda. It didn't matter; it hadn't been following her.

Nor had the silver Ford Expedition that the church probably used for hauling people or supplies, delivering meals to the housebound or the like.

Maybe Westin Stark wasn't the only driver of the vehicle.

Maybe someone associated with the Birds of Paradise or one of the elders had the keys or borrowed the Ford for church business.

Maybe Westin wasn't the bad guy she thought he was. There was a chance he had really reformed and was a true believer.

She reminded herself that the Expedition she saw parked in the church lot might not be the vehicle she thought had been following her.

"Give it up," she told herself, physically exhausted yet wired, her amped-up brain not in sync with her weary body.

She could take a sleeping pill and knock herself out for a few hours, then start again later in the morning. With a clear head, she might be able to figure out what she was missing. If only she could catch a few hours of uninterrupted sleep.

She still had the impression that there was a religious angle to the murders. Something to do with the numbers . . . in Hebrew and Arabic. That was a clue. Why bother etching the numbers two different ways? The killer was trying to tell the police something. Taunting them.

She left her office and went downstairs. Lily and Phee's room wasn't quite dark, the flickering light from the TV visible beneath their door, but that didn't mean they were awake. More likely Lily had fallen asleep with the remote in her hand.

As for Nikki's daughter, Chloe was sleeping soundly, tucked into her skirted crib, her blanket wadded near her feet. Sleep tight, Nikki thought, but didn't dare whisper the words for fear of waking her daughter, as she adjusted the blanket, which, of course, would be kicked off again before morning.

After double-checking that all the doors were locked, she made her way upstairs again and found her sleeping pills in the medicine cabinet, a prescription she barely used. Even though the medication was past its pull date, and probably not as effective as it once was, she filled the glass by the sink with water, told herself, "Bottoms up," and washed the pill down with a swallow of water.

Now, if it worked, in twenty minutes she'd be dead to the world, and when she woke up, she'd be refreshed and ready to take on the world again, her emotions under control, her mind clear enough to figure out exactly what it was she was missing.

Wouldn't it be great if she could unmask the damned Savannah Slasher? Not only could she help the police to get the monster off the streets, but she would get her exclusive for the paper and have the story for her next book.

Yawning, feeling the effects of the sleeping pill taking over, she tumbled into bed and was only vaguely aware of Arlo curling up in his dog bed near the window.

As slumber overtook her, the questions still spun in her mind, the faces of the victims, their names intertwined, floating in and out of her consciousness.

Why were they targeted?

What did the rocks and numbers mean?

How did All Christian Church connect to the murders?

As she drifted off, she remembered Mavis Greenlee's funeral and everyone who spoke and the fact that Duke Wheelan brought up the Ten Commandments. She'd memorized them once, long ago, when she was in the sixth grade. What had she learned in Vacation Bible School?

She tried to think, to remember the passages from Exodus, but her thoughts swirled, and the commandments were jumbled in her drowsy mind.

Thou shalt have no gods before me . . . Thou shalt not make any graven image . . . thou shalt not take the name of the Lord thy god in vain . . . Remember the Sabbath day . . . Honor thy father and thy mother . . . Thou shalt not steal . . . Thou shalt not bear false witness against thy neighbor . . .

Much as he hated it, Reed had to agree with his partner.

It certainly appeared that Jamison Kittle had taken his wife's life, then staged the scene at Jeanne LaRoux's hut in the swamp.

And yet it didn't fit. Not all of it.

He said, "You're not suggesting that Jamison Kittle is the Savannah Slasher," he said, as he heard more cops walking through the hallway outside their office. Men, their voices low, discussing some ball game.

"Nope," Sol replied with a shake of her head. "But I sure as hell think he killed his wife and set it up so that we'd think the murders were linked, that she was another one of the Slasher's victims." Her expression was cold. Calculating. "And you do, too."

He didn't deny it. Couldn't. Because the evidence was stacking up against Jamison. They'd discovered that Jamison was the beneficiary of his wife's substantial insurance policies. They'd found Naomi's burner phone, deep in a hidden compartment in her Mercedes, and had seen how often she'd contacted Knox Quinlan. In his initial interview, Knox had not only made a statement, but his alibi, of being at his brother's house with the brother, his wife, and children, had proved to be airtight. Reed planned to interview the man again, but he seemed devastated and horrified at Naomi's bizarre and untimely demise.

And that was the thing. To Reed's knowledge, never once had Jamison Kittle shed a tear for his wife. At least not that Reed had seen. Jamison had seemed sad, even appeared grief-stricken, and looked to be emotionally unraveling. But no tears had fallen

Reed had tried to give him a pass, telling himself that Jamison, an army veteran who had seen action, witnessed war, and lost friends could have an iron grip on his emotions. Jamison was the chosen son, taught by a strict father who believed in stoicism and rarely showed his own feelings.

But Reed didn't buy it.

Nor did Sol.

"The trouble is," she was saying, "he did a piss-poor job of trying to connect Naomi's murder to the others, to make her look like another victim. There are just too many inconsistencies."

"He didn't know about the nature of the blood."

"No, he killed her before we found out what it was made of. But it was like he was rushed and tried to take advantage of the fact that we had a psycho running around the area doing these bizarre killings." She cracked her neck and stared out the window to the dark night beyond. "My guess is that he killed her, maybe even by accident, and then he panicked and tried to cover it up." Her smile was as cold as an arctic blast. She met his gaze in the watery reflection of the glass. "That's what they say, you know."

"That it's not the crime. It's the cover-up."

"Amen."

Reed ignored the bile rising in his throat. He had to face the truth, no matter how painful it was.

"But you already had this figured out." It wasn't a question.

"I didn't have all the evidence," he said. "Not the differences in the blood on the stones, and I had no idea that Naomi had had her tubes tied, but even so, everything was pointing to Jamison." He rubbed his face as if he could scrub away the truth, but all night long, he'd come back to the same grotesque theory that Jamison Kittle, the man who could never lose, whose political ambitions were evident, would never have accepted the public humiliation that his wife was in love with another man.

"Okay, then." Sol reached for her sidearm and checked it. "Wha'd'ya say, Detective?" She pushed back her chair. "Let's go get him."

From his hiding spot across the street, he surveyed the house.

Nikki Gillette's home was situated on a large lot across the street and catty-corner from Forsyth Park. Aside from an upper-floor window, the house was dark, everyone inside presumably asleep.

The warm night was quiet, just the occasional sound of a car engine passing over the steady chirp of crickets.

The husband, the cop, had left.

And had been gone for a while.

He'd lucked out on that count.

Having the cop out of the house would make things easier.

He'd watched Detective Reed drive out of the garage earlier and had waited to make certain the Jeep didn't return, that he wasn't out going to the store for some middle-of-the-night emergency whatever.

So far, he hadn't come back.

No surprise, there, he thought. Detective Pierce Reed was busy these days. The Savannah Slasher had seen to that. He felt more than a little bit of pride, of satisfaction that he'd foiled the police, then quickly dismissed the feelings, as this was not about him nor his ego. What he did, he did for God.

And it was time to get to work.

He stared upward to his point of entrance, the one window on the third floor where a light was visible. He'd seen no one in the room for over an hour, and, he'd noticed, that particular window was always cracked a bit.

A lucky break.

He'd already scoped out the house on his previous nocturnal visits and noticed the cameras that covered the front and back entrances, and he assumed the house would be locked. But a large magnolia tree was close enough to the home that, with some effort, he could climb to the upper story and transfer to the window. It would be difficult, but he was up to the challenge.

He had to be.

The next problem would be the dogs, including that cur that had belonged to Billy Huber. He'd observed the mutt in the car with her a few times when he'd followed her, sometimes in his vehicle, other times in the church's SUV. He'd also seen that the dog's rear end was healing. Unfortunately. That was his fault. He'd been careless when the stupid mutt had put up a ruckus at Billy's house on the night he'd sent Billy to his maker.

He hadn't taken the time for a kill shot, and the creature had survived.

To be taken in by the reporter.

Well, not this time.

He patted his pocket, felt his pistol with its silencer, and smiled to himself.

Bye-bye, Arlo, you miserable cur.

"I need to do this on my own," Reed said, thinking of Jamison Kittle, what their friendship meant, how deep was their bond.

"What? No!" Sol kicked back her chair and stood. "You can't be serious! You want to go alone?"

"He's my friend." That did sound a little lame, like a whiney seven-year-old.

"A friend who killed his wife and went to a lot of trouble to cover it up. You can't—"

"This is personal, Sol."

"And dangerous." She was already grabbing her bag. "We'll need backup, too."

"Jamison Kittle is an officer of the law."

"Who has sharpshooting medals and killed his effin' wife." Sol was adamant. "He's desperate. Backed into a corner."

"He wouldn't try to kill me," Reed insisted, even as he thought about the fight near the pool the other day. For a few minutes, Jamison had been out of his mind with rage.

"Tell that to his wife. I bet she said the same thing. Now, come on. Let's go."

He knew she was right. All his training, his every instinct told him to follow protocol, to ignore the emotions running hot through his blood, to block the memories of brotherhood he'd shared with Jamison Kittle, but deep down, he had to fight this one out by himself. "I need to—"

"You need to shut up and quit being a hero. Shit, stop listening to your heart. Use your damned head!" She stopped then, crossing her arms over her chest as she stared at him as if he'd grown a second head. "You know what? I've got a better idea: You stay here. I'll go. I'll get whoever's on duty to come with me. I think Deputies Maddox and Freeman are on tonight."

"No!" He wasn't going to let her bully him. "This is my battle, Sol."

She cocked her head to stare at him. Long and hard. "Are you out of your frickin' mind?" she demanded, not backing down an inch. "Maybe I should have you put in a cell until this all goes down."

"I'm the senior officer."

"Oh, crap, Reed, don't pull rank on me. I'll tell everyone you're having an emotional breakdown. That you've lost it. That I can't trust you."

"You wouldn't."

"Try me." She started for the door.

"Do it, and I'll let the sergeant commander know that you go to crime scenes unauthorized. Alone. To do whatever."

She froze. "You . . . You'll do *what*?" Her eyes thinned, and her face was hard.

"Look, I don't know what you do, and it seems to work, but yeah, I was pretty sure I saw you on a bike on CCTV by Mavis Greenlee's house. I think, if I go over all the tapes of the roads near the homicide scenes with a fine-tooth comb, I'll find more footage of you on your bike or maybe in your pickup with a bag of some kind and then you'll have to explain yourself."

"Damn," she muttered, her lips barely moving, her eyes growing dark. They both knew her unauthorized activity could cost her the badge and job she'd worked years to achieve. There would be an investigation, and what she did at the scenes would be exposed and possibly get her fired, while also ruining her chances of being hired by another department.

"You'd go down, too. For not coming forward earlier."

"So be it."

For a minute, she didn't say a word, then uttered, "I'm coming with you. Don't argue with me. It won't work. I'll stay in the car for a few minutes. Give you some time alone to bring him in. But if you go inside his damned house and aren't back to the car in five minutes, I'm coming in."

"Guns blazing?"

She ignored that. "Final offer."

"And no backup? No FBI."

"Unless things go bad."

"Okay," he finally agreed. "Let's go."

Climbing the tree was easier than he'd imagined.

Getting through the window proved more difficult. It was tight, his shoulders brushing against both sides as he held on to the jamb and swung his legs across a wide desk to land on the floor of this converted attic room. Thankfully, the lamp was lit, so he'd been able to see what he was doing. With some difficulty and a lot of dexterity, he'd avoided knocking over the computer mouse, a cup of pens, and several legal pads that had been left on the desk.

Once inside, he saw that he was in the reporter's office. Bookshelves lined the walls, her own books filling one shelf, *The Third Grave*, with its author photo visible, her latest publication.

He knew.

He'd done his research.

He caught sight of the empty dog bed and reminded himself again to be wary. He figured that he could walk through the house easily and no one would become alarmed. Enough people lived here that a footstep or a creaking floorboard wouldn't cause much concern.

But the dogs were a different story.

As quietly as possible, with his nerves strung tight and his pulse pounding in his ears, he crept down the spiral staircase to the hallway on the second floor. Double doors on one wall. The primary bedroom. Where he'd find Nikki Gillette. He eased along the hallway.

Another door.

The bathroom with a night-light softly glowing in ever-changing colors.

He peered inside.

Empty.

At the end of the hall, two more doors and what appeared to be a closet between them. Blue, flickering light from a television appeared under the door of one—possibly the sister's room, and the other must be the child's room. Did the toddler share it with the preteen he'd seen? Or was she alone?

He withdrew his pistol, held it tightly, his finger on the trigger.

His heartbeat ticked up as he reached the final door.

Oh so quietly, he turned the knob.

Heard the latch click.

Shoved the door open and stuck his head in first.

Another night-light provided some illumination.

Only a crib.

No other bed.

The older girl must be bunking with her mother or somewhere else in the house. Good.

Better yet, no dog. To be certain, he swept the beam of his tiny flashlight around the perimeter of the room.

Nothing.

He let out the breath he hadn't realized he'd been holding, turned off the flashlight, and pocketed his gun. Silently, he crossed the carpet to the crib.

The child was lying on her back, one little arm flung out, her mop of curls framing her face. Dead asleep. Her tiny lips moved on a quiet sigh. So angelic. And perfect bait.

He took out his roll of surgical tape to cover her mouth and prevent her from screaming.

As he leaned over the crib, a strip of tape stretched taut, he heard a low growl.

The dog?

Where?

But he'd checked. He didn't move a muscle.

Swallowed hard.

Nothing.

But . . .

He reached into the crib.

Another warning growl.

What?

He was sweating. But all he had to do was grab the kid.

Oh, no, she was moving, and her eyes were open.

Big and round.

She started to scream, and he slapped the tape over her mouth.

All hell broke loose!

A huge graying animal, barking like mad, burst from beneath the skirt of the crib. Snarling, it leaped up, knocking him over, white teeth flashing.

The kid—trying to scream, tearing at the tape—scrambled to her feet.

He jumped up and grabbed her.

The old dog, the half-crippled one he hadn't paid much attention to, clamped onto his leg.

Teeth sunk through his jeans.

Pain seared his calf.

"Aaah!" he cried, biting off his own scream.

Too late!

He heard running feet in the hallway.

Whirling, holding the wriggling, panicked kid in front of him, he saw Nikki Gillette.

Standing in the doorway.

A pistol leveled at his chest.

"Put her down," she ordered, though her words seemed a little slurred and she swayed sightly. "Duke Wheelan, put my baby down this second, or I'll blow your head off."

"You wouldn't dare," he said, holding tight to the frantic toddler, his little human shield with one arm, his pistol with its silencer now in his free hand. All the while, he was kicking hard, trying to dislodge the damned dog. Still, the fierce monster held on.

"I said, 'put her down!'" But Nikki was leaning against the doorjamb now, whatever was wrong with her taking over. The gun wobbled in her hand, and he knew she wouldn't shoot, wouldn't risk harming her child.

He gave another sharp kick, slamming the dog onto the floor. With a yelp, it let go, and he gave it another swift boot, sending the old thing flying into a dresser, where a lamp in the shape of a rocking horse tumbled to the carpet.

The dog didn't move.

He'd planned on abducting the kid and luring Nikki out of the house, using this screaming imp as bait, but this chaos had ensued. He had to think fast.

"I'll hurt her," he declared. "Get out of my way or, I swear, I'll hurt her. I'll start with her fingers, or maybe her eyes."

The girl struggled, wildly pitching her surprisingly pliable body this way and that, flinging her arms, kicking as hard as she could, sometimes a little fist hitting his cheeks.

Still he didn't let go.

Nikki ordered. "Put. Her. Down."

"And what? You'll let me go?" He didn't buy it for an instant. "You'll kill me."

And he saw it in her eyes, the light of motherly fervor, the natural instinct to put her own life before her child's. If he let the kid down, she would fight him to the death. "Get out of my way!"

She didn't budge.

"No? Okay. Let's start here." He took a mouthful of the girl's hair and snapped her head back, yanking out some of the curls by their roots. Beneath the tape, the kid shrieked bloody murder, just as more frantic footsteps sounded.

"What the hell's going on?" the sister cried and pushed a wobbly Nikki out of the way. "You let her go!" In that instant, she leaped at the attacker.

The toddler wriggled and screamed.

Nikki cried, "Lily! No!"

He tensed.

Lily twirled lithely in midair, looking as she did in ballet class years before. She pirouetted agilely to the far side of the crib.

He fired, just as the crib rammed into him. The rails slammed against his back. He lost his grip. The kid slid to the floor next to the unmoving dog.

The shot went wild, blasting into the ceiling.

Nikki didn't wait.

She pulled the trigger.

Blam!

Wheelan fell back against the crib, and though he felt the sting of a bullet and the stickiness of blood as it oozed through his shirt, he braced himself on the top rail and took aim again.

Directly at Nikki.

Chloe cried and covered her ears. Nikki fired again, then scooped up her crying child. He tumbled to the floor, scrabbling on the carpet for his gun. In one swift, instinctive motion, Nikki spun, her bare heel catching Wheelan under the chin.

His head snapped back, and for a second, the world went black.

His gun went spinning away.

Nikki struck again. Her heel slamming into his face.

Crunch.

The cartilage in his nose collapsed, turning into pulp.

"Take that, you bastard," she said, ready to kill the prick and heard scratching and whining, then sharp barks from Arlo, whom she'd unwittingly locked in her bedroom down the hall when, still half asleep, she'd come to investigate. Even now, through all the chaos and the adrenalin pumping through her system, she felt some lingering effects from the sleeping pill she'd downed. But the pieces were falling into place. Wheelan knew all of the victims. He was a religious nut. Her mind spun as it was all beginning to make sense. With an effort, she kept her gun trained on the writhing man—Duke Wheelan, elder at All Christian, and finally unmasked as a serial killer.

Lily, apparently unharmed, slid from beneath the crib and snagged Wheelan's gun. While Mikado finally staggered to his feet, she leveled the pistol at Wheelan with one hand, and dialed 911 with the other. "Phee, take Mikado downstairs," she ordered, but her daughter stood rooted to the hallway just outside the bedroom door. "Now!"

Lily ordered, and Phee, blinking, complied, holding on to the old dog's collar and starting to drag him down the hall.

Lily didn't waver, just kept the gun aimed directly at Wheelan, the psycho who Nikki was starting to believe was the Savannah Slasher.

But his murderous spree was over.

Wheelan was holding his face, blood pouring through his fingers as he writhed on the ground. "You're heathens," he spat. "Heathens. God will punish you."

"And you!" Lily said, her lips barely moving, rage glittering in her eyes. "I'd love to be there when you meet good old Saint Pete at the pearly gates and you try to explain all your sins. Good luck getting in."

He forced out, "Thou shalt not . . ." But his voice faded.

Nikki finished for him. "Thou shalt not mess with mothers protecting their babes," and she carefully removed the tape from Chloe's mouth.

"Blasphemy!" he spat, and then his eyes rolled back into his head, and she hoped he didn't die. Duke Wheelan needed to face a court of law before he went on to his final judgment.

Nikki had a child to care for.

And a story to write.

She figured God could wait.

Chapter 40

Sol had lied.

Right through her teeth.

She'd promised Reed that she would stay put, that she would wait in his Jeep for five minutes while he tried to talk some sense into his friend, the deranged killer who had murdered his wife.

But that was crazy.

She didn't like the plan, not one bit, even though Reed assured her that he could handle the situation, and if push came to shove, he had his pistol. It wasn't enough.

So while Reed was walking up the front steps of Jamison Kittle's Georgian-style home to try to face his friend, to do the right thing and give the murdering son of a bitch some dignity, she texted for backup, slipped her pistol from its holster, and reached for the Jeep's door handle.

Even so, she was too late as Reed knocked on the door, and it immediately swung open.

He stepped inside.

"Damn it." She opened the door and slipped out of the Jeep. She'd been a fool to let him come here, she knew it. She should have called his bluff, arrested him on the spot, and cuffed him to his desk.

Or maybe sent him to the psych ward. Or done anything to stop this madness.

What was it about male friendship?

The "bro" pact or whatever?

There seemed to be some testosterone-fueled pride involved.

She knew Reed thought he was giving his friend a chance to come clean and confess, to explain himself and turn himself in. In truth, he was a patsy. And she was a fool to have agreed to this screwball, dangerous plan!

She'd made a mistake.

And now she had to rectify it.

Whether Reed knew it or not, Jamison Kittle was all about Jamison Kittle.

Period.

His wife's life hadn't mattered.

Nor would his best friend's.

Jamison answered the door.

Bleary-eyed, unshaven, his hair tousled, he stood in a T-shirt and sweatpants, his feet bare.

And he reeked of booze.

As if he'd drunk half a fifth of whiskey before tumbling into bed and was now sweating out the alcohol. He was a mess. Again. Pierce had thought it was due to the loss of his wife. Because of his grief. Now, though, he knew better and understood what was eating at him.

"What're you doing here?" Jamison asked and glanced beyond Pierce to the darkness beyond his porch.

"I think you know."

Jamison's eyes narrowed a bit. "You caught the Slasher?" he said, but he didn't believe it.

"Not yet."

"Then . . . ?"

"I think you know."

"Naomi," Jamison said and stepped out of the doorway to allow Pierce to pass.

"Right."

He let out a long breath and ran stiff fingers through his unruly hair. "I assume you found her phone."

"You mean the burner phone?" Pierce said, nodding as they walked through the main hall to the game room off the kitchen, Jamison leading the way and snapping on lights. "Yeah, it was hidden in the car. Under a panel. And it was the number that matched the calls we found on Knox Quinlan's."

"So they were really having an affair?"

"You know that already."

Jamison motioned to the arched opening to the dark kitchen. "You want coffee?" he asked. "It's early, but I can—"

"No. Look. This isn't a social call." Pierce took the two steps down and into the game room, where, once Jamison snapped on the lights, the Kittle collection of weapons and trophy kills was on full display. Rifles and shotguns, long bows and automatic weapons behind glass and mounted on the walls, long-dead prey with glittering glass eyes that seemed to glower down on them, and from the front hallway, he heard the steady ticking of the grandfather clock.

Counting down the seconds.

Tick. Tick. Tick.

"Not a social call?" Jamison repeated. "Well, I guess not, considering the time."

Feeling the weight of his pistol tucked at his back in the waistband of his jeans, Pierce nodded. "Right."

Jamison walked to the bar, where a half-full bottle of Maker's Mark stood open. "Then why are you here, *friend*," Jamison asked, "if not to join me in a very late nightcap or a really early pick-me-up?" He reached under the bar, and Pierce tensed, thought about whipping out his weapon.

But Jamison came up with two glasses. He set them down on the bar so hard, the bottle of whiskey rocked a bit.

"No thanks," Pierce said.

"You sure?" He poured three fingers in each short glass.

"Absolutely."

Tick. Tick.

Jamison eyed him, then shrugged, though beneath his seemingly cool exterior, he was tense, the cords in his neck visible, his jaw set and hard. "Your loss." Never letting his gaze leave Pierce's, Jamison tossed back the first drink in one large gulp. "What's up?"

"We found your insurance policies and checked with the companies."

"Yeah?" He lifted a shoulder.

"You had major policies on your wife. Total of nearly two million dollars."

"I know. Those were taken out when the kids were born."

"But a new one was bought recently. Just a month ago."

"I told you we were planning on another child." He picked up the second drink.

"A boy, right? An heir."

"Hopefully." Nervously, Jamison fidgeted with the second glass, the amber liquid sloshing a bit.

"About that, Jamison," Pierce said. There was no reason to keep beating around the bush. "It doesn't work."

Tick, tick, tick. The clock was relentless in counting down the seconds.

"What do you mean? What doesn't work?"

"We know Naomi had surgery, a tubal ligation."

"The autopsy?"

"Will confirm," Pierce said. "We noticed the scars on her abdomen."

He didn't argue. "There are ways of reversing the surgery. Medicine's come a long way in the last few years."

"If the woman is willing."

"She is—was," Jamison said, but Pierce noticed a vein bulging near his temples, jumping in counterpoint to the damned ticking of the clock.

Jamison gulped from the second glass.

"She was willing to have another baby."

"Wanted," he cut in.

"Okay, wanted another baby."

"I told you we were trying to patch things up. Save our marriage."

"Even though she was still seeing Knox Quinlan?"

"She was going to break it off with him."

Pierce stared at his friend, right through the lie. "I thought you didn't know about the affair until I brought it up. But you're saying she admitted it? Was going to call things off with Quinlan?" He saw Jamison realizing that he'd misspoken, that his lies were unraveling. Pierce recognized the panic in his friend's eyes, but he didn't stop. "We're having a more in-depth interview with Quinlan today."

"Why? Do you think he'll tell you the truth?" Jamison asked, his cool facade slipping. "He's an ex-con, Pierce. An adulterer. A liar. He probably killed Naomi. For all you know, he's the Savannah Slasher! There was a rock found in her hand, for the love of God. Why the hell are you not arresting him?"

"He didn't kill Naomi," Pierce said. As Jamison stalked across the room, knocking into the coffee table and swearing, Pierce kept his eye on him. "You know it."

"I know it? How?"

"Because you killed her."

Jamison stopped dead in his tracks. "What did you say?" He turned to face Pierce. "You think I killed Naomi? My wife? The mother of my girls?" If he was trying to appear incredulous, he failed.

"Yeah, I do. As an officer of the law, I'm asking you to come of your own volition down to the station with me. As a friend, I'm suggesting you get a lawyer."

"Oh, right, the husband is always the first suspect."

"Especially when all of the evidence points to him."

"Shit, man!" Jamison held his gaze, and just as he had the other day at this very house, out by the pool, Pierce felt a fight coming on.

"I came out here as a favor to you," Pierce said with measured, practiced calm. "So you can come in quietly. With some dignity. So we can handle this without the press, without a lot of fanfare."

"You're married to a fucking reporter! What do you mean without the press?"

"Come on, Jamison, don't make this any harder than it is."

"You're fired, Pierce," Jamison spat. "Do you hear me? You've just kissed your career goodbye. Who do you think you are, coming here with half-baked theories instead of doing your damned job?"

Without waiting for an answer, he stalked to the bar and picked up his drink. "Now, get the hell out of my house."

"It's over, Jamison."

"For you." He drained the drink, and more of his steady facade slipped. "Not for me."

"You're gonna make this hard? You're gonna make me arrest you?"

"I'm not going anywhere! This is crazy. I'm a fuckin' ADA. And when the DA retires, I'm getting her job!"

"I don't think so," Pierce said. "But come on down to the station and explain yourself."

"Fuck you!" He slammed his empty glass down and, swift as lightning striking, reached under the bar again. This time he pulled out a pistol. Not an antique or collectible like the weapons displayed in the cases. No, this was a semiautomatic handgun.

Deadly.

Accurate.

In the hands of a sharpshooter.

"I hate to do this, Pierce, I really do. But you're giving me no choice here. I'm not going down for this. Get it? I'm not going down for any of it."

Pierce shifted and reached behind him for his sidearm.

Jamison took aim.

"Drop it!" Sol commanded from somewhere in the darkened kitchen.

Jamison glanced toward the sound.

Pierce withdrew his pistol and caught a glimpse of Sol, standing full-frontal, two hands on the pistol she had aimed straight at Jamison.

Too late!

Jamison fired.

The muzzle of his gun flashed.

Blam!

Pierce snagged his weapon and took aim at his friend.

Stumbling backward, Sol pulled the trigger.

Bang!

Jamison's body jerked once.

Sol collapsed onto the steps.

Blood showing on his T-shirt, Jamison took aim at Pierce. "I'm not going down."

Pierce pulled the trigger.

Jamison fell backward.

Against the slider door.

Took aim again and fired.

The shot went wild, the bullet burying itself in the thick neck of an already dead buck.

Pierce's gun was leveled, directly at his friend, his finger on the trigger. "Give it up!" he ordered, and for a second, Jamison's eyes flashed with defiance. He seemed about to shoot again, but the pistol fell from his hand. Still leaning against the slider, Jamison sank to the floor, a smear of blood streaking the glass behind him.

"You . . . you . . ." Jamison rasped, blood on his lips. "You . . . goddamned fuckin' detective . . ."

Shaken, Pierce held on to his gun, keeping it trained on his friend as he walked closer and kicked Jamison's gun out of his reach. The man, his once-upon-a-time best friend, was gasping for breath, splotches of red blooming on his T-shirt.

Sol, too, lay on the floor, her body stretched over the two steps into the room, head near the kitchen, feet in the trophy room.

Pierce called to her, but she didn't respond. Her eyes open. Unblinking. "Sol!" he shouted. "Augustin! Come on. Stay with me," he begged, on his knees, seeing the blood oozing from a wound on her shoulder He couldn't lose another partner. Couldn't! "Sol! Sol!"

She moaned, then.

Blinked, her eyes seeming to focus as he reached for his phone.

"They're coming," she said, with obvious difficulty, realizing that he was about to call for help. "Backup. I called. They're coming. Listen."

He heard nothing but her labored breathing and the frantic beating of his own heart. He dialed, one eye on Jamison, who still wasn't moving, the other on his partner.

"911," a crisp female voice answered just as he heard the first siren, faint but bleating and heading this way. Nonetheless, he told the operator what he needed, insisting she send two ambulances to the home of ADA Jamison Kittle, one-time golden boy and now just another cold-blooded murderer.

Only when he ended the connection, against the operator's instructions, did he see the text from his wife.

We got him.

We got the Savannah Slasher.

Now you come home, Detective.

We need you.

Epilogue

Life had finally quieted down, Nikki thought, as she climbed into the passenger seat of Pierce's Jeep. It had taken a while, but she felt like she could breathe again.

Duke Wheelan, the Savannah Slasher, was in prison, awaiting trial, and still protesting that he was just doing God's will when he'd taken the lives of Billy Huber, Mavis Greenlee, and Jeanne LaRoux. He had taunted the police with his Hebrew and Arabic numbers. Hebrew for the Old Testament from which the commandments were originally written. Arabic as a clue for the modern man not versed in the Bible. Now, along with murder, Wheelan faced assault and many other charges. On top of that, he was now a prime suspect in his own mother's death, as the police had proven through DNA analysis that the blood that he'd mixed in his sacrificial concoction was hers. It was not only his sister Frannie's blood that confirmed it, but his own as well.

They'd discovered his lair, a spot his sister had just considered Duke's "man cave," and though Frannie had had suspicions about her brother being involved in their mother's death, she hadn't linked him to the recent homicides or the terror that had reigned over Savannah when he'd been on his killing spree.

Nikki had stupidly assumed Frannie was Duke's wife as they

didn't resemble each other, but it made sense. A wife would have seen the man's scars from self-flagellation; a sister was less likely to notice.

"Ready?" Pierce said as he slid behind the wheel.

"As I'll ever be." She caught a glimpse of Lily standing in the doorway to the house, Phee next to her, Chloe in her arms. Nikki waved to her daughter and blew her a kiss. Chloe responded by blowing her own and nearly slapping Lily in the face by throwing out her arm.

"Okay, let's go."

Pierce backed out of the drive. He placed his hand over hers for a second. "This is a good thing," he said.

"I know. You don't have to convince me."

"Good."

They drove out of the city, and Nikki rolled down her window, letting the fresh air invade the interior and waft through her hair.

It had been a rough two months, but things were looking up. Sol, Pierce's partner, had sustained a wound to her shoulder in the apprehension of Jamison Kittle, but she'd survived, claiming the scar as her first "war wound" and back on the job. Thankfully, Pierce hadn't been injured. Nor had she in her final battle with Duke Wheelan.

Chloe's hair was growing in where the monster had yanked out a handful, and she seemed none the worse for wear. Two nights sleeping with Nikki and Pierce and no more nightmares. Nikki was still upset that a monster had broken into their home and assaulted their child, probably to kidnap Chloe and use her as bait, so he could lure Nikki out. For all his proclaimed faith, Wheelan had no soul.

As for Phee, the girl had been more traumatized, but was seeing a child psychologist and healing. She had also shown an interest in ballet and karate classes, having been impressed by her mother and aunt's prowess in taking down the Savannah Slasher.

Luck had been with them that night.

Nikki had gotten her exclusive.

Tom Fink had been pleased, up until the point where she turned her last story in and told him to shove the job. Well, not in such blunt terms, but he got the message, and her only regret was that she would miss Roy, who had been horrified that she was leaving him. "How can you do this to me?" he'd asked over beignets and coffee. "You're leaving me in the lion's den!"

"Please, no references to the Old Testament," she'd said.

"Too soon?"

"Waaay too soon," she'd said. "And it probably always will be."

"Oh, not for you, Nikki Gillette," he'd argued. "You rebound faster than Tom Brady."

"He's a football quarterback, not a basketball player, for the love of God, Roy," she'd said and caught the twinkle in his eye, as he took a sip from his coffee "Oh, I see, you're just messing with me."

"Well, you deserve it for abandoning me."

He'd survive, she thought now, and she wasn't abandoning him. She'd make a point of keeping in touch while she wrote her next book on the Savannah Slasher, to her agent, Ina's, unending joy.

Yeah, life was settling back to normal.

Whatever that was.

Maybe she was about to find out.

She braced herself.

"You're sure about this?" Pierce asked as he parked the Jeep in front of Bart Yelkis's home, a cabin-like house on a few acres not far from the city.

"Yes." Nikki took a deep breath and reached for the passenger door. "Let's go."

"There's no changing your mind," he reminded her as he cut the engine. "Once the deed is done—"

"Yeah, yeah, I know. I said I'm fine with it." She opened the passenger door and stepped outside.

"Okay, then."

"Look," she said, as they walked up a cracked concrete path, past a carport that housed an older-model Chevy truck and an electric bike. Toby's bike. Pierce had said the kid had moved back home after couch surfing and living with his aunt, but being here with his dad didn't work.

"Let me do the talking," Pierce said, as he rapped on the bent screen door.

"Sure, Detective. You take the lead." They'd already discussed this, so she didn't really understand why he was bringing it up again.

She heard footsteps, then the door opened, and Bart Yelkis stood on the other side of the screen. No introductions were necessary.

They all knew each other. A television was on somewhere inside. Nikki heard the smooth voice of a sports announcer.

"What's goin' on?" Bart asked, eyeing them both with more than a little suspicion. He was a short, stocky man whose graying hair had receded while his belly had expanded.

"Is Toby here?" Pierce asked.

"Yeah, but I asked you what you want."

"To talk to him."

Bart muttered something under his breath, then called over his shoulder. "Toby! You got company!"

No response.

"Just a sec," Bart said, but still didn't unlatch the door. "Toby!" he yelled more loudly.

"What?" came a response from deep inside the house.

"I said you got company!" He walked away from the door, and then she heard him say, "Well, shit, son, take those damned things out of your ears, so you can hear. What's the matter with ya? I told ya, someone's here to see ya."

Less than a minute later, Toby appeared on the other side of the screen, and even through the mesh, Nikki saw him pale at the sight of her.

"Okay, he's here," Bart said, catching up to his son and planting himself firmly by the kid's side.

"I'd—we'd—like to talk to him." Pierce looked directly at the boy.

Bart snorted. "Okay. So talk."

"In private."

"That don't sit well with me," Bart said.

"He's seventeen," Pierce said. "I think he can speak for himself."

"About what?" Bart said.

Toby cleared his throat. "I can handle it, Dad."

Bart scowled. "I don't think—"

"I said, 'I can handle it'!" Toby glared down at his shorter father.

Bart hesitated, then rubbed his jaw, scratching a few days' worth of the silvery whiskers that covered the lower half of his face. "I really don't—Oh, hell! Go on, talk if ya want. But I'll be right here in the livin' room watchin' the game." He peered through the mesh and repeated, "Right here."

"Fine," Pierce agreed.

Bart then glanced up at his son. "Toby? You okay with that?"

"Yeah." Toby didn't bother hiding his irritation as he opened the screen door and stepped onto the porch, while his dad disappeared inside and opened the blinds to the picture window that looked onto the porch.

Through the blinds, Nikki saw Bart sink into his recliner that sat next to a table with a top crowded by a bottle of beer, an ashtray, and several remotes.

"So you wanted to talk to me? About what?" Toby asked, a little insolence still in his words.

Nikki motioned to Pierce. This was his show.

Pierce said, "We saw your bike when we came in."

"Yeah. So?" He jammed his hands into the pockets of his battered jeans.

"It's the same bike that we caught on CCTV the night Nikki's car was vandalized."

Toby shook his head. "No, it wasn't."

"Yeah, it was," Pierce argued, still calm. "We have the tapes to prove it."

Color infused the boy's face. "I wasn't—"

"Yeah, you were," Pierce said, cutting him off. Firm, but in control. "You're angry at Nikki, and probably at the whole world, and no one's blaming you for that. But you lashed out, and this time you committed a crime."

"So what're you, now?" Toby said, leaning back against the window. "A shrink?"

"You know what I am," Pierce said calmly.

"Yeah, my mom's damn partner, and you didn't save her," he charged, his voice cracking a little. "Isn't that what partners are supposed to do?"

"It wasn't Pierce's fault," Nikki said, unable to hold her tongue a second longer. "It was mine. I made a bad mistake and she . . . she tried to save me."

"And ended up dying!" he said, his chin wobbling before he clamped his jaw tight and kept the tears glistening in his eyes from falling. "And you're right. It is your fault. All your fault!"

Nikki crumpled inside, all her guilt knotting her stomach, but it was something she had to live with. Toby had to live with. Everyone had to live with. "I know this sounds trite, and might not mean much to you, but I'm sorry. Truly sorry." Her own damned voice caught, and she cleared her throat.

"Big fuckin' deal! Sorry isn't good enough! It won't bring my mom back, will it?" He sniffed and glared at Pierce, his jaw beneath his thin beard shadow rock hard. "And now, so what? You're here to arrest me?" His voice was rising again, and through the window, Nikki saw Bart leap from his La-Z-Boy and storm to the door.

Pierce said, "I'm here to make you an offer."

"What?" Toby asked. "Like a plea deal? I've seen those on TV."

"No. It's different. Nikki is not going to press charges, and we're going to forget the incident with the car ever happened, but you need to consider moving into the garage apartment at our place."

"Hey, what?" Bart yelled as he shoved open the screen door and it banged against the house. "He's not goin' anywhere!"

"I think it's up to him," Pierce said, his voice firm but calm. What Nikki referred to as his "cop voice."

"He's a goddamned minor!" Bart's face was flushed, his eyes glittering, his right hand fisted. "You tell them, boy; you tell them you're not goin' anywhere!"

"He can emancipate himself," Pierce said. "If he needs an attorney—"

"Who the hell are you, puttin' ideas into his head like that? I'm his fuckin' father. His legal guardian!" Bart's face was flushed, his nostrils flared, his fist still clenched. "He ain't goin' nowhere."

"Is it really my decision?" Toby asked.

"It could be, yes." Pierce was nodding, but his eyes were on Bart. "And I told you we have a place for you. Attached to the house, but your own apartment."

"Oh, no way!" Bart growled.

Nikki said, "We talked it over. You're welcome to stay there, go to college once you graduate, or trade school, or get a job. Whatever you want."

"Now wait a fuckin' minute," Bart cut in and jabbed a thumb at his chest. "I'm the one who makes those decisions."

"Until he turns eighteen or takes you to court," Pierce pointed out. "Either way, it's only a matter of months."

"I don't know," Toby said.

"Of course you don't." Bart glowered at his son. "You're just a kid."

Nikki held the boy's gaze. "It's up to you, Toby. No matter what your dad says. You're almost an adult."

The kid was actually teetering, but she didn't want to push.

"Now wait a damn minute," Bart said, trying to take control. "I'm his guardian, and the government says so."

Nikki's heart sank. This was about money, just as Pierce had predicted.

"That doesn't need to change," Pierce said. "Toby's got a few more months of social security coming his way, and you'll get it. We won't interfere. It's just that I know you aren't always getting along, so this is a way to make things easier. For both of you."

Bart's face tightened. He wasn't buying it. "His benefits stay with me. And you get . . . ?"

"Someone in the apartment over the garage. If he wants to make some money, he can do yard work or walk the dogs."

"You're not going to charge him rent?" Bart asked, clearly astounded.

Nikki reiterated, "No rent."

Bart clarified. "And he can come and go as he pleases?"

"They'll be some house rules," Nikki replied.

Pierce added, "He has to finish school. Go everyday, and we'll get reports."

"But I keep the money?" Bart wanted to nail that fact down.

"Right." Pierce nodded.

"Dad?" Toby asked.

"It's up to you," his father said with a snort. "They're right, I guess. You're almost an adult. Do what you want!" And since he'd locked up what he wanted in the bargain, Nikki guessed, he went inside. Nikki watched him through the window as he lit a cigarette, then, using the remote, turned up the volume on the TV.

"Okay, so there you have it. It's up to you," Pierce said. "Just let us know. Come on," he said to Nikki, taking her hand and starting for the Jeep.

"Hey! Wait a minute."

They stopped midway in the yard. "You're not pressing charges? About the, well, you know, your car?"

"The vandalism?" she said. "No, not yet." She raised her eyebrows. "But it better not happen again."

He didn't reply, but she saw his Adam's apple bobble as he swallowed hard.

"And please, Toby, think about our offer. You'd be safe there, and it's relatively private." She offered him a bit of a smile. "And the price is right."

Again, he didn't answer, but at least she thought, or more truthfully, she hoped, that she and Pierce had gotten through.

Fingers crossed.

Two days later, she got her answer. She'd taken the girls to the horse barns, where Phee had announced that she was getting a new riding instructor. "Miss Annabelle" was no longer giving lessons. "It's because she's gonna have a baby," Phee said, sounding disgusted as she tossed her gear into the back seat.

"Is she?"

"Yep. And she's getting married to some old grandpa!"

"Archer."

"She calls him Archie," Phee said and slid into her seat.

"Of course she does." Nikki knew that. "So who's your new instructor?"

"Gia." Phee sighed theatrically as she stuffed her earbuds into her ears.

"Don't you like her?"

"She's okay." Phee shrugged and snapped her seat belt over her lap. "I just really like Annabelle."

"Maybe she'll come back," Nikki said, but she was talking to herself, as Phee had already plugged in. It had been a long two months, she thought, since the night she'd squared off with Duke Wheelan, unmasking him as the Savannah Slasher, and Pierce had nearly been killed by someone he'd considered one of his best, if not his very best, friends, a man who now swore he hadn't meant to kill Naomi, but they'd fought and he'd panicked.

Which only added to his lies.

Looking through bank records, the police had discovered that he had paid Stoney a large sum of money to carve the rock found in Naomi's hand at the crime scene. And there was the matter of a neighbor's rooster going missing, probably one Jamison had killed and drained its blood, dousing the rock with it and not realizing that the type of blood would trip him up.

A brilliant lawyer.

A not-so-brilliant killer.

They had new evidence against him in the form of enhanced video images that showed him driving his wife's car, but he'd been wearing a blond wig, in the hope that no one would figure out he'd been behind the wheel, while she was probably in the trunk of her own car. Then he'd taken her back to their place or somewhere nearby. He'd strangled her, hung her at the LaRoux place, then ditched the car in the river, leaving the windows down so it would sink, before he swam upstream, then jogged home.

At least that was the prevailing theory.

Jamison Kittle, once a shining star in the DA's office and touted as following his father's footsteps into a judgeship or further, now sat in prison after a monthlong stay in the hospital getting over his wounds. But Pierce was still beating himself up for not knowing how duplicitous the man could be.

Now, Jamison's children were without a mother, and a father awaiting trial. Naomi's sister and brother-in-law had taken in Lara, Michelle, and Shana, so the girls were living in Charleston now, away from the pain and heartache of the Savannah media circus that surrounded Jamison Kittle.

Pierce had vowed to be a part of their lives. If they let him. Lara, the oldest, blamed him for her father's incarceration, and the younger two were confused. It would take time for their lives to get to some kind of normal, if that ever happened. Nikki had tried to form a bond with Roxie, Naomi's sister, and had said she'd like to help out, especially with Shana, as she and Phee shared a love of horses and riding.

Time would tell.

Currently, Roxie and Naomi's parents were overwhelmed, though Reverend Stark and the Birds of Paradise were helping out. It turned out that Westin was a true believer, but he'd trusted Duke Wheelan with the keys to the church's SUV. Wheelan had made himself a spare set so that he could take the vehicle out whenever he wanted, though it was usually legitimate, and with the reverend's approval.

But Nikki and Pierce were trying their best.

They'd talked it over time and time again.

Just the other night, while lying in bed and watching Jimmy Kimmel, Pierce had said, "You know, if things break right, we'd have a ton of kids. Most of whom aren't ours, but who we feel responsible for." He was right. Morrisette's two and now, if they were allowed, the Kittle girls.

"And none of them want us," she'd said, snuggling closer as the late-summer air had wafted through the bedroom on that hot evening.

"Maybe that'll change."

"When pigs fly," she'd murmured.

Now, as she pulled into the drive, she wondered if she'd been wrong, if boars and sows had sprouted wings and were navigating the clouds.

Because Toby Yelkis was waiting for her, staring down at his phone, his electric bike leaned against the side of the garage, a single duffel bag patched with duct tape at his feet. Arlo was lying in the dirt of a flower bed nearby.

Toby had been texting, but he looked up when the noise of the garage door lifting caught his attention. His eyes met hers for the briefest of seconds as she drove inside.

"Take Chloe into the house, please," she said to Phee before climbing out of the car.

"Why?" Phee whined before she spied Toby, shoulders hunched, obviously waiting.

Nikki said, "I'll be in soon."

Phee looked about to argue, but finally rolled her eyes. "Fine. Okay." She put her boots and gear away while Nikki unstrapped her daughter, promised to be right in, and watched as Chloe happily followed Phee into the house.

"Hi," Nikki said, walking outside.

"Hi." He barely looked up. Embarrassed, maybe? Ashamed? Something.

"So, did you have a change of heart?" she asked when it seems he wasn't up to starting the conversation. She motioned to the bag.

He flipped his hair out of his eyes. "Dunno."

But he was lying. "You want to see the apartment?"

"Yeah." He lifted a shoulder, as if he didn't care. Yet here he was. Waiting. "Okay."

"Let me grab the keys." She went into the house, quickly explained to Lily what she was doing, then found Toby in the garage, admiring the Caddy. "This yours?" he asked, touching the shining hood.

"Pierce's."

"Sweet ride," he said under his breath, a boy who appreciated an antique Caddy but could scratch the hell out of her Subaru.

As if he read her thoughts, he dropped his hand and blushed.

She let it pass. "This way." Waving for him to follow, she led Toby up the stairs that ran up the side of the garage. "It's not exactly finished because we really hadn't decided what we wanted to do up here." She unlocked the door and snapped on the lights, three single bulbs dangling from the sloped ceiling.

"Oh. Wow." Toby followed her to the huge room, with its plywood walls and massive dormers. The only furniture was an old futon, a table, and a lamp with a broken shade, items she had planned to donate or throw away.

"We've got the Sheetrock and flooring ordered," she told him. "And there's some tile that needs to be laid in the bathroom, but the plumbing works."

He peered into the one room that cut into the space and housed a tub/shower, sink, and toilet, then returned to the main room, where Nikki was touching the wall that was attached to the house. "There's no door into the inside yet, but eventually it would go here," she patted the wall; on the other side was a closet at the end of the second-floor hallway, the space between Chloe's nursery and Lily and Phee's room.

"But not now," he said, making certain the attic over the garage was private.

"That's right. Not now."

"And you're not using it."

"Not yet." They'd talked about it off and on. The discussion had ranged from an apartment for Lily and Phee to a bonus room with a pool table or even a podcasting/recording studio for Nikki. "We've had lots of ideas, but Pierce and I agreed; you could stay here, rent free, until you finish college or whatever. After you graduate, then we'll re-evaluate."

"You'd do that?" He was still skeptical. Still didn't trust her.

"Yes. The question is, would you?"

"Don't know."

"Then why are you here?" She wasn't buying that he was just checking out the space. His duffel bag belied that flimsy excuse.

"Priscilla told me to come. Told me I'd be a . . . an effin' idiot not to take you up on it."

"Your sister sounds like a wise woman."

"Nah. She's just tired of me crashing on her couch every time Dad and I get into it."

"How's it going with your dad?"

"Fine!" Toby was instantly defensive, but he didn't meet her eyes.

"Well, if you moved here, he could only come over when you invited him," she said.

"I'll think about it."

The garage door rumbled open, and Nikki heard the familiar sound of the Jeep's engine as Pierce parked beneath them.

"Your husband?" Toby asked.

She gave a little laugh. "Well, I hope."

Less than a minute later, Pierce appeared in the doorway. At the sight of Toby, he grinned and stepped inside. "Priscilla called and said you'd probably show up."

Toby's eyes darkened. "Yeah?"

"She said you and your dad had another fight. That he threw you out."

"He didn't throw me out. I left."

"Okay." Pierce, nodding, didn't argue. "Well, if you want to stay here, you're welcome."

"Not sure," Toby said.

"Tell you what. You take your time deciding. You don't have to do it today. We'll give you a key, and you can try it out. If it works for you, great, we'll fix it up a little, make sure you've got the basics like towels and some more furniture. And I'll work out an allowance with your dad."

"He won't go for it."

"We'll see," Pierce said.

"My husband can be pretty persuasive. I'll leave you two to figure it out."

Then she left. She hoped Toby would take them up on their offer, but only time would tell, she thought as she went into the kitchen, where Lily was looking at a takeout menu. "We're DoorDashing tonight. I couldn't get dinner together." She looked up. "I'm thinking . . . barbecue? Work for you?"

"Sure."

"Do we have . . . a guest?" she asked.

"Possibly." She walked into the garage and opened the door. Pierce and Toby were inside, where Toby was again admiring the classic car and Pierce was telling him all about it. "Barbecue from Dixie's tonight. Toby? Would you like to stay?"

"Oh. Yeah. Sure." He looked from Nikki to Pierce. "If it's okay."

"We'd love it," she assured him, and then before he could change his mind or she interrupted their car-man-talk any further, she ducked back inside. "Just order what you think," she said, "but whatever it is, double it." Then she walked outside, where the hot Georgia sun was beginning to lower, shadows chasing across the yard. Mikado, a little stiffer than he had been before Duke Wheelan had broken his ribs, was lying in the shade, while Arlo chased the girls around the birdbath and a squirrel scolded them all from the thick branches of a live oak.

"Anyone in the mood for lemonade?" she asked, seeing Chloe's red face as she tried to keep up with her cousin.

"Me, me!" her daughter said and ran up to her, lifting up her little arms.

"You got it, Princess," Nikki said, picking her up and holding her close.

Life, for now, had become calm again, but, Nikki knew from experience, this could just be the calm before the storm. If so, she'd deal with it.

"So be it," she whispered into her daughter's hair. "So be it."